# Angel in Black

Bill Rapp

 Pittsburgh, PA

# Angel in Black

ISBN 1-56315-376-9

Trade Paperback
© Copyright 2007 Bill Rapp
All rights reserved
Library of Congress #2006922181

Request for information should be addressed to:
SterlingHouse Publisher, Inc.
7436 Washington Avenue
Pittsburgh, PA 15218
www.sterlinghousepublisher.com

Pemberton Mysteries
is an imprint of SterlingHouse Publisher, Inc.

SterlingHouse Publisher, Inc. is a company
of the CyntoMedia Corporation

Cover Design: Jamie Linder
Interior Design: N. J. McBeth

All rights reserved. No part of this publication may be reproduced, stored in a retrieval system, or transmitted in any form or by any means—electronic, mechanical, photocopy, recording or any other, except for brief quotations in printed reviews—without prior permission of the publisher.

This is a work of fiction. Names, characters, incidents, and places, are the product of the author's imagination or are used fictitiously. Any resemblance to actual events or persons, living or dead is entirely coincidental.

Printed in the United States of America

# Acknowledgment

There are many I must thank for their help in bringing this novel to print. Francine Mathews, Acher Mayor, Carolyn Banks and David Lorne were instrumental in teaching me to write a readable prose that contained a voice and vision of my own, while also telling a story worth hearing. My agent, Jennifer Piemme at Lee Shore never lost faith in the manuscript and knocked on any door she could find in the conviction that someone would eventually like it as much as we do. Many old and dear friends in Naperville were always available with a story, an insight, or a suggestion on how I could improve the setting of the story, and without the hospitality of Larry and Jan Baumgartner I would probably have lost touch long ago. Most of my thanks, however, must go to my wife, Didi, and my daughters Ellie and Julia, without whose patience, understanding, and support this manuscript would never have come to life. It is to them that I dedicate this book. Of course, all shortcomings are mine alone.

# Chapter 1

It was Saturday night, but I was a long way from uptown. Hell, I wasn't even near the Interstate. But the murder brought me a lot closer. And it brought me back to parts of my past I thought I had forgotten.

I had been tailing Steve Courney off and on for five days, and on this night we had landed at the Skylark Inn, a bar on the outskirts of Naperville, Illinois, my hometown. His wife suspected him of infidelity. She had for some time, actually, but it had taken her weeks to summon the courage to call a private detective.

I hated domestic investigations, even if they did pay the bills. I had seen this sort of thing too often. I tended to sympathize with the wives. They looked so alone and vulnerable, and this made the job a little easier. Still, I knew next to nothing about most couples' marital problems, so I tried not to judge. The two parties would have to sort out their own guilt and retribution. But I knew one thing for certain—death is definitely too heavy a price to pay.

"For the last month he's refused to take me out with him on the weekends," she'd confided in our first meeting. Lisa Courney sat huddled in the middle of her sofa, her shoulders pressing toward a chest hidden under folds of pink cotton. A long skirt with a bright floral pattern fell nearly to her ankles, and her knees looked like they had fused together beneath the fabric. Two fists rested on top of her lap, a crumbled wad of tissue trapped between them. Every so often the knees bobbed, and white knuckles rode on waves of nervous energy.

"What's his behavior like during the week?" I asked. "Distant? Cruel?"

"Oh, everything's fine during the week. He often has to work late...." The tissues floated between face and lap. "But I've always been able to check that by calling his office or talking to a co-worker. That's what makes this all so strange."

I stifled a yawn and jotted more hieroglyphics on a pad as she fed me information on her husband's behavior, associates, schedule, and so on.

"And...there's something else. He may be in some kind of danger."

That got me to sit up straight. "What kind of danger?"

She shrugged between sniffles. "I'm not really sure. He hasn't said anything to me. But I can tell he's worried about something."

"But you don't have any idea what it is? Couldn't you try to be a little more specific?"

"I'm not sure I should. I don't want to mislead you. But I thought you should be aware of it."

"It would really help if you could give me a little more to go on."

She just shook her head and refused to say anymore.

On that particular evening the surveillance had carried us to a hotel bar, some fashionable pubs, and even a restaurant or two. But Mister Courney never seemed to have much luck with women. Men either, but he didn't appear to be interested in those. Nor had I seen any bogeyman.

The Skylark Inn buzzed with its usual Saturday night party of boomers and twenty-somethings who were fueling the area's economic growth. Its two stories of mauve stucco and deep brown trim looked like a cross between a Tudor pub and one of the bi-levels that had spread through the town after World War II. On three sides, residential skylines of sloped, black shingles sprouted where waves of corn and alfalfa had once grown. Years ago, my hands had helped till this earth, hallowing it with sweat and grime and the lost summers of youth. Now the fields belonged to the residential zones and shopping meccas built for the sons and daughters of Midwestern prosperity.

The Skylark had settled next to a slow fork where Route 34 and Oswego Road run together, just before they begin a mutual journey to Aurora and other points west. Surrounding the bar was a moat of gravel and weeds that passed for a parking lot. About half of the available spaces were claimed by the Jeep Cherokees and Chevy Blazers that provided the baby boomers with a sense of accomplishment and security as they navigated from one suburban driveway to another. An occasional Saab and BMW added a touch of exotic flavor.

My green Volvo waited in the last lane next to the highway, its 130,000 miles hidden by the unchanging style of the 240 model. After more than an hour, I had grown antsy, watching spots of light from passing vehicles bounce off the windshield and disappear along the slope of brown grass and dry dirt at the edge of the lot. It was time to head back into the Inn to use the can, cuddle a Sprite, and check on my mark.

As I pulled myself up from the door, I noticed Steve Courney on his way out and moving quickly. Draped along his left arm was a woman with a sea of raven hair that cascaded past her shoulders like a sheen of black silk. Unfortunately, I didn't get a chance to check on Courney's tastes now that he had finally scored because I couldn't see the face. The head was bent forward, the eyes intent on finding a path through the gravel and rusting beer cans.

I jumped from the Volvo and ran to the edge of my lane, struggling to get a better view as the two floated away among big tires and wide-bodied vehicles. I caught only a thin nose and more waves of hair as the couple seeped through a haze of insects surrounding the street lamp on the corner. Tan skin glistened against the night, but her eyes and mouth disappeared as the couple turned their backs to my side of the parking lot. Two more rows and they would reach Courney's Lexus.

I ducked back into my car and retrieved the 35mm Olympus I carry on surveillance. That's when I heard the sound I can never forget. It's one you hear only on rare occasions in suburban Illinois. But I knew it well enough from basic training, and from Vietnam. The shot barked across the parking lot like someone had just snapped a two-by-four in half.

I leaped up, banged my head against the door frame, and bolted toward the noise.

"Oh my God!" a woman shrieked, her voice on the verge of panic.

A Chevy Corsica hurtled onto Route 34, bounced into the middle lane, then raced through a yellow light before speeding off in the direction of the Tollroad. A web of dark hair sprouted over the rim of the steering wheel. I whipped my camera at the car like I was brandishing a Remington 12-gauge and rolled off three shots from chest level.

"Jesus fucking Christ."

I glanced up, hoping to find the owner of the heavy male voice. Then I heard a woman's sobbing.

I ran towards the sound and found a crowd of about half a dozen spectators. The soles of Steve Courney's feet stared up at the night, their black shadows receding into the twin pant legs of brushed brown cotton. The masculine voice belonged to a hefty six-footer, whose broad shoulders were draped in a Hawaiian shirt that ran to a pair of pleated khaki slacks. He spun behind one of the 4-wheelers and sprayed his dinner along the sideboard of a beige Cherokee. His date tried to pat his back while dancing out of the way to avoid getting his filet on her red miniskirt.

I tiptoed closer, afraid of what I knew I was going to find. Steve Courney had been a good-looking man, with well-groomed hair running straight back in neat waves from deep-set eyes and a square jaw. It made me wonder why he had such a hard time committing adultery. But there was no way he'd be able to do so now. Not with that big chunk missing from the side of his head, parts of it spread along the Ford Taurus at the side of his Lexus. From a first impression it looked like the bullet had entered just below the ear and taken parts of his skull and brain with it on the way out. I knelt beside the body.

"For Chrissakes." It was all I could think to say.

My internal organs danced as though they were trying to rearrange themselves.

I gulped for air and slumped against the trunk of Courney's car. The humidity of a mid-July night closed in like the sticky jungle air that had followed me everywhere I went in Vietnam. That was the last time I had seen anything like this. There had been more of them, then. Some had even been my friends.

"What the...?" The lines of a man's face twisted into a long, ugly oval. "You know this guy?"

"Knew," I corrected.

"Yeah?" The speaker was dressed for summer in Miami with a blue and white striped shirt and faded blue jeans that topped his shiny black loafers. With his build he looked like a relative of the guy retching to the side. A woman with short blond hair called him Tom and tugged at his sleeve. She looked as though she was ready to join the guy hugging his ribs behind the Cherokee.

"Not really," I confessed. "It was a long time ago. I was just getting to know him again."

I pulled myself up and glanced around.

"Anybody see anything?" I asked. "The shot maybe, or a woman who was with him?"

Vacant eyes and swaying heads peered at Steve Courney's open skull. A few people looked at me.

"Some broad was moving like a banshee down that aisle." The speaker was the guy named Tom. He pointed to the row that ran along the side of the Lexus. "I think she's the one who pulled outta here like she was running from a ghost." Tom had one hand thrust deep in his pants pocket, while the other rubbed away hours of styling from the straight brown hair that rose from his forehead and fell over the tips of his ears.

"But did you see if she's the one who fired the shot?"

Tom just shook his head and chewed on his lower lip. His date tugged some more.

The couple slid into the night, Tom edging his way backwards as his feet trudged through pebbles and dust. The police sirens grew louder in the background as they sped along Aurora Road and turned onto Route 34. I wouldn't have much to say. Preliminary background checks hadn't taken me very far, not yet anyway. Place of employment, local driving record, some employment history. Nothing remarkable. I hadn't even had time to check into the domestic situation, or peek at the Courneys' financial state. Basically, I had been hoping to catch the wayward spouse in the sack, collect the rest of my fee, then back off.

Now it was too late for that. And I still didn't know whom he had been sleeping with—if anyone, which I had come to doubt.

But this wasn't what bothered me the most. What I had really wanted to learn was why his wife had hired me to follow someone from my old unit back in Vietnam, a soldier and a man I had known only casually. As I remembered it, we had been in the same company, Alpha, but different platoons. And he had bugged out a short time after I arrived. Maybe she hadn't known that our paths had crossed once before, that there had been issues I wanted to leave buried in that particular hell. But if he wasn't screwing around, why had I been asked to step back into his life?

The flashing red and blue lights rushed through the parking lot, announcing the arrival of Naperville's finest. I pondered why anyone might want to kill Steve Courney and what I was going to tell the police. I didn't know much yet. That would change, though. In fact, if I had known what was coming, I would have gone into the Skylark for a drink.

# Chapter 2

"So, you never really saw the shooting? You only heard it?"

"That's right. But everything points to the woman I described. At the very least, Frank, she's got to be your most important witness."

Frank Hardy, the chief of Naperville's three-man detective squad, towered above my chair, his hands resting on his hips and his badge clipped to a brown leather belt. His broad chest was hidden beneath a white cotton dress shirt that struggled to escape from a pair of pleated blue slacks. A blue and yellow striped tie hung loose at the collar. His hands rose slowly from his waist, then drifted to the edge of the table. They rested there on the flat, wooden top, absorbing the light from the ceiling for about a minute before he spoke. When he did, Hardy's face dropped until his light brown eyes met mine. Unfortunately, he hadn't had a chance to shave yet. Or brush his teeth. His breath carried the scent of a wet dog.

Mine wasn't much better, but that was small consolation. If I had had the energy to move away I would have. But I was too exhausted.

"Let's go over it again. Tell me about your week together."

"It was more like five days, and we weren't together the whole time."

"Why not?"

"Because I had other commitments. Some of us still work for a living, Frank."

"Not very well, apparently. Now go on. Tell us more."

So I went over it again. The places we had been, the people Steve Courney had met, the times, and what he liked to drink. All the mundane things your learn when you intrude into another man's life.

"And you never saw anything while you were tailing him to suggest that someone might want to kill him?"

"Hardy, we have been over this enough already. You guys have had me here for I don't know how many fucking hours. You expecting me to slip up and confess?"

"Humor us."

"No, goddammit, I did not see anything of the sort. The guy couldn't even get laid, from what I saw. Maybe he paid someone to shoot him out of frustration."

"Now we're gettin' into your territory."

"Oh, thanks, Rick. Just what I'm in the mood for. Bad marital humor."

Rick Jamieson sat in a chair just off to my right. We had known each other since childhood-the third grade, actually-and I was familiar with his jokes. I was also familiar with his marriage. I'd been his best man. His left arm snaked around my shoulders. He hadn't shaved either. Early morning murders can be hell on your appearance.

This one hadn't done much for mine. But then, a couple of fifteen-minute naps and three cups of vending machine coffee aren't much to go on.

"Bear with us, Bill. You can understand that we're looking for something to go on here," Jamieson said. "At this point, you're probably our most reliable witness, and you haven't given us much so far. I mean, you were a big part of his life for what, the better part of a week?"

My hands griped the edge of the table. When I pulled them away, the fingertips had left their outlines in sweat on the light brown grain. It matched the moisture beading along my forehead. The whole damn room felt heavy and damp, like the days and nights thirty years ago. The memories had started to trickle back the moment I'd got on Steve Courney's tail, and I had found myself thinking more and more frequently of that time and place I had tried to leave behind. But there was no way I was telling these guys about our mutual past with the 25th Infantry at Tay Ninh. Not until I had a better idea of what was going on here myself.

Hardy straightened and then stepped back, his face a fat frown. I glanced up at the man, sighed, then waved my hands.

"I've given you what I've got. I told you what I was doing there, how long it had been, and what I saw. In fact, I've done it several times. The guy looked like he was finally going to score, but somebody else did not have sex on her mind." I blew out my stale, tired breath. "Or so it appeared."

"And you say the wife hired you to follow him? No one else had an interest in what he did with his free time?"

I shook my head. "Not as far as I can see."

"Which wasn't very far," Hardy pressed. "By the way, where was his wife?"

"Probably at home. But then how the hell should I know? I wasn't following her."

I resisted telling them any more than I had to. At least until I had a chance to sort some of this out myself.

Hardy leaned back on the table, his fingers splayed across the wood. "Habermann, you need to open up on this. Hell, she's got to be a prime suspect.

She's got a motive-and with no alibi, an opportunity. Shit, you give us what we need to nail her ass and we might even let you go home."

"If I ever get to call a lawyer, Hardy, you're going to have to let me go home. As it is, I'd hate to see the face on the commissioner when he reads the complaint I'm going to file."

"You know we can go to a judge and have him suspend your license until you divulge the information. Hell, Habermann, you're a murder witness, and it wouldn't take much imagination to argue that it is relevant."

He was right. But I owed my client at least the benefit of a doubt. Until I spoke with her, anyway.

"You guys do what you have to do. I'll cooperate wherever and however I can."

Hardy smiled and pulled away from the table. Jamieson climbed from his chair and strolled over to his boss. They stuck their heads close together, as though that might keep me from hearing what they said. Hardy's eyes left my face, studied the plate glass window separating us from the hallway, then focused on his deputy. He actually seemed to be listening to what my friend had to say.

"His testimony corresponds to what the others at the scene had to say, Frank. Let's let him go home for now."

Hardy's finger pointed at my head like a saber. "I'm willing to bet you a pair of Bulls' tickets that your buddy over there knows more than he's told us. He was workin' on one of his fuckin' marriage-on-the-rocks cases, and he knows something more that he hasn't divulged. I bet he's got a pretty good idea who the shooter is."

"And you think he won't tell us?"

"For some goddamn, hairy reason he won't. And it's pissin' me off."

"All in due time, detectives." I didn't want them to forget I was still there.

"You didn't pick anything up, did you?" Hardy asked. "You don't have any physical evidence, do you?"

"Christ, Frank, I'm not that stupid. I do know a little about proper police procedure and the law. I used to work here, ya know." I thought of the camera on the floor of my car. But if the picture did implicate Lisa Courney, I wanted to check that on my own first before passing the evidence to the police. I'd think of some excuse later.

"Then get the fuck out of here," Hardy barked.

"And I promise not to skip town, chief."

Hardy smiled. "Where the hell would you go anyway? And don't call me 'chief.' Not anymore."

Jamieson ambled over and took my arm, pulling me toward the door. "Let's go before he changes his mind."

We wandered into the hallway, and Jamieson glanced at his watch. "I hope you don't mind if I don't see you to the door. I've got to start writing this shit up."

"Later, Rick. I know my way out. My best to Susan. I doubt I'll make Sunday dinner at your place today."

"The way this day's goin', we won't be havin' one. Not with me, anyway."

"Stay in touch, Habermann," Hardy called. "We'll be calling if anything else pops into mind."

Halfway to the front desk I stopped and turned toward my old boss. I had spent a little over two years with the local P.D., and Frank Hardy and I had not always seen things through the same lens. Still, he was a good cop, and I hoped there had been no hard feelings when I left to set myself up as an independent operator. I waved goodbye. Hardy's hands were back on his hips, sleeves rolled to the elbow, his eyes following my path like a bird of prey. He did not wave back.

The sun was just beginning to sear into an earth parched from weeks of dry, July heat when I left the police headquarters at seven-thirty. It reminded me once more of that time way back, when the tropical heat and human stench had kept me company everywhere I went, along with the bugs and snakes and rats. And Charlie, too. Good ol' Charlie.

I fell into the front seat of the Volvo, threw on a pair of sunglasses, and slid away from the station, two-stories of light brown brick and dark glass that met at odd angles beneath a blue crystal sky.

I knew I would have to visit my client sometime this morning, but I needed to shower and change clothes first. I was going to have to tell Lisa Courney the circumstances of her husband's death and answer some questions. Like why I hadn't uncovered any liaisons, and why I hadn't been able to prevent his murder. Then, I would have to figure out some way to see if she had been aware of our brief, mutual history in Southeast Asia. Of course, that didn't mean it was all related to Courney's death or my presence on the case. But I've learned to distrust coincidences. In any case, it seemed like a good idea to wash away the scent of murder first.

I pulled into the garage next to the alley behind my building. Like many of the garages in Naperville's oldest neighborhood, the structure had originally served as a carriage house to one of the Victorian homes that dated from somewhere in the last century. It had become fashionable several decades ago to invest a lot of work and money into these things, and many owners did the same with their garages. I was an exception. Mine still needed a coat of paint and a new pane of glass for the window on the alley side. And one of these days I would pull the weeds thriving in the shade next to the yard. I also did not own a Victorian.

After parking the Volvo, I ambled along the stone pathway that bisected the yard behind my apartment. The ubiquitous Mrs. Bachmann strolled to the edge of her walk, wrapped in a full-length cotton bathrobe almost as blue as her hair. I tried to move quickly to escape detection, but she must have spied me when she bent over to retrieve her morning *Tribune*. Mrs. Bachmann owned the white three-story on the other side of the alley behind my house, and sometimes she served as a self-appointed, one-person neighborhood watch committee. She must have had a busy night, too, because she had forgotten to knot her belt this morning. Not that it mattered much. She had to be at least seventy-five years old. I glanced away and waved.

She waved back, the fingers of her right hand tickling the air in front of her chin. The *Tribune* swung back and forth like a broken pendulum in its plastic sack. She wrapped the robe tighter around hips heavy with age and Midwestern cooking. Then she wagged a thick index finger.

"You'll do yourself no good with these hours, Billy."

I shrugged.

She frowned and turned toward her front porch. She worried too much about the people in her neighborhood. It was a quiet place, most of the time.

I climbed the stairs to my flat on the second floor of a building younger than most in the neighborhood. My parents had purchased the house and turned its management over to me when they'd sold the family farm out near Eola and fled the Midwestern winters for the heat and humidity of Florida. Whatever its age, the years on the house were camouflaged, not so cleverly, under a layer of camel-colored siding wrapped around three sides and a fresh coat of beige paint that covered the bricks in front.

My happy little nest sat above a delicatessen run by an Iranian, Ahmed Valyati, a nice enough fellow who made wonderful gyros and the richest pan of blondies this side of Lake Michigan. He claimed to be related to high-level officials that had served under the Shah. I wasn't sure I believed him, not that I cared a whole hell of a lot. The rent from his shop came as a welcome addition to the money I earned investigating wayward husbands, insurance cheats, or prospective employees at any one of a dozen high-tech firms in the area.

The neighborhood was crowded this morning with parishioners from Saints Peter and Paul, the Catholic church across the street. It was also my church, just as the school had been my school from grades one through eight. Then I had joined the Protestants at the local public high school. But that was a long time and many confessions ago. The eight o'clock mass had just let out, and a crowd milled about on the long concrete steps that ran the half block in front of the church. I left all that behind me on the wooden porch of leaky sealant and fading paint, the boards groaning when I slammed the door.

Next week, I told myself. Maybe an afternoon service. And I might even toss a few bills onto the collection plate. Small ones, probably.

When I reached the bedroom, I lay down on my bed and told myself I would rest my eyes for about fifteen minutes. The next thing I knew the bells for the 11:30 mass were dragging me back into consciousness.

After a quick shower, I changed into a blue blazer, light gray slacks, white shirt, and blue and red paisley tie. It was the most somber outfit I could construct from my closet's holdings. I tried to wash the taste of dust and depression from my mouth with a cup of reheated coffee and some vanilla yogurt, but they only made my stomach grumble. Then I wrote a letter requesting a copy of the records of a Mister Steven Courney from the Veterans Administration. On my way out the door I grabbed an apple and decided to hit Ahmed up for a real cup of java.

The Courneys lived across from Naperville Central High School in the River Place luxury condominiums. These seven-story apartment blocks sat back from the road among a flock of trees rich in green foliage. Outside the gate, you couldn't help but confront the noise and bustle of traffic navigating its path around the high school or into the downtown shopping district. But once inside, you were swallowed in a garden of residential delights, with a vista that opened like a broker's brochure as soon as you parked your car. I left mine in one of the spots set aside for visitors near the rental office just to the left of the front entrance. When I climbed from the Volvo, the noise from the traffic on Aurora Avenue faded away.

I strolled to the right, toward the green acres of rolling lawn in Riverwalk Park just beyond the last building in the complex. Strategically placed sprinklers shot jets of water across the grass, and the morning sun glistened in the dew of well-tended sod and shrubbery. The scent of moist earth mingled with the humidity of a mid-July heat wave.

When I reached the last set of apartments, I marched through a glass door held open by a heavyset visitor on his way out, then across the marble floor and over to the elevators behind the reception desk. I tipped my hand to the security guard, who stood leaning against the counter top, eager for company and conversation. His gray hair sat hard against a skull covered in skin that looked like parchment. Waves of wrinkles around his eyes and a sagging chin failed to hide blue eyes looking for something to do.

"Can I help you?" he pleaded.

"No thanks. I'm just on my way to number 520. I've been here before."

"Ah. I thought you looked familiar. I rarely forget a face," he assured me. "Yours sort of reminds me of a guy on the force in Wichita...."

The words trailed off my shoulders as the elevator opened, and I escaped into the paneled coolness of the cabin that would deliver me to the grieving widow. I prayed for a slow ride while I rehearsed my lines.

I continued rehearsing as I strolled along a plush carpet of deep scarlet. After about twenty seconds, I reached the heavy wooden door with the golden numerals planted on a field of dark brown mahogany.

It took a minute or so for someone to answer the door after I knocked. In fact, I had raised my hand for another knock, a little louder this time, when the door swung open to reveal a woman somewhere in her mid-thirties or early forties silhouetted against a ray of sunlight. She wore a white cotton shirt and seemed to disappear in the morning haze that burst from the window behind her. Only her black stirrup pants stood out clearly, and they framed a pair of thin, muscular legs.

"Can I help you?"

"You can close the drapes. I think I'm going blind."

The figure retreated into the apartment but left the door open. I assumed it was all right for me to enter. She didn't go anywhere near the windows.

"Thanks anyway," I said.

Ms. Black Slacks had taken a seat on the white leather sofa next to a shrunken Lisa Courney. She draped her left arm around the widow. Once I could see again, I noticed an attractive face underneath a sheet of deep brown hair. The face looked like it was struggling to escape from the prison imposed by its owner when she had pulled the hair straight back like a layer of paint, ending in a tight bun at the back.

"I'm sorry for intruding, Mrs. Courney, but I wanted to express my condolences over your husband's death." No one offered me a seat, so I stood at the edge of the sofa. I shifted my weight from one foot to the other. "I'll return the balance of your retainer with my report."

Ms. Black Slacks clung to my client, who sat glued to the same middle cushion where I had seen her last.

"So, you're the investigator my sister hired to follow Steve." She glanced from me to Lisa Courney. "Just what were you supposed to do? Follow him around, spy on him? Write up little reports on his misbehavior?"

She gave the impression of a woman with tremendous confidence in herself, someone with a bright mind, quick judgment and a smart mouth. She looked like someone who liked to take control. And she looked like trouble.

Lisa Courny lifted a tired face toward mine, her cheeks streaked with tears. Light brown hair hung in uncombed clumps over her ears, and her thin bones seemed to retreat beneath a light skin all the more pallid from grief and anxiety.

"Perhaps I should come back later," I suggested.

"No, wait." Lisa rose from her seat and extended a hand toward mine. "You must forgive my sister. She cared deeply for Steve. It's been a shock. I...you keep the money. I can't blame you for what happened."

A sigh escaped from somewhere inside Lisa Courney's sunken chest, and her gaze drifted down toward a deep white rug. The walls were white too, and they absorbed the sunlight pouring into the room. Two broadleaf plants against the far wall on either side of the fireplace seemed to enjoy the photosynthesis. A hint of disinfectant lingered

"Thanks very much, Mrs. Courney, but I haven't really earned it. I never did find the information you wanted. I'll just take enough to cover my expenses."

"Bravo!" The sister leaped from the couch and snaked an arm around Lisa Courney. "Spoken like Philip Marlowe."

I was beginning to dislike this woman. "He was a very good detective," I reminded her.

"How about you? How good are you?"

I shrugged, looking for a way to get the hell out of there.

The sister turned her face toward Lisa Courney. "I think that the good shamus here might be able to earn his keep after all."

"What...what do you mean?" Lisa Courney's mouth hung half open, and her words drifted in the air between us. Light brown sparks of recognition slipped from the depths of her eyes. "Oh no, Debbie. That won't be necessary."

Then Lisa Courney shrugged and collapsed into a pile in the corner of the sofa, sloping shoulders hidden underneath a white cotton pullover. She clasped her hands together in her lap. A thick, gold chain hung at the base of her neck, picking up some of the sun from the windows and reflecting random beams of light around the room. Lisa's eyes seemed to follow these, wandering from her sister to me.

"Why don't we hire your private eye to help find Steve's killer? I mean, he's sort of started on the job already. The question that remains is whether he's capable of finishing it." Lisa Courney's sister waved her hand in the air like some sort of magic trick. Just like that. Presto. A murderer discovered.

"That sort of thing is usually best left to the police," I cautioned.

"Are you saying you can't handle something this challenging?"

"I'm just saying what's best for my client. The police have the manpower, the equipment, and the experience to handle an investigation like this."

"Well, consider me your new client." She extended her hand. She seemed to like having her hands in the air. "I'm sorry we got off to such a rough start, but today has been difficult for me." Her smile softened. "I'm sure you can understand that. My name is Deborah Krueger."

I shook her hand. "Bill Habermann. This is kind of sudden. Is there some reason you don't want to leave this to the police?"

She shrugged. "Let's just say I want to have as many minds as possible working on something this important to me and my sister. Do you have much experience?"

"Enough. But I'd like to have Mrs. Courney's approval first."

Lisa Courney had pulled her feet up under her, the soles as clean as the leather of the sofa. Her eyes drifted out across the balcony, past the green, tubular lawn table and chairs, and down onto the park below. She sighed, then nodded.

"Good! Then it's settled. How much do you charge?"

"My going rate is $75 an hour."

"That's not bad. But do you bill like a lawyer? I mean, as soon as I call or whenever you get a bright idea do you add on another $75? That could get to be expensive."

"For something like this I prefer to work for a daily fee."

"And that would be?"

I hesitated. "Four hundred dollars." I figured I'd see right off how serious she was.

She pursed her lips as though she was giving the figure some thought. "That shouldn't be too bad."

"Plus expenses."

"Oh? And what would that cover?"

"Tips for information, mileage, transportation if necessary. Things like that."

"Well, that sounds fair enough. Is our handshake enough, or do you people like to have contracts and all that? I mean, that makes it all sound so formal."

"I'll type out a statement we can both sign. That's usually enough. But I will need an advance."

She looked puzzled. I got the impression that confusion was rare for her.

"Kind of a commitment."

"Oh, of course." She marched over to a black leather bag lying in a heap on a dining room table of dark brown cherry. "How much should I make the check out for?"

"$1500 will be fine."

"Well, let's make it $2000. Five days worth." Her blue eyes snaked toward mine. "Starting with today, of course."

She ripped the check from the book with the flourish of a butcher, strode over and tucked it into my shirt pocket.

"Do you think you can solve this that quickly?"

"No. And I'll write a receipt."

"Oh, don't bother. But if you must, you can send it in the mail to me here, along with the little contract of yours. I'll be staying here with my sister for a few days."

I turned back toward Lisa Courney, who had not moved from her spot on the sofa. This didn't seem like the best time to begin interrogating the widow, but then it was probably not going to get any better for a while yet. I hesitated, moistening my lips, then squatted in front of her.

"Mrs. Courney, can I ask you a few questions about your husband? It might help me if I could review a few things now."

Vacant eyes stared in response for a moment before they focused. "The police have already been here. I've spoken to them."

"Yes, I know. But they're not going to share any of that. I realize this is hard, but perhaps we could try a question or two."

She nodded.

"First of all, can you think of any reason someone might have to kill your husband?"

Her mouth opened, then closed without a sound. The lips quivered. "The police have asked me that already." She shook her head. "No, of course not."

I hesitated again. This was not going to be easy. "There was a woman last night."

Lisa Courney's eyes jerked toward my face, and her hand dropped to her knees. "So, it was true."

"Perhaps the description sounds familiar? A thin woman, about your size, but with much darker hair, and more of it. I'd put her age somewhere in the late twenties or early thirties."

I went down on one knee but kept my hands folded together. "I'm afraid they left the bar together. But they never got very far." I leaned back to give her more room. The open lips and hard eyes of Deborah Krueger added pounds to the burden on my shoulders.

"No," she said. "That does not sound like anyone I know"

"If she wasn't the murderer, she is at least a witness." Another pause. "Did anyone try to contact you or your husband last night? Here at home, I mean." Very slick, I thought, trying to establish her whereabouts through an indirect line of questioning.

Lisa Courney shook her head. "No. There...there was nothing."

"That should do for now," Deborah Kreuger said. "My sister's been through a lot already, especially for one day."

I raised my hand. "One more question. Missus Courney, did your husband ever talk about his time in Vietnam?"

I thought Lisa Courney had looked pale before. But now she turned as white as her living room. For a moment I thought she was going to faint. Brittle, hazel eyes studied my face. I tried to see what was going on behind those thin, pointed pupils, but I might as well have been looking at the wall behind her. Her lips tightened and pressed together, separated by less than a crack. For a moment I thought she was going to spit at me.

"No."

It wasn't much. In fact, it was almost nothing. But it was enough to keep me curious. I stood and stepped away from the sofa.

Deborah Krueger took my arm, pressing her breasts into my biceps as she walked me to the door. Lisa Courney remained at her perch on the edge of the sofa, her face tilted toward the sun and away from the two of us.

When we got to the door, Deborah wheeled on me with a sudden, vicious stare. A spark of hatred bolted from eyes of deep blue fire. Everything about her—the slick hair, the modest white shirt and demure slacks, the easy banter—all of it fell away in a momentary flash of anger and aggression.

"What was that all about?"

"It was just a question. Why did she freeze up like that?"

"Look, it was a very difficult time for Steve. Things happened. I don't suppose you'd know anything about what that war did to some people, how it affected the ones who loved them."

That just about did it. This woman had hassled and misjudged me from the minute I entered the room. And now she was dismissing my character and history with a shrug. I found myself wanting to prove to her that I was as good a man as any, and a better detective than most, that I had good instincts and knew how to pursue a hunch as well as a clue. Hell, I was a survivor, too. My only regret was that I responded to her little speech with nothing more than professional courtesy.

"I'm just pursuing all the angles, Miss Krueger. I think there could be more at work here than somebody having a fling." I studied her face. "You seem pretty interested in all this. More than I would expect."

"What's that supposed to mean?"

"Nothing. How is it you know so much about Vietnam? Did he ever talk to you about the war?"

She paused while her eyes searched mine, then dropped toward the floor. In that moment she revealed a vulnerability I would never had suspected she owned. Not from her behavior thus far.

"Yes, he did. And there were things from that time he's carried with him ever since."

"Are they tied to his death? Is that why you hired me?"

Her eyes rose back to mine, and there was moisture there. But they turned hard while I watched.

"Don't dodge the real issue here." She opened the door and pushed me toward the hallway. "Steve was murdered. I want you to find that bitch for me, Bill." I stumbled backwards. "Find her," she spat. "I know you can. That's why I hired you."

The door flew shut. It missed my face by about two inches. I pitied any person caught in the sights of that woman. And for a moment I pitied whomever it was that had killed Steve Courney.

On my way to the parking lot I stopped at the reception desk. The old cowboy from Wichita jumped from his saddle behind a light brown teak desk and leaned across the counter until our heads were only about a foot apart. His breath smelled of peppermint, and gnarled, liver-spotted hands worked their fingers back and forth across a paneled countertop.

"Terrible news about the Courneys," I began.

His eyebrows soared, and he glanced toward the elevators, as though everything would be explained on a chalkboard over there.

"Is that what the cops were here for?"

I nodded. "Afraid so. It seems Mr. Courney met with an accident last night."

He looked at the floor by his feet and shook his head. When he met my face again, his eyes and cheeks were set in a scowl that looked like it would last forever. "And they were such a nice couple. Very nice tip at Christmas. Always a friendly word. Not like some folks around here. Place used to be a lot friendlier." Apparently.

"You from these parts? I thought you said something about Wichita."

He waved that off and smiled. "Aw, I just lived down there for a while. Worked as a patrolman, then a security guard at nights. Not bad money, if you ain't greedy."

"Did the other people around here feel the same way about the Courneys?"

The scowl returned. "You with the cops?"

"Sort of." I dropped a card on the counter. "I've been asked to help in this case. I was wondering if there was anyone in particular that was close to the Courneys. Someone I could speak to about them."

The scowl evaporated while he studied the card. His eyes narrowed as though I had handed him one printed in Arabic. "They were pretty new here. I did see the Courneys with the Hoffmanns once in a while. Usually coming in from the tennis courts, or the pool."

"Do they live in this building?"

Wichita straightened himself. "Naw. Over next door. Number 464."

"That's pretty good. Thanks."

His wrinkled face beamed. "It's my business to know that stuff. And think nothing of it. Always glad to help a fellow cop. Sort of." His gaze roamed the foyer, then settled back on me. "Don't tell 'em I sent you, though."

I winked and gave a thumbs-up. "Just between us, pardner. If you think of anything else, though...." I pointed to the card. He was still trying to read it as I slipped out the door.

On the way to my car, I was feeling pretty good about myself. I had begun work on a new case and even had a lead, or at least something to follow as a next step. Then I glanced back toward the Courneys' apartment. One floor below and several apartments to the side stood a man of average height but above average build, dressed in a white T-shirt and loose black pants, leaning against the metal railing of the balcony. He blended in with the building and the sky like a hunter in camouflage. I might have been mistaken, the distance was enough to obscure his face. But I could have sworn that his eyes followed my path to the Volvo, and that his lips curled in a sneer.

# Chapter 3

After about sixty seconds in the parking lot, the overbaked air clung to my body like an extra skin. I fled to the dark comfort of my car, waited with windows down until the air conditioning kicked in, then I steered the Volvo back onto Aurora Avenue. As long as I was this close, I figured I might as well check out the scene of the crime with the advantage of daylight. The engine let out a suspicious whine, probably complaining about the snarl of traffic backed up by all the stop lights along what had once been an open stretch of road. Years ago, the highway ran uninterrupted across rich farmland as far as the outskirts of Aurora, a quasi-industrial settlement that almost passed for a city. Now it was fighting Naperville for the distinction of local boom town. As far as I was concerned, the eruption of shopping malls along our old farm roads represented game, set and match.

The summer haze bounced with spiteful radiance along patches of gasping lawn and blacktop, then lingered just outside my car window. The Volvo wheezed and spit out a thin stream of cold mist, and I was grateful for the panel of well-cooled glass at my side. It didn't sound like the cold comfort would last much longer, though, and I fingered the cheque in my shirt pocket. In the residential plots I passed a few home owners struggled with a garden hose and bourgeois courage against the boiling summer air that was leaving their yards parched and yellow.

I cruised past the Jewel food store and pulled into the twenty-four hour Post Office building on Route Thirty-Four to mail my request to the VA. At the light by the fork at Oswego Road I swerved left and pulled alongside the parking lot at the Skylark. I left my car propped on the shoulder of the road and strolled toward the small crowd of Naperville officers and county technicians working the scene.

About half a dozen men milled inside the yellow ribbon strung around the front of the parking lot and hooked into the side of the Inn. It formed a square roughly half the size of a football field. Two cars were still parked inside the cordoned off area, Courney's Lexus and the Taurus that had been spray painted with his blood and brain matter. Two officers in civilian clothes circled the cars, peering at the ground as though they had lost something. I recognized them as the county forensic experts and figured they were re-inspecting the crime scene in daylight to be sure they had caught everything. Gravel baked dry by the sun crunched under their hard rubber soles, and flecks of dust coated their shoes. The stench of death had been swept away by the odor of stale beer. They were probably having a ball.

A patrolman stopped me when I approached the border of yellow evidence tape that hung limp in a windless sky. I called over to Rick Jamieson, who stood near Courney's car. He held up his hand, motioning for me to wait while he spoke with the technicians.

"Jesus, Willy-boy, you didn't have to get all dressed up to pay us a visit." The voice of Frank Hardy broke the heavy air in a false greeting. "Back for more? I woulda thought you'd had enough last night."

"I did," I said, meeting his false smile with one of my own. "But it's always great to see you."

Hardy sauntered in my direction, scratching his belly along the way. His navy blue slacks had succeeded in retrapping the bottom rim of his white dress shirt. The tie had disappeared, though. The sleeves were still rolled up to the elbow.

"Actually, I don't recall asking you to visit us at the crime scene."

"You didn't. But I thought that if I returned it might jog my memory."

"Uh huh." He eyed me suspiciously, his head cocked backwards at an awkward angle. The smile had disappeared.

I didn't respond. I wanted to see how long he could hold that pose. He had to be catching up to my own lack of sleep by now. After about ten seconds, his head rolled forward in one slow, luxurious movement, and I thought I caught a glint of recognition in his glazed pupils.

"Go ahead and look around," his stubby index finger gesturing at my feet, "on the right side of the tape." Then he winked, like the patrolman and I were two old poker buddies. "And I know you'll share with us everything you find, Bill."

"Why wouldn't I?" I started to walk along the border of the parking lot.

"Because you didn't last night," he called after me. Hardy had rotated his upper body to follow my movements. "Care to tell us anymore?"

I stopped and turned. "There isn't anymore, Frank." Give me time, though, I thought.

"Have it your way, Bill. But I'm warning you. I'm expecting you to cooperate with our investigation. That comes first now, not your spy games with some jerk-off husband and his jealous wife."

He marched over, halting right in front of my chest. One of the patrolmen started to amble over, but Hardy waved him away. He was about an inch taller than me, and he leaned his chin forward almost to mine to exaggerate the difference in our heights.

"You've never investigated a murder as a private citizen before, have you?"

I moved my head back an inch. He must have grabbed some breakfast after I left the station. His breath smelled of day-old scrambled eggs and dried-out bacon crisps.

"What's that got to do with anything?"

Another smile creased his lips. His right index finger jabbed my chest bone. It was a strong, hard finger. "I haven't forgotten the work you did for us, Bill, but that was long ago and far away." His index finger stayed upright while his hand swept the air around us. "This is different. You're not on the force anymore. Don't get in our way, and don't fuck anything up. Got it?"

I tried to stare him down while a smile slipped between my own teeth. "I know the proper procedures. You don't have to play hard ass with me, Hardy."

He didn't seem to hear. "Because if you do, I will fuck you up good." He jabbed my chest once more for added emphasis.

Rick Jamieson appeared out of nowhere, grabbed my elbow, and yanked me away.

"It's all right, Frank. I asked him to come over."

"What the fuck for?" Hardy was staring hard at his detective. I pitied Rick at this moment, and not just because he was my oldest friend in Naperville. He had just lied to his boss.

He dropped my arm. "I thought he might be able to help us reconstruct the crime now that there's light."

"What difference would that make? There wasn't any light last night." Man, but Hardy was relentless. We had never been the best of friends, but this was something else. I wondered if the murder had set him off and, if so, why he was taking it out on me. Maybe he just hated having to miss his Sunday service at the local Presbyterian meeting house. But I doubted it.

"Still, I wanted Bill here before his memory started to go stale."

Hardy slid his hands to his hips. "Just keep him on the other side of the tape."

Rick grabbed my sleeve again and pulled me further along the perimeter of the crime scene. My eyes refused to leave Hardy's navel, which threatened to break out between the buttons of his wrinkled white shirt.

When I swung my vision back to Jamieson, I was startled to see him in a blue cotton dress shirt. And he had a tie on. A nice yellow and red job with little elephants running up and down like escapees from a Republican convention. He must have gone home to change.

"I see that stick from this morning is still stuck up Hardy's ass."

"Forget it. You've got to expect that in this kind of situation."

"What the hell kind of situation is that?"

"Bill, we get maybe one murder a year here in Naperville. You know that."

"So?"

"So, the pressure's on to solve this one as quickly as possible. The press has already been out here, hounding us with a pile of questions. And I guess they didn't like the answers."

"So? Screw 'em."

"Bill, you know better than that. You know that people have come here from all over the region to live."

"Yeah?"

"And I don't have to tell you that the security of suburbia is one of the things they like about it. Chicago's only thirty miles away, Bill. You've been there. They don't want the violence that plagues the city to follow them here."

"You just said it hasn't. One killing a year is a pretty enviable statistic."

"Well, they don't want the fear that goes with it either. And they pay a lot in taxes to make sure it doesn't."

"I know the sociology of the region, Rick, but that still doesn't explain why Hardy has to be such a prick. Hell, I might even be of some help."

We glanced over at the two cars, and I could see that the Taurus had been cleaned, the blood and brains probably packed, sealed and already on their way to the lab.

"Your silence last night didn't help."

"I didn't have anything to say."

"He's also pissed because he had to give up a couple of Cubs tickets."

"So? They'll probably lose anyway."

"Don't tell him that." Jamieson laughed. "And it probably doesn't help that you slept with his wife."

My arm shot out and grabbed Jamieson's sleeve. "Goddammit, Rick. I did not sleep with her. We went out twice, and they weren't even married yet. We had a couple of nice, proper dates. Dinner and a movie. That was it, and you fucking know it."

Jamieson's smile broadened. He shook his arm free. "Hell, I know that. I also know about your luck with women. But Hardy probably thinks you're a real stud."

I just stared.

"I mean, you're still a bachelor, so he figures you're getting laid a lot."

"I'll bet he's on another one of those damn diets."

I turned my head and studied the front of the Lexus. Another technician was searching the ground several feet from Courney's car. He appeared to spy some black specks, dried blood perhaps, scattered about six feet from the car, then bent low to gather the gravel.

"Anything yet," I asked. "Prints, shells, a weapon? I doubt if you were able to find anything like tire tracks."

Jamieson shook his head. "Not in this stuff. There's so much crap in this lot, there's no way to tell what might be tied to the shooting." He kicked at the stones. Dust swirled, then sank. "We had hell to pay with most of the customers for making them wait while we prowled around the parking lot." He chuckled. "I think the last one got away around five o'clock."

"Any luck?"

Jamieson pointed to a spot in the gravel about several feet from the Lexus. "We found a casing over there."

"And?"

"It's a nine millimeter."

"Then you should be able to match it with a weapon, if you find one."

Jamieson nodded some more, his eyes still focused on the Lexus.

"Found a slug yet?"

"Nope. But we've been all over the lot." He shook his head and finally brought his eyes toward mine. "Guess we'll have to do it again."

I turned my face back toward my friend. "I don't know, Rick."

Jamieson's eyes shot toward mine. "What?"

"Well, the bullet had to go through a lot of bone to penetrate Courney's skull. Twice. And if it hit anything else, there might not be a whole hell of a lot to use for identification."

"So, what are you saying?"

"I'm not saying anything, Rick. I'm just wishing you a lot of luck, because I don't think this one will get solved in the lab. A weapon sure would help, though."

"Thanks for the tip. We'll keep it in mind."

I pointed at Courney's Lexus with my right arm. "I also think those guys are wasting their time."

"Oh, really?"

Two men were busy dusting the windows and upholstery for prints. "I doubt they'll find anything to lift, Rick. The lovebirds never made it to the car. It sounded to me like she—or someone—shot Courney before they got there."

"I thought you told us you didn't see the actual shooting."

"I didn't. But I could tell that much from the timing. It's not like they had time for any hank-panky in the back seat. You might be able to get something from the corpse itself, if it isn't too late."

"Thanks again, Bill. You know, we haven't forgotten how to do our jobs since you left the force."

"Yeah, okay. What about the bar? Anything from in there?"

"Nope. They wash everything as soon as they can to try to move more drinks. And can you imagine how many prints we'd lift from a barstool or ashtray? None of that shit would be any use in court."

"Anything else?"

"Not so far."

"How about the witnesses?"

"Nothing there either. The one guy...."

"The puker?"

Jamieson laughed. "Yeah, the barfer. He didn't see anything besides the blood and gore, or so he says. Claims he stumbled onto the corpse before he realized anything had happened."

"He didn't hear the shot?"

Rick shook his head. "Nah. Claims he doesn't remember anything special with all the noise."

"Bullshit."

"But to an untrained ear...." Jamieson shrugged.

"What about the one guy who told me he saw the woman running away? I think his name was Tom."

Jamieson shook his head. "No clear i.d. there either. Doubts he'd be able to pick her off a lineup or a mug sheet."

"Any help from the bartenders or waitresses? I saw Willy Romer behind the bar last night. He's a pretty solid type."

"Nothin' much there either. We're putting out a notice asking anyone who was here last night to come by the department if they have something to volunteer. It would be nice if you could contribute what you remember to a composite sketch."

"Oh, that should help." I rolled my eyes.

Jamieson shrugged again. "You'd be surprised."

In the intervening silence I could hear the traffic hum and skip along Route 34. Every couple of minutes the pop of a burst bubble would resonate through the early afternoon furnace. It's a sound I associated with summer, especially July, when the black tar soaks up the heat of the sun bearing down on us below, and small bubbles form along the surface just waiting for the hard rubber of an automobile tire to press them back and let the gas escape.

"So?" Jamieson asked.

"What?" I groaned. I had a pretty good idea of what was coming.

"So, why are you here? Why all the questions? Are you really looking to see if anything extra comes back to you?"

I looked long and hard at the face of Rick Jamieson. I had seen him interrogate witnesses and suspects before, and he was very good at it. Never betraying his emotions, never overplaying his hand. He knew just how to read each individual, how to find their most vulnerable spot. It's what made him such a good cop. And it's usually what made him such a good friend. He knew my vulnerabilities as well, and he knew I'd tell him just about everything I could, everything I knew. Even when I didn't want to.

"Not really. I haven't forgotten anything."

"I knew that much already."

"And now I have a new interest in the case." I glanced at Rick to see how closely he was watching me. His brown eyes held the piercing intensity of a hawk.

"And that new interest would be?"

I returned his stare. I knew I couldn't play games with him, especially if I hoped to get any cooperation from the police. Rick was a friend, but he was still a cop.

"The widow's sister just hired me."

"And why do you suppose that is?"

My right hand groped for my heart. "Out of love for and devotion to her sister, of course. At least, that's what it looks like at first glance."

Jamieson shrugged and turned his head to survey the line of thick blacktop fading in the distance somewhere off in the West. Iowa was rumored to be out there, a little farther on.

"Just remember, most victims knew their killers. The family is the first place we look."

"You think she hired me to throw you guys off the scent?"

Jamieson shook his head. "Probably not. Unless she's been watching too much TV. It's something you need to keep in mind, though. Her motives, I mean. Or else, why not just leave it to us?"

I glanced around the parking lot. The houses that ringed the fields on either side of the lot stood out against a blue-sheeted sky, their vinyl and brick sprouting from the rich earth like a harvest of ragweed. My head listed to the side, reminding me that I hadn't had much sleep in nearly twenty-four hours.

"Thanks, Rick. I tend to forget you guys are infallible. I'd better go."

Jamieson put his hand on my shoulder before I could turn to leave. "Bill, he's right, you know."

"Who is? And about what?" I could guess, and it made me irritable.

"Hardy. You were on this thing earlier, but your part's over now. Why hang on to this case? What's in it for you?"

I could see Jamieson squinting, even though the sun was at his back. His eyes avoided mine, searching the gravel like some Delphic oracle.

"There's a fee, Rick. I've got an insurance premium coming due and a shitload of bills." I stuck my finger in the air. "With my cooking skills I don't think I would raise a whole hell of a lot at a bake sale."

"Fuck off, Bill. Who's the one with the stick up his ass now?"

"Sorry, Rick. But there are some unusual aspects to this case, including my client who looks like she'll be a real pain in the ass. But she pays well, and she pays in advance. I plan to give her good service for good money. And it doesn't make my day knowing that you guys are not going to share shit with a civilian like me."

"Those are the rules, Bill. I'll help where I can."

"That's just how I see it, Rick."

"Don't make things worse for yourself, pardner."

His words rolled off my back as I walked to my car. He was right, of course. But I wasn't thinking of Rick Jamieson's advice any more. My mind had recalled an image of Lisa Courney shuddering from the pain and uncertainty of a loss she had yet to absorb. Then the vision disappeared with the shock of seeing Steve

Courney with a large chunk of his head distributed over the pub's parking lot. There were memories there that Rick Jamieson would never share, no matter how close a friend he was. And those memories lingered at the back of this case like a distant shadow.

But even more disturbing was the guilt I couldn't shake about Steve Courney's death, almost as though I had pulled that trigger myself. After all, I had been tailing him. I had experienced death in the past, enough to last me several lifetimes. I knew that Lisa Courney had to be struggling with a set of powerful and conflicting emotions, and the least I could do after being present at her husband's death was help bring the killer to justice.

There was also Deborah Krueger. And I couldn't escape the feeling that she was worth meeting again. A woman of beauty and contradictions, she had blown hot and cold over me like an early spring breeze, holding a promise of better things to come. I don't know what it is about the appeal of a difficult and attractive woman for so many men, but against my better judgment, I wanted to pit myself against the challenges I suspected she was going to throw my way.

I realized when I reached the Volvo that I had taken this case not only for the money. I had signed on partly because I wanted to see the two sisters again. But each one for different reasons. But more than anything, I had taken the case because of the man who bound them and the chance that his death was linked in some way to my own past. Like I said, you can't go through life trusting in coincidence. I wondered if a vision of Steve Courney would visit my dreams when I closed my eyes over the next few nights. And if he did, I wondered if Steve would meet any of the Vietnamese who occasionally came to call.

# Chapter 4

It took me while to fall asleep that night. I don't remember how long. Maybe an hour or so. But I do remember my mind drifting back to the jungle, the canopy looming in the distance, a silhouette under a shower of falling flares and a moonless sky of deep scarlet. A wave of black rags surged against the perimeter. Wide-brimmed straw hats danced across the open space as though in slow motion. When they got close enough I could see cheeks lined with dirt, and dark sockets of fear peering out of the distance. Small ovals shaped themselves to yell, but the little lips rose and fell in silence. Morter rounds and grenades burst to their front, then at their backs. Metal shards ate at their flesh, and their faces filled with pain and horror. A bell started ringing somewhere off in the distance. The sound held steady, piercing the darkness. Suddenly I saw myself out there, waving at all the people, at the explosions, at all the goddamn noise. I just wanted everything to stop.

My eyes popped wide, but I couldn't see a thing. It took about twenty seconds for my eyes to adjust to the darkness, then my hand found the alarm clock on the night table.

But the ringing didn't stop. It kept hammering away at my ears, and I realized it was the telephone. I kicked off the covers and rolled out of bed, fumbled for the light switch on the lamp at my bedside and glanced at the clock. Two o'clock in the morning. Now, what kind of asshole calls at that time of night? I banged my knee against the side of the bed, stumbled toward the door, then stubbed my toe against the sofa groping for a path through the living room. By the time I reached my desk I was pretty pissed.

"What the hell do you want? " I rubbed my eyes and ruffled my hair. "Do you know what time it is?"

"Yeah, I know the time, Habermann. I own a watch, you dumb shit."

I waited, trying to identify the voice.

"Hey. You there, Habermann?"

"Who are you, and what do you want?"

"You don't remember me?" He didn't wait for an answer. "That's too bad."

"Why not just tell me your name, tough guy?"

"All I'm going to tell you is not to get too smart on this one, asshole." The words crept out from a throat that sounded like it was lined with gravel and spite.

"Excuse me?"

"I know you, Habermann. Our paths have crossed before. Consider this a goodwill message from the past."

"So what is it?"

"Back off. If you stick around you'll get squished real easy. You may not believe this, but I'm tellin' you for your own good."

The click on the other end of the line fell like a shot. It must have taken me another hour to fall back to sleep.

It felt like I had been out for only a few minutes when the ringing started again. This time, though, I wasn't dreaming. I swung my arms in a wide arc. The alarm clock crashed to floor and rolled under the bed. Suspended over the edge, I groped through dust balls and yesterday's socks. I leaned further down, propped my upper torso on my elbows, spotted the clock and grabbed it.

The ringing continued. The damn phone again. I stumbled out of bed for the second time in god knows how many hours and hunted for my desk. I remembered the location of the furniture this time, and the morning sun lit the room with a haze that made the obstacles hard to miss. I squirmed through the light and grabbed the receiver.

"Jesus, Bill, who've you got with you there?"

"Actually, just trying to catch up on my beauty rest, Rick. To what do I owe the dubious pleasure?"

"I thought you might like to know there's a memorial service for Steve Courney this morning. At eleven o'clock."

I glanced at a bare wrist. "What time is it now?"

"A couple minutes past ten."

"How can they have a funeral already? Has the body even been released yet?"

"They're not. It's a memorial service. The sister laid it on. I guess she's one of those take-charge types. Wants to show everyone how much she and the widow care for each other."

"Can't say as I'm surprised."

"You should join me. We can look for faces in the crowd."

"Hell, yeah. Where's it at?"

Jamieson relayed the information, then I dropped the receiver back into place and marched into the bedroom. I had less than an hour to shower, eat breakfast, and get dressed before the service. I just prayed the blazer was still clean and another blue shirt hung ready and waiting in the closet. I figured my dark gray slacks would be clean. If not, the khakis would have to do. And coffee and a croissant from Ahmed's. If not, then a donut from 7-Eleven.

The service was being held at the First United Methodist Church, a quaint building of red brick and gray stucco set back from Washington Avenue behind a line of waist-high residential shrubbery. A handful of dwarf lilacs peeped out from a bushy green crowd at each corner. A winding stone walkway led from the sidewalk to the front entrance. I left the Volvo around the corner on Franklin Avenue, snuck through the double oak doors, and slid into the last pew next to none other than Rick Jamieson.

He nodded. I nodded. We both nodded again, and he wrinkled his nose.

"Hey, I showered."

I made a note to splash on some aftershave and deodorant after the funeral. Maybe even send some clothes to the dry cleaners.

After my run inside, the darkened interior felt cool, even refreshing. The white plastered walls stood out in a marked contrast to the dark brown rows of hard oak that ran through the middle of the church. Aside from a candelabra on the altar, the only source of light came from the rays of sun streaming through panes of stained glass, where angels of dust danced in panels of colored amber. I leaned back against the wooden pew and propped my feet on the padded kneeler on the floor.

About forty people sat scattered throughout the church, half of those congregating in the first three or four rows at the front. I assumed those people were family and close friends. The others were probably colleagues from work.

Lisa Courney sat in the first pew, her sister tight by her side. Periodically, Deborah Krueger would slide her arm around Lisa's shoulders and rest her head against her sister's. Seated and viewed from behind, they appeared to be of matching size and build, an impression different from the one I had gotten at the apartment. Both wore black dresses that covered their shoulders and crept up their necks, with wired veils that fell forward to their chins. They sat like ravens of mourning, merged in a sibling bond. If it had not been for the differences in hair color I would not have been able to distinguish one from the other. I could also tell Lisa by the occasional sobbing that seized her, the shoulders heaving as the head bent forward. In those moments Deborah hugged her firmly. Sitting together in the silence of the church pew they presented an image of shared sorrow I had not detected yesterday. And Deborah Krueger looked almost human, as though she might actually have some feelings aside from bitterness and pride.

Once the forty-minute service was over, I accompanied Jamieson to his Ford Thunderbird parked about two blocks away on Edgeworth Avenue.

"Look, I'm sorry I exploded yesterday," I apologized. "Pass it off as sleep deprivation."

"I understand," he murmured. "And I didn't mean to suggest that you shouldn't feel an obligation towards your clients, or that you can't help them."

"This case has gotten personal."

He smiled as his eyes darted through the maple trees lining the curb along Edgeworth. "Because the victim bought it on your watch? Or is there something else?"

I paused, my own eyes following his line of sight through the trees. "That's pretty much it." I didn't feel like filling him in on the shared history, the phone call, the widow's reaction to a simple question. He'd find out about some of that soon enough anyway.

Jamieson leaned back and rested his rear end against the grill of his car. "It's too bad. Your personal agenda is not gonna help."

"Why's that?"

"Because Hardy really does have a bug up his butt over this one."

I stepped forward and placed my right foot against the grillwork of his five-year old Thunderbird. "Why is this case so special?"

Jamieson shot a glance at my feet, then blew his breath out. "He's afraid all the money coming into the area will bring in a new kind of criminal, a new breed of parasite."

"People who want to cheat the prosperous engineers and lawyers?"

"Yeah. I told him those types would be more likely to work the white-collar scams, not blow somebody away outside a bar."

"What's his theory of the case?"

"I wouldn't say he actually has a theory yet. None of us do." Jamieson cocked his head back toward the church, while his blue pupils peered at me through half-closed eyelids. "Do we?"

"Absolutely not," I assured him. I wasn't lying.

"Than get your fucking shoes off my car." He shook his head in mild disgust. "Anyway, I think he'd be happy to discover that it really was just some domestic spat behind this thing. Is that the only reason you were following him?"

I shrugged. "That's all the widow told me." I nodded in his direction. "Does this mean you're handling the case?"

"You got it."

I paused for five, maybe ten seconds. "So what do you need from me?"

He shook his head. "This one isn't going to be easy. We're going to have to put our heads together to keep Hardy from taking both our scalps."

My shoe dropped to the pavement, and my hands made a compulsive tug at the hair along the back of my skull. "Well, my ties to the widow could come in handy here. If there's a family angle, I could have some unique access." I shook my own head. "And goddammit, Hardy has no cause to hammer my ass."

"Maybe he's jealous."

I looked away. "Oh, come on. Not that crap about me and his wife again."

Jamieson sighed. "Not this time. But you're being on the case does bug him."

"What for?"

"Look." Jamieson leaned forward, his hands resting on his knees. "Hardy's a good cop. Works hard and long. He leads by example. That's how he got to be chief of our division. And he probably would have been happy to stay a big fish in a small, suburban pond. But Naperville's not so small anymore. And now this killing happens."

"So why does he want to ream me?"

Jamieson sat back again and let his breath slide out. "Because you've played in the big leagues. You went back to Saigon after your tour as a grunt and got to work in the intelligence game."

"It was a lot less impressive from the inside."

"It still impressed a lot of people in this town. And Hardy's probably afraid you'll steal his big chance for some thunder, his shot at establishing himself here."

"Shit, Rick, it's only Naperville."

"He grew up here too, Bill."

"Has he spoken about this to you?"

Jamieson shook his head. "No. It's just my guess. But it's an educated one."

I shook my own head and surveyed the homes lining the street. "I still think it's those damn diets he tries."

"Maybe so, maybe not. But there's another reason for you to open up with me, Bill."

"And that is?"

"We're trying to find a murderer here. Remember? It wasn't that long ago. And I can't shake this feeling that there's something you're not telling me. I know you too well, Bill."

I took a turn studying the stately trees that formed a long column between the curb and sidewalk along Edgeworth. A canopy of green covered about three quarters of the street. Fingers of bright white sunlight poked the dusty lawns and steaming blacktop. A shaft of silver split the street down the middle. When I turned my head, Jamieson's eyes had not moved from my face.

"So what is it? Did you find anything? Did the guy have a dancing dick?"

I shook my head. "Not to any tune I could find."

"Was his wife just paranoid?"

"It's hard to say." I glanced at Jamieson and smiled. "It wasn't for any lack of effort."

"Did he make you?"

"Never acted like it."

Rick shook his head. "He probably wasn't gettin' any at home."

"I can't say. I didn't know them well enough to guess."

"Still, that could give the wife a motive. Did you get to know her at all?"

"Not really. Just the tearful, neglected spouse. Another victim."

"You think there's more there?"

"Usually is." I turned to leave.

Jamieson's voice followed. "Thanks, Bill. And here's something for you."

I glanced back at my friend. "So we are going to trade."

"Just this once. We found the weapon."

"No shit? What was it?"

"A Makharov. It turned up in some weeds down the road. The shooter must have tossed it there."

"Holy shit, Rick. Did it match the casing?"

He nodded. "Ballistics confirmed it this morning."

"Good luck tracing that bastard."

He shrugged. "We'll do what we can. Just remember this, pardner. You owe me."

"Yeah, right. Let's go find the reception."

I marched to my Volvo parked around the corner and waited for Jamieson's Thunderbird to drive up. He tailed me to the reception at the Courney's apartment, where we followed the dark-suited flow of somber faces. The crowd had nearly doubled by the time we got there. I figured more people from Steve Courney's employer, Americo Tech, had been able to escape during their lunch hour. An array of finger sandwiches and pastries covered the dining room table on about half a dozen trays, and tall pots of coffee and hot water for tea stood next to the arrangement on a small side table. A few people wandered in an out of the kitchen with soda or beer or a glass of wine before milling with the other mourners.

Jamieson and I staked out our positions at the edge of the dining room, then drifted over in front of the fireplace. I stuffed my hands in my pants pockets, hoping to look inconspicuous. Jamieson crossed his arms at his waist in a more respectful posture.

The widow leaned on her sister for much of the time, giving no sign of recognition to those milling around her. She pasted a frail smile over distant eyes when people came to shake her hand or kiss her cheek. Many of the women hugged her, and Lisa Courney appeared genuinely grateful. In those moments, she held her head high and back firm while her arms moved with restraint and dignity. Her bearing suggested a reservoir of self-confidence that just might see her through this crisis. I admired her.

So did her sister, by the look of pride on her face. At one point Lisa seemed to waver, as her knees bent and her face fell to her sister's shoulder. Deborah Krueger supported her sister with an embrace that wet quite a few eyes in the crowd.

Rubbing my own lids, I strolled over to the table and collected a plate full of breaded biteables, ham and turkey mostly, and searched the small sea of faces to see if anyone looked particularly aggrieved-or elated. Trying to choose between the pink and white pastries, I heard someone at the table introduce Karl Hoffmann to a Mrs. Swiggert. I glanced up to find a tall gentleman in his mid-to-late thirties who had packed his roughly 170 pounds into a well-tailored, two-piece blue pinstriped suit. His blond hair fell in loose curls over the tips of his ears and nearly to the shirt collar at the back. His red and blue checked tie was tight enough at the collar to hold his mustache in place during a heavy wind. After a few courteous words with the dowager Swiggert, Karl Hoffmann ambled toward the patio. I followed.

"Excuse me," I said, "but aren't you Karl Hoffmann? From here in the complex?" He nodded, too polite, apparently, to speak with his face full of turkey and gouda. "The Courneys mentioned your name on occasion, and I'm glad to meet you finally." I offered my hand.

Hoffmann hadn't swallowed yet, so he nodded some more, put the plate on the patio table, and took my hand. He stood with his back to the sun, which set his hair ablaze with yellow light and obscured his facial expressions. I moved to the side. In the interim, he gulped down his mouthful. "And you are?"

I introduced myself, embellishing my experience with the family somewhat, and slipped him a card. "I did some work for the Courneys once, and we stayed in touch." I surveyed Riverwalk Park, which spread behind us like a verdant green lake. Islands of newly planted trees dotted the landscape. "It really is tragic. I wonder who could have done such a thing."

He nodded vigorously while reading my card. "It is hard to believe. I really can't imagine myself." The card disappeared in his shirt pocket.

"You're not aware of any enemies Steve had, or anything he said that might throw some light on this, are you?"

Hoffmann's eyes narrowed. He retrieved his plate of food. "Are you interested professionally? Aren't the police handling this?"

I forced a smile and held my hands out palms up. "Just a natural inquisitiveness. I can't help myself. Anything I learn I pass along to the police, of course." I turned, then pointed to Jamieson, who was trying to cram the last parts of a ham-and-cheese croissant into his mouth without getting any crumbs on the floor. So much for diplomacy and tact. "There's one now. We came together."

"I see." His left hand held the plate while his right toyed with another turkey and gouda in a mini-Kaiser. "My wife and I never noticed anything unusual about the Courneys. We weren't very close, of course, but we saw an occasional film together. Dinner maybe once every other month. Things like that."

"Tennis? Swimming?"

"Oh, sure. But the conversations never got personal enough to reveal much."

"Why is that? I mean, people are usually willing to open up some once they get to know each other."

Hoffmann shrugged. "I can't really say. The Courney's were a friendly, hospitable couple, but they gave us the impression that they always wanted to maintain a certain distance. They claimed they couldn't talk about their past jobs."

"Pretty mysterious. Were they spies, or something?"

Hoffmann laughed. "Perhaps. But we never felt like pressing. I mean, there was enough to talk about here with the way the area is growing."

"So what else did you discuss? Hobbies, the weather?"

He nodded. "Mostly. They didn't care much for the winters here. And both seemed to read a lot."

"What sort of books?"

"Steve read a lot of history. I was always impressed by how much he knew about the world."

"Anything in particular?"

"Yeah, Vietnam. I guess he did some time there."

"What do you do for a living, Mister Hoffmann? If you don't mind my asking."

He shook his head between bites. "Not at all. I have an insurance agency here in town. In fact," he swallowed and pointed to his shirt pocket, "I might even be able to steer some business your way."

I smiled. "Sure. Always happy for that." At least the conversation wouldn't be a total loss.

A pregnant woman in a navy blue dress that sloped from her breasts in a gentle curve around her stomach joined our conversation. Her green eyes sparkled under a light blond scalp of short hair and an air of expectation.

"Happy about what?" Her left arm snaked around Hoffmann's waist.

"This is my wife, Cathy, Mister Habermann." We shook hands.

"We were just discussing your late friend, Steve Courney. Aside from some mystery to his past, I guess he led a pretty normal life."

"Yeah, pretty middle-class and all that," she agreed. "Except maybe for the occasional nose candy."

I leaned forward, setting my plate on the table. Someone over in the park flipped a switch, and the sprinklers shot jets of crystal water across rolling hills of green. "Excuse me? Nose candy?"

"Cathy." Hoffmann frowned. "This is hardly the time to gossip."

She ducked her shoulders, and her eyes danced back and forth. A sly smile crept out. "I suppose you're right. But it's not gossip. Besides, who cares? It's not like they're going to arrest him now, is it? I saw the dust and mirror in their apartment once." She looked up at her husband, the smile gone. "Sorry."

"Oh, that's okay. I won't tell him." I pointed to Jamieson, who was leaning against the wall by the fireplace. "We all have our vices."

Hoffmann's frown refused to disappear, so I excused myself and returned to Jamieson. Along the way, I detoured to the dining room table and collected three of the pink pastries.

For his part, Jamieson appeared to have spent most of his time studying the crowd, and Deborah Krueger in particular.

"Who's the salesman?"

"Karl Hoffmann and wife. Neighbors and friends of the family."

"Learn anything?"

My words fell out between bites of sweet little vanilla cupcakes with a hint of strawberry. "Only that the deceased may have had a recreational drug habit."

"What kind?"

"The words 'nose candy' were used."

"The lab work should tell us something. I've got to head over to Wheaton this afternoon for the autopsy." Jamieson tilted his head toward Miss Krueger. "Your new source of income is a very attractive woman, Bill."

She had freed her hair from yesterday's imprisonment, and dark waves swept back to a pair of high and square shoulders.

"Yes, she is, Rick. I see you cops can be perceptive every once in a while."

"Do you know anything about her yet?"

"Not really. Not sure how much I want to learn, either."

"Why not?"

"My first impression was that of a real bitch."

"Well, maybe you can put her in touch with her feminine side."

"It might be worth a try."

His eyes sparkled at the thought. "You private dicks have all the fun."

"Sometimes. We just don't get any respect from the bureaucrats."

"Well, you'd better be careful on this one."

I glanced at Jamieson. "What have you found out about her?"

He shook his head. "Not much beyond a messy divorce. It seems she signed a prenuptial agreement that cut her off from a nice settlement."

"That was quick."

"I told you we always start out with the family. Her stuff just popped up first."

"So, she married rich? Some old guy?"

"No, a young one. But he came from a wealthy family. The guy was a doctor who inherited a lucrative practice in upstate New York. She moved back here to start over."

I thought of the ease with which she had signed my cheque. "Hasn't done too badly."

Jamieson's eyebrows bridged under his hairline. "Certainly fills out an expensive dress nicely. Overcame the abuse well."

"From her husband?"

"Apparently. You have to wonder about her reasons for hiring you, though. You're not cheap, you know. Stupid maybe, but not cheap."

I gestured toward the crowd with my head. "Well, maybe that's one area where I can help you out. She just might shed some light on this thing."

"What else can you tell me on Courney? Did you ever find much on the guy's past?"

I hesitated. "He was a vet. A trace also brought up some obscure reference to a job in the Pentagon and an address in Alexandria, Virginia."

"Have you looked at his VA records yet?"

"Nope," I mumbled.

His eyes stayed with the crowd.

"Didn't think it would be necessary," I continued. "I mean, I was only trying to see if he was dipping his stick in somebody else's shrubbery, not write a biography."

"Fair enough. We'll send away for them. What about the Pentagon thing? Don't you still have some friends in the Washington area? Friends from Vietnam, or something?"

"Yeah," I nodded. "Or something."

"Do any of them work at the Pentagon? You still in touch?"

"Yeah," I repeated. "Where you going with this, Rick?"

My old friend studied my face. "Let's check on the vet's history. I'll request his VA file and you can check out the Pentagon. Maybe there's something there."

"You really think so?"

He shrugged. "There's an interesting coincidence here. We pulled the guy's phone records, and it seems he made several calls over the last couple weeks to a number in Arlington, Virginia."

"Private or business?"

"Private. Apparently a Vietnamese residence."

A mild, involuntary shudder shook my chest and shoulders. "Maybe you're right. I guess I owe Sully another visit."

By now, the dark-suited mourners were turning away to return to the world of the living. A few stragglers held their own lonely silhouettes out on the patio against the shimmering summer sky. Empty plates lay scattered among the rooms like pebbles on a white sea.

Jamieson and I strolled away from the fireplace and deposited our plates in the kitchen near the sink. After paying our respects, I cast one last glance at the Courney sisters. They were seated in two winged-back chairs at the edge of the living room. Deborah had wrapped her arm around Lisa, who sat stock still, her head in her hands.

Then, as though moved by a sudden thought, Deborah Krueger looked up and across the apartment. Our eyes locked for a brief moment, no more than a second. She let a faint smile escape and nodded lightly, almost imperceptibly. I tried to swallow, but the muscles in my throat locked. I felt suddenly adrift.

When I looked away, Jamieson's gaze caught me square in the eyes as he slid on his sunglasses. "I mean it, Bill. Keep your proverbial ass in gear on this one. Or you'll have Hardy climbing all over your back."

"Fuck Hardy."

"That," he noted, "is a very unpleasant thought."

We strolled out the building and over to our cars. Wichita nodded and winked, acknowledging our earlier cooperation. Jamieson and I did not say anything more. I was happy for that. I knew I wasn't going to be able to keep my past ties to Courney a secret much longer. But before I said anything, I hoped the stranger would call again.

# Chapter 5

After the reception I drove to the Lantern, one of Naperville's oldest watering holes. Its red brick facade had locked the busy intersection of Washington Street and Chicago Avenue together for as long as I could remember, a real landmark. I and most of my friends had tried at various times to get served there as teenagers, and most of us celebrated our twenty-first birthdays there. The new owners had covered it in a coat of light brown paint. Everywhere I looked, I encountered varying shades of beige.

Willy Romer had pulled lunch duty behind the bar that day, as he did most weekdays. He had also been working at the Skylark Inn the night of the shooting. Willy was a tall, lanky guy in his early thirties, whose frizzy red hair sprouted on all sides of his head and fell over the tops of his ears. I had known Willy for a long time. My sister had even baby-sat for him. Willy had survived that and gone on to become a pretty fair basketball player at Marmion Academy, a Catholic high school over in North Aurora.

It was just after one o'clock, and the lunch crowd had thinned. I sat down on one of the red vinyl stools that lined the front of the bar just as you walk in the door and rested my feet on the metal tubing at its base. The booths at my back were still full, but about half the tables in the back room were vacant. The new beige exterior hadn't changed the inside all that much. The dark paneled wall to my front was still covered with ancient beer advertisements for such long-ago brands as Dreweys and Falstaff. The Hamm's bear posed beside a neon stream promoting the miraculous taste produced by the sky-blue waters of rural Wisconsin.

Willy sauntered over in his afternoon uniform of jeans and a T-shirt, this one advertising Bradley University from out near Peoria. I ordered a hamburger-one of their half-pounders-and a plate of fries.

"Do ya wanna try a Bass Ale with that today? We just got it on tap. Or will it be one of your regulars?"

"You'd better make it a Coke today."

"Rough night?"

"Rough day is more like it."

He walked away to settle someone's bar tab, and I took out my notebook. Willy Romer supplemented his income from the Lantern by working at different night spots around town on the weekends. He had once explained that the Skylark was his favorite, since the tips were highest there. In fact, he probably earned in one night at the Skylark what he received over the course of a week at the Lantern. That made a lot of sense when you considered the difference in customers at the Lantern, mostly blue-collar types and students from North Central College in town.

Willy set the Coke in front of me. "I'll have your burger and fries in a sec."

When he returned with the food twenty minutes later, I laid a twenty dollar bill on the bar.

"Willy, do you mind if I ask a few questions?"

"Go ahead." He studied the twenty.

"They have to do with last Saturday night."

"Oh, yeah. That." He averted his eyes, studying the wooden pallet at his feet. "I already explained everything I could remember to the police. Can't Jamieson fill you in?"

"No, Willy. There's a lot the police won't tell me. Besides, they might have missed something."

His eyes widened.

"Hey," I said. "It happens."

"Are you workin' this case for someone?"

"Yep. How long did they hold you?"

"Until four o'clock. I felt like shit when I got outta there." He yawned. "And I'm still catchin' up on my sleep."

"I believe you, Willy. This shouldn't take nearly as long. I just want to clarify a few points."

He shifted his weight from one foot to the other, then back again while his eyes examined the length of the bar. "Okay. But I gotta keep waitin' on the customers." A bar towel wound itself around his wrists.

"Sure. What kind of night was it out at the Inn?'

"The usual." He shrugged his shoulders and rolled his head toward the door when two customers walked in. A shaft of light followed from the street.

"What do you mean by that? Was it pretty crowded?"

"No more than every other Saturday night." The lean shoulders rotated once more underneath the loose gray T-shirt. "The real crowd doesn't start coming in until a bit later. Eleven o'clock or midnight is when it really gets hoppin'."

"Did you notice the murder victim at all? How about when he came in?"

"No, I didn't notice him at first. I was too busy. But I saw him later."

"You did?"

"Hell, yeah. He was hard to miss, after a while."

"What do you mean?"

Willy leaned forward on the bar, his elbows resting on the smooth wooden countertop. "Man, that guy was all over the place. He was talkin' up chicks like a real pro."

"Do you mean he was trying to pick someone up?"

"Yeah, but he wasn't havin' much luck."

"Didn't the women find him attractive?"

"I wouldn't go that far."

"How come?"

"Well, they looked pretty interested."

"Then what was the problem?" I bit into the hamburger before it went cold. The fries were already lukewarm.

Willy looked down the bar. "Excuse me a minute."

He sauntered to the other end and filled a waitress's order with two Bud lights and two Sprites. He topped off somebody else's Miller Lite, then returned to our conversation.

"Man, I don't know how anybody can drink that crap."

"I know what you mean. They might as well save themselves the trouble and drink water instead of anything phoney enough to be called 'lite' beer."

"No. I meant the Sprite."

"Oh yeah, that." I ducked behind the hamburger and took another bite. "Anyway, what do you think the guy's problem was?"

"There was no follow through."

"Come again?"

"Just when one of the babes looked ready to go, he would wander off and chat up another one."

"Maybe they weren't all to his taste."

"Hey, most of these chicks were good lookin'. Good enough for me, anyway."

"Well, maybe he was just more particular."

"Maybe. He seemed to prefer dark-haired women."

"He spoke only with brunettes?"

Romer nodded. "Pretty much. The darker the better."

"Did anything else about him strike you as odd?"

"Whadda ya mean?"

"Well, was he drinking heavily, or just sipping to be sociable? Did he appear to be inebriated?"

Willy shrugged. "Hard to tell. I was pushin' a lotta liquor over the bar."

I fingered the fries and studied the plate before looking up at Willy again. "Don't take this the wrong way, big guy, but have you ever noticed or heard of any drug activity out at the Inn?"

Willy backed away from the bar. "Where the hell is that comin' from?"

"Relax, Willy. I'm just trying to explore all possible angles."

Willy Romer's angular frame returned to the bar. "No, Bill. No drugs that I'm aware of. No child prostitution either."

I popped a few of the fries into my mouth while Willy surveyed the other customers at the bar. "Okay, okay. So what finally happened with the one he did choose? Did you see her come in the bar?"

Willy shook his head. "Sorry. She must have come in when I went to the cellar for some more vodka. That stuff was movin' real fast"

"Okay." I chewed some more. "Then what?"

Willy grinned and shook his head again. The towel found its way to his brow, while Willy's eyes explored the grains running the length of the bar top. "One minute I saw him talkin' to this delicious number with hair the color of a crow. Then I go downstairs, and the next thing I knew, he was headin' out the door with this same chick. I thought, man, it's about time."

"Did you get a look at her face?"

Willy's eyes found mine, and his grin beamed across the countertop of polished wood. "Nope. Too much hair. But she never really looked at me." Willy wiped the bar counter with long circular strokes. "Shit," he exclaimed. "I probably woulda taken her."

"Why is that?"

"I dunno. She seemed different, kind of exotic. I like that.

"I believe you, Willy. But you gotta be careful these days."

He glanced up from the countertop. "You mean AIDS and shit?"

I chewed thoughtfully, then swallowed. "Semi-automatics, too."

I pushed the twenty in his direction and told him to keep the change. I finished the burger, including the tomato and lettuce-my mother would have been so proud-but left half the fries lying on the rim of the plate.

Willy studied the floor. "Amen to that," he said. "And thanks for the tip."

"Sure. Just one more thing. Was there anyone else working that night I could talk to?"

Willy's hand rose to his forehead, where it rubbed his eyebrows, then ruffled his hair. Not a strand moved. His eyes seemed to peer right through me and follow the traffic as it collected at the corner of Washington Street and Chicago Avenue outside. His bit his lower lip.

"Don't tell her where you got the name, okay?"

"Who is it, Willy?"

"No. You gotta promise first."

"Okay, okay." I held my hand up. "Scout's honor."

He leaned back against the cabinet with the four long rows of hard liquor, a wry smile spreading across his thin face. "You were never in the fuckin' scouts, man."

"Well, I promise on their honor anyway."

Willy weighed this thought for a moment like a rare coin. He folded the bar rag, then tossed it at the sink to his right. "Her name's Wanda," he mumbled to the floor.

"Wanda what, Willy? And I could use an address."

"Wanda Rathko. And she lives in the Camelot Apartments down by Moser Highlands."

"Do you know the apartment number?"

Willy studied the ceiling fan. "Three hundred something." His eye fell to mine, and his shoulders heaved. "Sorry."

"That's okay. I'll check the mailboxes."

Willy's face brightened. "Not bad. For a detective."

"Thanks, Willy. Anything you want to tell me about her?"

Again, Willy stood mute for about a minute. Then he held up a finger, strolled to the end of the bar near the cash register and filled another order. When he returned, Willy's eyebrows had pulled together in a red hedge.

"Look, Bill. I'm not sure how Wanda will react to you, but I know she doesn't like cops."

I drained my coke, then twisted the glass in my hand. Ice cubes rattled like dice. "Why is that? Trouble with the law?"

He took the plate and set in the bucket with the other dirty dishware next to the cash register. He massaged his forehead with his right hand, ignoring a customer who waved an empty glass.

"It's just some stuff she's said in the past. She was real nervous before the cops got there. And she didn't have a whole lot to say to 'em. She bolted as soon as she could."

"Do you think she had anything to do with the killing, Willy?"

He shook his head. "Wanda's a good kid. She's just had some tough luck." He looked up, the lines of his face straight now. "Just be careful with her, okay?"

"Sure, Willy." I slid off the stool. "I'm basically a nice guy. Even dogs like me."

Willy didn't have to tell me how to find the Camelot Apartments. Several friends of mine had rented flats there when they were just out of college, earning their first paychecks full time. We had thought we were all such hot shit.

As I drove up to the three-story complex with its fake Tudor styling of black timber and white stucco, it struck me how well the buildings had survived four decades. The cars in the parking lot had changed, though. I noticed quite a few four-wheel drive vehicles along with the Cavaliers, LeMans, the Geos and Honda Civics. The parking lot bore a slight resemblance to the Skylark's in taste and variety, but without the higher-priced European models. This one was paved, however. And nobody's brains littered the pavement.

Wanda Rathko lived in Number 363 in the building to the right when you entered the complex from Washington Street. I left my Volvo where it could get friendly with a dark red Ford Explorer and wandered up the outside stairs to Wanda's apartment. Willy had guessed that she'd still be home, since her second job as a waitress at the Willard House didn't start for another couple hours.

Wanda answered the door after my second knock. I shoved a copy of my license toward the minuscule crack between door and frame.

"Hi. My name is Bill Habermann." I held the copy as close as possible to my face to convince her of the authenticity of my claim.

Silence bounced back in response, framed by the canned laughter of daytime reruns. A pair of light brown eyes ringed in pink fluttered in anxiety and suspicion.

"I was hoping I might be able to talk to you about the shooting the other night at the Skylark."

"Who sent you? Was it that bastard Willy Romer?"

"Willy who?" I lied. "I was there myself, and I remember watching you wait tables. You seemed to be very good at it." My awkwardness must have disarmed her. The eyes blinked a couple of times, and the door opened another inch. "I'm working with the Naperville police on this case, and I was wondering if you might be able to answer a few questions."

The eyes rolled, and the door shut. A chain dropped on the other side, then the door opened again, releasing a scent of potpourri that wafted through a sparsely furnished living room. I watched the Wanda Rathko's backside, packed in a pair of blue jean cut-offs, stroll to a yellow sleeper couch, where her white polo shirt settled against a rich floral pattern splattered across the cushions. Beige carpeting melted under her bare feet, leaving a light set of imprints behind her. The only other pieces of furniture in the room were a light brown coffee table, a color television with a Panasonic VCR, and a stereo. The two sets of electronic equipment had their own stands. The television and VCR had one of those light brown teak jobs with shelves in the bottom for tape storage. The room reminded me of a college dorm but without the posters. Instead, French Impressionist reprints hid behind bare metal frames and reflecting glass streaked with light.

Wanda's blond hair had strips of brown and was rolled in a rough bun at the back of her head. She slumped across half of the sofa, then looked up at me with a face marked by a deep blue bruise running from her right eye to the middle of her cheek. She sniffed and patted her nose with crumpled white tissue from a box of Kleenex on top of the coffee table. Hers was the first summer cold I had seen during this heat wave. I took a seat on the edge of the table and shoved the box closer to Wanda. Sunlight streamed in from a window at the apartment's front, bounced off my shoulder and sprayed the wall behind Wanda.

"If you're from the cops maybe you can get this son-of-a-bitch. Thanks to him I'll probably lose about a week's work now."

"I'm not from the police. I'm a private investigator. But tell me, which son-of-a-bitch? This Willy guy?"

"No, not Willy Romer, silly. He's an angel. The other one. The one with the dark hair." She dabbed at her nose, then her eyes rose hopefully to mine. "Can you arrest him?"

"Who are we talking about? Does he have a name?"

"He never said. He claimed it was Raphael. Probably more like Ralph."

"So what happened?"

She sat upright against the arm of the sofa. "He came by the Willard House around closing time, Sunday night. Said he noticed me waiting tables at the

Skylark the other night, and was wonderin' if he could buy me a drink or somethin'."

"And you agreed?"

"Why not? We close early on Sundays, so it was only nine o'clock. After a few margaritas at this Mexican joint out on Ogden, we came back here."

"Did you offer to show him your prints?" I motioned toward the frames hanging on the walls.

"If you're going to be such a smart-ass, you can leave, Mr. Private Detective." She dabbed at her nose again with the balled remnants of tissue.

I shrugged and held out my hands. "I'm sorry. But it does look kind of predictable."

"Yeah, well, all he wanted was information on the shooting. I figured he was a reporter or something."

Wanda stood up and swayed back towards the kitchen.

"Or something?" I called after her. "Got any other ideas?"

She returned a minute later with an ice pack stuck to her face. "Hell, I don't know. I thought he might even be a cop. You know, like an undercover guy."

"But he wasn't, was he?"

"Guess not. When I told him I didn't want to talk about it, that's when it happened."

"What happened?"

She pulled the ice away and pointed to her cheek. "This, jag off. What do you think happened?" She replaced the ice pack. "The asshole hit me."

"What was he after?"

"Damned if I know. But I started screaming, and he ran the hell outta here."

I leaned forward to inspect the bruise. Wanda winced as I neared her face, as though it was painful even to have someone look at it. Although the edges were beginning to turn a yellowish green, the blue still formed a deep pool at its middle.

"You were lucky, Wanda. This guy could have done a lot more damage."

"How do you know? Do you know him?"

"Not really. But I know the type. Can I get you anything? Would you like to see a doctor?"

"No, that's alright. I could use the week's tips, though."

I moved closer and sat on the opposite corner of the couch.

"Did you notice anything strange about this guy? His looks? His voice?"

"Naw. He was tan, though, and pretty muscular. Good looking, too."

"Was he short, tall? You said he had dark hair?"

"Oh, he was about your height. Maybe an inch or two taller. And he had thick, dark hair, and it looked like the blow-dried type. Not like yours." She laughed. "He tried to sound real smooth, too, but I could tell it wasn't natural."

"What do you mean?"

"He had this fake tone and false manners. Probably got 'em from watchin' TV."

"Do you think he's from around here?"

Wanda shrugged and ran the tissue past her nose. "I wouldn't be surprised."

"Would you care to guess at his age?"

She shook her head. "Not really. But older than me. Closer to you, probably."

"Do you think you could pick him from some photographs if we went to the police?"

She shook her head. "No way. I ain't goin' anywhere near a cop station."

"Why, Wanda? What are you afraid of?"

"I'm just not going to. That's all." Her lips pushed themselves into a pout, while the eyes studied my face.

"Is there someplace you can go for a few days?"

"Like where?"

"Your parents', perhaps? Where do they live?"

The pout disappeared. Fear shone through the sudden widening of Wanda Rathko's eyes. "Oak Lawn. Why? Do you think this creep will come back?"

"He might. I'm not sure you qualify as a material witness, Wanda, so I don't think you can get much in the way of police protection. Particularly with as small a department as Naperville has."

"I...I'm not sure I want to go back home." The ice pack floated away and came to rest on her thighs. After a minute, it returned to her face.

"What did you leave behind, Wanda?"

Her eyes sank to the floor. Disembodied voices droned on from the television set. "I followed a guy. I met him out at Western Illinois, and we went steady for a year. I was only a sophomore when he graduated and got a job here, but I didn't want to lose him."

"And it happened anyway?"

A smile broke through her tired, battered face for the first time since my arrival. "Yeah. As always. But I had a pretty big fight with my folks about it."

"Are your parents still pissed? Can't you go back to school?"

"Not with my folks' money, I can't. That's why I'm workin' in this town and livin' like this."

I sat back against the sofa arm. Wanda's sad eyes retreated behind a haze, like a fading Renaissance portrait. She studied my movements, and I saw the fear and pain that lived with her now. But I also saw the emotional hunger that comes with loneliness. I wanted to help. I also wanted to keep my distance.

"Wanda, is there anything you want to tell me that you didn't tell the police? I'm sure that whatever may have happened in the past...."

"No." Her head rolled back and forth. "No. I can't."

"What's wrong, Wanda?"

"Why should I tell you anything?" Her lips were pressed together, the muscles of her jaw set like concrete.

"Excuse me?"

"Why the hell should I tell you anything at all, much less what I told the cops?"

She leaned away from the light and rested against the arm of the sofa. She pulled a cushion around her back for support. I studied her face, pointing to the bruise.

"Because I think you're afraid, Wanda. I think you could be in danger, and I think you know that. I can help. The police can help."

Wanda sat sullen, chewing her lower lip.

"Look, Wanda, I'll stay in touch to see that you're alright." I dropped a card on the table. "If you need to get in touch with me, or if you think of anything else, please call." I scribbled Rick Jamieson's name and office number on the back of it. "If you can't reach me, this is the officer working the case. He's an old friend."

She picked up the card, studying the print.

"What do you think this guy was after?"

"Damned if I know. But I think I got a good look at the bitch that killed the guy."

Bingo. "Did you see her shoot him?"

"Well, not really. But she was the one he left with. Who else could have done it?"

"Lots of people, Wanda. But she is definitely an important link in the chain. Do you remember what she looked like?"

"Well, she had pretty nice hair. Real dark."

"Black?"

"Yeah, but kind of shiny."

"How so?"

"Kinda like a bird."

"A raven, or a crow?"

She nodded. "I think so."

"What else, Wanda?"

I was jotting everything down in my notepad, and Wanda leaned forward to see what I was writing. I held the hieroglyphics up for her to study. "Just notes, like all good detectives do."

"Well, she was also kinda skinny. But not like she had that disease, you know."

"You mean anorexia?"

"Yeah, that one. But she looked like she worked out a lot. Probably a jogger. God, I hate joggers. And she didn't have much in the way of tits, if you ask me."

As Wanda said this, she tucked her legs up under her lap and thrust two round breasts forward, as though for comparison. The buttons of her polo shirt were undone, hinting at deep cleavage.

"That's too bad," I mumbled. "How about her age? Her size? Things like that?"

Wanda pursed her lips and studied the ceiling. "I'd say in her thirties, but late. Hell, maybe the early forties. And she was a little taller than me."

"Did you hear her speak?"

Wanda shook her head. "Sorry. But I can tell you one thing for sure. She wasn't from around here."

"How do you know?"

"Because we don't have any Chinese in Naperville."

I sat up straight. "Chinese? Are you sure?"

"Well, Asian at least. I could tell that much."

"Thanks, Wanda. That really helps. Anything else?"

She shook her head.

I crammed my notebook into my jacket pocket. "Why are you mad at this Willy guy?"

"Because he's the only other person I mentioned it to."

"Mentioned what?" I stood up.

"That I could tell the woman had somethin' wicked on her mind."

"How can you tell something like that?"

Wanda lowered the ice pack to her lap, where she cradled it in both hands.

"You must not know much about women, Mr. Private Detective."

"I try."

"Well, I knew because her eyes never left that guy, from the moment she entered. She followed him around the bar and kept gettin' in his way. You know, tryin' to get him to notice her."

"Maybe she was really attracted to Mr. Courney...."

"Who?"

"Courney. The dead guy. Was she interested in anyone else?"

"I couldn't really tell. I was workin', ya know. But I did see her give one guy the brush off."

"You don't recall what she was drinking? Or how much?"

"Naw. But it wasn't beer or wine. It was a clear cocktail. Probably vodka and tonic, or something like that. I never waited on her."

"Did she smoke?" I held my hands out, palms up. Searching at this point.

"Not that I noticed."

"But you saw them leave together?"

"Oh yeah. And they were movin' like they couldn't wait. It was like she had marked him from the start."

I told Wanda I didn't know what that was like at all. I could not remember a woman having marked me for anything. Not yet, anyway. I closed the door softly behind me.

---

The heat gave me a taste for barbecue, so I stopped at a ribs joint in a shopping center next to the Camelot complex. The Greek owner actually specialized in his country's native dishes, but few Napervillians had cultivated a taste for mousaka or pestitsio. Not yet, anyway. To stay in business, Andreas had created a spicy barbecue sauce that would have made NASA proud. Probably save some money on fuel, too. I left a trail scented with red pepper and chili sauce in the parking lot on the way to my car, while I licked the last bits of dinner from sticky fingers.

I rode home with the front windows down, one arm propped on the window to work on my farmer's tan, the other resting on the steering wheel. I wanted to go easy on the air conditioning, which had been struggling of late. And our heat wave showed no sign of abating in the near future. Besides, the barbecue had put me in a lazy summer mood; I was just some good ol' boy cruising with the sleeves rolled high, wind in my hair and a toothpick in my teeth.

It also put me in a frame of mind to ponder the elements emerging in this case. Steve Courney's drug use, if confirmed, offered one possible explanation for the killing. He could have gotten involved in dealing, or screwed somebody out of a payment. I'd have to explore that part further, despite Willy Romer's defensiveness about any action at the Skylark. Of course, the location of the murder could have been pure chance.

But what about our time together in Vietnam? Jamieson also thought there could be a connection, and Wanda's attacker pointed to a man's involvement-possibly my late night caller, someone with enough interest to produce a nasty violent streak. Was he trying to frighten off a potential witness? Was he the jerk-off who had phoned me in the middle of the night? Was that even related to this killing? Was our mutual past also tied to Vietnam?

And then there was the woman from the Skylark parking lot, a woman who seemed to have vanished. And an Oriental, if Wanda was right. Had she been acting alone, or with Wanda's assailant? That reminded me of the roll of film in the glove compartment, which I dropped off at one of those kiosks in a shopping center before I turned up Chicago Avenue for home.

The Volvo slid into the carriage house garage like it was happy to be home. I knew I was. I grabbed the camera, hopped free from the car, then shoved the double wooden garage doors shut. The camera dangled from my shoulder, the strap hooked over an index finger. Dark shadows lurked under the back stairs and at the corners of the house, where fences on either side left several feet of open space. I thought of Wanda's recent attack and decided I'd have to install some lighting in the back. It would be easy enough to run some wiring through the back. My friend and old Army buddy Jamie Krug could always help. He was handy with that sort of thing. My paced slowed as I neared the steps, my eyes trying to penetrate the darkness.

If you're away from combat and training long enough, the instinctive edge those drill instructors drum into you starts to fade. And I was well past that stage. I mean, you don't normally need it, not in civilian life. Most of us don't, anyway.

I didn't hear a thing before the first blow fell. With the second and third all I heard was a ringing in my ears and my own voice cursing in the still suburban night. A blow to the back of my knees buckled my legs, one to my kidneys doubled me over, and another to the back of my skull sent me to the pavement.

There had to be more than one. The punches and kicks came too quickly. The air swam with rays of light and blurred images. I covered my head and rolled over to get a glimpse of my assailants. Dark shapes danced in the night air. A long thin arm reached down, picked up the camera, and ripped it open.

I worked myself to my knees, one hand holding the ground at a safe distance, the other holding my stomach in place. One attacker was within easy reach. Three more stood maybe ten feet away. At first I thought they were high school kids, their size and builds appeared so slight.

Then I saw a face, and horrible memories flooded back.

"What the fuck do you guys want?"

The camera sailed against the back side of the house.

"Mister Habermann, you've made some mistakes. You need to pay for those."

The accent sounded Vietnamese, and the one closest skipped toward me. His right foot ripped into my ribs. I rolled away to escape most of the blow and felt my back ram against the legs of another. His formless shape slipped back into the shadows.

The nearest one, apparently their leader, pulled a Colt .45 from a side pocket and held it in front of my face. I guess he wanted to be sure I saw it in the poor lighting and all. But he never aimed it at me. He just waved it back and forth, as though calling the weapon to life.

"Remember this thing?"

I didn't answer. I just stared through a haze of pain and bad memories. If the weapon had been in my hand, I would have shot the bastard right there.

"You should, Mister Habermann."

The gun lowered itself until the end of the barrel was even with the space between my eyes. Then a voice broke the silence. I fell deeply in love with my neighbor, Mrs. Bachmann, that night.

"What's going on down there? You boys, what do you think you're doing?"

A full, round silhouette stood outlined against the light of an upstairs window. Mrs. Bachmann leaned forward, and she appeared to have a phone in her hand.

"I'm calling the police right now. So don't you dare make another move."

My attackers retreated with sure deliberate steps that broadcast their confidence. They were clearly in no hurry.

"Good night, Mister Habermann. We'll meet again."

The four shadows backpedaled toward the alley. I listened to their footsteps retreat through the gravel, then pulled myself up by the banister. A car engine roared, then tires squealed on an invisible road. I limped over to the camera lying on its side in front of the rear entrance to Ahmed's shop. It didn't look broken, but I couldn't tell what sort of damage might have been done to the mechanism inside.

I waved at my guardian angel and told her everything was alright. Upstairs in my apartment I set the camera on the table and made sure the door was bolted. For good measure, I pushed one of the kitchen chairs against the door. There were no signs of forced entry, and nothing appeared to have been disturbed. The chair was unlikely to stop a determined intruder, but I thought it might create enough noise to give me some additional warning.

Then I walked back to the bathroom and filled the tub with steaming water. Not the best thing for a July night, but pretty comforting after a beating. I soaked for about twenty minutes, soothing aching bones and a wounded ego. After I dried off, I climbed into a clean pair of boxers, then pulled my Browning 9mm and the fully loaded clip from the night table next to my bed. I rammed the clip home and set the semi-automatic on the table within easy reach.

It took me a couple hours to fall asleep, and my night was interrupted repeatedly by sounds outside my windows. Cars, mostly. Occasionally a cat. I got up to check on them all. And every time, that voice echoed in my ears. It was a voice with a Vietnamese accent. It sounded like so many I had heard years ago.

# Chapter 6

I was lost again. Bodies pressed everywhere. Little brown limbs of sweaty flesh flowed under loose black tunics. A wave of brown faces spilled off the sidewalks, swept into the streets, dodged motorbikes and rickshaws. Here and there a blond head, or dust mop brown, or one that looked curly red danced above the mob. Sun and heat weighed down on everyone. I thrust my hands and elbows forward to make a path, while the heat burned the air around my face and my lungs struggled for oxygen. Rotting wood and dirty laundry hung in alleys lined with metal sheeting. Then the ringing began again. There was always too much heat, too much fucking noise.

When I opened my eyes I was no longer in Saigon. The sun was still there, though, pouring over the edge of the window shade and painting the walls with streaks of light.

The ringing continued. I grabbed the alarm clock and fumbled with the switch until I turned the damn thing off. Then I returned the clock to the night table and let my head sink back into soft folds of my pillow.

When I opened my eyes again I saw the Browning. I normally do not carry. I've always believed that guns give a false sense of security, and that there's a greater danger in relying on one too much than not at all. But it had definitely provided some comfort last night. And I sure wished I'd had it earlier. I decided to carry it with me for the next few days.

Last night's dream had been a new one. I had never found myself lost on the streets of Saigon before. I wondered how a shrink would interpret that. For $120 an hour somebody with a Ph.D. in introspection might tell me I was reliving a different aspect of my time in Vietnam-the second tour, when I had returned a crisp new lieutenant right out of Fort Benning. Perhaps my subconscious was still struggling to come to terms with all the events of my time over there and their place in my life. I thought I had already done a pretty good job of readjustment in the years after I returned. But I guess there were still a few things left to resolve.

I glanced at the clock again. Eight-thirty. Enough reflection. Time for coffee. So I started a pot, then headed for the can. After a shower and some breakfast I'd pay a call on Jamie Krug, an old buddy from Vietnam who lived in nearby Oswego. I could discuss the case, the telephone call, the attack, and the flashbacks. And Jamie wouldn't charge anything.

When the knock sounded at the back door, I finished dressing and slipped the Browning in my back pocket. But instead of a dark shadowy figure on my doorway, Mrs. Bachmann stood before me, holding out a white china plate with what looked like a dozen cinnamon rolls.

"I thought you might need these this morning."

"Excuse me?"

"I heard a commotion outside last night and saw you with some friends. Later you had to stagger up the stairs." Her finger rose, and her face went hard. "Billy, I want you to promise me you'll stop spending so much time in that damn Lantern."

"Oh, thank you, Mrs. Bachmann. You're right, of course. And these look wonderful." I figured they weighed almost as much as she did. "But did you by chance get a glimpse of anyone else out there last night?"

The jowls under her chin shook with the rest of her head. "Nope. And I don't want to."

"Excuse me?"

The finger rose once more. "I don't want to know who all your friends are." Her finger sank and took aim at the rolls. "I can only bake so many of those, you know."

After my effusive thanks, she waddled back down the stairs and out of the back yard. If only she was a little more observant and a little less judgmental.

I tore off one of the rolls, which left a string of honey and cinnamon from the plate to my mouth. The damn thing tasted like an early slice of heaven, so I grabbed some paper towels and freed another one for the ride to Oswego. Then I slid the clip from the Browning's magazine, stashed it in my pocket and carried the pistol to the car. Protection is always advisable, but so is caution. That's why I also slid a piece of Scotch tape over the lower corner of my door.

The porch and back yard yielded nothing from the previous night's adventure. The same was true in the alley. My visitors had been careful, as well as cautious. That suggested some real professionals. I set the Browning in the glove compartment, then backed the Volvo out onto Benton Avenue.

By nine-thirty I had eased the Volvo onto Ogden Avenue for the drive west along Route 34. I knew from experience that if I simply followed the white lines buried in the blacktop, they would take me through the southern edge of Aurora, past farmlands and strip malls, past housing developments with new sod and tender saplings, past a new golf course and convenience shops. The lines would even take me to Oswego, one town that had yet to cash in on the prosperity that was sweeping this part of Illinois like a well-timed tornado.

Jamie Krug lived in a worn out split-level tucked into a warren of tight residential streets that crossed in neat squares. They ran just shy of the Fox River. The white paint on Jamie's house looked like it hadn't stopped peeling since my last visit on Memorial Day.

Jamie had a harder time than I did readjusting to civilian life after Vietnam. At least initially. We both struggled to put the war deep in our pasts without losing the camaraderie that grows among men in combat. I had tried education and apathy. He had turned to alcohol and drugs, then therapy and rehab. Of the two of us, Jamie looked the worse for psychological wear. It hadn't helped when he lost his job at the Burlington Northern Railroad for showing up for work drunk. Nor had his wife's departure, but at least they were talking about getting back together. His job with the railroad, though, was gone forever.

The front door stood wide open, so I pounded for about twenty seconds on the screen door. It hung loosely on its hinges, the old wood warped by years of exposure to a harsh midwestern climate. I noticed a small rip in the rusting screen at the bottom left corner. Someone had painted the floorboards on the front porch a medium gray years ago. Only streaks and patches of fading paint were left. Beads of sunlight escaped from the foliage of the oak tree in his front yard and danced along the boards. Jamie's dented, red Chevy pickup roasted in the gravel driveway.

"Hold your fucking horses, Habermann."

Jamie approached the front door in torn blue jeans and an off-white T-shirt that concealed the bulky frame of a man who never quite got his 6 feet and 3 inches of casual manhood into solid shape. He was drying his hands on a black and white checkered dish towel. He had also shaved this morning. Jamie was nothing if not hygienic.

"Then let me in, Corporal Fuckhead."

"Piss off, Sergeant Dickface."

Old Army buddies love this sort of pseudo-intellectual banter. The screen door swung out.

"Come on in. I just finished with the breakfast dishes. There's still some coffee. You look like you could use some. Are you into S and M these days, or just short on your sleep?"

I followed Jamie as he strolled toward his kitchen. "The latter, Jamie. And I could use some more coffee."

He poured two mugs full of a dark liquid that looked something like tar from a Mr. Coffee machine next to his sink. "Milk, right?"

I winced. "Yeah. And lots of it, for that stuff. How long has that been on the burner?"

Jamie shrugged. "I don't know. Maybe an hour, maybe two." He slid the mug across the table without adding any cream.

I dropped into a seat at the table next to the refrigerator, wincing at the pain in my side. I drummed my fingers across the white-flecked Formica top to the tune of the Rolling Stones song "You're Out of Touch," still running in my head from the car radio. I surveyed Jamie's kitchen. He refused to change anything in the house from the way he remembered it as part of his childhood. He had grown up in this house and had inherited it when his parents died. The yellow paint on his kitchen wall, for example, had first darkened and then faded over the years to the tone of light urine. Not very yuppie.

We were still in the Army when he got the message about his folks. Vietnam, in fact. Jamie had only a month left to his tour when the letter about the car accident arrived from an uncle living in Elgin. I had just gotten to Saigon for some hard-earned leave when Jamie showed up at my hotel room carrying about a case of whiskey in his belly and a load of sorrow on his shoulders. I found the crumpled letter in his shirt pocket. It took me another forty-eight hours to get him sober and back together emotionally, plus every possible connection and favor I could think of to get the AWOL charges dropped. His unblemished record and bronze star had helped. Jamie always thought he owed me for that, but I had only begun to repay the debts I'd accumulated during the periods of hell that punctuated our days of boredom in the elephant grass and endless nights on the hilltops.

"Don't be such a pussy, Habermann." Jamie sat down with his back to the sink. "Not everyone gets to sleep in."

I sipped from a white mug, browned by years of bad coffee. I feared for my intestines. The coffee sent me into a spasm-like gasp, and I lunged for the refrigerator. I pulled out a half gallon of two percent from the top shelf and let a handful slosh into the mug.

"You are a wuss, Habermann."

"Jamie, I have work to do. I cannot spend the day running from one toilet to the next trying to rid my system of this crap." I put the milk back and sat down. "Speaking of work, how is the search going?"

"I went out to a site this morning to check on a job for a frame carpenter."

"And?"

He shook his head. "No such luck. But there's another possibility out by Batavia. I'll check on that this afternoon."

"Good luck."

"Thanks. But tell me what happened last night. You look like shit."

"Feel like it, too."

I stretched my legs under the table, while my fingers played with the ring on the mug. I sipped some more. Still pretty awful. It even drove the Rolling Stones away. I studied Jamie's face. His wide brown eyes betrayed the innocence and optimism that he had lost years ago, then somehow found again. Sometimes I marveled at his capacity for renewal. Envied him, too.

"I need to bounce a few things off you, Jamie, for a sanity check."

He raised his eyebrows in anticipation.

"I had another dream last night." His eyes did not move. "And some visitors."

"That why you couldn't sleep? I thought the dreams had stopped a while ago."

"They had."

"Then why now?"

"I'm not sure. And last night's was different."

Jamie waited for several seconds. The hum of his refrigerator drifted between us. "How so?"

"We weren't on the hill anymore. I was in Saigon this time. At least, I think it was Saigon. I was stuck in a crowd of Vietnamese."

"The woman wasn't there anymore?"

"No. This time it had nothing to do with that night, not that I can remember." I sat upright and cradled the mug in my hands. "But you know, I still felt desperate."

"What for? You've been through all that, Bill. It wasn't your fault. There was nothing you could've done. Shit like that happens in war. It happened to a lot of us over there at one time or another."

"You still carry it with you, Jamie. Anyway, this was different. It felt more like my second tour, when I was in Saigon."

Jamie sat forward and pushed his own mug to the side. "How the hell can you tell? It's only a fuckin' dream. Probably lasted what, twenty seconds?"

I shook my head. "Maybe so, Jamie. But there's more. Some asshole called me two nights ago to warn me off a new case." I explained the circumstances of Steve Courney's death and my employment by Deborah Krueger. "Said he was actually trying to do me a favor, in so many words."

"It doesn't have to be connected to your dream. Maybe you're just nervous about the new case. Sounds like a tough one."

I shrugged. "Maybe you're right. But there's more. Courney served in the 25th and was even stationed at Tay Ninh. I've sent away for his VA records, but I'm not sure how much they'll help."

"Why?"

"Well, I expect they'll just list his assignments, promotions, shit like that. If there's anything in his past tied to the crime, I doubt I'll find it listed there in black and white. And then on top of that, I got jumped last night."

"You got jumped? Where?"

"At my place. They came from the shadows. I'm pretty sure they were some young Vietnamese thugs."

"How sure?"

"Absofuckin'lutely sure. I got a pretty good look at the ringleader, and he had one hell of an accent when he spoke my name."

"Any ideas why?"

"Hell no. But at the end he pulled out a Colt .45 and waved it around like some ancient relic."

"It probably is. You say he knew you?"

"He knew my name, anyway."

"Was there anything familiar about him?"

I shook my head, then sipped some more coffee. "Not really. All I can say is I am one lucky bastard to have such a nosey neighbor." I told him about Madame Bachmann's timely intervention.

"You think it's related to the shooting?"

"It's kind of early to tell. But the thought has occurred to me."

"What's the story with the wife and sister? Any possibility it could be tied to them?"

"I don't see how. I mean, why hire me just to have pricks beat me up and threaten to kill me?"

"But if you think this caller and the thugs are linked to the shooting, then how else could they know about your involvement?"

I shoved the coffee away. "It doesn't fit, Jamie."

"What doesn't fit?'

"The killing, the sisters, the telephone call. The whole fuckin' mess. It's all so jumbled and confused. There's no thread. I just wish I could find some kind of motive for Courney's death."

"Did you tell Rick Jamieson or the other cops about the call? Have you reported the beating?"

I shook my head. "No. Not yet."

"Is Jamieson working on the case?"

"Yeah, but he's only gonna be so much help. His boss will be all over him to keep the details inside the department and me at a distance."

"Why? You used to work there. Doesn't this guy trust you anymore?"

I waved at Krug. "It's a long story."

"So, why tell me all this?"

"Can you check out your networks of 'Nam buddies and see if anyone remembers Courney, or even kept in touch after he left the 25th?"

"You sure you want to bring me into this?"

I stood and watched beads of sweat build along my friend's upper lip. "Jamie, I wouldn't ask if I didn't have to. It's been a long time, and I've been able to put a decent distance between me and that time. I don't have the connections anymore."

I pushed a path out from behind the table and strolled to the sink. I stood without speaking for a minute, staring out the window at a square of fading green dotted with circles of yellow. I could hear Jamie's mug tap against the table as he lowered it.

"Your dandelion patch is doing well."

"Forget the lawn." His chair slid across the floor. "You've got to go back there sooner or later, Bill. Whether this case takes you there or not, you gotta go if there's still stuff you need to resolve. We all do." I heard a grunt that resembled a laugh. "Hell, some would say we never really left it."

"I'm not goin' back there alone."

His hand reached my shoulder. "Shit, man, you know I'll always be there."

"Yeah, I know that much, Jamie. I know you."

I turned to face my old war buddy. He leaned back against the table.

"You did some good work over there, Bill. And not just the Civic Action stuff. It wasn't all bad. Not all the time."

"But that's what I remember, Jamie. Certain things stick with you." I looked away. A neat pile of grass clippings waited by the back door. "You must have mowed this morning. I'm surprised the grass is growing at all in this heat."

"Fuck the grass, Bill. You've got to learn from our days back there. Pull the positive out. You can't just disconnect that part of your life, that night on the hilltop, from everything else."

"So, what the fuck am I supposed to do?"

"Try growin' up, for starters. Then find out who these assholes are that're after you. And why. Maybe it's tied to 'Nam, and maybe it isn't. But it sounds like there's a real good chance it is. And I'll do what I can."

I stared at Jamie Krug for what seemed like minutes. He was as good a man and as reliable a friend as I'd ever meet. I blew out a lungfull, not realizing I had been holding my breath. Then I glanced into his coal-dark eyes. They shone hard and looked brittle with anger.

"Thanks, Jamie. I'll be in touch."

Jamie Krug did not respond. He followed me in silence onto the porch, where he watched me drive away through the overhanging oaks that lined his ancient street. His gaze hung in the rearview mirror all the way back to Naperville. I kept waiting for the look on his face to soften, perhaps with some sorrow or maybe even a little support. Not only did I have a murder to solve, but now I had a psychological puzzle as well. I'd get to all those problems eventually, and Jamie would certainly help. I knew that much. I just wasn't sure yet how soon the murder and my memories were going to cross.

---

That afternoon I sat in a shower of heat, perched in the third row of the small, open-air theater at one end of Naperville's Riverwalk Park. Throughout my childhood, the grounds bordering the DuPage River as it runs through downtown Naperville had possessed the run-down look of a strip mall. But about thirty years ago the city fathers had renovated the section between the central business district and the old stone quarry known as Centennial Beach, a gift to the people of Naperville from FDR's New Deal. The result? A mid town relief package of green hilltops, a covered bridge, and a scattering of benches along wandering stone walkways. Just to the business side of Centennial Beach, an open-air theater lay nestled between two green mini-hills. Naperville as the Athens of the suburban Midwest? I hardly think so. But I found it a comfortable place to think while I digested a pastrami on rye from lunch.

Around two in the afternoon, I gathered my waste paper from lunch and deposited it in one of the dark blue trash bins along the pathway back to my car. I swung the Volvo through town and out along Ogden Avenue to catch the East-West Tollroad. Just before I turned off Ogden, I pulled into a liquor store to restock my home supply with a twelve pack of Heilemann's Special Export.

The Tollroad had first opened to traffic in 1958. It was originally hailed as the major artery linking Chicago with its outlying suburbs like Naperville, and indeed, both it and the Burlington Railroad had done a lot to open the area. Together they changed Naperville from a settlement of German farmers to a bedroom community of professional commuters and technological wizards.

You could see why when you drove along the Tollroad, rechristened as "The Illinois Research and Development Corridor." The stretch of highway between Aurora and Oakbrook had sprouted a New Age panorama of brown glass and white cinderblock that looked like a testimonial from Architectural Digest. And the office buildings all had titles with words like "Technologies," "Advanced," and "Institute" emblazoned across their archways.

It had all started about thirty years ago, when AT&T and Amoco built their new research laboratories just outside town. Then, the Fermi lab went up over near Batavia. The close proximity of these new scientific facilities to one another led the management of other firms to consider relocating to the area, and the state offered attractive tax packages as further incentives. Growth, prosperity, and exploding real estate prices soon followed, not to mention the loss of acres of rich farmland.

Just east of Naperville I drove onto an exit ramp, then caught the frontage road to a square building set amidst twin rows of rectangles and more squares, all of them somehow connected. I steered into one of the slots reserved for visitors directly in front of the entrance to United Americo Technologies. A vista of white metal and dark glass reflected the rays of the sun like a tunnel of mirrors. The whole complex looked like it was floating atop patches of grass, garden, and blacktop. I got the impression that the managers could pick the buildings up and move whenever they wanted.

# ANGEL IN BLACK

Americo's headquarters sat inside a low-slung building with thin rows of horizontal white concrete separated by plates of green glass. I selected the Lisle water tower and the Hyatt Hotel across the highway as my landmarks. The latter was hard to miss: a tall crescent shape of pink concrete with broad cylinders of brown glass running along either end. I navigated through the twin sprinklers working the garden that fronted the entrance, then stepped into an air-conditioned paradise of glass, tile, and potted trees.

The air conditioner in the Volvo had not been able to match the demands of the July heat wave. My forehead was beaded with sweat and my blue and white striped shirt stuck to my back like flypaper. The Swedes apparently hadn't invested much in air-conditioning. They probably only needed it about two days out of the year. The cool air in the building's foyer let me slip on the navy blazer to cover the dampness. I wasn't sure of the smell.

"Can I help you?"

A perky blonde in a bright flowered dress sat behind an oval reception counter. Her partner, a redhead in a dress of blue silk, had a telephone receiver attached to her ear. She considered my presence with a professional detachment.

"Yes. I have an appointment with Mister Davis in Personnel."

"And your name?"

"Habermann. Bill Habermann."

"Do you have some identification, Mister Habermann?"

I flipped open my wallet to show her the copy of my investigator's permit and my drivers license.

She got busy on another phone at her part of the desk. A wooden cup held an assortment of pens and pencils, while an appointment book and telephone directory lay spread before her. She hung up the receiver, and indifferent eyes glanced up. Then a smile snuck through.

"Come with me please."

She stood and strode through an opening at the back of the cubicle and waited for me at the elevator.

"Clip this to your jacket please, Mister Habermann."

She handed me a badge with a huge "V" in the middle and the number 201 below it.

"What's this for?"

"It indicates that you need an escort while you're in the building."

"But what for?" I was trying not to sound too stupid.

"We do a good deal of contract work for the Pentagon, sir. And much of that is classified. As part of our contract with the government, we have to institute certain security precautions."

"And it's a good thing too," I added, just to let her know that I was a loyal American. Early during my surveillance of Steve Courney I had learned that Americo was an engineering firm specializing in electrical systems, and that they did a lot of work on missile systems. Guidance, targeting, important stuff like that. Still, it sounded like Americo Technologies was taking itself a bit too seriously.

We rode in silence, while a suite of strings butchered the Beatles' "Lovely Rita." I detected a faint smell of musk that I had missed below. She glanced at me and smiled again.

We stepped off the elevator at the third floor and sauntered together down a long, well-lit hallway of vanilla plaster board. My feet slid along thin industrial carpeting that looked like the ocean floor. Framed pictures of Chicago punctuated the walls after every other doorway. Our journey ended in front of a door with the name "Davis" embossed on a silver plate at eye level. Below that was printed the title, "Assistant Director for Personnel." Blondie knocked.

"Come in," a heavy voice boomed.

We breezed through the doorway like we belonged. The office struggled for distinction, with walls just a little less white than the hallway. The occupant had a window at his back that looked out over the parking lot and framed his body in a bright glow. A print of the Rocky Mountains covered a large section of the wall next to the door.

A heavyset man sat behind the desk in a white shirt with rolled up sleeves and a striped tie of green and gold. He consulted a desk calendar next to a row of three small photographs set at an angle on a far corner of the desk. The pictures showed two children in individual shots like the ones kids bring home from school, and one group photo with Davis and a dog. He didn't look like a cat person.

He stood. "Jack Davis." His right hand shot out. "You must be Mister Habermann." A draft of English Leather lingered for a moment.

"That's right." I extended my hand as I approached the desk. "Thank you for seeing me on such short notice."

Davis pointed to a chair in front of his desk as he sat down. I followed his example. When I glanced behind me, the blond phantom had disappeared.

"Now, what can I do for you?"

His voice was heavy, but smooth. I crossed my legs to look more officious, extracted the notebook from my jacket and pulled down a Bic from my shirt pocket.

"I'm investigating the murder of Mister Steven Courney, and I need to ask you a few questions."

He leaned back, rubbing the stubble of black hair and advancing gray along the top of his head. "Are you with the police?"

"Occasionally I assist in their investigations." I handed him my card. "Have you met Rick Jamieson? He's the detective working this one for the Naperville police."

"Jamieson?"

"Yes. He's an old friend of mine."

He studied the card before tucking it into his breast pocket. "Not yet. But I have an appointment with someone later this afternoon." He wrote something on a pad next to his desk calendar. "What would you like to know?"

"Basically, what I'm after here is information about Mister Courney."

"About Steve?"

"Yes. It might help get a lead on who would want to kill him."

Davis frowned. "What can you learn here? I thought some goofball shot him."

"It's always best to examine all possible angles, Mister Davis. What sort of worker was Steve Courney, for example?"

He frowned again and rolled his shoulders. I wondered if he was having trouble remembering his recently deceased colleague. Flecks of sunlight danced across his desk when he moved.

"I'm not asking you to speak ill of the dead, Mister Davis. But it would help to know if he had any friends, or," I hesitated, "enemies here at work."

"Hm...." He stared at the print of the Rockies. "No. Steve didn't seem to have much of either." I stopped writing. It was my turn to frown. "I mean, he kept pretty much to himself. You know, sort of quiet like."

"Was he anti-social? Unfriendly?"

"Oh, I wouldn't say that. Steve was always friendly enough. In fact, I attended a very nice Christmas party at his place last year. It's where I met his lovely wife. But he was the quiet sort."

"Yes, she is nice. I imagine she's having a rough time of it right now."

"That's too bad. I'll have to stop by to pay my respects. It seemed she was actually more open and friendly with the folks around here than Steve was. I think she was a lot happier about coming back here."

"Mister Courney didn't want to live here?"

He frowned again and waggled his hand.

"He was unenthusiastic?"

"Sometimes I got that feeling." He leaned forward on his desk. "But it never affected his performance here. Steve was well thought of, professionally. He'll be missed."

"How much did you know about his work before he came here?"

"You mean at the Pentagon?"

I nodded.

Davis smiled, then wheeled around in his chair and looked out his window. "It's funny, you know. I had my doubts about hiring a government bureaucrat."

"Why is that?" I directed the question at the back of his head.

"Oh, you know. Three hour lunches. Always going home early."

"Is that how they work in the government?"

"Sure it is. At least that's what I hear."

He shifted his weight in the chair and swung it to the side so that he now faced the wall to my left. I noticed four diplomas encased in black wooden frames arranged in a diamond pattern around some sort of an award at their center. Two of the diplomas came from Northern Illinois University, and two more signaled success in business courses. They hung right where he could point them out to any visitor.

"Anyway, I was glad to see that I was wrong. Steve was a hard worker, always willing to stay late. And his connections to the Pentagon didn't hurt, either."

"That's good to hear. What sort of connections did he have?"

"Well, with his old office in procurements," he nodded toward the window, "and several others."

"Such as?"

Thick fingers worked their way across Davis's brow. "I'd rather not say right now. We're working on some classified stuff that Steve helped arrange, and I'd prefer not to discuss it."

"I understand." Like hell I did. I had heard the word "classified" dropped too often in the Army. It was necessary about half the time, if that.

It was my turn to lean back and affect a more relaxed manner. I glanced at the print of the Rockies. The sun from the window at Davis's back seem to set the scene on fire. I was beginning to feel warm.

"How did Mr. Courney come to work here at Americo?"

"Well, a couple years ago we advertised in several regional newspapers, and Steve applied." Davis formed his right hand into a pistol, pointed the index finger at me and pulled an imaginary trigger. "Knocked our socks off in the interview, too."

"And you say he was a dedicated worker."

"Yeah, I'd say Steve probably worked late two or three nights a week. On average."

"Is that unusual?"

"Yeah, I suppose so." He holstered his fist with the other one and brought both to rest on the desk. "Don't get me wrong. When it's crunch time, like at the end of the fiscal year, we all put in our fair share of overtime."

"What sort of things did he work on those evenings?"

Davis leaned back and studied his shoes. "Oh, government contracts, mostly. That's the kind of things he had responsibility for."

"Could you be more specific?"

His eyes met mine for only the second time in the conversation. "I'm afraid not. We're stepping on confidential turf again."

"I see. But you're fairly certain that Mister Courney had no enemies to speak of. No one that would want to do him harm?"

"Oh, yeah. I'm pretty certain of that."

"Do you recall anything odd or peculiar in his behavior the week or so before his death?"

Davis shook his head and frowned.

"Any unexplained absences from work? Telephone calls? Things like that?"

Another shake.

I put my pen and notebook away. Time for some balls. "I'd like to see his personnel file."

Davis frowned again.

"I promise not to remove or copy anything."

He was still frowning. His face had the look of someone who had eaten a bad lunch at a very low price but couldn't decide if he should regret it.

"And I won't even take notes."

Davis rubbed his chin for another ten seconds. A hint of shadow was beginning to emerge. "No, I'm afraid I can't do that. It would be against company policy."

"Really?"

"Yes. It's one of things we had to promise the government. All our personnel files are confidential."

"Could I possibly see the recommendations from his superiors at the Pentagon?"

Davis shook his head.

"Not even their names?"

"Sorry. I'd like to help, but...."

I leaned forward and put on a great big smile. "You're sure about that?"

"Yeah, absolutely." He shrugged and tossed his hands in the air. "I'm sorry."

"Have the police asked for them?"

"Not yet."

I found that hard to believe. I'd have to call Jamieson when I got home.

Davis swung his chair around to the face the diplomas again, shook his head, then wheeled to the front. He punched a button on the console at the corner of his desk. I motioned toward the card in his shirt pocket.

"Please call me at that number if you think of anything else. Day or night."

Davis retrieved it and examined the printing. "Sure. Is this a local number?"

"Yes. I live in Naperville."

The blond reappeared in a breeze of scented musk to escort me to the entrance.

I held out my hand. "Thanks again, Mr. Davis. You've been a great help."

He stood and took my palm in a hard grip. "Oh, sure. Sorry about the file thing."

"Don't worry about that," I laughed. "I run into that sort of thing all the time."

At the front door, I paused and turned to the blond. "What sort of guy is this Davis to work for?"

She closed one eye and pursed her lips. "Well, I don't work for him myself, but I hear it's been pretty rough over the last year."

"Why is that?"

Blondie leaned forward and whispered. "Messy divorce."

I leaned far enough in her direction to catch a whiff of lilac from hair that shone like threads of gold. I nearly lost myself in a pool of sweet daydreams.

Instead, I let a sentence slip from the corner of my mouth. "Was there another woman? Or man, even?"

She frowned. "I doubt that. I'm not really sure. But he's had two secretaries leave."

I slipped my card into her hand and managed to get the name 'Brenda' before she threw a smile and a wave in my direction as I walked to the car. Sitting in the driver's seat, waiting for the air conditioner to revive, I was certain now that Mr. Davis had been avoiding my eyes for a reason. I examined the stained windows on the third floor and had a spooky feeling that United Americo's assistant director for personnel was watching me from behind the green glass that stood between his office and the world outside.

Perhaps he was wondering if I would try to see other files on Steve Courney, now that he had denied me access to Americo's. Or maybe he was wondering if I'd touch base with the police, or try some other way to get into Americo's files. He might also be asking himself if I was the person he let into the Courney's apartment building Sunday morning. If so, he was right on all counts.

The sun was fading but not yet gone when I got home. No shadows had formed yet to hide nasty surprises. I pulled the Browning from the glove compartment and shoved the ammunition clip into place anyway. Then I snuck from the garage to the back door with new caution. I also checked the deadbolt and tape to see if anyone had tampered with the door.

Satisfied, I pushed through the back door and into a kitchen as comforting as an old garage. Cursing, I remembered that I had forgotten to turn on the air conditioner when I rushed out that morning. At the peak of summer I try to leave at least the window unit in the living room on to keep the place habitable. Either that or leave a window open, and I had forgotten that, too. The heat and humidity clung to my body like an extra set of clothes.

First thing's first. I tossed two bottles of Special Export into the freezer for a quick chill. Then I threw open every window and plugged in both my fans to get some air circulating. After that I switched on the air conditioning units in the living room and kitchen. The familiar hum swept the apartment with the promise of cool relief. The rest of the beer ended up on the bottom row of the refrigerator next to a week-old tuna casserole and some left-over pizza. The Grateful Dead's

American Beauty album started to spin its own peculiar path around my twenty-year old phonograph, the music drifting through a twin set of speakers at opposite corners of the living room. I have often pondered the benefits of a compact disc player: better sound and tonal quality. Stuff like that. But then I'd have to get all new discs. I kicked off my shoes and swung my feet over the arm of the blue sleeper sofa that held up the back wall of my living room, which also served as my office.

It was time to reflect, but I didn't have much to go on. I had one dead mark, an ex-client who was also a grieving widow, and a new employer, her sexy bitch of a sister. The dead man had been a serious but quiet worker, not disliked but not about to run for student body president. Hubby had allegedly been playing around, but not like you would expect. Or else his standards were incredibly high. So high, in fact, that they had killed him. I knew a little bit about his personality, but if Davis could be believed, it was not enough to get him killed. Then again, Davis's evasive behavior suggested there was something in Courney's work or background that could throw some light on the case. Or dirt on Davis. Maybe both.

I hustled over to the desk and dialed John Sullivan's number in northern Virginia. His wife Hannelore answered, and she informed me that my old Army buddy was working late at the Pentagon. I told Hannelore of my travel plans, and she assured me I was always welcome.

"John would love to see you."

"I'm sorry he's working late, but I'll sleep better knowing our national security is under his special care."

"Oh, hush. Your coming should at least bring him home on time."

"Thank God for small wonders, eh? I'll also need a favor from John. In fact, it's my other reason for coming East." I told Hannelore of my new case and passed along the relevant information I already possessed on Steve Courney. "And please, Hannelore, assure John that at this stage every little bit will help."

"Can he reach you at home, if he needs to?"

"Absolutely. Any time. The answering machine is always on when I'm out."

We said our good-byes, then I hung up and headed for the bathroom to get rid of some beer. Halfway there, the telephone rang. Too hot and tired to bother, I let the recorder take a message.

After the beep, silence hung on the line for about five seconds. A guttural note of disappointment followed, then "Shit!"

My phantom caller. I lunged for the telephone, grabbing the receiver.

"Who the hell is this?" I yelled. My heart hammered against the front of my ribcage. My body slammed into the front of the desk. Papers swam across the top and seeped over the edge.

The voice laughed. "You mean you don't know? You are a stupid fuck, Habermann. Did you enjoy yourself last night?"

Points of sweat rolled along my forehead. "Goddammit! Who are you, you fucking coward?"

"Coward?" A pause. "There's more in store if you don't back off. It can get a lot worse, Habermann. You were lucky. Some people think it's payback time."

"Anytime, asshole."

The eery hum of the dial tone answered. But his words hung in the air.

Somewhere, some time ago, I had known that voice. I couldn't place it yet. But there was one thing I did know. By now, I knew I hated that bastard.

So I settled in for the evening to see if he or his friends would return. I kept a beer in one hand and the Browning in the other. Now I was armed and dangerous. Luckily for me and anyone else who might wander by, the reunion never happened. Around eleven o'clock I turned off the TV, rid myself of some more beer, then went to sleep. I could always count on company in my dreams.

# Chapter 7

The next morning the sky burned blue and cloudless, but that didn't help my timing. I needed to speak with Lisa Courney to learn what I could about her husband's past, even though the emotional scars of her husband's death were still deep and painful. I doubted his murder had stemmed from any cating around he might have done. I simply hadn't seen any evidence that he fallen into a relationship with that kind of consequence. Maybe he had gotten involved in something pretty heavy before I arrived, and he had kept a safe distance during the period of my surveillance. If so, his wife would hopefully be able to point to a few indicators. Mostly, though, I wanted to get to know her better and get a better feeling for her reaction to the question about Vietnam.

After a few hours chasing witnesses to verify accident reports for a local insurance agent I called Lisa Courney. We agreed to meet for lunch at the Cantina, a Mexican restaurant on Jefferson Avenue. After dropping my notes at home, I drove downtown and withdrew the balance of her retainer-350 dollars-from my account with Naper Bank. Then I hustled across Washington and down the brick sidewalks that line this part of downtown.

By one o'clock, the Cantina had assumed the lazy, vacant air of a siesta. At two tables, customers lingered past the traditional lunch hour into the tedium of a mid-afternoon in mid-week in mid-summer. I strolled toward the back and seated myself where I had a clear view of the street.

Fifteen minutes later Lisa Courney hovered outside the front door. My report on her husband's surveillance rested on the edge of the table, safe inside a manila envelope. I had tucked the money inside one of those narrow white envelopes you find by the teller's window and slipped it inside the larger package. She looked uncertain about coming inside, so I glanced around. It looked safe enough to me. Clean, too. I was actually proud of my choice. Her voice had sounded hesitant over the phone, and the pale skin and haggard features peering through the front window suggested she could use the fresh air.

Eventually, she made up her mind. The door made one of those tinkling sounds when it opened. Once inside, Lisa's hand rose to her head and groped at a head of hair that looked like it hadn't seen many brushings lately. She stuffed a pair of metal-framed Foster Grants into a baggy canvas purse. I motioned with my hand to catch her attention. She nodded, her eyes darting around the room. She had tossed on a loose-fitting summer dress colored in dark blues and greens that looked like it was woven of light cotton. A gold necklace captured the light from the ceiling fixtures, its brightness a sparkling contrast to the somber colors of her dress and her vacant stare.

Her thin frame shuffled through a maze of chairs, past tables covered with checked cloth and colored glass bulbs wrapped in white plastic netting. Brightly colored pictures of tropical foliage hung from the walls. Sunlight spread behind her as she approached the table. I stood in welcome, a big smile on my face. This was going to be tough. The scent of frying onions and chili peppers circled at my back.

"Can I get you something to drink, Mrs. Courney?" I asked. "Coffee, or a Coke?"

"Yes, that would be fine. Thank you."

I guessed at Coke and ordered her a glass, plus a bottle of Dos Equis for myself.

"I hear the food's very good here if you're hungry." I glanced at my wrist and pretended surprise. Anything to relieve the tension. "Good Lord! You must be. It's past one o'clock."

"Oh, thank you. But I'm not very hungry. Perhaps I'll just have a burrito or something."

When the waitress brought our drinks I ordered an enchilada platter to keep the burrito company. I handed Lisa Courney the envelope.

"I realize it's been such a short time since your husband's death, Mrs. Courney, but I wanted to give you my report and discuss my observations. Perhaps ask a few questions. I've also enclosed the remainder of your money, minus my expenses. I've enclosed a detailed list of those."

"Thank you again. I'm sure everything is all right. This is all so overwhelming." She brushed a strand of undisciplined hair back in place atop her forehead, then covered her eyes for about ten seconds. "I...I never thought it would end like this."

I sat back in my chair to study my former client. Lisa Courney was much prettier than I had realized. Perhaps it was the resemblance to her sister, which was not striking but noticeable all the same. Lisa was thinner and smaller breasted, but the muscles of her arms stood outlined in clear relief against the loose sleeve of her dress. She was a woman who took care of herself. Again, I wondered why her husband had felt the urge to cat around on such an attractive wife, and one who seemed to care for him as much as this one did. I guess some studs just have to play around.

"As I wrote in the report, Mrs. Courney, I never encountered anything that would confirm your suspicions."

"Until Saturday night." Her eyes caught a spark of energy. A spot of color leaped to her cheeks.

"Yes, until Saturday night. But there's a lot that doesn't add up about Mr. Courney's death."

"What do you mean? What have you found?"

"Well, nothing yet." I ran my finger across a line of blue squares on the table cloth. "That's just the point. Did you ever notice anything that would have pointed to a particular liaison? With one woman, I mean."

"You mean an affair?"

"Yes. Things like unexplained withdrawals from the bank or expenses on credit card statements. Or long business trips. Anything like that?"

She seemed to consider the options. "No. Nothing really."

"Well, there are a number of things I'd like to check out. Why there was no robbery, for example. That eliminates the most obvious motive for the shooting."

"I see."

"There's also some more I'd like to know about your husband. Where he came from. His work...."

The waitress set our plates on the table, warning us that they were hot to the touch. We both picked at the food with our forks while the heat ebbed. Finally, Lisa grabbed her burrito with her fingers. She spoke between bites.

"Are you sure this subject is necessary?"

"Yes, I'm afraid so. It might help me establish a motive for the killing. If this is too difficult, we can talk about it some other time."

"No, that's okay. I'll try." She put her burrito down and wiped a slab of hot sauce from the corner of her mouth. The color faded from her cheeks and eyes again. "I told you. He worked for United Americo Technologies."

"Yes, but his employment record prior to Americo is kind of spotty. Can you tell me any more about his previous work?"

"He worked at the Pentagon for the Department of Defense. Something to do with procurements." She set her hands in her lap and studied the air. I thought she might be struggling to keep her composure. "It's how he made the contact that got him this job."

"What contact was that?"

She shook her head. "I don't remember the name. But it was someone who put him onto Jack Davis."

"I thought he responded to an advertisement."

Lisa Courney's eyes searched mine. "Oh, he did. But he inquired first, and a business associate put him in touch with Mr. Davis."

"What sort of things did he procure?"

"I'm not really sure. He never told me that much about it."

"That's odd."

"Not really. You see, I never cared that much to learn the details of his job. Besides, he said it was all classified. He worked in some new office established during the early Reagan years, when the new administration began its big arms buildup. I always assumed the job had something to do with weapons."

"Why is that?"

"Well, it was the Pentagon. What else would they be buying?"

"Just about anything, I imagine."

"How do you know that?"

"I spent some years in the military."

"Oh. I wasn't aware of that."

"I don't talk about it much. But I do recall that you could find just about anything in the Army."

She resumed her work on the meal. If she wasn't hungry now, I'd hate to pay for her groceries when she had an appetite. The burrito was just about gone. She started on the refried beans.

"Yes, I suppose so," she agreed.

"So, you lived in the Washington area? In Alexandria, right?"

"Yes, that's right. In Alexandria. How did you know?"

"I got a look at your husband's application for a driver's license when you first hired me, and it listed your previous address."

"Oh, really? Well, we loved Alexandria. We lived in the section known as Old Town."

"I know it. It's been a long time, but I spent a few evenings there when I was in the Army."

Her eyes lost their vacuous stare and brightened just enough to catch a spot of light and color. "Where were you stationed?"

"I wasn't. I was visiting friends."

"When was that?"

"Back in the early seventies."

Her eyes shot up toward mine. "Were you over there?"

"There?" I studied her eyes, which had clouded over again. "You mean Vietnam?"

She nodded and her eyes closed. She seemed to concentrate on some rare scent.

"Yes, I was."

Lisa's eyes opened, and she rocked in her chair. Her face slid off center to study the tropical plant life in the wall hangings. "How long were you in the Army?" Her hands worked a napkin through all ten fingers.

"A couple of years. Military life and I did not agree with each other."

Her eyes roamed the blue and white tablecloth and found a patch of Spanish rice that had escaped from my plate. "I'm sorry."

"Don't be. The Army was much better off without me. Anyway, I'm sure it's changed."

Her eyes leaped to mine. "The Army?"

In spite of myself, I laughed. "Well, maybe. But I meant Alexandria."

"Oh, it's much nicer now. The older homes have all been rehabilitated. And there are some very nice restaurants. And clubs."

"Did you and your husband stay in touch with any friends back there?"

She shook her head. "No, I didn't find it easy to make friends there. Everyone was so ambitious, so serious."

"Why did you leave Washington and come to Naperville?"

She mopped the last clumps of beans on her plate with the remnants of her burrito. I guessed she hadn't eaten much sitting in her apartment. I congratulated myself again on getting her out and wondered what her sister was doing to help.

"Well, it was October, 1991. With the Cold War over, Steve was pretty sure that career prospects in his line of work would be limited."

"And why did you come here? Was it only the job?"

"Well, no. Steve and I met at the University of Wisconsin. He's from LaCrosse, but I grew up around here. Over in Wheaton." She flipped her head toward the back of the restaurant.

"Wheaton, eh? The town that stole the county records so it could become the county seat."

"Excuse me?"

"It's a bit of local history," I explained. "It's why our towns are traditional rivals."

"Yes! Now I remember." She smiled for the first time since I had met her. "Why didn't Naperville try to get them back?"

"We did. Chased the wagons all the way back to Wheaton. Some of the ledgers fell off, so our boys grabbed 'em and shipped 'em off to Chicago for safekeeping."

A small, polite laugh escaped. "I guess we won that one."

"Probably. But we're about to swallow you guys whole."

"It certainly looks like it."

Lisa Courney had a pleasant and easy smile. Her face, her whole presence, seemed to swing open with a wave of friendliness that was a welcome contrast to the bitterness and sorrow she had been carrying. I hated having to bring the conversation back to the business at hand.

"Just what did your husband do out at Americo? They were pretty tight-lipped when I was out there yesterday."

Her face clouded over again, and she hesitated for a moment before answering. "They put him in charge of overseeing contracts with the military. It seemed like a natural fit."

"Was it legal work, then? I don't recall seeing anything in his background related to law school."

She shook her head. "No, no. Steve was no lawyer. I'm not sure what he did, exactly."

I wet my lips and studied the colored lights behind the bar. "Now that really is odd."

"Excuse me?"

"No one seems to know or wants to provide details about his work. It's the kind of thing that makes you wonder."

"About what?"

"About what he did for a living. About how it could be related to his death."

The only response was a shrug. Her eyes evaded mine.

"Was he happy with the shift from government to private industry?"

"I believe so. He said once that he appreciated having the chance to make his own decisions. But...."

"Yes?"

"Well, as I said, we never talked much about his work. But I could tell something was on his mind, that something was bothering him."

"But he never confided in you? You have no idea what it might have been?"

"No, I'm sorry." She looked back at me. "But Steve grew increasingly withdrawn. Like I told you when I first hired you."

"And you feared for his safety, correct?"

Her gaze wandered off to another part of the restaurant again. "Yes, I thought so."

I looked past Lisa and out onto the street. It was still deserted. The other tables were also empty. We were sitting in a plastic oasis, where the smells from the kitchen seemed to fit the suburban desert just past the front door. Outside, I could make out the edge of the old Naper Theater, where my friends and I had spent many a Friday night watching the Hollywood version of American life. Movies had only cost 35 cents then. The building housed an antique emporium now, and I got the feeling that Lisa Courney was leading me through old furniture of her own choosing. For one thing, the husband's behavior at home was not what I noticed on his nights out.

"He didn't make any enemies, did he? Or have any run-ins with, say, difficult people?"

"I don't believe so." Her look returned to me, relentless now and unmoving. I looked away and brushed at my hair, then met her gaze.

"Did your husband ever talk about Vietnam?"

She sat rock solid, her muscles tense. "Why?"

"I think there's a chance it might be related to his death."

"How do you know that?"

"I don't, Mrs. Courney. It's just a feeling I have. A few things have come up that point in that direction."

"Such as?"

"I'd rather not go into it yet. It's all pretty vague. Were you aware that we served in the same unit? The 25th Infantry Division. Our tours even overlapped."

"Did you know Steve?"

"I think I may have met him. Did he ever talk of that time?"

Her head jerked to the side, then returned to her soda, which was nearly full. "No. I gather that was hard for Steve."

"How long did he stay?"

"The usual tour, I guess."

"That was one year. Are you sure you don't know?"

"Not really. He may have extended it."

"I find that odd that you wouldn't at least know the length of time he spent there."

She shook her head. Tears had formed at the rims of her eyes, which had grown pink. She wiped a line of moisture away with the back of her hand. "I'm sorry. This is very hard for me."

I leaned back in my chair. "I'm sorry, too, Mrs. Courney. Perhaps we should continue this some other time."

I believed in her ignorance as much as I believed in mine. There were other ways to check on Steve Courney's military career. I paused to let the emotions settle before moving on.

"Perhaps a cup of coffee."

"Yes, thank you."

I signaled to the waitress, then drained the rest of my beer.

"Would it be possible for me to check some of your financial records?" Her eyes leaped to mine. "Credit card bills, cheque stubs. Things like that. I couldn't get access to your credit records when I tried earlier."

"Why did you do that? And what do you think you'll find there?"

"Back then I was looking for evidence of your husband's philandering. I hate to pry, but now I might find something unusual, or a pattern of some sort."

A soft smile slipped out. "I'm afraid you're too late, Mr. Habermann. The police already carted off most of that. You'll have to ask your friend, Mr. Jamieson."

It figures. Some cops are too damn thorough.

"Is there anything else?"

"Yes. Did you know your husband was calling someone in Arlington, Virginia?"

The blood seemed to drain from her face. "It never showed in our phone records. I know, I paid the bill."

"He used his cell phone."

She nodded, relief flooding back to her cheeks with the color. "That was his work phone. I'm sure it was related to his job."

"Sure. Just one more thing. Have you and your sister always been close?"

Lisa Courney looked at the waitress as though seeking relief "What do you mean?"

I shrugged. "I don't know. Siblings usually quarrel at some point. Was there ever any sort of friction between you? Say, over your marriage?"

"Of course not. She resented Steve's taking me away to the East, at first. But she was extremely happy when we moved back."

The waitress brought the coffee, and Lisa Courney took it eagerly. She added cream, then settled back, cradling the cup in one thin, alabaster hand. Her other hand groped for the necklace, massaging the gold links just below her throat.

"How could you tell?"

"She helped us get settled, for one thing. She even recommended Naperville. Said it was the up and coming place to live in the area."

"Did she visit you two often?"

"Not really." The coffee cup dropped to the saucer with the clang of heavy, industrial china. "I really don't see what this has to do with anything, Mister Habermann." She fumbled at her side for the loose canvas purse slung over the back of the chair.

"I'm just trying to determine why your sister showed such an unusual interest in having me investigate this case."

"Perhaps she loves me, Mister Habermann. And perhaps because of that she wants to see that justice is done."

"I'm sorry." I sat up straight and nearly burped out a mouthful of Dos Equis. "But most people trust the police for that. I'm just trying to establish the motives of everyone involved."

Lisa Courney's spine stiffened against the back of her chair. Her hands came down hard on the rounded edge of the table and pressed into the plastic covering. Her eyes bored through me like I was made of cheap plaster. I sat back in my chair as far as I could to escape the unexpected burst of emotion.

"There is something you should know, Mister Habermann. I was and still am opposed to my sister hiring you to continue this investigation. I don't think it's wise or necessary. You can stop any time, as far as I'm concerned."

"Why do you think she did it?"

"I'm not completely sure. But you also should not assume that Deborah is as hard as she likes to appear. She's soft inside. Very romantic."

"Is she given to impulsive behavior? Was that how she married?"

Lisa Courney blinked, then seemed to remember my presence. "She was a fool. She worked to help put that jerk through med school and stuck by him during his internship and residency. And his family had plenty of money. I warned her."

"Of what, Mrs. Courney?"

She blinked again. "That he'd take advantage of her devotion. Men can do that."

I didn't want to press the next question so soon after her husband's death, but the connection was too obvious.

"Is that why you hired me to investigate your husband?"

The hands dropped to her lap, and Lisa Courney's eyes dodged past mine. "I was lucky with Steve. At least, I thought so. I was hoping you'd prove just that, Mister Habermann. I'd like to believe it still."

I couldn't say anything to that. Lisa Courney rose to leave, assuming a military stance with her legs planted at shoulder width, her hands on her hips.

"I've been over all that with the police," she said, "and, frankly, I'm tired of it. In fact, I'm tired of all of you."

With that, Lisa Courney wheeled around and marched toward the door. At least I had brought some spunk back to her. But I was more convinced than ever that she was hiding something of her husband's past. And after this outburst, I wasn't sure what to make of her sister's relationship with her and her husband. Hell, I wasn't sure what to make of her sister at all.

I paid my tab, then strolled outside to bake in the afternoon heat. The town was like an oven, hot air just hanging there. The heat and conversation brought back more memories of Vietnam, but none of them shed any light on Steve Courney's history.

I shook all that away and marched past the Rexall Drug Store, then crossed the street. I dropped a quarter into the pay phone at the corner of Main and Jefferson. Some kid in a scruffy beard and his straight-haired girlfriend stared at me from their seats at the window bar in Starbuck's. I dialed the police department and waited through three rings.

"Jamieson here."

"Rick, it's me. Bill."

"Nice of you to call in, Mister Habermann. Checking up on your telephone service?"

"What are you talking about?"

"One of your waifs called here. You must be developing a taste for young meat these days."

"Rick, this is not amusing." The eyes inside Starbuck's had not moved. I spun away.

83

Jamieson sighed into the receiver. "Wanda Rathko called me. She was checking up on you, my boy, and the adjectives she used were very complimentary. She must be blind."

"She's scared, Rick. Someone beat her up over this Courney killing. You guys should go out and talk to her."

"We already have. At the bar. On Saturday night. You remember, the scene of the crime and all that. Have you gotten anything worthwhile out of her? Related to the crime, I mean."

"I just found out about her myself. Incidentally, I also had a visitor. Several, in fact."

"Come again?"

"Somebody jumped me outside my place two nights ago."

"Did they do any damage? And why are you reporting this now, and not two days ago?"

I thought of the camera. "My ego, mostly. I've gotten slow as I've aged, Rick."

"That means you'll have to rely more on your brains than your brawn, my friend. This could be trouble for us all."

"Yuck, yuck."

"Seriously, Bill. I want you to ease off this case. Come on by and tell us about your visitors. Then let us handle the murder."

"No way, Rick. I was hired, paid a retainer, and now I'm pissed as well. I'm not going to let anyone run me off."

"There are some new complications, pardner."

"Such as?"

"Such as, let's talk. We need to clear a few things."

"Sure. But first, how about filling me in on the Courney's financial records?"

"Who told you about those?"

"The widow. I asked to have a look at them."

"You sure have a great sense of timing."

"No time like the present. Have you found anything yet?"

Jamieson ignored my question. "I have another appointment with her tomorrow. I like to let grief subside a bit, Bill. It usually makes people more willing to talk. It also gives the memory time to recover."

"Well, I don't think you'll have to worry about that with our widow now."

"What have you noticed, Sherlock?"

"I must have lit a fire under her today. She got pissed enough to walk out on our lunch and do a little shopping."

"Did you say anything egregiously stupid?"

"No, I don't think so. What have you found out about her history?"

"Well, she came from your usual middle-class, midwestern family. She and her sister were the only two kids, although a brother died at birth."

"Sorry to hear it."

"Old man was a lawyer but died when the girls were in junior high. Mom was a high-school math teacher."

"Sounds like there were some rough spots underneath the suburban bliss."

"Yeah. She also gave up her own law studies to follow her husband to Washington. Or, I should say, future husband. They married in northern Virginia."

"What did he study?"

"American history. A man after your own heart, Bill."

I glanced over my shoulder. The kids had disappeared from Starbuck's, and some mid-fortyish guy in a beard was regaling a couple of coeds with great piles of wisdom. I swung back around.

"How does she impress you, pardner?"

"She's a strong woman, Rick. Stronger than I realized. I have to wonder, though."

"About what?"

"About why she claims to know so little about her husband's work and his time in 'Nam."

"That is weird. Anything else?"

"Yeah. Did you guys ask to have a look at Courney's records out at Americo?"

"Yes, and they told us those files are missing. Why?"

"Just curious. I'm going to Washington tonight. I might be able to run down a few things about Courney's background there. Have you gotten anything from the autopsy report?"

"Oh, yes. According to the written report, Courney died from a gunshot wound to the head."

"Well, whatta you know. It's amazin' what science can do these days. You didn't attend the autopsy yourself?"

"Unfortunately, that comes with the job. Hardy was there, too."

"Anything from the labs?"

"You betcha. Traces of alcohol and cocaine in Courney's blood."

"So Mrs. Hoffmann had a point. Anything from the car?"

"Minute traces of cocaine in the trunk. He was a careful cokehead...."

"But not careful enough."

"That's right. And he wasn't alone."

"What do you mean?"

"I mean your little friend Wanda has been known to snort a line or two as well."

"Says who?"

"Says a local reformed coke dealer and a tidy little rap sheet. She's been nailed for possession, pardner."

"No wonder she got all shaky when I tried to get her to talk to you guys. Probably afraid you fascists will torture her."

"Not right away. We usually wait for the second visit. Look, Bill, I'm serious. I'm not sure it's such a good idea for you to run off to Washington."

"Gotta go, Rick. I can't stop now. I'm following a hunch here while you guys do the boring stuff."

"Don't do this, Bill."

"I'll tell you what, pal. Give me what you've found on Courney's service history and the financial records, and I'll hustle on by."

"I'm still waitin' on the feds, pardner."

"We all have to do that at some time, Rick."

I didn't plan to wait much longer, though. I hung up before he got mad enough to send a patrol car.

# Chapter 8

The receiver settled into its cradle. I waved goodbye to my friends at Starbucks and trotted to the Volvo hiding from the sun in an alley not far from the phone booth. Once inside, I fired the engine, lowered the windows, and drove back out to the Illinois Research and Development Corridor. This time I cruised all the way to Oak Brook, five or six miles past Lisle. I took the exit before the shopping center and drove down the frontage road between gleaming towers of white steel and brown glass. The architecture was a bit older here, and even more boring. Just piles of rectangles. Very functional.

The check from Deborah Krueger had listed her business address in the upper left hand corner. I wondered why she had chosen not to print her home address. It was as though she had no private life, or one that she wanted to keep well hidden.

Her office building stood at the end of the road, right next to the highway. The title "Roelling Industries" stood chiseled in stone over the front entrance. I pulled into a two-tiered parking garage that nestled tight against the office building and found an empty space on the ground level near the back wall.

Unlike Americo Technologies, no rounded cubicle rose to welcome you as you entered. Instead, tiny islets of green bloomed all over the foyer, and twin plantings arranged behind knee-high brick walls sat on either side of the entrance. The reception area was a small office off to the right behind a glass partition that separated the staff from the visitors. I felt like I was headed for the principal's office. The receptionist, a young man in his mid-twenties, wore a light gray suit and sported short black hair and a cusp of facial hair along his upper lip. He told me Miss Krueger's office number was 826. I thanked him and left to find Deborah. I had no escort this time.

An invisible band inside the lift played a pathetic rendition of Elvis classics, heavy on the strings and without any vocals. Three people shared the elevator with me, and my companions seemed oblivious to the butchery underway on the other side of the speakers. One businessman must have been counting the tiny red flowers that dotted his bright yellow tie, while another brushed his hair in time to "It's Now or Never." The only woman in our group kept her eyes glued to the door. The elevator stopped twice to let people off, and each time I debated getting off myself to walk the last few floors. But the enchilada from lunch was still at work, and I didn't look forward to the extra exercise. Finally, at the eighth floor I pushed my way through sliding doors that opened at a glacial pace.

Number 826 sat across the hall and five doors down. I sauntered down a paneled and dimly-lit hallway that had a heavy carpet the color of spilt burgundy wine. It was several grades above industrial, and I could feel my feet press into the padding underneath. The air was blessedly quiet. No name stood on the door. I knocked and entered without waiting for a reply.

An attractive blonde in her mid-to-late twenties greeted my arrival with a cheery smile and sparkling eyes of bright hazel. Her teeth gleamed, and the blond hair fell to a broad set of shoulders. Heavy breasts lay over the top of the desk as she leaned forward on her elbows.

"Can I help you?"

"I'd like to see Deborah Krueger, if she's in."

"I'm Miss Krueger's secretary. Was she expecting you?"

"Not really," I explained. "But I was hoping she'd see me on a private matter." I handed her my card.

"Have a seat, and I'll see if she's free."

The young lady strode through another door to my right and left it open while she stood in the doorway and spoke with a disembodied voice. Her summer dress of white and pink checks fell to mid-calf, barely hiding a pair of hips that matched the breadth of her bosom. I heard the words, "Yes, of course."

"Miss Krueger will see you now," she said on the way back to her desk, gesturing toward the door. She no longer had my card.

"Thanks," I said, tossing another one on the edge of her blotter as I passed.

I entered Deborah Krueger's office and sucked in my breath. The room had two of its walls paneled and stained in a dark mahogany. It was probably plywood, but it still looked pretty impressive, even when the sun shone through the window that looked out over the Oak Brook shopping center at her back. A set of oriental carpets covered her floor, lending a rich tone of reds and blues to the office decor. Framed photographs hung on the walls to either side of her desk, several of them featuring her sister and brother-in-law, both alone and paired together.

She sauntered around one of those executive desks of dark cherry and pointed to a Queen Anne sofa set against the opposite wall. She told her secretary to hold all calls, closed the door, and then walked back to her desk and leaned her nice rear end against the front. Not a sound intruded from the rush of traffic outside. Soft strings from a Mozart concerto drifted from a Toshiba stereo behind the desk.

"Mister Habermann, this is truly a pleasant surprise. What can I do for you? You haven't solved the mystery already, have you?"

Although her eyes seemed to drift from me to the door every minute or so, her tone caught me by surprise. It sounded as though she had put on her cheery persona, so I decided to play along.

"No, I'm afraid not. But before I incur any major expenses, I like to check with my client."

"Can I get you anything to drink?"

I tapped my stomach. "No thanks. Lunch wasn't that long ago."

"Then what will it be?"

What indeed. The bitterness and hostility she had thrown up when we first met had disappeared. There was still an edge, a nervousness present. But she looked very professional in the two-piece red dress and low black heels. And very attractive. Still free of that damn bun she had worn on Sunday, her hair fell across her shoulders in thick coils. The long tresses set a natural frame for her oval face and tanned skin, the result, I assumed, of lots of poolside lounging. When her gaze met mine, rich blue eyes called from somewhere far away. It made me wonder just how deep this woman's personality ran.

"I'd like to fly to Washington to check into a few things."

"Our country's capital? What do you hope to find there."

"I think your brother-in-law's death has something to do with his past."

"Interesting. What makes you so sure?" She started to pace and played with my business card, flicking its edge between the thumb and forefinger of her left hand.

"I'm not. But do you remember your sister's reaction to my question about Vietnam?" I didn't wait for an answer. "Well, I got something similar when I raised the subject at lunch today."

"I know. She called. She sounded pretty upset." The pacing and finger flicking stopped. "Why do you think his time in Vietnam is tied to his shooting?"

I weighed whether I should tell her about the calls or the assault. I had to admit that I didn't have much else to go on yet, at least nothing concrete. "You'll have to trust me on this one, Miss Krueger. I wouldn't go so far from the scene of the crime if it wasn't necessary."

"I take it then that your investigation is not getting very far back here."

I averted my eyes and found myself focusing on one of the pictures on her wall. Deborah stood between and slightly behind her sister and brother-in-law, an arm draped over each one's shoulder. All three wore magnificent smiles. From the cut of Steve Courney's hair and the length of his sideburns, I'd say the photo dated from the mid-to-late seventies. His right hand rested on the hip of his cut-off blue jeans, and a silver I.D. bracelet caught a glint of sunlight as the camera snapped the moment's memory. The promise and hope of youth shone on faces two decades younger. I thought of how different the emotions of that face were from what I had been feeling back then.

"Mr. Habermann? Is something wrong?" Deborah Krueger stood in front of me now.

"I'm sorry." I shook my head free of the image. "You asked about the investigation?"

"Yes." Deborah Krueger sat herself in a green leather wing chair next to the sofa and crossed slender legs wrapped in black stockings.

"Well, to be honest, I'm a bit stymied by Steve's past and the unwillingness of those who knew him to open up. It's been difficult to get a picture of the sort of person he was, the kind of things that made him tick."

"That's a surprise. He always seemed like such a popular person."

"His employer said he was a bit of a loner."

She shrugged. "Maybe he didn't care for his colleagues."

"Do you have any idea what sort of work he did at the Pentagon?"

"I'm afraid not. I do know that he spent some time overseas, though."

"Do you remember where and when?"

"Oh, not really. I think it was some sort of attaché work, or something. Over in Europe. I gather there was some kind of trouble at one post, however."

"What kind of trouble?"

"I never really pressed. I'm afraid that sort of work is a bit complicated, and, frankly, not something I've had the time to explore. I believe Lisa pressured Steve to return to Washington. But I doubt you'll find much on it back there."

"Why is that?"

Her eyes glanced away, and her shoulders shrugged. "I got the impression it was hushed up, somehow."

"That's an interesting aspect of this case."

"What's that?" Those blue eyes narrowed and focused on mine.

"How little people seem to know about the victim and his past. Or are willing to divulge."

Deborah Krueger spread her hands. "I've been too absorbed with my own work. Besides, I could tell Steve and Lisa didn't like to talk about it. Where do you plan to stay out there?"

"I have a friend who lives in Arlington, Virginia. I'll call him tonight."

The smile returned. "Well, that should cut down on the expenses somewhat. Where do you plan to look for this information?"

"I have a few contacts left from my days in the Army."

"Oh, yes, the Army. I'm afraid I misjudged you earlier. You also spent some time in Vietnam, didn't you?"

"How did you hear about that?"

"I've done some checking on my own. I know all about your time in the jungle, and later, in military intelligence." She crossed her legs once more, and my eyes accompanied the hem of her skirt as it rode on her thighs. "You even made it to Officer Candidate School, right?"

"You have done your homework."

"Your detective friend, Rick Jamieson, told me about you."

"I hope he was charitable."

She nodded. "Oh, he was. He came by yesterday to interrogate me, and we talked some about you. He thinks very highly of you. He also thinks you should return to the police force."

"I don't deal well with authority. It's kind of a holdover from those earlier years."

Deborah threw her head back and laughed. "Me either. We have something in common."

"Well, I hope it helps on this case."

"Oh, I'm sure it will. I'm developing more confidence in you all the time. You're much more interesting than I first imagined." Her right hand massaged the leather arm on her chair. "When do you plan to leave?"

"This evening, if I can find a seat. American Airlines has several flights a day to the capital."

"And how long do you plan to stay?"

"This should take no more than a day, two at most. I'll check in when I get back. Before I go, though, can you tell me anything about this incident overseas? Could it be connected to your brother-in-law's death?"

She shook her head. "I don't think so. That goes pretty far back, and it was far away."

"Distance and time aren't always much of a barrier. What about Steve's behavior? His relationship with your sister? I take it you know why she hired me."

Deborah Krueger waved the question away, like some minor discomfort. "Lisa has always been a jealous girl, overly suspicious. I'd say that at times she was far too possessive. You didn't find anything did you?"

"Not really. How about drugs? Some witnesses have pointed to drug use."

"Steve?" She shrugged. "Perhaps. But I'm sure it was no more that the recreational thing you find among the young and prosperous these days."

"How about you?"

Deborah Jaeger laughed. "Hardly, Bill. I have too much to lose. Besides, I tried it a few times and never found it very appealing."

"May I ask a personal question?"

She smiled while one leg rocked back and forth over the other. It was very disarming. And very effective.

"That depends. What would you like to know?"

"Just what do you do here?"

"Of course. You should know something more about your employer."

"It usually helps."

She ran the edge of my card across her chair. "I'm the Vice-President of Sales, Midwestern Division."

"You must be doing well."

She winked and her lips parted in a smile. "Don't worry, Mister Habermann. Your cheque won't bounce."

I waved at nothing in particular. "Oh, I'm not worried about that."

The smile grew and a light laugh escaped. "I know. But I've been without, Bill. May I call you Bill?"

I nodded. "Please do."

"Well, I've encountered my share of hard times, Bill, and I want to be sure I've left them behind. I work pretty hard at what I do."

"Are you referring to your marriage and divorce?"

The smile faded for a moment. A shadow passed somewhere behind her eyes, then daylight reappeared. "So, you've been checking up on me as well?"

I shifted in my seat. She leaned forward and wrapped her palm around my forearm.

"No, don't feel uncomfortable. I'd expect you to look into my background. After all, you're a private investigator." She settled back into the chair. The leather moaned with delight. "Yes, the years after the divorce were tough. There were some other rough patches as well. But I'd rather not go into that right now. Perhaps later."

"It takes a strong personality to bounce back as well as you have, Miss Krueger."

Her eyes stared hard at mine. "Please. Call me Deborah. And I'm not always strong. Occasionally, I look for that in someone else."

I shifted my weight on the sofa. "One last question, if I may."

She shrugged, still smiling. "Why not?"

"Can you tell me any more about Steve Courney and Vietnam?"

Her eyes clouded, and the hand came to a rest in the middle of the chair's arm. "What would you like to hear?"

"What did he talk about?"

"He never said much."

"Even so, what did he say?'

"He told me of things he wanted to forget, things he hoped he could leave behind."

"Did he? Or did they follow him home?"

"Isn't that what you're supposed to find out?'

"What kind of things?"

Her eyes glanced toward the window. "He never went into specifics."

"Do you think it has anything to do with his death?"

The eyes came back to me. "I hope you'll find out. You were there, too. That should help, shouldn't it?"

"Is that what you think? That I have some sort of bond, some special access or insight?"

"I should hope that you'll at least have a special sort of understanding."

"I guess we'll find out. I'll check in when I return."

"Please do. Here's my number at home in case you need to reach me there."

She walked over to her desk, wrote something on a pad, then slotted the pen in a gold holder set upon a marble slab. Her deep blue eyes caught a flash of the late afternoon sun when she looked up from her desk, the pupils intent on my own. She strolled back toward the door.

I stood and followed her lead like a obedient puppy. The card with her number and address floated in a palm of smooth skin. Nails as red as her carpets held its edge.

"Another Naperville resident." I tucked the card into my shirt pocket.

"Yes. And not too far from you." She held out her hand. "Good luck."

"Would you like an accounting of the case thus far?"

She escorted me to the door. "No, I don't think that will be necessary. I trust you. Now, I really must go. I have a lot to do."

"Oh, by the way...."

"Yes?" Deborah stopped in mid-stride about halfway to the door.

"Is there any chance I could get a list of out-of-town guests attending the funeral?" I spread my palms. "Every little bit helps. You never know who might have a motive."

She frowned, her lips molding to a seductive pout. "Sorry to disappoint you. I'm afraid none could make it on such short notice."

Her secretary stood at the outer door, holding it open when we emerged from the inner sanctum. She strolled over to her boss to pass along a phone message, and I glanced at the appointment calendar on the secretary's desk as I passed. After a busy morning, Miss Krueger's day looked like it was slowing down.

At the door, I paused to look the young secretary in the eye.

"I'm sorry, but I didn't get your name."

"Julie," she bubbled, her head rocking to the side as she spoke.

"That's a very pretty name. What exactly does Roelling Industries do, Julie?"

"Oh, we do a variety of things. This is not the corporate headquarters, you know. Here, we oversee the Midwestern manufacturing operations."

I paused at the door. "What do you manufacture?"

"Lots of things. But out here mostly electronics and appliances."

"I see. What else does Roelling do?"

"Well, we do quite a bit in the import/export business."

"Of course. That's where I heard the name before. Thanks very much." Just outside the door I pivoted, then poked my head back inside. "Oh, by the way. A Jaguar in the parking lot had its lights on, but fortunately the door was unlocked. If that was Ms. Krueger's car, you might tell her to be more careful."

The secretary pursed her lips, rested her chin on her fingers, then shook her head. "No, I don't know who's that would be. Ms. Krueger drives a BMW. A nice red one."

Slick. Very slick, indeed, I thought. "Thanks again."

I climbed into the Volvo and slid down low behind the steering wheel. I couldn't be sure that Deborah Krueger hadn't seen my car at her sister's last Sunday, but I'd have to take that chance. A red BMW sat across from my car and about a dozen spaces down. She had pulled in front first, so I figured I'd have plenty of time to sneak out behind her.

After a twenty-minute wait, I had my reward. Deborah Krueger never even glanced at the Volvo. She headed straight for her Kraut power machine, coaxed the engine into a soft roar, then backed up without even looking. Women drivers. I waited for her to round the corner in the direction of the exit, then slid out of my space.

Deborah Krueger was not difficult to tail. She pulled onto the Tollroad, heading in the direction of Chicago. Traffic flowed with its usual moderate-to-heavy, midafternoon crush, an ideal pace. I had plenty of cover, but not too many obstacles to a clear line of sight. It also helped that she restrained that powerful German engine to a steady 65 miles an hour. I did have to cut off a Chevy Cavalier and Ford Explorer at one point. The drivers did not appreciate my intensity, and I did not have the time to explain that I was investigating a murder. Life's tough in the big city.

And that's just where our journey ended. The red BMW hugged the middle lane until it reached the Eisenhower Expressway. That she followed into the heart of Chicago, turning off on State Street. After a block, she dropped her car with a parking garage. I lost her momentarily when I circled the block, looking for a parking space.

I never found one. But I caught a glimpse of Deborah heading for the tracks of the Elevated. I followed in my car from a block's distance until I saw her climb the stairs to catch the southbound train.

The tracks rumbled, and I knew I had lost her for the afternoon. I thought hard, and I tried to be imaginative. But I couldn't think of how this little trip would fit into her responsibilities as a Vice-President of Sales for Roelling Industries.

It was almost six o'clock when I got home. I stopped along the way to pick up my mail and the film, but the kid behind the counter claimed it wasn't back yet. I reminded him that his company promised twenty-four hour service. He shrugged and returned to his copy of the Sporting News. At least the VA records had arrived.

The back door lock still looked clean, and the piece of tape was unbroken. Nothing in the apartment appeared to have been tampered with. Someone, however, had slid a sealed white business envelope underneath the door. I picked it up and ambled into the bedroom, where I placed the Browning and clip back on the night table. Then I carried the envelope back to the kitchen and pulled another Special Ex from the refrigerator, sat down at my rolltop desk, and called American Airlines to book a reservation. The woman on the other end told me there was also nothing open until the ten-fifteen flight tomorrow morning. Next, I left a message with the Sullivans, giving them my approximate time of arrival and promising to show in time for dinner.

After hanging up, I sat back and lifted my feet to the edge of the rolltop desk, envelope in hand. I had inherited the desk from my parents when they'd sold the family farm. Their condo on the golf course at St. Petersburg was too small for all the furniture the family had accumulated over the years, especially the heavy oak and maple pieces that had filled the living and dining rooms. This was the one item I had requested. It was where I conducted most of my business, and where I kept the phone and recorder.

I expected to be gone no more than a day or two, but I was already looking forward to seeing Sully. John Sullivan had been a close friend in Saigon, where we both worked in military intelligence. I had spent most of my time on order of battle crap; Sullivan had started there and then moved into counterintelligence. My discomfort with the military had grown to an active dislike after that additional year in intelligence. Something to do with ignoring the inconvenient on the part of my superiors. I had been soured enough by the absence of good intelligence in the bush, where it always seemed that some jag-off at division headquarters was sitting on stuff because of a "need-to-know" obsession that he used to keep the information to himself. I mean, who the hell needed it more than us? Saigon didn't change my perception that we just led ourselves in circles over there.

So I bolted at the first opportunity. Sully, however, had always been a more organized individual than me, and his distaste for authority never reached my anarchic levels. In fact, he had gotten pretty comfortable in the army, and after ten years he had decided to make a career out of it. Now he was assigned to the Pentagon, a colonel probably fully engaged making coffee and delivering donuts.

My attention wandered back to the envelope. I held it up to the light streaming in from the window to the side of the desk, searching for unpleasant surprises, like wiring or packing that resembled an explosive. All I saw was the outline of a 3 x 5 index card. I tore the seam, and the card fell into my lap. I retrieved it by the edges and held it back up to the sunlight. Someone had scrawled four sentences in block letters worthy of a pre-schooler. "Steve Courney was a traitor who deserved to die. Leave him alone. Lots of people will be happy to see him dead. Others too, if you are not careful." And the author had written it in pencil.

I picked up the receiver and dialed Rick Jamieson's office number. He had already left for the day, so I left a message that he should get in touch with me as soon as possible. Then I called him at home, but his wife Susan told me he hadn't arrived yet. I left the same message with her.

Next came Paul Justin. Paul and I shared a mutual respect, and we occasionally shared tasks, like surveillance work or insurance fraud. Two cars and two sets of feet can always do more than one. He was a good detective, very careful and thorough in his investigations, something he probably learned from his days at the FBI. He also enjoyed excellent contacts with the insurance companies in the area. He had offered to set up a partnership about a year ago, but the work, while regular, sounded a little too predictable.

"Justin Associates."

"Associates? Since when did you go corporate?"

"Hello, Bill. I haven't, really. But it sounds more impressive."

"Well, damn. I, for one, am certainly impressed. In fact, I'm so awed I'm going to ask for a favor."

"I never intended it to be that impressive." The window air conditioning unit settled into a cozy hum, and a cold breeze tickled the back of my neck.

"Seriously, Paul. I'm going to be away for a couple of days on a case. Could you look after things for me?"

"I suppose so. What's up?"

"First of all, I promise to finish that report on that background investigation you farmed out to me before I leave tomorrow."

"The one for Amoco?"

"Yeah. I'll type it up tonight. If I don't drop it off before my flight, check with Ahmed downstairs."

"I was wondering if I'd ever see that thing. In fact, I was wondering when I'd see you again. You must be busy."

"Yeah. And there's something else."

"I was afraid of that."

"Are you still well connected to a lot of those firms out along the Tollroad?"

"I don't know if I'd put it that way. Why?"

"Does anyone owe you a favor?"

"I don't like where this heading."

"Could you see if anyone knows anything about a Steve Courney? His firm was antsy about letting me have a look at his file."

"You mean Naperville's very own dead guy? I'm not surprised."

"Why is that?"

"Because a lot of those firms have pretty strict security policies about their personnel files. Especially those involved in government work."

"Yeah, I'm aware of that. That's why I'm looking for someone who can call in a chit, Paul."

"It will take more than that. This kind of thing requires some tact."

"Try the favor route first, Paul. Hell, bribe someone if you have to."

"Your ethics suck, Habermann. But I'll see what I can do."

"Thanks, Paul." I leaned back in my chair.

"You know, if we had joined forces permanently this sort of thing would be much easier. You wouldn't have to beg for favors."

"I'm not begging. Just requesting a professional courtesy."

Justin continued like I hadn't said a thing. "It's getting harder and harder for independent operators like us to survive, Bill. Everyone's going corporate, and the kind of firms setting up shop out along the Tollroad feel a lot more comfortable with that sort of investigator."

"I promise I'll think some more about it, Paul. In the meantime, I've got some real live surveillance work for you while I'm away."

"Who's the mark, and where are you going?"

I gave him Deborah Krueger's name, description, and working address, and then told him where I was going and for how long. I asked him to keep tabs on where she went and whom she met.

"You'll be paid for your time, of course. I'll check in when I get back."

"Of course."

I didn't tell Justin everything, though. This was the first time in the years we had worked together that I didn't give him all the information I had. I didn't tell him I was putting a tail on my own client.

Rick Jamieson arrived around nine-thirty. I handed him the note. "It looks like someone did not care for Mister Courney," I explained.

He weighed the card in his palm like it was gold dust. "More drugs stuff, you think?"

I shrugged. "Hard to tell. But why would recreational drug use make him a traitor and make someone want him dead? Dealing, of course, would be a different matter. And who are the 'others' mentioned here? It sounds like there could be more trouble on the way."

Jamieson nodded. "Yeah, and it could be something else entirely."

"Yes, it could. We're both masters of the obvious tonight."

"I'll have this checked for prints." His gaze shifted from the card to me. "You alright here? Any chance of another visit?"

I thought of the Browning and the tripwire I planned to string across the hallway. "I may be losing a step or two. But this time I'll be ready, if they come back."

"In any case, I'm glad you cancelled the trip east."

I shook my head. "Not cancelled, Rick, just postponed. I couldn't get a seat until tomorrow."

Jamieson frowned like he had caught me cheating in school again. "You really need to lay off, Bill. I can't go into it yet."

I leaned forward, starting to speak. His hand shot up. "Bear with me, pardner. But there are some new angles, some new information. I'm trying to keep you from getting in worse trouble, as well as getting hurt."

"Rick, I can't sit here. This thing is already pointing to paths I need to follow."

"Like where?"

"I can't, Rick. I got a secret, too. But believe me, this is something I've got to do and only I can do it. I'll tell you everything once I work it out."

When Rick Jamieson left that night, he was very pissed and very disappointed. He was still my best friend, of course, but I wasn't sure how much he still trusted me. I just hoped he hadn't seen the manila envelope from the Veterans Administration on my desk.

I picked it, ripped the flap open, and read. It didn't take very long. As I had feared, the records were woefully incomplete.

# Chapter 9

"Enjoy your stay, Mr. Habermann, but be careful," the attendant at National car rental had warned. "You're in Washington now."

I didn't see any crooks or politicians that I could identify as such. Just a minor crowd of exhausted shoppers and tourists trying to flee the heat and humidity of Washington. It actually made Naperville's weather seem pleasant. We were all enjoying the mist that sprouted from a fountain in front of Alexandria's town hall, a large four-story office building in a mock colonial style attached to another structure that looked like an oversized firehouse from the previous century. The fountain sat directly in front of the hall and right in the middle of a square pool a little larger than what one might find in a rich man's backyard. A continuous spray of water shot about thirty feet into the air.

What I did see, though, were red bricks. Lots of them. In fact, I wished I owned the brick store. The city hall was constructed entirely of red bricks, as were all of the buildings on the surrounding streets. The plaza in front of the hall was also made of brick, just like the sidewalks. In fact, in the two blocks from Queen Street, where I had squeezed the little teal Geo the folks at National had given me, I had walked on nothing but bricks, except to cross the streets. The only other man-made colors came from the mixture of whites, reds, and pinks with trims of tan, blue, and black on the rowhouses clustered in the streets of Old Town. Scottish flags and flowered pennants waved to the pedestrians strolling by on their way to the shops and restaurants closer to King Street and the Potomac River. But back here, the bricks had won out. It was like a desert of red rock.

I sat just beyond the water's reach, studying the map the attendant had given me. According to Courney's license application in Illinois, his last residence here had been on Saint Asaph Street in Alexandria. I had driven down Saint Asaph, but the street was not as I had remembered it from my earlier visits. That's why I kept checking the damn map, to be sure I had not mistaken the street for another one. As I recalled, there had been a county prison there, surrounded by two-story tenement homes, part of the city's housing projects.

Not anymore, though. The prison had been converted into a row of upscale rowhouses with BMWs, SAABs, and Jaguars parked at curbside. In fact, the whole neighborhood had leaped several notches up the socio-economic ladder. Lisa

# ANGEL IN BLACK

Courney had been right about one thing, at least-Old Town Alexandria was much nicer and probably a whole lot more expensive than I'd remembered it. I figured I'd better check on the Courney property while I had the chance and before I headed to the Sullivan's for supper.

A large black woman greeted me from her seat when I walked through the door of city hall. She was planted behind a reception desk to the left of the entrance, and it looked like she was there for the long haul. A paperback romance and knitting bag occupied about half the countertop. She informed me in a pleasant voice that the office with the personal property tax records was on the third floor. I decided to skip the crowd waiting for the elevator underneath a row of brick arches and trotted up the two flights of stairs to Room 315. If the Courneys had lived here, this was as good a place as any to start building a portrait of their personal and professional lives. The personal property taxes are not normally available to the public, however, and I wasn't sure how far I could get on my wit and charm.

Inside, a gleaming white counter ran for about twenty feet until it hit a wall. Somewhere behind that, a buzz of activity hummed while a small line of people waited for assistance. A long, thin glass tube on the ceiling filled the room with brightness and a steady sigh. I loosened my tie and undid the top button of my shirt. After about twenty minutes, a middle-aged woman with gray hair and a pale green dress tossed me a smile that looked like she had been carrying it all morning. She had done a superb job holding the creases of her mouth in just the right places for the four people in front of me. I guess it was her way of mastering a numbing administrative routine.

"I was wondering if you could help me locate some personal property records for a given year."

"Are they yours?"

"Not exactly."

The smile faded, and her brown eyes darkened with suspicion.

"They belong to a dead man," I explained.

"Are you his next-of-kin?"

"Not exactly."

This time she frowned.

"I'm a detective investigating a murder."

She folded her hands. "I'm afraid those records are not for public viewing. For whom do you work?"

"My name is William Habermann. From Chicago. I'm investigating a killing, and I was hoping something from the victim's history might help reveal a motive for the murder."

"The victim's name?"

"Stephen Courney."

"And you have some identification?"

"Sure." I flashed a Photostat of my license.

"Could I look at that more closely?"

"Of course." I tossed her own bright smile back at her and threw in some extra wattage of my own.

"But you're a private detective. And it says here Naperville, not Chicago."

"Well, yes...." I strained to hold the smile in place. Just for added emphasis, I leaned across the countertop and spread my hands to show her how sincere I was. "But the license entitles me to work throughout the great state of Illinois. And I've been asked by the local police force in Naperville-that's just outside Chicago-to assist them in this matter. You can call this number, if you need to verify that."

I wrote down Rick Jamieson's name and number on one of my cards.

"Just a minute, please."

She seized the card and disappeared behind the wall. The percussion and buzz of earnest activity from computers and civil servants kept a steady beat, the noise echoing off the linoleum floors to the audience outside. Periodically, a face would appear, and then an entire body. I smiled at the people in line behind me and drummed my fingertips on the counter. Periodically, one of those disembodied bureaucrats would take human form to wait on a customer. After about five minutes, Ms. Green Dress returned.

"Detective Jamieson was not in. Nor was his superior, a Mr. Hardy?" Thank God for small favors. "But it was the Naperville police department, as you said. And they claimed to know you. They also verified the case. But I'm surprised the police would bring in a private investigator. Is it even legal?"

"Well you see, I know the family, and I promised to check out a few things. So, I thought as long as I'm here...." I shrugged to affect some innocence.

She hesitated, pondering the scrap of paper held between both thumbs and forefingers. "I'm going to take a chance. I'll see if there are any records here, but you may not copy them, or take any notes."

I nodded.

"What was his name? And you're sure he lived here?"

"Oh yes. Stephen Courney," I repeated, spelling the last name in a slow, measured cadence, and gave her the address I had gotten from the Illinois DMV. "And it would actually help me the most if I could see a copy of his records from, say, 1980 to 1991."

"I'll see what I can do. But you will not be permitted to copy these records until I get authorization from my supervisors. And that will require a written request from your-I mean, the Naperville police department, as well as a court order."

"Of course. Detective Jamieson was supposed to file the request with a judge today," I lied. "It shouldn't be too much longer." I smiled some more. "But this will do for now."

It took another ten minutes before she returned with a green and white computer printout that was about an inch thick.

"You may sit at the desk over there," she pointed toward the wall behind me, "to examine these."

I carried my prize over to the designated spot, a small brown and gray desk of oak and metal that looked like it had been remanded from the local elementary school. The records began in 1983, when I presumed Steve Courney had first moved to the area, or, at least to Alexandria. The District and Maryland do not have a personal property tax. Only the lucky citizens of Virginia get to file that particular claim in the fall. And the records do not give a listing, or even an indication, of total income. The only thing the records in front of me covered was the make and estimated cost of possessions like cars, boats, and airplanes. I doubted if Steve Courney had owned any of the last two. I also thought these records would be more accessible than anything the IRS would have.

The address I had was correct, and I had been right about the boats and airplanes. So much for conspicuous consumption. The gaps, however, were intriguing. He had not paid a property tax every year. There were no records on his cars for the years 1985 through 1987, and from 1989 through 1991. And he had started out with a Chevy Nova, but after each interval, he reregistered with a new Saab. Not bad. I figured those missing years must have been the ones Deborah Krueger had spoken of as overseas assignments. Then I remembered her comment about trouble at one of the posts. Whatever it was, the trouble did not appear to have dented his purchasing power.

I returned the records to the matron behind the counter. She resurrected her smile, which now had the look of worn paint. The afternoon was wearing on. The room felt even brighter and warmer than before, as though someone had increased the wattage in the lights and cut the air conditioning. Most of the other customers were gone, though. Only one other gentleman, an elderly black man in a white T-shirt and blue jean overalls, remained.

"Are there any records for Lisa Courney?" I asked. I tried to sound real apologetic when I continued. "I'm sorry. I realize I should have asked before. But I'd hate to have to fly all the way back here again."

"Is she a relation of the deceased?"

"She was his wife." I cast my eyes at the floor.

"No," she sighed. "I would definitely need legal cover for that one."

I looked up. "How about the real estate records?" I was pretty sure those were available to the public.

The woman pursed her lips as she studied my face. Then her eyes brightened, and the smile returned. "Yes. Those may help." She pointed to someplace outside the door. "They're right down the hall."

"And the city real estate index?" A hunch worth following, since I was already here.

"Same office. Number 344."

"Thank you."

Miss Green Dress actually smiled. I nodded and smiled back. If I wore a hat, I would have tipped it. I shuffled my way into the hall and headed for Room 344.

---

The black woman at the entry was engrossed in her novel and did not raise an eyebrow when I passed through the door and out into the brick-lined yard. From the looks of the cover of her book, at least two people in the world were having one hell of a good time, cavorting on the sands amidst tropical pleasures, hair tossed and shirts ripped. I dropped down at the edge of the fountain and spread copies of the real estate records for the Courneys' last three years in Alexandria across my lap. A heavy, fetid air hung like a tropical tapestry. I could almost hear the booming echoes of an artillery barrage along the perimeter.

The Courney's house had not been cheap. In fact, it had cost a pile of money in 1991. The city of Alexandria had valued the property at $350,000. Not bad for a two-bedroom squatter, stuck in a row of packed houses, none of which looked like they topped 2,000 square feet. The price of prestige.

The city's real estate documentation recorded the sale in 1989 for an affordable little sum of $225,000. A real bargain. Maybe the house had needed a lot of work. The previous owner was a man named Sean Cavanaugh, a self-employed consultant. Lord knows there were plenty of those running around Washington, and probably always would be. There was also no mortgage company listed, which I found very odd. Moreover, the Courneys had purchased the house during their second overseas tour, which meant they had probably rented it out, perhaps to Mr. Cavanaugh, or left it vacant until their return. And the real estate index indicated they had resold the property in 1992 for $365,000. Not bad at all.

A fine mist sprinkled my back. It felt pretty good, and I was not alone. The crowd had grown to about a dozen people, all of us watching the pedestrians wander past. Occasionally we saw some jerk on a skateboard or rollerblades. A handful of idiots were cycling toward the Potomac. I might as well have joined them. Steve Courney's background got more mysterious the deeper I dug. The guy had held on to a valuable piece of real estate for about half a decade, some of which he spent elsewhere, most likely overseas. What had he been doing those missing years? What had he done when he came back? What had happened at that last posting? How had he managed to climb that ladder of yuppie purchasing power to move from a General Motors reject to a Saab? And how had he been able to make such a nice little real estate investment?

It was three o'clock, and the Washington summer was in full blast. The taste of brine bit through my lips as sweat rolled along the rim of my cheek. The Baskin-Robbins up the street beckoned, its bright letters leaping out from the staid red masonry. A double scoop of mint chocolate chip sounded like the thing I needed to break free of the heat.

I settled for a single scoop, then strolled back to Queen Street to retrieve the Geo. My fingers fumbled with the keys as I tried to balance the cone, then I dropped them on the blacktop. When I looked up from my crouch, I spotted a woman with a dark nest of hair and a body like the one that had escorted Steve Courney to his death. In fact, she could have passed for a twin. She wore tight black slacks and a black tanktop, and she moved like slick licorice.

She darted down an alley, and I bolted after her. When I reached Princess Street two blocks away, the dark hair flowed past in a shiny black Honda Civic. Her body and the car's seemed to merge and disappear at the same time. I ran to the Geo, fired all four cylinders, then raced off in pursuit.

The Honda came into view again three blocks south of King Street. She turned right on Franklin, towards Washington Boulevard, where I figured she'd try to lose me in the crush of early rush hour traffic. She caught the light at Washington and continued north. Some slob in a Ford Escort insisted on braking at the red light, and I had to swerve to keep the Civic in sight.

We continued north as the Parkway snaked along the edge of the Potomac until she caught the exit that ran past Arlington cemetery and Fort Meyers, through Rosslyn and down Wilson Boulevard. This should have been familiar territory, but too much had changed. Shiny new office buildings gleamed on either side of the street, and a string of Vietnamese restaurants, grocery shops, and department stores ran for about five blocks. It had all the appearance of a miniature Saigon, the kind of neighborhood that sprouted as the Vietnamese refugees settled into America's urban landscape when they fled the war and the aftermath of defeat.

The black Civic slid into an alley off a side street and parked behind a restaurant, the Nam Dinh. I circled the block, grabbed a metered spot on the main street, and trotted inside. A wrinkled old woman, the top of whose head barely reached my chest, told me in a high-pitched shrill that they would not be open for dinner for another hour.

I tried to tell her I was looking for an old friend. I'm not sure she understood me.

"You come back later. We open later."

"But I'm not hungry. I'm looking for someone."

"Come back later. When you hungry."

We went on like this for two or three minutes. Through it all a set of deep dark pupils surrounded by a maze of silky hair followed my movements with the stealth and suspicion of a black cat. An image returned. Two, actually. One from the jungle and one from the other night, in Naperville. My head swam, and I struggled for breath. One of those women was dead, and the other had walked at Steve Courney's side the night he was shot. Now I was really confused, and not hungry at all. The two images were so similar it seemed they were the same. And I could have sworn that one of those women, maybe both, held me in her vision from the back of that restaurant.

# Chapter 10

I stumbled out of the restaurant and back onto the sidewalk along Wilson Boulevard. The sun beat down on me like the memories and images that kept returning when I least expected them. Traffic swam past in a flow of white and blue and brown, most of them coming from more goddamn SUVs. The exhaust and noise combined with the heat to create a web of nausea midway between my stomach and throat. At least the Sullivans lived nearby. I knew John Sullivan would not be eager to hear about recurring phantoms from my military past, but he'd still listen and try to help.

John Sullivan and his wife Hannelore lived in a scenic part of northern Virginia separated from Georgetown by the Potomac River and the national park surrounding the George Washington Parkway. When I flew in, the river had risen like a fat silver thread rippling over green upholstery. Up close, its pale, placid water looked like a narrow lake struggling to hold off urban development and self-serious politics with a current that was too weak and water that was too shallow.

I retraced my path down Wilson, through the plate glass office buildings in Rosslyn, and back onto the George Washington Parkway. Just past the Key Bridge I veered onto a two-lane exit that swung up and away from the Potomac and through a small forest that overflowed into a residential area of undulating lawns and sturdy oaks. The Geo struggled to the top of a hill called Lorcum Lane, and then I heaved the little car around a corner, past a Protestant Church, and into a cul-de-sac listed as Randolph Street. Another four or five blocks further on Lorcum, and I would have hit Route 29-a Washington area replica of Ogden Avenue, complete with car dealerships, Mexican restaurants, banking establishments, and 7-Elevens. And more rush-hour traffic to go with all that neon scenery.

I landed in the Sullivans' driveway, climbed out of the car, and swam in a pool of suburban bliss toward a colonial with white siding, black clapboard shutters, and a sloping shingle roof. It was a house one could find almost anywhere in Naperville. Hell, the whole neighborhood belonged in Naperville. Fifteen minutes later, Hannelore Sullivan had me inside the kitchen chopping vegetables for the evening salad. My overnight bag lay at the foot of the stairs in the living room.

I had just finished dicing the carrots and mushrooms, when the screen door opened. A drab olive uniform rushed toward me, topped by the closely cropped light brown hair and wafer-thin mustache of John Sullivan.

"Sully, you old asshole!"

Hannelore winced.

"Colonel Sullivan to you, butthead."

"Now, that's impressive. So much authority. And with so little talent."

We shook hands, then embraced.

"When did you get in?"

"About one. I'd forgotten that you lose an hour when you fly in this direction."

"Do those big wheels in the driveway belong to you?"

"Jealous?"

Sully frowned and shook his head. "Not really." He peeked in the salad bowl. "It looks like Hannelore is keeping you gainfully employed." He winked at his wife. "Glad to see someone is, finally."

He strolled over to Hannelore, slid his arm around her waist and kissed her on the lips. Then Sully broke from his wife and pulled a thin brown bottle from the refrigerator.

"Habermann, you look like you need a beer."

"I usually do." I glanced at the bottle he handed me. "What the hell is Dominion Lager?"

"It's actually pretty good. It's one of the few local beers Hannelore will drink."

Sully examined his own bottle and passed it to his wife. He opened the refrigerator to pull out another. "This is one of their lagers."

Hannelore sipped from the bottle, placed it on the table, then stepped to the cupboard for a glass. She glanced over her shoulder while she poured her beer. "I'll finish in here. You two go catch up in the living room."

Sully led the way past the kitchen table of light colored pine into a living room decorated in varying shades of blue. A matching sofa and love seat with a deep, navy color and a similar floral setting occupied a strategic location near the front picture window. Two white arm chairs faced off across a glass-topped coffee table.

"How's your buddy Jamie Krug these days?" Sully collapsed in one corner of the sofa.

"Better. Still trying to line up steady work."

"Is he laying off the booze?"

I dropped my own frame into one of the armchairs. "I think so. At least, the last time I saw him he was."

"So, tell me about this case and what it has to do with me."

"I'm not sure it does, Sully. But there are a few things I need to check out."

Sullivan's eyebrows arched as he took a swig from his bottle and shrugged at his wife, who peeked in through the doorway. He pointed at me like I was some escapee from a mime troupe.

Sully had met his wife during his tour in Germany at Bad Kreuznach. She was an attractive blond, almost as tall as me, which put her just under six feet, probably around 5' 10". We had gotten to know each other during my brief stint at the Abrams Headquarters in Frankfurt shortly before I left the Army, and she had spent most of that time lecturing me on the evils of the American military intervention in Vietnam. I had told her I wasn't too crazy about it, either.

"She hates it when I talk about the war." Sully studied me for a moment. He drank.

I shrugged. "Me too. But we all have to face our demons sooner or later."

The skin tightened around Sullivan's eyes. "There aren't any demons in this house."

I leaned forward. "Sully, I didn't mean it that way. You know that."

"It wasn't the military's fault, Bill. You weren't alone, you know. A lot of people suffered." He sipped again. "Most dealt with it and got on with their lives."

An awkward moment interceded. I tried to drown it with some of my friend's local beer.

"I'm not looking for a lecture, and I'm not looking for sympathy. Just help on a case."

"So, tell me about it." He took another pull on his beer. "How did this Courney guy buy it?"

"A bullet through the forehead, and then some. We saw worse, of course, but still not a pretty sight. It seems he spent some time out here. At the Pentagon."

Sully shook his head. "I don't think so."

I set my bottle down. "What do you mean? Several people have told me so."

"Like who?"

"Like his wife and his sister-in-law. And his employer."

He put his own bottle on a coaster of a famous Civil war battlefield-Bull Run, I believe-and leaned forward. "I asked around today. 'Procurements' isn't much to go on, Bill. I checked in the office of the Secretary of the Army, since I know some folks in there. No one has ever heard of this guy."

"Maybe the crowd has changed. Did you get to look at any records?"

"Nope."

"Why not?"

"Bill, it's not like I have a lot of free time these days, and I need to know where I'm supposed to find the damn records if I'm supposed to go looking for them. There is no special office for procurements. I need to know if he was associated with a particular service."

"His wife said something about a central office set up during the Reagan years. Perhaps you could check in there. What about the work number I pulled from his DMV records?"

Sully smiled. "Do you have any idea how many reorganizations and office moves that building has gone through over the last decade? That number got me some secretary in the Joint Chiefs' office." He shook his head. "No, I asked several people to get some direction, and all I drew were blanks. Even then, the records would not be that easy to obtain. I'd have to call in a lot of chips."

"Yeah, I realize that. That's why I asked you." I tried to smile. I grabbed my beer and gulped.

"Well, afterwards I did manage to find some old Federal Registries for the years you mentioned."

"Federal what?"

"The Federal Registry for the Executive Branch. And he wasn't listed in any of them."

"So?"

"So, it doesn't mean he never worked here, but it does make him a lot harder to locate. And I certainly could not go looking in every cubbyhole at our place to find some file that may, or may not, exist. What about a military record?"

"I had a look at some VA records, but they were incomplete."

"What do you mean?"

"They stopped around 1970, shortly after he left my unit."

Sullivan paused and sipped his lager. "You said he was also involved in some intelligence shit afterwards, didn't you?"

"That's right. I think he was working out of one of the units in the Saigon Military Assistance Mission. Like us."

"But you don't remember running into him there, do you? No unit designation, or anything like that?"

I shook my head between more sips of beer.

"I could check around on that. I still have some contacts in J2. But as you know full well, Bill, that stuff's not going to be easy to run down. Depending on what he did, there's not likely to be much of a paper trail. Care to take a guess at what his job was?"

"I'd say he was running agents in the north."

"Why?"

I shrugged again. "Nothing else fits right now. Our paths would have probably crossed if he had worked at a desk in Saigon."

"Then there won't be much I'll be allowed to see. I'll have to rely on word of mouth stuff. You sure our paths never crossed?"

"Pretty sure. I mean, you and I were order-of-battle and CI types. I think the closest we ever got to people like him was reading the reports his people put out."

"What about when you were working on exfiltrations near the end?"

"Hell, I don't remember anything about individual cases. I just wrote some memos."

"Shit, Bill, that's not all there was, and you know it. Those memos could be used to scuttle an operation."

"Sully, I just put down what most of us believed. Those networks were not feeding us any worthwhile information. They had probably all been turned a long time before. We never should have let them run for so damn long."

"Do you think the stuff that may be tied to your case came after he left the 25th?"

"Shit, I don't know. I'm groping here. I also don't know what he may have done in between, either." I considered the rug for a moment. "There may also be a drug angle."

"How so?"

"I haven't told anyone this, but I think I remember him as a user and small-time dealer back at Tay Ninh. I don't know what else he may have done afterwards. But it looks like he was at least a recreational user at the time of his death."

Sullivan shifted his weight on the sofa. "I'll leave that stuff to you and your Naperville cops."

I nodded. "Thanks. But I could really use your help to narrow down his duty assignments."

Sully was silent for a moment, the mouth of the beer bottle resting on his lips. When he spoke again, his gaze wandered from the picture window to my face. "What did you find in Old Town?"

"That he lived here and paid taxes. He spent most of that period at an address in St. Asaph Street."

"Whereabouts on St. Asaph?"

"The 300 block. Why?"

Sully rotated his upper torso in the direction of the kitchen. "Hannelore? Isn't St. Asaph the first street on the river side of Washington Avenue?"

A faint "yes" echoed from the kitchen.

"She's my almighty encyclopedia." He shook his head and took another swig of beer.

"Not to mention your conscience."

Sully's relationship to his wife had always been difficult for me to understand. It never ceased to amaze me that a woman who had matured in the closed world of impassioned, left-wing German student politics should find her happiness with an American Army officer. But she did.

"Anyway, that piece of property sounds like it falls into the high-priced category. Anything in the two quadrants to the river side of Washington Avenue is bound to be expensive."

"I sort of figured that. The sale price for the Courneys' place listed in the real estate records was not that high for the area, though. It came in over $100,000 under the tax assessment. The resale, however, more than made up for the difference."

"That's pretty strange, especially since that area underwent rehabilitation back in the 70s. Even then, I doubt he owned a house like that on a civil servant's salary. Not just one anyway. The taxes alone would be pretty stiff, and he couldn't have been more than a GS-14. Did he have any other income, that you know about?"

"Just one more in a growing list of questions."

I looked out the front window at two squirrels scampering up the oak tree in the Sullivan's front yard. His blue Corvette was blocking my Geo.

"Did you check out his wife?"

"She may already have lied to me about his employment. I doubt she'd tell me the truth about their household finances."

"I don't suppose there's any way you can get a look at their bank records."

"Not without her consent. Or that of the Naperville police. They've already collected bank statements and credit card records." I shook my head "I doubt the cops in Naperville will let me look at them without a very pressing reason. And probably not even then." I told Sullivan about my new run-ins with Frank Hardy.

"Are you going to let that stop you?"

"Well, I would like to keep my license for a little while longer. I'm not looking forward to joining the Army again."

"I'm not sure we'd take you again. We don't have the draft for an excuse, you know."

"Yeah, I remember reading something about that."

Hannelore carried in a huge platter heaped with mounds of sauerbraten and steaming potato dumplings.

"Sit down you two while I get the red cabbage. And Bill's lovely salad."

She forced a smile out and rolled her eyes. I returned the favor. Sully and I stood and stretched. I drained my beer and carried the empty out to the kitchen, then returned to the dining room.

Hannelore followed and handed me the bottle of Virginia chardonney I had brought for dinner. "Here's something more in your line of work."

"There was something else that happened today. I'm not sure it's related , but it sure gave me a funny feeling in the pit of my stomach."

Sullivan's eyes studied my hands as I worked the corkscrew. "How so?"

Hannelore took the chair facing her husband across the middle of the table, leaving the place of honor at the end for me. The cork popped free of the clear glass. I poured the wine, then sat down.

I told the Sullivans about the Vietnamese woman I had seen in Alexandria and followed to Arlington. "The funny thing is, Sully, she looked a lot like the woman from the other night, at the shooting." I paused. "She also reminded me of the one on the hilltop, back in 'Nam."

Sullivan slid into his chair. "Christ, Bill, let it go. It wasn't your fault. You've tortured yourself enough. You're not going to tie that to this case too, are you?"

"Shit, Sully, I don't know what all's going on here. It is weird how this should start coming back now, though. You know how I feel about coincidence."

Sully held his hand over his place setting and tilted it back and forth. "Bill, forget the shooting. The woman had no reason for being there." He glanced over at his wife. "Bill's unit was camped at one of the old rubber plantations and the NVA hit the perimeter. Some civilians got caught in a cross fire."

"That's not all, though." I told Sullivan about the calls and the fight in my back yard.

"You sure you don't recognize the voice?"

I shook my head. "No."

"Did you report the assault to the police?"

"I just let my friend, the detective Rick Jamieson, know about it."

"And you think it has something to do with your time in 'Nam?"

"Well, for one thing, they were Vietnamese. And the head honcho waved an old service revolver in my face."

"An old .45?"

I nodded.

"Ouch." Sully winced. "Sorry about that."

"What do the police think?"

I shook my head enough to ward off flies. "No way I'm running this part of it by them."

"You may have to, Bill."

"How so?"

"Think about it, man. Somebody back there could be setting you up. And the police are bound to find out sooner or later."

Sullivan raised the wine glass to his lips, and I glanced at Hannelore. Her own eyes were on mine, her pupils as piercing as blue ice. She reached for her wine, and her husband's glass floated back to the table. I tasted some myself.

After she drank her wine, Hannelore's gaze shifted to her husband. "If you think that, John, then you must help him."

Sullivan glanced at his wife and winked. The he turned to me. "What are your plans for tomorrow?"

"I'm going to see if I can shake something loose at the passport office."

"Good. I'll see what I can find at work. I can run Courney's name by some people at J2 and see if they know where I might be able to look further."

I sipped the fine Virginia chardonnay, studying my old friend over a rim of long-stemmed crystal. Maybe he was right. Maybe I was being set up. Or maybe I was just getting jerked around. Whatever the case, I wasn't about to get trapped in those steaming fetid jungles again. I'd make damn sure of that.

"And pay more attention the next time that asshole calls, " Sully warned. "You never know what may be sneaking up on you. That, at least, was one thing you were good at over there."

# Chapter 11

I remembered Washington's rush-hour traffic as some of the worst in the country. I did not want to get stuck in the flow of steaming metal that pours into the various agencies and offices in Washington from the Maryland and Virginia suburbs. So the next morning I lingered over breakfast after John and Hannelore had left for work.

By ten-thirty, the city had already begun to bake under the pressure of the summer sun and its heavy air. A steady stream of cars still crawled into our nation's capital, a giant colored snake of frustrated ambition curling its way over the Memorial and Teddy Roosevelt Bridges. But at least they were moving.

I maneuvered the Geo through the throngs lining K Street and pulled into a parking spot in front of a castle of stone and glass labeled the Franklin Towers in bright, golden letters. It stood just off of 14th Street. Back around the corner, the passport office was hidden in a warren of coffee shops, convenience stores, and airline offices. I had been here before, several times. My last trip had been with Sullivan, who had needed to renew his tourist passport to accompany Hannelore on her annual pilgrimage to visit her family in the Nahe region of western Germany. That was a decade ago. I wasn't sure how the place operated anymore, but I knew the information was not open for public viewing. Still, I figured my chances of obtaining the information I needed were much better here than at the State Department offices in Foggy Bottom. I'd be lucky to get through the door down there.

I sauntered past the camera booths advertising special one-hour offers in loud, obnoxious posters and grabbed a cup of coffee from a sidewalk vendor to keep me company. I knew the lines would be long and the progress slow.

A series of glass-paneled doors on the second floor opened to reveal an office the size of a small restaurant. The atmosphere was one of air-conditioned comfort, and the shades were drawn. The room had the faint smell of a gift shop and an archive. The minute hand was pushing two on the clock over the door, and the little one rested on the eleven. I had six hours to lose before my flight back to Chicago. About twenty customers milled in four different lines. I sipped the coffee, hoping the delay wouldn't be too long.

After about an hour I approached the counter and was met by a tall, thin black clerk. He was conservatively dressed in tan slacks, a white dress shirt, and blue and red striped tie. The shirt sleeves were rolled just past his wrists. He looked right through me with gold-rimmed glasses and a gaze of long-standing indifference.

"Can I help you?"

"Yes. I'm looking for records pertaining to the late Mr. Stephen Courney of Naperville, Illinois. He probably has a passport dating from his residency in Alexandria, Virginia, however."

"Did you say 'late'?" He stepped back from the counter, his eyes widening.

"Yes, but it wasn't contagious. Bullet wounds never are." I peered at him from underneath my own narrow eyelids, then leaned to my right and tossed the empty Styrofoam cup in a waste basket by the door. "Unless, of course, you're standing too close."

"Nice shot. But on whose authority are you asking for these records?"

I repeated the routine from the Alexandria city hall.

"I'm sorry, sir. Those records are not for the public. I'll need something in writing, preferably from a judge."

He shrugged, and his tired eyes rolled with a false sympathy. He lifted his left arm to rub his eyes, and that's when I noticed it. A tattoo of crossed sabers with the inscription, 'The Real Cav.' His age looked about right, so I decided to follow a hunch.

"Rough night?"

The customer behind me strolled to the next line. The clerk's eyes followed him, then took in the other customers, wandered over to his three colleagues busy at the counter, and finally returned to me. I read a story of bored days in weary brown pupils.

"No shit, man." His voice carried a weight equal to that of his eyes.

"Was it worth it?"

"Not right now, it wasn't."

"Long days, too, I'll bet. And slow."

He shrugged. "It's a job. And one I want to keep. Is there anything else?"

He glanced over my shoulder to see if anyone else was waiting in line behind me.

"Things were a lot different once," I added. "And more dangerous too."

Light burst somewhere at the back of his eyes. They locked on my face like a clamp.

I pressed ahead. "You a vet?"

"Yeah. What of it?"

"'Nam?"

"So?"

I smiled and raised a fist to shoulder's height.

"You too?" His eyes narrowed with a hint of suspicion. But a faint smile escaped.

I nodded.

He hesitated, then re-approached the counter. "Where?"

"Northwest of Saigon. 25th Infantry." I extended my hand. "Bill Habermann. And you?"

"The Central Highlands. First Air Cav." We shook. "Joshua O'Shea. And no, I ain't Irish." He stared at the window looking out over K Street for a moment. "Been to the Memorial yet?"

"Nope. One of these days, though. The deceased was in 'Nam too."

"Well, shit, man! Why didn't you say so? How'd the guy buy it?"

"Gunshot to the head."

"Man, that will ruin your whole day. Why'd it happen?"

"Don't know. That's what I'm tryin' to find out."

He leaned forward, and his voice dropped to a rough whisper. "So, how's this gonna help?"

"I need to find out more about his background. What he did here in town. How he lived." I raised my eyebrows. "And where all he lived."

"What's so hard about that?"

"I keep runnin' into a fuckin' wall."

"Can't you get the authorization?"

I shook my head and rammed my fist against the countertop. "Takes too damn long. I don't want to let this one slip away."

He straightened himself and let his eyes roam the room again. There were only two lines of customers now. Two of his colleagues from the front had joined about half-a-dozen others at their desks. The index finger of his right hand shot up, while his left hand beat a drumroll on the counter.

"I'm off for lunch at noon, man. Meet me in the park across the street, behind the bronze dude on a horse."

"Sure. Whose statue is it?"

"Fuck if I know. Some dead dick."

"At twelve sharp?"

"Yeah. I'll see if I can find anything. What was the guy's name?"

"Stephen Courney. I'd place the year of birth around 1950." I wrote the name out on the back of one of my cards.

"Let me see what I can find." He studied the writing. "We're gettin' ready to move to our new offices. It might give me an excuse to poke around."

"Whatever." I tossed an off-hand salute in his general direction.

My former comrade-in-arms marched to his desk, where he dropped into a chair. After about 30 seconds of paper-shuffling, he began to punch his keyboard and squint at his screen. I glanced at the clock, then swung myself through the double doors and into the hallway. 11:30. If I had survived Vietnam, I guessed I could take another July afternoon in Washington.

Outside, waves of cotton and silk in charcoal grays and navy blues ebbed up and down K Street. Patches of bright pastel and baggy madras broke the dull monotony of somber, bureaucratic color. Washington would not be our capital city without the mixture of tourists and civil servants in summer. Before long, most of the bureaucrats would be stripped to their shirtsleeves. The heat could be a great equalizer.

I strolled in front of shop windows to take advantage of the shade under their awnings and inside their doorways. One was a camera store, and I priced the new Olympias and Leicas. Maybe it was time for a Pentax, or some Japanese model. Another window opened onto a men's clothing store. The stuff on display looked very serious and very stiff. None of the attendants seemed to notice me. The prices were too high for my taste anyway. And the heat crept into any available space along the sidewalk, sunny or not.

At five minutes to the hour I wandered to the park, where I claimed a spot on the corner of a bench resting in the shadow of General McPherson. From there, I possessed a clear line of sight to the passport office. One of Washington's many homeless eyed me through shifting pupils, one arm clinging to belongings crammed into half a dozen paper bags and piled in a rusting shopping cart. Several blankets lay rolled in a bundle on his lap. I tried to avoid eye contact.

Within ten minutes, my fellow vet scrambled out the door, then disappeared into a Subway shop. He emerged after about ten minutes, holding a sandwich with the paper rolled back uncovering the upper third. Lettuce, ham and tomato peeked over the edge of a long bread roll. He was also walking back toward his office.

When the light at the corner changed, however, he shifted course and trotted across the street toward my bench.

"That was swift."

"No sweat, man. I did forward artillery in 'Nam." He slid onto the bench next to me.

"Congrats' again, brother. What did you find?"

"Here you go." He pulled a folded sheet of white paper from his shirt pocket, then dropped it in my lap. His face beamed with pride as he bit into his sandwich. "Always happy to be of assistance. Even if you weren't a blood."

"I appreciate it all the more."

I bent low over the bench and opened the note.

Steve Courney had received several passports, the most recent ones in 1985 and 1990. And they had been diplomatic passports, not tourist ones. That meant that Steve had been abroad on government business. So far, his sister-in-law's story was checking out.

"How well did you know this dude?"

I glanced up. The homeless guy had gone back to sleep. Or, at least he pretended to sleep.

"Not well at all. I was tailing him for his wife."

His eyes grew wide, then narrowed. "And you couldn't keep him alive? Shit, man," he laughed. "You must have been a better soldier than you are a dick."

"That wasn't my job. I'm not an escort service." The piece of paper felt like lead in my hands.

"And a good thing, too. But at least you survived 'Nam." He laughed again. "I ain't so sure you're gonna survive this one. Here's somethin' else for you."

He held another slip of folded paper in front of my face while he took another bite of his sandwich. About half had disappeared

"It looks like they're related."

I took the page. "Husband and wife," I replied.

Lisa Courney had also acquired a passport. Two of them, in fact. The first had been an official passport, issued in 1980. The second was also a diplomatic version, issued in 1985 and renewed in 1990.

"Did the records list place of employment?"

"You bet. The Pentagon, dude. Good 'ol D of D."

Great. I'd have to let Sully know. "For both?"

"Uh huh. Good luck, brother. And don't let the ghosts get to you."

When I looked up, Joshua O'Shea was already halfway to the street. It was no mystery that this man had survived his tour in the jungles of Vietnam as a forward artillery observer. He moved with a stealth and grace that bordered on instinct, like an animal evading beasts of prey, a man rid of his own phantoms.

The sun continued to blaze its path through the busy crowd of tourists, civil servants, and lobbyists, all of them oblivious to the other. The jackets were already evaporating in the early afternoon haze. I searched the faces, but my mind wandered to images of Steve and Lisa Courney walking these streets, or ones like them in foreign capitals. And what had they been doing that was so important that they had to lie about it, and keep it hidden?

Before I went to the airport, I decided to swing by the Alexandria DMV and fill out a request for some information on Sean Cavanaugh. Washington bubbled with consultants and lobbyists, but I didn't think there were many solo flyers around. The competition could be pretty stiff. And from the sale price of the house, he must have wanted one hell of a tax write-off. I hadn't been able to get at the Courney's credit records to see what kind of financing they had available, but the absence of a mortgage company on the title to the property pointed to cash or a gift. And that did not add up.

Then I got to thinking about my comrade's Subway sandwich. It had looked pretty damn appetizing, and my stomach reminded me that I needed some lunch, too. I trotted to the car, then swung the Geo back in the direction of Arlington, Virginia. I drove south, through the upscale neighborhood of Foxhall, where comfortable-looking two-stories sat in the middle of well-groomed half-acre lots, all of them probably starting at three-quarters of a million. The route brought me to Key bridge just north of Georgetown. I followed the flow of traffic back across the Potomac and up along Wilson Boulevard.

The lunch crowd at the Dam Ninh was a busy one, and I had to wait twenty minutes for one of the small formica-topped tables against the wall. I figured the food had to be pretty tasty, since the décor couldn't have drawn in much of a crowd. The tile floor was bare but clean, and the walls had only faded posters of Caribbean resorts hanging as decoration. When I saw the menu I realized that the prices certainly helped; they were easily as low as anything I was going to find in this town.

The same was true of the food. I mean, it was really good. I worked my way through an orange chicken dish with noodles and a German beer, a Warsteiner. Not your usual mix, but if the best is available I say go for it.

## ANGEL IN BLACK

Unfortunately, what did not appear to be available was the young, dark-haired lady I had followed home from Alexandria. My waiter, a husky young Vietnamese in his mid-twenties, brushed off my inquiries, and the old woman from yesterday sat with her eyes staring straight ahead at the traffic outside from behind the counter at the back. It almost looked like she was afraid one of the customers would raid the cash register if she moved or showed any sign of life. And the register looked like some antique she had found at a department store fire sale. When I paid my bill I tried to peek into the kitchen behind her, but grandma just shooed me away. "You go," she said. "No trouble." I bought an O'Henry from the display case under the register and walked out, glancing back over my shoulder every third table or so.

Outside I wandered to the Geo, which was cooling in a garage about three blocks away. Then I pulled the little teal thing back onto Wilson Boulevard but couldn't find a parking spot with a clear view of the restaurant. I circled the block until I located a spot just off Wilson and around the corner. I had a couple hours yet, and I wanted to see if the young woman showed. I figured I could always mail in my request on Sean Cavanaugh to the local DMV.

My luck held. Around two-thirty, the old woman, the girl, and one of the waiters spilled out the back door and climbed into a silver Cadillac in the lot at the back of the restaurant. At least that boat would be easy to follow, even at a safe distance. The girl wore black slacks and a matching black shirt that buttoned down the front. The similarity to the Vietnamese peasant woman many nights ago on a hilltop in Southeast Asia was striking, and eery. The hollow feeling somewhere in my midsection returned. I listened for the sound of gunfire but heard only the muffled roar of an oversized engine as the Caddy pulled into the street.

The trio drove west until they reached Glebe Road, then followed that north through another picturesque neighborhood much like the one surrounding the Sullivans' home. Compared to Foxhall, these places sat on lots about half the size, and I figured you could knock about $200,000 off the starter price. The caddy pulled into a parking lot behind a Catholic church that looked like it had been transported across the Atlantic from an English country village at the time of the Tudor monarchy. It sat across the street from Maymount College, a small liberal arts school for women. I kept going, driving past the church and down a side street lined with oaks and maples that looked like it had been cut from a faculty brochure. I turned around in what was probably some professor's driveway—a Volvo station wagon was parked in front of the garage—then retraced my path back to the church until I found a spot in the shade, about a block from Our Lady of Victory.

The two women had disappeared, but little brother was still hanging out by the car. He stared in my direction, puffing his way through two cigarettes in quick succession, then he paced back and forth along the length of the car. After about a minute of this, his steps brought him across the street and in my direction. He stopped at my window.

"Why are you following us?" His voice was high pitched and sounded very angry. "You think you going to fuck my sister? Huh? No way. No way, mister."

His fist pounded the roof of the Geo twice to punctuate the last two sentences.

"Hey, watch it, asshole. It's a rental."

"So? What you want? You a fucking agent or something? You from the government? The CIA?" Bam, bam on the hood.

"Buddy, I don't know what you're talking about. And lay off the damn car."

"You leave us alone. We've done enough for this country. We belong here now. We came here fair and square."

"Glad to hear it. Now piss off."

This time his fist ricocheted off the window. Then his foot beat the door. That was enough. I threw open the door, pushing him back toward the sidewalk.

"I told you to leave the fucking car alone. What's it gonna take, asswipe?"

In spite of his tirade, I actually liked the kid. I had to give him this much; he was willing to take on a total stranger to defend his family at the slightest hint of danger, inconvenience even. He stood his ground at the edge of the grass, his hand open and pressed against my chest. Sweat had broken out along his brow, and his white shirt clung to his underarms.

"No, you leave us alone. My sister is not for you. We did what we had to do. My family helped your government. You go ask the CIA or the Army. And what did you do for us, huh?"

"What the hell are you talking about? I don't even know you."

"You're not so funny, mister. Now leave us alone. Don't come back to our restaurant."

"Hey, I haven't done anything wrong. Just what the hell is your problem?"

"Yeah, yeah. I know you."

Then his eyes shot to the side, where the old woman and his sister stood on the sidewalk next to the church parking lot. The girl had her arm in that of the old lady's. Her eyes peered across the blacktop and looked open and curious, almost friendly. She nodded at her brother. The muscles of his face relaxed, and he slipped a card from the restaurant into my shirt pocket.

"Here. Take this and go. Maybe you learn finally."

Grandma was something else. Her eyes showed only a bitter hatred, deep and dark like the barrel of a gun. I decided to visit Alexandria's DMV office before going to the airport after all.

On the way I pulled out the card the brother had given me. As I thought, it was a business card from the restaurant. On the back was a telephone number. And there were two things about that vague note that struck me as odd. First, the handwriting looked remarkably similar to that on the note I had received just before I left Naperville. Even more surprising was the telephone number. There was no area code, so I couldn't be sure. But the telephone number listed on the card was the same as Steve Courney's cell phone.

# Chapter 12

My flight home arived at O'Hare around six-thirty. All that running around in Washington made me hungry, so I stopped at a Pizza Hut on the way home from O'Hare. Afterwards, I retrieved the developed roll of film and called on the sister-in-law to set some things straight. If Sully was right and someone was setting me up, I wanted to make sure they didn't have an in with the family.

Deborah Krueger's house sat in a new development near the Burlington train tracks and hard up against the old Saints Peter and Paul cemetery, just off Columbia Avenue. Not surprisingly, the neighborhood bore the name of Columbia Estates. By the time I reached it, the sun sat low on the horizon, and a broad ban of orange fused the ends of the earth and sky together in a soft glow. Her house sat deep in the shadow cast by the onset of evening, about twenty yards back from the sidewalk. The streetlight popped on while I drove around the block, and a shaft of bright yellow cut the bricks in the two-story Dutch colonial with a ragged, diagonal slice.

It was not the house-or the neighborhood-I had associated with Deborah Krueger. It was so damn suburban. I had expected a high-rise, with doormen to carry shopping parcels and walk the poodles. The sidewalk and cement pathway to the front door divided the lawn into even squares, and the grass shone from a recent watering. It was clipped and manicured. A spray of rhododendrons lined the front of the house; a patch of spruce and birch trees gathered by the corner of the garage. Dogwoods screened the far side of the house from the neighbors.

The Volvo sat at the curb while I strolled to the front door. I wondered if Deborah had watered her lawn earlier in the day. Perhaps when she had come home from work, hose in one hand while the other angled against sharp hips in blue jean cutoffs. Somehow, I didn't see it. I swallowed hard.

The driveway was bare. As I passed the garage door, I noticed the red BMW parked inside. A light shone from a back room, probably the kitchen. Another one marked a room upstairs. I guessed she was home, and I hoped she was alone.

The doorbell punched the silence with a loud double-toned jab, first high, then low. Nobody answered. I glanced back at the Volvo, ran my fingers through my hair, and rang it again. Footsteps echoed inside.

"Who is it?"

"It's Bill Habermann. I just got back from Washington, and I was hoping we could have a word." I waited about five seconds. "That is, if it isn't too late." My watch said eight-forty five. "And if you're free."

A deadbolt tumbled, followed by a sliding chain. The door opened to reveal Deborah Krueger in a blue and white striped terry cloth bathrobe. She stood there barefoot with her hair fluffed, as though a blow direr had just worked it over.

"Well, I just got out of the shower. But I am glad you stopped by."

She stepped back with a confident smile, head cocked in the direction of her interior, holding the door while I entered. Only then did I notice the cocktail glass in her hand. About half an inch of something yellowish drifted around tiny ice cubes. I walked inside. The image of her standing in the shower lingered. I tried to concentrate.

"I'm sorry. If this is a bad time, I can always get in touch tomorrow."

She ambled towards the living room to my left. "No, no. Please come in. I'm sure it's important."

"Actually, it is."

"Can I get you a drink?" She hefted her glass and glanced over her shoulder as she walked. "I'm almost ready for another."

"Okay."

"So, what's your pleasure?"

"Make it whatever you're having."

I passed a stairway leading to the second floor that lay under a runner with a blue and red oriental design, about eighteen inches wide. The rug was held in place by a brass rod tucked into the back of each stair. At the foot of the stairs twin coat racks of oak stained in light brown contained a mirror and umbrella stand. The runner extended to the door, and the floor underneath glistened with varnished hardwood.

The wallpaper in the living room was a mirage of green and blue stripes against a deep yellow background that ran to the floor, where it met a plush wall-to-wall carpet of light brown. The sofa, love seat, and four armchairs displayed a mixture of solids and patterns that managed to pick up every color in the walls. Another mirror hung on the far wall, reflecting back against the one in the foyer. This one was also surrounded by a an array of ancient-looking prints from somewhere in the Middle East. They looked like Dave Roberts sketches. I wondered if they were originals. A collection of Meissen plates and figures stood scattered throughout the room.

"Not bad," I conceded. "A cut above my place."

"Thank you. I hope you like single-malt." Deborah passed me a glass half full of a golden liquid resting on ice. When she handed over the drink her eyes rose to mine. I found dark rims, like circles of fear or anxiety. Still, a warmth seemed to linger just beyond their edge, and the Scotch drifted with invitations behind clear-cut lines of Waterford crystal. I couldn't tell how much was simply my imagination. She turned and dropped into one side of the love seat.

"Is something wrong?"

She tried to smile. "That's okay." She gave up. "Well, actually, I don't know."

Her gaze drifted while her left hand chased some disobedient hair away from her forehead. Then rich, blue eyes settled on mine.

"So, how was Washington? Did you find anything?"

"Yes and no."

"Sounds mysterious."

"There are problems, both here and there. And the ones in Washington highlight the ones back here."

She sipped her drink and crossed her legs. My eyes could not avoid the knee and flash of thigh that snuck through. "It's late. You'll have to be a little more clear."

I picked up my drink. The water from the ice drifted slowly upwards, like a river of dreams. I took a quick sip to check on the quality. Very good. At least ten years old, and definitely single malt. The heat of the drink gave me a burst of courage as it settled in my stomach.

"First of all, there are still a lot of holes in your brother-in-law's past."

"What do you mean?"

"I mean, gaps in his professional history, like what he did for a living, where he spent the last ten years of his life, where his salary came from and how large it was."

"I don't understand. Didn't Lisa tell you everything?"

"Apparently not." I took another sip of Scotch, smaller this time. "And I'm beginning to wonder about her role in all this."

Deborah leaned back, her eyes shifting to the mirror on the wall and then back to me again. "Just what did you find?"

"Well, I found that your sister and her husband lived in a very nice, almost exclusive neighborhood in Alexandria. That in itself isn't necessarily suspicious.

But I haven't been able to find any kind of records of what it is he did at the Pentagon and when he worked there."

"That's why Lisa worked. So they could afford to live there. Did you find anything about their time overseas?"

"What did she do?"

"Something for the Pentagon as well. I believe Steve got her the job."

"But you don't know exactly?"

"No. I told you, I never paid much attention to that sort of thing."

My finger rose. "You see, that's one of the problems on this case. Normally, that sort of information is readily available. Place of employment and job titles are listed on most records, like those at the DMV. It's standard procedure on most cases simply to request that sort of thing."

"And you have access to those?"

I nodded. "Just about anyone does. But in Steve's case, I'm finding it difficult to get much beyond some vague reference to the Department of Defense and a work number that now goes nowhere. And when you consider that Steve and Lisa apparently spent a lot of time out of the country on official business, it's unlikely that I will find any records."

"Why is that?"

"Because it probably means they were involved in intelligence work. Which is something he worked back in Vietnam after his infantry tour."

"And you think it's connected to his death?"

"I'm not sure yet. But there are more and more signs pointing in that direction." I blew out some breath and rolled my eyes. "And then there's that damn house. There's no mortgage listing. Was it a gift or something?"

"Bill, I really don't know. My sister and I did not discuss her family's accounting."

I pressed my glass down on the coaster. A spoonful splashed over the rim. "Well, I think it could be important." I mopped at the small puddle with my handkerchief. "I'm sorry."

She waved at the liquid with disinterest. "How can you tell?"

"Because anytime you have unexplained income, it points to something that could tie into the killing." I leaned back against the sofa cushions and avoided her eyes. "You see, that's the problem here. There's too damn many 'could be's' and 'maybe so's.' Until I get some solid information, there won't be any 'can't be's.' And I'll just keep swimming in circles."

"Do you think people have been lying to you? Or hiding something?"

She sat forward, her legs uncrossing themselves. Both feet came down hard on the floor. Her arms went rigid, the palms glued to the edge of her knees.

I did not go into her afternoon foray into Chicago. "Some people are not being as open or as honest as they need to be with me. I can't work against some unknown killer and the victim's family. And that includes you."

"Just what is it you need to know?" She remained unmoving, her eyes twin azure flames.

I leaned forward. "I'd like to know why your sister hired me. Her husband was not fooling around, and I think she knew that. I think there's something more serious at work here. She once expressed concerns for his safety, but never followed that with any specifics. And I'd like to know just what your concerns are, why you're not willing to leave this to the police."

Deborah Krueger relaxed a bit, her eyes darting toward the mirror again. They were dimmer now, their blue clouded with a touch of night. She drained the Scotch, then sat back in her chair, the glass resting in her lap. "Lisa told me she had hired someone to follow Steve. That's all. She said Steve had mentioned your name once, that he thought it was funny how you two showed up in the same town after Vietnam and all."

I stood up, then emptied my glass of its Scotch, well watered by the ice. "Yeah, I laugh about it every night."

"Are you sure he was not philandering?"

"Steve was not engaged in some pick-up action last Saturday night, or any other night I was with him. He wasn't killed by some irate husband or lover. He was set up. For one thing, it went too smoothly. And for another, I would not have gotten the crap kicked out of me if that was the case."

Deborah Krueger's eyes grew wide and white. "You were attacked?" She started to stand. "When? Where?"

I waved her concern away. "I'm fine. Just pissed. A waitress was also beaten."

"Why?"

"Someone was afraid she might have seen something."

Her body crumbled as she bent back, her eyes sweeping to the picture window behind me. "Did she see who shot Steve? Was it that woman?"

"That particular woman seems to have vanished." I thought of Washington. "Pretty much, anyway."

"What about the police? Have they found anything?"

I looked toward the window. The sky had changed to a dirty gray. It would soon disappear completely under a shroud of black. I turned back to Deborah. "Not all killers are found. In fact, I think less than half are. And with each passing day the chances of finding the killer shrink further." I shook my head. "There's nothing wrong with the Naperville police. They just don't have much to go on. It's almost as though it was a professional hit."

Her eyes found their brightness again. "What do you mean?"

"It was too clean, for one thing. No solid leads that I've heard of. No prints, no reliable witnesses. Nada. That's one of the things that leads me away from the crime of passion angle."

She fell back into the seat. The legs re-crossed themselves, and her eyes glanced around the room. "So, you think it's tied in some way to Steve's background. To his work, or his time in Vietnam?"

"Yes, I do."

"Do you think Lisa's safe?"

"I'm not so sure. It all depends on how much she knows, and whether the people who killed Steve see her as a threat."

Deborah Krueger's hand pushed at her hair, while her eyes explored the floor. "I think you're right about they're having worked in intelligence. Lisa always refused to tell me anything about their work overseas. She said it was classified, whatever that's supposed to mean."

I studied Deborah Krueger's face, something I found myself doing more frequently each time we met. The shadows I had seen in her eyes back in her office returned, a momentary passing of some painful memory.

"I need your help on this one, Deborah. Don't shut me out."

Her head rose. The light returned to her eyes as she studied my face.

"I'm pretty sure Lisa was frightened about something. That's really why she hired you."

"What was I supposed to do?"

"I think just sort of watch over Steve. Make sure nothing happened."

"How was I supposed to do that if I didn't know what to look for?"

She shook her head. "I...I don't know. You'll have to ask her."

"Goddammit, Deborah. It makes no sense."

I rolled the empty glass in my hand. Deborah blew out her breath like she had been holding it in since childhood. She held up her own crystal to examine it.

"Can I get you another?"

"No thanks. I'll just help myself to a glass of water."

I walked into the kitchen, lit only by a small lamp on a breakfast table. I poured myself a half-glass of water from the tap resting over double metal sinks. The refrigerator hummed at my back. It must have masked the sound of Deborah Krueger as she entered behind me.

When I turned, she was nearly upon me. She moved steadily, quietly, gliding like a lost swan until she was close enough to slide her arms around my waist. Her head fell to my chest. Her breasts felt firm against me. Her hips exuded warmth, an unspoken invitation. Her fingers dug into the muscles of my back.

"Help us, Bill." I could smell the fresh scent of lavender from her shampoo. "I am so frightened. I can't wait for the police. I need you to find the killer now." Her chest heaved like she had stifled a sob.

"What are you frightened of, Deborah?"

She burrowed her face deeper into my chest.

"If you won't tell me, I can't help you."

Her face rose, the lips probing my neck. When her eyes met mine, they had lost their hardness. Tears shone over the dull glow of fading sapphires.

"I'm afraid it won't stop with Steve. I'm afraid there's more death out there."

I rocked back on my heels to pull her hips away from my crotch. This was not what either of us needed. I had to think this thing through with my brain.

"When and where, Deborah? Do you know why Steve was killed?"

"I only know that someone is trying to frighten me."

"What's happened?"

She sucked in her breath. "There have been calls. On the telephone. Two of them."

"What did the caller want?"

"To meet me. In the city."

"And?"

"And no one showed."

"How did the voice sound?" I grabbed her shoulders and searched her eyes. The person behind them was slipping away. "Did you recognize the caller? Did he say anything else?"

"Only that your time was coming, too."

"Do you know what he meant by that?"

She shook her head. The back of her left hand wiped at the tears along the lower rim of her eyes.

"Do you have any idea who it might be?"

She stood silent for several seconds before she spoke, her voice a faint whisper. "You have to find him, Bill. Please find him."

Her arms circled my neck and she collapsed against me. The sobs came slowly, building until they shook her entire body. I patted her shoulders and pressed her face into my chest.

I carried Deborah upstairs and laid her on a queen-sized bed in what looked like the master bedroom. Her arms refused to let go. I pulled them apart. Her robe fell open, revealing full breasts still glistening after her shower. I sighed like a man lost in a forest, closed the robe and covered her with a quilt of overlapping green, black, and red squares. Her body curled, then burrowed into the mattress.

"Stay with me. I don't want to be alone."

A single hand crept from underneath the covers and found mine. The light from the streetlamp invaded the room, pestering the air with a sharp, brittle quality. We sat on the bed for what seemed like hours, until her breathing became slow and regular, and I was sure she had fallen asleep. I crossed the room to close the drapes. After that I returned to the edge of the bed and bent low, stroking her rich brown hair. She looked vulnerable and innocent, a different woman than the one I had encountered during the day, out doing battle with the world. I wondered which of the two sisters was the stronger one, and what their lives had been like together.

Then, I stood up, turned out all the lights in the house, locked the door behind me, and walked to my car.

---

Moonlight shimmered across the blacktop on Benton Avenue. The streetlight on our corner was out again. The red and brown bricks of Saints Peter and Paul retreated behind a surge of shadows set by a full moon. The conical spire of the steeple rose like a lighthouse in the darkness. Stillness seeped across the grounds of North Central College, the summer students all gone or fading into the hallowed halls of small-town academia.

I walked through the door of my apartment, a fresh six-pack of Special Export cradled in the nook of my arm. I didn't bother to flip on the light switch, however. I lived here. I knew my way around.

I set my packages on the table, then shuffled through the kitchen and into the living room. My foot kicked a chair standing between the table and the doorway. I didn't remember leaving it there, but I was not the world's greatest housekeeper, either. I swept my arms in front of me, and my feet probed for more obstacles. I shuffled to the wall next to the kitchen and reached for the light switch.

A shaft of light burst through the living room. My desk loomed off in the corner, a mound of brown wood resting in black shadows. Everything else appeared to be as I had left it. I ambled over, threw up the roll-top cover, then searched the desktop and drawers. Nothing was missing. The telephone, too, had stayed where it belonged. I wrote the suspicions off to anxiety. I wondered if my imagination was starting to get the better of me. My fingers found the telephone, and I punched in Lisa Courney's number. I dropped into my chair.

There was no answer. After half-a-dozen rings, her husband's voice came on the line.

"Hi, we're not at home right now. But if you'd like to leave your name and number, we'll get back to you as soon as we can. And please, don't hang up. Your call is important to us."

Not anymore, Steve, I thought. At least not to you. Lisa was definitely going to have to change that message. I wondered what else from her recent past she had left hanging around her psychic neck. I pronounced my name and business number carefully, then hung up.

And there was Deborah. Hers was the voice I wanted to hear again. I also wanted to see her again, terry cloth robe or not. If she wanted to pile her hair in curlers that would be alright, too. I asked myself if I should have stayed the night to watch over her, to protect her from the dangers she also faced. Convenient rationalization? Perhaps.

When I checked my answering machine, there were two messages. The first was from Ahmed telling me he'd be late with his rent. No sweat. I figured I'd take it out in sandwiches and brownies. The second came from Deborah Krueger.

"Hello," her voice cooed. "Please call me as soon as you get home. I really want to hear what you may have found in Washington."

I replayed the message, searching for a note of desperation, fear even, in that voice. There was no way to be sure. It sounded like a tone of interest, with a hint of seduction. Then again, maybe she was still putting on the brave front: the independent woman, the valiant entrepreneur, sure of herself and of her world. It was the image she had conveyed when I first arrived at her house this evening, but one that had fallen away as night arrived.

I tossed the receiver back in its cradle. The sisters continued to intrigue me. I felt certain there was much more to both than they wanted to reveal to the world. But I wondered how much I would ever learn, and how much I really had to know. And which one had the answers I really needed?

I peeled myself from the chair, slipped into the kitchen, and pulled a beer from the paper bag. The lukewarm liquid stung my throat, but it still felt better than the pounding in my toe.

I searched through my briefcase and found the photographs I had picked up on my way home from the airport. My touch of pity for the pimply sixteen-year-old trapped behind the booth on a summer night had evaporated when I paid the rip-off price for the pictures. I had cursed in silence and let him go back to sleep.

With my rear going stiff, I strolled to the window for a stretch. Sucking on the warm green glass of the Special Export, I held the pictures against the light reflected from the street lamp next to the church. Outside, a Pontiac Grand Am the color of moonlight cruised from the curb like a lost lunar moth.

The three pictures from the parking lot at the Skylark Inn were lousy. I would never make a combat photographer. The shutter speed had not been set for a moving picture, especially one with so little light. Blurs and streaks were the principal result, especially in two of the shots.

But the third was different, if only just a little. I trotted to the desk and pulled the desk lamp closer to throw more light across the picture. Squinting with an eye just inches from the paper, I could make out the letters and numbers of a license plate on the Chevy Corsica that had hurtled from the lot through a maze of gravel and dust.

With that last photograph tucked neatly in my shirt pocket, I drifted into the bedroom for a full night's sleep. I peeled down to my boxers, flipped on the air conditioning, jerked back the covers, and fell into bed. Just in case my late night visitor returned, I tugged open the drawer of the night table. My hand froze, then I practically threw my head inside the drawer. Someone had broken into my place, after all. And the son-of-a-bitch had taken my Browning.

# Chapter 13

The little people in their black pajamas kept coming closer. Two boys, thirteen, maybe fourteen years old, led the pack. About ten feet behind, a young woman struggled toward us, a baby on her right arm, its hands clinging to the back of her neck. She couldn't have been more than twenty, the baby less than a year. But I couldn't really tell through the dirt and noise and pain. Then more emerged from the tree line behind them. There were so many. It was too dark to count them all. So damn dark. Just a black mass, ebbing in the distance. Flares burst in the air, bathing the ground in a sickening brightness. Then the dark earth seemed to swallow everything. Mortar fire erupted. Dirt leaped toward the sky. A magazine slammed into Jamie Krug's M-16, and a nervous finger probed his trigger guard. I leaned forward. My shoulders and chest reached over the sand bags.

"Habermann! You stupid shit! Get the fuck down!"

A hand pawed at my bulletproof vest, grabbed the collar and pulled me back. Artillery fire broke out behind me. My ears were pounding, and my head throbbing. My whole damn body shook.

Then I heard slamming doors and rustling chairs echo in the distance. I opened my eyes and met the brilliance of a new morning. The familiar dark brown poster ends of my bed loomed like lonely wooden sentinels.

The noise came from somewhere in my own apartment. It sounded like the kitchen. It also sounded pretty dangerous.

I rolled over from the middle of my queen-size bed and groped in the top drawer of the night table for the Browning. My fingers came up empty. Then I remembered the theft.

My heart pounded against brittle ribs, and I struggled to breathe. Bright morning light snapped the stale air over my bed. The surge of adrenaline swung my legs to the floor. I made sure the bare feet halted just shy of the hardwood. I inched my upper torso off the mattress to prevent the springs from singing. It was an old mattress, and it yawned anyway. But at least it didn't scream, and the clown in my kitchen was making more than enough noise to drown out anything from the bedroom.

I searched for something to use as a weapon. My palms were moist with perspiration, and I rubbed them against my boxers. My eyes spotted the baseball bat in the corner of the closet. I had quit playing sixteen-inch softball a couple years ago, but the wooden bat was still a lot harder than the skull of the clown roaming around my kitchen.

I stalked the hallway outside the bedroom, creeping toward the back of the apartment with all the stealth of an out-of-shape infantryman.

"You planning to hit a home run this morning?"

I leaned against the light switch next to the kitchen entrance.

"I mean, with your batting skills, Habermann, that thing is hardly a threat."

"You got a search warrant, Jamieson?"

I set the bat in the corner by the door. Rick Jamieson was dressed like he had already been at work for hours. The paisley tie hung loose at the collar, and the sleeves of his yellow cotton shirt were rolled up at the elbows. He had probably left his jacket in the car. For as long as I had known him, Jamieson had hated to wear a sport coat or suit jacket. The July heat didn't help, either. The shirt clung to his side where the holster and service revolver hung.

"Don't need one. I got a key."

"One of these days I'll remember to take that back."

"Then I'll get a search warrant."

"Fuck you. Have you made coffee?"

"Couldn't find any. You are one shitty housekeeper, pardner."

I dropped into one of the captain's chairs at the side of the kitchen table. "There's instant over by the sink. Put some water on. I'll stop later at the grocery store." I resisted the urge to scratch my crotch. "What time is it, anyway?"

"Seven-thirty. And there's no need to. Not right now anyway." He held up two white Styrofoam cups, steam rising over their rims. "I got a couple cups of some gourmet brew from Ahmed when he opened up."

I shuffled over to the stove, where Rick had set my coffee next to one of the burners. "Do I have any milk?"

"Some," Jamieson said. "But it doesn't smell too good."

"Marriage has spoiled you, pardner."

I opened the refrigerator, pulled out the carton of two-percent milk and poured a spoonful into the rich, black pool. After stirring, small bits of white floated undissolved on the top of the coffee. I raised the deep brown liquid to my lips anyway.

"You're right. He does make a nice cup of coffee. Tastes a little sour, though."

"That's your milk. The coffee comes from Costa Rica, I believe. Or maybe Ethiopia. The milk is probably from Wisconsin. Looks like it's traveled some, though."

Jamieson moved over toward the kitchen table. He hesitated, chose not to sit down and leaned against the wall next to the door.

"How'd it go in our nation's fair capital?"

"All right. I found out something about our murder victim. It seems he lived overseas for a couple of years. Several times, in fact."

"What time did you say you got back?"

"I didn't. But it was around dinner time. Why?"

"Did you meet with anyone? Your client, maybe?"

"Yeah, maybe. Don't you care about what I found in Washington? Like the real estate information. Or the dead end at the Pentagon, which I suspect leads elsewhere."

"All in due time, Bill."

I sipped again. "Shit!"

"What's wrong?" Rick bounced his shoulders away from the wall.

"I just burned my tongue. I'm going to have to raise Ahmed's rent to pay for my medical expenses."

Jamieson leaned back again and raised his cup to his lips. "I wasn't aware he paid any."

"He doesn't always."

Rick's eyebrows arched over the rim of his cup. "What time did you get home last night?"

My own eyes shot toward Jamieson. "I'm not sure. Ten, maybe. Why all the interest in my night life?"

"Alone again?"

I blew on the coffee. "Yeah, unfortunately. But somebody came by before I got here."

"Too bad. Your earlier visitors again?"

I shrugged. "Perhaps. Wouldn't be a bad guess. Whoever it was, he wasn't about to wait."

"What was he looking for?"

I shrugged, thinking of the gun. "Can't really say. Nothing was missing from the desk. The papers were all in order."

Jamieson whistled. "First an assault, then an anonymous note, and now a forced entry. You've had some tough luck on this case."

"Kind of looks that way. Found anything back here yet?"

"The widow opened up a little."

I raised the Styrofoam. It felt a bit cooler now. "Congratulations. Sister Alcuin would be proud."

"Sister Alcuin hated my guts. She always liked you better because you played basketball." He smiled and drank some more of his coffee.

"She was a wise woman." I took a banana from the wicker basket in the middle of the table. It felt soft to the touch, but there were no black patches on the skin. "What else did Mrs. Courney tell you?"

Jamieson recounted her tale about Steve Courney's career at the Pentagon. He still worked on procurement. She had elaborated, however, on what he was supposed to have been procuring.

"Electronic components? What for?"

"Anti-missile systems."

"What kind?"

Jamieson shrugged. "How the fuck do I know? I was an infantry grunt. Just like you."

"For a while. Couldn't his wife tell you any more?"

He shrugged. "I'm not sure she's all there. The shock hasn't worn off entirely."

"I guess not. Especially since the office she told me her husband worked for never exited."

Jamieson just shook his head. "What else did you find in Washington?"

"I may not be sure what he did for a living, but he lived pretty well in Virginia." I told him about the tax records and the real estate.

"Yep, this guy is a real mystery." He drained the last of his coffee, then tossed his cup at the waste basket between the sink and the stove. The cup sailed away from the edge of the plastic container and floated to the floor. "Like some others around here."

"Well, I may have found something that will help us get a lead on the shooter. Or at least the mystery woman."

"What do you mean?"

I walked into the living room to retrieve the pictures from my desk. When I got back to the kitchen I pushed the photograph with the license plate number toward his outstretched hand.

"It seems that at least one of us is doing some detective work around here."

He held the picture up to the light to make out the number. "Not bad for an amateur."

"Leave the picture, okay? You can write the number down."

Jamieson shook his head. "Sorry." He tucked the photographs into his shirt pocket. "Where'd you get this?"

I studied my friend's face. "I guess I took the picture Saturday night."

His features hardened, and his lips looked like they had turned to metal.

"I must have forgotten to mention it. Sorry."

Jamieson peered at the license plate number. "Man, Hardy's going to screw you front and back on this one."

"What the hell for? This could help."

He held the picture at the corner, flipping it back and forth. "This is just one more strike."

"Just what the hell is going on, Rick?"

"You'd better get dressed, Bill." He motioned toward the bedroom with his head as he took a seat by the table. "There's something else I want to show you."

"What is it?"

"You'll find out soon enough."

"Dammit, Rick. Tell me what's wrong. Just what the hell has happened?"

He looked up. "We only agreed that you wouldn't keep secrets from me. Now people will realize that you have. Which isn't making any of this easier on you. Or me."

"What do you mean?"

"Just hurry up," Jamieson waved his hand at me. "You'll find out soon enough." His eyes studied the Styrofoam cup on the floor. "If you don't know already," I heard him whisper.

I hustled back to my bedroom, chewing the last bits of banana. That would have to do for breakfast. I threw on a pair of blue jeans and a short-sleeve madras sport shirt. I figured that would cover whatever Jamieson had in mind. Everybody was turning out to be a damn mystery on this case.

I rode with Jamieson in his Thunderbird west along Aurora Road. The route was getting to be very familiar. This time we drove all the way to Route 59, then turned right and headed north. We cruised past new developments of half-built houses, clean sheets of plywood wrapping their frames in a semi-protective coating. From a distance they looked like unfinished school projects. Here and there, you could still see patches of farmland, most of it under weeds and mounds of bulldozed dirt.

Jamieson crossed the bridge that ran over the Tollroad. Down to the right, in the direction of Chicago, the Amoco Research Center beckoned eager young engineers. I knew; I had done background investigations on some. To my left, open fields disappeared against the horizon in the direction of Aurora. I wondered for how long.

The Thunderbird pulled into the parking lot that stood between the road and a large, five-story building of white concrete and black glass, headquarters for Northern Illinois Gas. The managers of the utility had chosen an architectural style cut from the same cloth as Americo Technologies. In fact, it was the same blueprint used by most of the companies along this road: postmodern pseudo-elegance. Without a map you could get lost from the lack of distinguishing landmarks.

Several cruisers from the Naperville and Dupage County Police Departments sat in the front row of the parking lot, and I noticed a large, official-looking group in civilian clothes milling just outside the tape with a host of uniformed officers. Not all of them came from Naperville. The brown, broad-brimmed hats bobbing up and down on two of the men told me the state police had arrived. And two of the men in civvies were carrying nice-looking Leicas. I figured them for forensic technicians. Two cars belonging to the state police were parked along the edge of the Tollroad.

We aimed for the row of reserved parking spaces next to the police cars. The nose of the Thunderbird's grill nudged the yellow tape extending across the edge of the lawn. Our spot said number 36. The yellow numbers rested in the shade of a large maple. Probably someone important, I told myself, until I saw the bird shit littering the ground. It was only eight-thirty, but the temperature felt like it had already soared into the nineties.

"It feels like Florida around here."

"It's supposed to rain in the next few days," Rick said.

"Great. That will make it even more like Florida. Hot and humid."

He looked through me with cold eyes. "Follow me, Bill."

We ducked under the tape and marched to the edge of a pond set under a sweep of willows about one hundred yards from the highway. Most of the heads turned in our direction as we approached. Frank Hardy emerged from the crowd, marching toward us.

"Glad you could make it, boys." His voice dripped with a false cheerfulness that was becoming familiar. I was starting to resent it. Hardy's sleeves were rolled up to the elbows again, like Rick's. He probably wanted everyone to know that he had been hard at work.

"It must be a pretty special occasion for you guys to bring me inside the yellow line," I said, tilting my head back toward the tape marking the border of the crime scene.

Rick tugged at my sleeve, then pointed to a white sheet at the edge of the pond. I did not need to go any closer to see there was a body underneath.

"Why don't you take a look, Bill?" Hardy suggested.

"Sure. Is it okay if I go all alone?"

I strode through the full green grass. It was still wet from the morning sprinkling, and the water beaded along the tops of my sneakers.

When I got to the sheet, a row of uniformed officers parted like the Red Sea to make way for my entrance. I felt like I had just assumed center stage, and that they were expecting some deep and profound revelation. In a flash of irreverence, I was tempted to look up to the heavens and cry "Stella." Fortunately, though, I hesitated. The thought came to me that it might actually be someone I knew. Like Wanda Rathko. Or Deborah Krueger. The scent of stale water and algae hovered.

I gulped, then squatted next to the corpse and peeled back the plastic. The body was fully clothed but wet. There was another chunk of head missing, much like Steve Courney's. I did not recognize what was left. But it had the thin nose and long black hair I remembered from the night outside the Skylark Inn. It had been just six days, but it was beginning to feel like an eternity. Although pale and bloated, the face had some clear Oriental markings, mostly around the eyes. Hard, dark pupils stared skyward like pebbles of cordite. The face of the young Vietnamese woman in Virginia floated into my thoughts, along with that of a woman on a hilltop years ago. From what was left of her face, this woman looked remarkably like them. But I was pretty sure she was somebody else, another mystery to add to the others.

I shivered. My eyes refused to leave the corpse on the ground. She also wore a Saint Jude's medal, like the one I had seen on the irate brother back in Virginia. Finally, I glanced up and saw the brown concrete of the National Education

Training Group on the other side of the Tollroad. I wished I worked there right now. I had a lot to learn.

"Sorry. There's a good chance it's the woman from the Skylark, but I can't make her for certain."

"Why not?"

I glanced up into the sun and saw Hardy's barrel belly and sloping chest through squinting eyes. Jamieson stood in silence behind him, his head bowed, his eyes searching the grass. A weeping willow behind the men dampened the glow from the sun.

"She looks vaguely familiar. But it was dark, and I only caught a glimpse of the woman before she sped away."

"Not very good detective work, Bill."

"Still as good as your police work, Lieutenant."

Hardy balled his fists and glared. He stalked closer. "We'll see about that. The lab should be able to tell us later if anything here matches the hair or fibers we found on Courney."

Then he wheeled and marched over to a man I recognized as the county coroner in a tan blazer, navy blue slacks, and brown loafers, all of which struggled to complement the checkered shirt and striped tie. He was the only coroner I had known who could make a fashion statement like it came with the job. He also had a hairpiece. I wondered sometimes how he ever got elected.

Hardy returned holding a brown paper bag. It was too early for lunch.

I stood and smoothed the jeans around my knees. "So, who found the body and when?" I asked.

Jamieson stepped forward. "Apparently, it was the cleaning crew. They were leaving about four this morning, and one of them noticed the lower torso of this lady extending up out of the water at the rim of the pond."

"It was right in front of where you see her now, Habermann," Hardy added. I guess he wanted me to know that they had only moved the body as much as necessary, in case I ever had to handle this sort of thing again, and in case I doubted that he was in charge. I thought of Jamieson's earlier comments at my apartment, looked at the corpse, and realized I was stuck in some very deep shit.

"Hell of a way to finish a night's work." I wiped the sweat beading along my upper lip and forehead. The underarms of my madras shirt were stuck to my skin.

Hardy resumed his glaring through eyeballs of white steel. One of the state cops had joined him, his hands on the holster at his hips. His sunglasses prevented me from seeing if he was glaring, too.

"How long was the woman dead?"

"Coroner here believes about an hour." Jamieson had resumed his role as intermediary.

"And I take it you've had no luck identifying the body, or locating other witnesses."

"Not yet. We've already sent the prints off to the lab, with copies to the FBI and down to Springfield for our own Bureau." Very thorough, but that was Jamieson's style. Hardy's, too. And I hoped that would help me, eventually.

Hardy stepped forward again. The brown bag swung at his side. His head nodded toward the Thunderbird.

"Your friend drives a nice car. Yours is nice too. Old, but nice. How long you been drivin' it?"

"About five years now. Why?"

"I'm still tryin' to figure you out, Habermann. Your parents had a good patch of farmland."

"Nobody's farming it anymore, Hardy."

"So you can't be hurtin' for money. And I don't know how much you bring in with this line of work."

"Enough for gas. Repairs would be tough, though. That's why I drive a Volvo."

"And you've never finished any of the special schooling you tried. Never finished law school. Never wrote that dissertation on American history."

"So?" I knew where this asshole was heading.

His smile was as wide as his belly. I wanted to split them both. Jamieson bit his lip and refused to raise his eyes off the ground. I stared hard at the Lieutenant. A thin wisp of light brown hair fell across his forehead.

"So, it makes me wonder what kind of person you are. Just where you're goin' with your life. What you're up to and how you pay for your beer." He paused. "What time did you get back from Washington?"

"Between six and seven. Why?"

"What did you do when you got back?"

"I had dinner, then I called my client."

"Who is?"

"You already know who it is."

"Fuckin' right we do." A wicked smile pushed at the corners of his lips. "You're not having much luck with the ladies these days, are you, Habermann?"

A strange, elliptical smile shoved the corners of the state trooper's mouth almost to Lisle. The wide green ovals over his eyes did not move from my face. I tried to look over at Jamieson with a mixture of exasperation and disappointment. He shrugged. I turned back to Hardy. I refused to take the bait and make a comment about his wife. This thing was threatening to get ugly enough as it was.

"Just what the hell are you getting at, Frank?"

"You were around and available at three AM this morning. That gives us opportunity." Hardy turned toward Jamieson. "What kind of shape was he in when you got there this morning?"

My friend shrugged, his eyes moving from his boss to the ground again.

"I asked what the fuck his condition was when you saw him this morning."

"He had just gotten up. Other than that, nothing out of the ordinary."

"Could anyone vouch for his whereabouts last night? I doubt he had a broad up there. What about Ahmed, or the neighbors?"

"Ahmed's deli isn't open at three in the morning, Hardy."

Hardy's eyes shot in my direction. "Shut the fuck up. No one is talking to you right now."

Jamieson shook his head. "None of the neighbors heard anything either way. I did get a lecture and a nice cinnamon role from one, though."

Hardy stared hard at his deputy for about a minute. Then he turned back toward me. He held out the bag. "Does this look familiar to you?"

I took the bag and peeled the edges back. The parcel was heavy, much heavier than a sandwich and a bag of potato chips. It was just about the right weight for a pistol. I peeked inside. There sat a Browning that did indeed look familiar.

"Well, Habermann. Does it?"

"Yeah, it looks like mine."

"It is yours. We ran the number."

"Where did you find it?"

"In the grass near the body."

"And?"

"And we'll know more when we get the tests back. But my guess is that your weapon killed her."

*Bill Rapp*

"Perfect, Hardy. I shot her and conveniently left the weapon for you to discover."

"Well?" Hardy pressed.

"Well, that would be about the only way you could solve it, big guy. It would just about have to fall in your lap."

Hardy stepped forward and rammed his fist against my chest. Air burst from my lungs, and the state cop dropped his smile. Rick grabbed his supervisor's arm. Hardy glared at me with a look of contempt.

"You've been hiding too goddamn much from us, smart ass. We know about you and Courney, and now we'd like to know why you kept that from us." He smiled again. "Hell, I could ram your ass into a cell for obstruction of justice alone."

Hardy broke free and marched toward the parking lot, followed by about two-thirds of the people there. "Ziegler."

"Yes, sir."

One of Naperville's uniformed officers, the one I remembered from the Skylark, trotted over.

"Drive Mister Habermann to the station. He'll be spending a few hours discussing the merits of this case with us this morning."

Hardy brushed the yellow tape in front of the lot up toward his shoulders and bent underneath. The others followed in turn. Jamieson hung back for a minute, his eyes glazed with a distance I had never seen before.

"Do you think I did it?"

It took him about ten seconds to answer. "No."

"Sister Alcuin would never accuse me of doing such a thing."

He waited about twenty seconds more. "Sister Alcuin's dead, Bill." He looked up. His eyes remained hard and distant. "And she was never that smart, anyway."

---

Ziegler cast periodic glances in my direction while he drove. I buckled myself in with the shoulder strap so he wouldn't think I'd try to escape to Missouri or something on the way to the station. I also figured it would be easier to pump him for some information if he was the one preoccupied with traffic.

"Things have gotten pretty much out of the ordinary for you, haven't they?"

He nodded. "Yeah. Press is gonna go ape shit when they find out about this one."

"Well, that explains Hardy's happy mood."

"Yeah, I suppose so."

Eloquent kind of guy. "Of course, the early hours suck. Don't they?"

He shrugged. "I can always use the overtime."

"Notice anything unusual? Aside from the dead bodies suddenly sprouting up all over Naperville, that is." I only had about five minutes, so I had to work fast.

Ziegler rolled his eyes in my direction. He squinted against the glare washing the windshield, then slipped his sunglasses on while his right held the wheel steady. It looked like he got lots of practice. He shrugged again, and a smile cut the air between us. I might as well have tried to mine gold from the excavations lining Route 59.

"Hardy told me not to discuss the case with you. He said you'd try, though."

"Why not? We're all working toward the same end."

The smile broadened. "I doubt it. You're in a lot of fuckin' trouble now."

# Chapter 14

The interrogation lasted nearly three hours. Until the night of Steve Courney's death, I had never spent more than half an hour at the Naperville Police Department, outside of my work as a cop. I was fourteen then, and an overweight desk sergeant had hauled me in for a curfew violation. And that had all taken place in the old police headquarters, downtown, in a yellow brick building with a Renaissance clock tower that now served as a pizza parlor and gourmet coffee shop. I kind of missed it.

Time passed. Sometimes quickly, and sometimes slowly. And it seemed to be slowing down while I made up for my lack of interaction with the police as a child.

These three hours had dragged on like a job interview. Hardy and his crew worked me pretty steadily with maybe five minute breaks here and there to take a leak. The overhead light beamed hard enough to give me a sunburn. I started sweating after about ten minutes into the interrogation. I went over my excursion to Washington several times, four to be exact. They wanted every detail about the trip: who I saw, where I stayed, flight information. More than that, though, they wanted to trace my movements after I got back. It made sense, but professional pride and my sense of obligation kept me from revealing everything. I wanted to decide what information I gave away. I mean, these guys were not exactly cooperative and forthcoming with their knowledge. And they had no need to know everything from my conversation with Deborah Krueger.

"Come on, Bill," Jamieson said. "That's not going to help now. We need to have it all out in the open."

"That cuts both ways, Rick."

I looked at my friend, searching for an ally. I found a cop. But at least he wasn't an antagonist. Hardy was another matter.

"Goddammit, Habermann. You know we're going to check everything with your client." Hardy's cheeks sprouted red. At one point a dash of spittle formed at the corner of his mouth. I thought of dew on a rose, but the image didn't fit. "Now, when did you see the Krueger broad?"

"I am not prepared to discuss the private aspects of our conversation."

"Yeah, I'll bet there was plenty of that."

"And I'm not going to say anymore unless I get a lawyer." So, blow it out your ass, Hardy, if you're going to make cracks like that.

Hardy's bulk loomed at the edge of my chair. "You're fucking yourself, Habermann. You're destroying any alibi you might have."

"I seem to remember three AM given as the approximate time of death."

"Roughly three AM," Jamieson added.

"Not that rough."

"So, where were you after your meeting with this client?" Hardy continued.

"Home in bed. I made a few phone calls. Check the records from ma Bell."

"At three AM?"

"Well, no...."

They probably wouldn't have kept me that long if it hadn't been for the photograph and the story about the theft of my gun. The case against me was pretty weak, but Hardy hit his boiling point as soon as Jamieson gave him the snapshot. I almost expected to see steam seep out between the buttons of his shirt.

"Habermann, you motherfucker. You've been withholding evidence. What else have you got?"

"Bullshit. You got that picture as soon as I did. I picked up the prints on my way home from the airport last night and passed that one to Rick when he paid his nice little social call this morning." I sent a cold stare at my dearest, oldest friend in Naperville. He stared back like we had just met. "What did you guys pull off the index card? Anything conclusive?"

"The card had only your prints, Bill. The one we received...."

"Come again." I started to stand.

"Easy, Habermann. You heard right. We got one, too," Hardy explained. "The same wording, the same writing. But no prints."

"And the weapon?"

"Oh, hell, Bill," Jamieson said. "You know that weapon doesn't have shit for prints. We found it in the grass about twenty yards from the body, and it had been wiped clean."

"Which any self-respecting murderer would have done," Hardy added.

"What's that? Wiped it off and then left at the scene of the crime, where it can be traced to me?" I asked. "That would be absolutely brilliant. The whole thing stinks, and you guys know it."

"Maybe so," Hardy conceded. "But now we've got two murders. And you were tailing one victim–"

"And your weapon may have been used in the second," Jamieson chipped in.

"-and now this," Hardy said. He tossed a plastic baggy with an American Airlines boarding pass inside on the table in front of me. I leaned forward and studied the printing. "That's right, Habermann. It's from a Washington-to-Chicago flight yesterday evening. Guess where we found it."

"How many chances do I get?"

"None, asswipe. The stiff had it in her pants pocket."

"You two didn't hook up out there by any chance, did you?" Hardy asked.

"No, we did not." I let it go at that.

"It makes me wonder," Hardy pressed, "what else you're not telling us. Like all the details of your past with Courney."

"It's coincidence. We served together in Vietnam, but we didn't really know each other. Hell, the first time we saw each other again was when I started tailing him. Just an unlucky coincidence."

"I don't believe in coincidences, Habermann. We got the dates on both your tours. You two weren't that far apart. It doesn't take a whole lot to hook you two together."

"Goddammit, Bill," Jamieson said. "You knew we'd make that connection."

"That's right," Hardy added. "We've gotten smarter since you left the force."

He flipped the photograph on the table. It landed about six inches from my left hand. I picked it up by the edges and studied the rear end of the blue Corsica. Lights sparkled across the horizon, and a black smudge covered the inside of the car.

"I want the rest of the film, Habermann. Negatives too."

"Sure," I nodded.

"Any more anonymous notes or telephone calls?" Jamieson asked.

"Just one. Call, I mean. It was the same stuff, warning me off." I looked at Jamieson. His eyes had softened, and the distance in his stare had diminished. "When do you think Springfield will finish the lab work? It would be interesting to see if there are any traces of drugs in the blood."

Jamieson shrugged. "Why didn't you mention the theft of your weapon earlier? It sounds pretty suspicious to tell us about it now."

"I didn't like your manners, Rick. You never said 'may I?' when you entered."

Hardy's fist slammed the table so hard it shook. My head bolted in his direction and met eyes that looked hard enough to split diamonds.

"Get the fuck outta here, Habermann. We're not gonna charge you with anything yet. But I want you to stay out of our way. I don't want your face anywhere around the Courney murder, or this one. If you take just one more false step, I will have your license and haul your ass in here on a murder charge. And don't go anywhere."

"May I make one suggestion?"

Jamieson glanced up at me, his eyebrows arched. Hardy shook his head and stared with iron eyes at my friend. "No more help for this guy." Hardy's finger jabbed at nothing in particular, but it pointed in my direction. Then he turned to Jamieson. "And I want you to stay away from him. You're in almost as much shit as this asshole. This fucker has a history with Courney, and we're gonna run it down."

Hardy shook his head in disgust and pushed his way through the door.

I tugged at Jamieson's sleeve and whispered softly enough to avoid the ears of an angel. "Have Wanda take a look at the corpse. If she IDs her from the Skylark, that will at least close that particular chapter."

"You think she's one and the same?" Jamieson's voice was no louder than mine.

"Yes, I do. The build and hair look pretty similar, but Wanda got a good look at the face."

"If the mystery woman is dead, though, that means there's someone else behind Courney's killing. And this won't help."

"True, Rick. But it's one less shadow in the case."

---

Ziegler drew the short straw and had to drive me back to my car. After I got home, I popped in on Ahmed for a steak and cheese sandwich, my first real meal of the day. For good measure I had Ahmed throw in a couple of blondies. I figured I'd need the extra energy.

Then I went back upstairs and phoned in a request to the DMV to run the license plate numbers from my foray into action photography. The nasal-like feminine voice at the other end of the line insisted I fill out a request in person. And pay the fee, of course.

That cost me another hour and a half, after which I swung by the Ace Hardware store on South Washington for another dead bolt, a chain lock, and some security bolts for the windows. It was getting to the point where I'd have to move into one of those gated communities.

On the way home I stopped at the Skylark to see if Wanda had gone with Jamieson to Dupage Central Hospital in Winfield. That was where the county stored the dead bodies before it built the morgue over in Wheaton. Serves 'em right, for stealing our records all those years ago.

Willy Romer was tending bar again. He informed me that Wanda had returned but had left work early.

"Man, she couldn't even finish the lunch shift."

"Feelin' poorly?"

"Pretty green at the gills, if you ask me."

"I can understand why. Thanks, Willy."

I slid out the front door and hopped into the Volvo. I raced through two yellow lights so I could get to Wanda's before anyone else visited.

She answered the door after the third knock. She wasn't green, but she did look pretty pale.

"God. It was awful, Bill."

I followed her toward the sofa as she left a trail of nausea and depression in her living room. Her body moved like wet cement under the light pink bathrobe as she rolled toward the sofa. She sat down, then propped her bare feet on the teak coffee table. I let her talk, just to get it out of her system. I remembered my first death in Vietnam. A kid from Dalton, Georgia, as I recalled. Both his legs had just evaporated from a mortar round that landed near the front of our column. I couldn't keep any food down for about twenty-four hours.

"You friend came by. The nice cop. Rick, I think."

"That's right. Rick Jamieson."

"He drove me to the hospital, and there was this young guy there. Pretty young for this job, it seemed. He was about twenty-five. Something like that."

"Was he the lab technician?"

"He said he was an intern. He was all dressed up in a green smock and stuff. They were getting ready for the autopsy. That's when I wanted to leave. But your pal said no." She raised her arm and stared at the elbow. "He had a pretty firm grip, too."

"Rick's under a lot of pressure right now. Two deaths in this town is very unusual. You didn't see the coroner?"

Wanda shook her head, then shrugged. "Maybe. I don't know what the guy looks like. Anyway, they had the body laid out in this storage room in the basement. It was pretty cold, and all the metal and tiles made it seem even colder." Wanda shuddered.

"I'm sorry you had to go through this." I stroked her shoulder to offer some warmth and reassurance.

Wanda patted my hand, then wrapped her arms around her body, as though to insulate it from the cold world around her. "Christ, it was gross, Bill. There was another guy standing there all dressed up, like for an operation. Maybe that was your coroner guy. Anyway, the body was under this sheet, and it was in the middle of the room. The table had these raised edges that led to a drain at the end. I can't believe anyone would do that for a living."

"It is necessary, Wanda."

"And when they pulled the sheet back, I nearly puked."

"Nearly?"

"Yeah, I almost tossed my cookies right there. What with her head all shot up, and her skin so pale." Wanda shuddered again. "Instead, I blew 'em all over the parking lot when we got outside."

"I hope Rick was some help."

"Yeah, he tried to be nice. He even gave me his handkerchief. And he didn't ask for it back."

"So how'd it go?"

"What do you mean?" Her arms came loose, and her hands found each other in her lap. Beads of water sat in the corners of her eyes when Wanda looked at me. Her feet rubbed against each other for comfort.

"Did you recognize the dead woman? Was she the one from the Skylark?"

Wanda's eyes studied my face. A tear broke free and formed a tiny stream that ran as afar as her cheek before it disappeared. Her mouth opened and closed.

"What is it, Wanda?"

"I'm sorry, Bill."

"What do you mean?"

Wanda leaned forward and pulled a tissue from a box of Kleenex on the coffee table. She dabbed at her nose and two more tears that had escaped. "I know I should have told you earlier."

"What is it, Wanda? What happened?"

She glanced away, then her eyes found me. "I knew the dead guy. Steve."

I loomed over her. "What did you say? Was he there that night because of you?"

She shook her head. "No, Bill, honest. We had done some coke together. Maybe a couple times."

"Jesus Christ, Wanda. Why didn't you tell anyone?"

Her hands fell to her side. "What the hell was I supposed to say? I'm not going to confess any more of that shit to the police."

"Wanda, did you sleep with him? Was he screwing around?"

"Hell, I don't know. I never slept with him. From what I could see he just liked to snort once in a while. I got the impression he went home afterwards and jumped all over his wife. He talked about her and her sister a lot."

I sat next to her. "Wanda, this connects you to the killing more than you know. We've got to be careful. This could also be why that creep came over here."

"You, too. At least that's how your friend sounded."

"What did he say?"

Wanda dabbed some more, then pulled a new tissue from the box. She wiped underneath her eyes, but new tears filled the vacant spaces almost immediately.

"He didn't say anything much. I guess he can't. He mostly seemed to mumble to himself. Something about drugs coming into it."

"But what did he say about my part in all this?"

"Something about how he hoped the other evidence didn't point to you too."

The room swam. I stood, then stumbled against the wall that led to Wanda's kitchen. I pressed my hand against the plaster to steady myself.

"But what about the corpse, Wanda? Was she the woman from the Skylark last week?"

Wanda moved with light, almost imperceptible steps. Her hips swept from side to side as she neared. She took my hand in hers, then led me to the couch. I fell into the corner seat. Wanda sat down with her back against my chest and pulled my arms around her shoulders.

"Hold me for a minute, Bill."

My arms hung like lead limbs on her soft, round shoulders. "What about the woman, Wanda? Was she the one from last Saturday night?"

"I'm sorry, Bill. It was awful hard to tell. I couldn't be sure, but I think so." Wanda strangled a sob. "She looked so young to be dead. But I think it was her. Why would she do it, Bill?"

"I'm trying to find out, Wanda."

We sat together for a long time. At least it seemed like a long time, like hours had passed. When I got up to leave, I noticed that only forty minutes had elapsed on the clock on the kitchen stove.

# Chapter 15

When I left Wanda's apartment, I swung back onto Washington Street. The Volvo wandered through town, past Hallmark stores, real estate firms, delis, and coffee shops. The blank windows of the old Nichols Library stared out from remnants of stone and brick. Constructed around the turn of the century in an elaborate ranch style, the library had served generations of housewives and schoolchildren. Now, however, the town had outgrown its original library. A handful of pedestrians wandered past from the municipal parking lot at the rear. Next door, a turn-of-the-century YMCA building of red brick and iron railings sat nearly vacant. I swam there for the local team as a kid in a pool not much larger than a back yard pond. Now, it served only the loyal few who continued to come here rather than use the newer building out along Route 75.

I needed to keep driving, so I pressed on until I reached the eastern side of Naperville. Here, Ogden Avenue begins its long run through car dealerships, fast food joints, and hotel chains that make it indistinguishable from about a million other streets in suburban America. It's an endless sea of neon and metal, a consumer's paradise where every outlet and parking space lies within easy reach of your car and a gas station.

The dinner hour approached and neon signs beckoned, offering processed food at minimal cost. But I had a different kind of hunger. I needed to talk to Rick Jamieson. Uncertainty and frustration gnawed at my insides like a cancer. I noticed white knuckles strangling the steering wheel. The air conditioning died with a gasp, and by the time I rolled the driver's window down, beads of sweat ran down the sides of my face.

Before I reached the curve in Ogden that leads to the Tollroad, I turned right and drove through a neighborhood of modest houses on tiny plots to Jamieson's two-story, three-bedroom bungalow. It resembled most of the others that filled the streets, which ran in neat perpendicular lines from the old Kroehler furniture factory. Many predated the Kroehler business, but the building boom that had rippled through this section of Naperville once the factory had opened had attracted new workers. This was right before the war. Rick's dad had wandered down from Geneva, a town in the Fox Valley overloaded with Swedes, back in the 1940s to work there. Rick had grown up in this house, and he had inherited it from his father. His son would probably get it, eventually. And by then the real estate value would have increased about a thousand percent.

The place had a long front porch that ran the width of the house, and the overhanging roof looped down under pale gray shingles until it reached the twin pines on either corner. The second floor looked like the architect had set four triangles facing outdoors, a window in the middle of each. A collection of overflowing evergreens as tall as a man ran around the front and down the right side of the house, all the way to the back. Although most of the houses on the block had been built with red brick, Rick's had beige siding and white trim. I had often envied the suburban, domestic bliss that emanated from this house. Not today, though.

I parked the Volvo against the curb in front, hiding the number painted on the curb against a black backdrop. I marched up the three cement steps that bisected the slope of lawn next to the sidewalk, then walked down the long, stone pathway that ran past the front porch and around to the kitchen door at the side. The large oak in the middle of the front yard broke the late afternoon heat with a canopy of shade that enveloped half the lawn like a prayer tent.

Rick Jamieson's wife, Susan, told me he was out back in his work shed. I resumed my line of march down a white stone path through patches of yellow lawn and sprouting crabgrass until I reached the carriage house at the edge of the alley. Most people still used these to shelter their cars, but his Thunderbird was parked in front of the shed, having long ago been displaced by an assortment of tools, workbenches, chain saws, and miters. A half-dozen unfinished projects kept these company. I snuck through the double doors, exchanging the late afternoon sun for the damp shade of the garage. A gray cloud of dust hung in the air over the worktable. Tools lay spread across the wooden top, only four or five still set upright in the slots Jamieson had constructed for them along the wall at the table's edge. A window looked out across the alley. Jamieson stood at the table sanding what looked like a birdhouse, his ten-year-old son at his side.

Jamieson looked up long enough to nod. Then he returned to his rhythmic work on the birdhouse. "What brings you to this part of town, pardner?"

"You really need to ask?" I selected a spot to the right of the entrance and leaned against the far end of the table.

"Would it do any good to ask you to stick around for dinner?" He turned to his son. "Ricky, go ask mom if she wants some brats tonight. If so, you can take your bike and wagon down to Kroeger's and pick up about half a dozen for me. Have them put it on the tab."

# ANGEL IN BLACK

His son started out the door with the energy and enthusiasm of any ten-year-old eager to please his father after a tedious thirty minutes of woodworking.

"You sure you can afford to have me in your house nowadays?" I stared at my friend.

Jamieson set the small bird house down, then tossed the sandpaper after it. He pulled out a drawer, selected a piece of finer sandpaper, and began to smooth the corner of a china cabinet. He worked the rounded crown of the cabinet, brushing the dust away with his bare hand, then inspected his handiwork.

"I promised Sue I'd finish this by fall."

"You've got time."

Jamieson sighed, then set the sandpaper down on the lap of the cabinet. He dropped into one of the unvarnished chairs that stood at the side of his work table.

"I knew you'd be by, sooner or later."

"I prefer sooner."

"Yeah, well. It's all in a day's work." He shrugged and reached for a can of Miller on the floor next to his feet. He tipped the edge of the gold aluminum can back toward his mouth. Beads of moisture spotted the sides.

"Kind of early to be drinking that rabbit piss."

"I've been up since four, Bill. I plan to crash right after dinner." His eyebrows arched, and the jaw dropped while he studied me against the backdrop of his garage door. "You want one? I'm all out of Special Export. Augsburger too. Sorry."

The heat of the sun burned at my back. The light penetrating through the windows in the garage door worked my body like a crooked cop.

"Goddammit, Rick, you set me up out there today. I would have thought our friendship meant more than that."

"I'm not going to discuss this with you here, Bill. You know better than that."

"You know damn well I'm trying to catch the killer as hard as you guys. I deserve better than the shit I got out there today. I used to work with you fuckers. Remember?"

"Look!" He bolted up from the chair. "Hardy gave me strict orders not to let on about anything. You know damn well I had to ask those questions and check with your neighbors."

"You know it was a setup. That planting of the gun was bullshit, Rick. And you know it."

"Goddamit, Bill. Hardy has been having shit fits about the Courney killing. And now this one occurs. The press is gonna go nuts over this."

"I can help, and you know it. This thing goes beyond Naperville. This thing reaches way back into Courney's past, and I'm in the best position to find out where."

The muscles of Jamieson's face worked back and forth. "Hardy and the rest of us think Courney's past is important, too. But that past includes you, Bill, something you tried to hide. How do you think that looks? Why do you think I was trying get you to come to the station instead of flying off to Washington? And holding on to the photograph didn't help."

"Okay, okay. So that was a mistake. But I'm not giving up on this case."

"Don't let Hardy catch you." He tossed the empty beer can in the direction of his trash bin. "And I didn't hear you say that, either."

"You've gotten everything from me I could give you. Hell, Hardy's not stupid. I know he's a good cop. A prick at times, but steady and thorough. Shit, I even liked him when I worked there. Even he doesn't think I'd shoot someone and then leave the murder weapon lying nearby where any idiot could find it."

Jamieson's own finger thrust out at me. It was like High Noon in the Naperville Corral. "It's still your weapon. There's a link there somewhere, and we have to find out what that is. If someone is trying to set you up, then we have to figure out why."

"Oh come on!" I threw my hands up in the air. "For Chrissakes, Rick! If something significant turns up, you'll get it. You know that."

"Why didn't you report that your gun was stolen?"

My hands flew back in the air. "I didn't know it was missing until last night. I had planned to report it first thing this morning. But I was interrupted. Remember?"

"That's still pretty damn careless, Bill."

"I don't like to use the fucking thing, Rick. It had been months since I had it out of the drawer, and only then after I had been jumped behind my place the other night."

"Yeah, I know all about that." He averted his eyes. "We all do."

My temples pounded with anger. I hadn't leveled my weapon at anyone since those days in Vietnam. And I had certainly not shot anyone since that horrible night on the hilltop. I walked to his worktable and slammed my fist against the soft pine. For a brief moment I pondered the birdhouse, saw it shatter under the force of my fist. Then I saw the tears in his son's eyes. Ricky Jamieson was the son of my best, my oldest friend. Hell, I was the kid's godfather.

"So, whoever it was came when you were in D.C.?"

"That's right."

"Do you think that's why the dead woman was here? To follow you? And if so, then why was she killed?"

"To shut her up. I don't suppose you'll tell me if anything you found on Courney was a match for her."

Jamieson shrugged.

"Never mind. Wanda confirmed it, sort of. But I think she was back in town for another reason."

"Which is?"

"Either to finish a job someone else started, or warn me."

"About what? And why you?"

"I'm still not sure. But some Vietnamese I ran into back east knew I was there. They knew where I was from. If we can trace this corpse, something else might fall into place."

"How so?"

"There's some kind of family history at work here. And they knew the Courney's. Have you traced all his phone calls?"

"Yeah. The ones to Arlington were to a private residence."

"I'll bet it's someone connected to the family I met." I told Jamieson about the restaurant. "Did the cops back there have anything?"

"They just ran some traces for me. They were a dead end. Are you sure nothing else is missing besides the Browning?"

"Yeah, pretty sure. What's the story on the drug angle? Have you guys found any substance there yet?"

"I can't go into that, Bill. Hardy would have my ass. He's on the warpath."

I frowned.

"Bill, Hardy needs this one bad. Real bad. These murders are the biggest thing to hit Naperville in a long while. It can make or break his career."

"What did I ever do to him, besides date his wife? Note too, Rick, the operative verb I used."

"Nothin', that I know. But he's grasping, and a lot of things are suddenly pointing at you. And this latest killing has everyone looking in your direction. You've got to expect that."

"Is there any other evidence beside the gun? You said there were no prints. What about the lab work? The autopsy?"

Jamieson just shook his head.

"Help me on the drugs shit, Rick. I need to close off options if I can. Is there new evidence leading you guys in that direction?"

"It's something we have to follow, Bill. I can't say anymore than that."

"Goddammit, Rick. Don't play that game with me. We go too far back for this to happen."

"Don't, Bill."

"Don't what?"

"Don't start pulling on our friendship. You know I'll give you the benefit of every doubt I can. But I gotta do my job. We've got to go after this stuff if we're going to find who killed Courney and the other woman. And why. It's our job, too, Bill."

"What about Courney's wife? Have you given up on the family angle?"

"She's got no motive or opportunity that we can see to kill her husband."

"Adultery has caused a lot of death over time, Rick."

"You said you couldn't find any. Besides, she's got an alibi."

"Which is?"

"The movies. She still has the ticket stub."

"So? People can get up and leave."

"Her sister confirmed that she went to a show that night. Said they met afterwards for a drink."

I rolled my eyes.

Jamieson shrugged. "I know it's not airtight."

"So, what about the license number? Didn't that go anywhere?"

"Not yet. I just found out as I was leaving this afternoon that the plate belongs to a rental car."

"Well, which one?" I pressed. "And where?"

"You know the number. Call the DMV."

"I did. But I'm not a cop, Rick. That takes time."

"Budget. Out at O'Hare." His finger probed the air in front of my chest. "But you didn't hear that from me. Hardy will have my ass."

"Rick, nobody wants your ass. It's too skinny."

"I'll take that as a blessing, where you're concerned. Just be sure to watch your step, Bill. Stenson went out there as I was leaving to check it out. He doesn't like you as much as I do."

# ANGEL IN BLACK

"So there is a drug angle." Stenson normally worked narcotics for the Naperville Police. His beat had yet to get him out beyond high school parking lots and occasional forays onto the campus at North Central College, however. "Man, I hope he doesn't screw things up out there."

"In what way?"

"He likes to play the hard ass, Rick. It can turn a lot of people off."

Rick climbed out of his chair and picked up his beer can. He strolled to the trash bin he had set against the wall of his shed and slammed-dunked the empty can. I was happy to see that at least his aim had improved since his visit to my kitchen.

"Stenson's just doing his job, Bill. We all are."

"Yeah," I nodded, as I headed toward the alley. "That's what Hermann Goering said."

Footsteps pounded the dry earth behind me. Jamieson's fingers locked themselves onto my shoulder and spun me around. His face snarled, the muscles taut and the eyes like blue marbles.

"If you're so goddamn smart, why haven't you solved the murders, hot shot? From where I stand it looks like you've had your chance, and you've blown it. Another choke job."

I shook the fingers loose and backed into the open air. The sun hit my neck with a blow almost as heavy as Jamieson's grip. My hand seemed to rise of its free will, the index finger thrust forward like a dagger.

"Don't, Rick. Goddamit, don't you walk down that road. I don't want to hear that from you. I am going to solve this fucking thing, if it kills me."

I pulled myself away from my friend and walked down the alleyway. I did not want to cut across his lawn to return to my car. Straight ahead I saw the red brick outline of the old Kroehler factory, now a set of condos, chic shops, restaurants, and a brew pub. But I didn't recognize the change. Instead, I remembered the old four-storied manufacturing plant whose prosperity had faded as the town had thrived, and I spied old ghosts beckoning from an abandoned relic.

My stomach was growling again, so I stopped at the Lantern for another burger. I finally took Willy Romer up on his offer of a Bass Ale, but during the two cups of coffee I resisted his attempts at friendly conversation out of deference to the case.

It was sliding into a swamp of history and deceit. What did I expect? This was a murder investigation. Since it had been such a rough day and I was in no hurry to return to my apartment, I treated myself to Dairy Queen afterwards. Soft vanilla, which I had to slurp faster than I like because of the intense July heat.

The steeple of Saints Peter and Paul cast a forbidding shadow across the Volvo's path when I rounded the corner on Benton Avenue. After I had tucked the car in for the night I stood on the back porch, remembering the years I had spent growing up under their tutelage. Voices of long-forgotten nuns floated in the night air, and I listened like an obedient child for their message.

I checked the locks on the door, and there was no sign of tampering. Of course, there hadn't been when I'd returned from Washington either. I set the bag from Ace on the table, pulled out a screwdriver and power drill from underneath the sink, and got to work.

About two hours later I had installed a new deadbolt and chain lock on the door, which did not look any the worse for my poor craftsmanship. Nothing that a little paint wouldn't fix. Then I began to drill holes in the window frames so I could bolt those shut.

I thought about the two killings to see if I could determine how they were linked together. There wasn't much doubt in my mind. But why would someone try to set me up? Unless the burglar was involved in that killing, and just dropped my weapon by mistake. But then why steal only a gun? There had to be some other evidence out there, since the gun was not going to go very far. And if so, had the cops found it? And was that what had opened the narcotics angle? Had they found a stash somewhere? Was there something in the Courneys' financial records? And who had known I was going to Washington? Deborah Krueger for one, but she was the one who had hired me in the first place.

The telephone interrupted my ruminating and my carpentry.

"Where the hell you been, guy?" John Sullivan's voice called me back to the present. "I've left any number of messages for you."

The message light blinked red.

"I've had a lot to run down since I saw you last, Sully."

"That's good. And that's bad."

I sighed. "Sully, I've got mysteries enough. What's up?"

"Well, you got even more now, my boy."

I sat in the swivel chair, then pulled a pen and notepad close. "Let me have it."

Paper rustled somewhere back in Virginia. "Your dead guy, this fellow Courney...."

"Yeah?"

"I drew blanks with the Navy and Air Force people on the procurement angle."

"Why am I no longer surprised?"

"But I did ring some bells over at J2."

"And?" My pen was poised.

"Some guys there remembered him from working intel at the end of the war."

"What was he doing?"

"He was an agent handler. He picked up some of the long-term cases that were feeding info from the north."

"How long-term?"

"One guy claims they went way back. All the way to Landsdale's time. You know, the stay-behinds."

"Man, that puts them at the very beginning. No way they couldn't have been turned."

"Yeah, I know. That's what a lot of us thought."

A light blinked somewhere in the back of my head. "Oh shit, Sully."

"What?"

"Those groups drew heavily on the Catholic population in the North, didn't they?"

"Yeah. Ethnic minorities, too. So what?"

"Something may have just clicked."

"I'm glad. One other thing, though."

"What's that?"

"There's a big gap after '69 in his VA records."

"Yeah. I noticed that, too. What's your thought?"

"You just might find something else at work there. I doubt he was working at the agent game the entire time."

"Thanks, Sully. This has really helped."

"Anytime. And watch out for those demons, pardner."

I set the receiver back in the cradle, then swung the chair around to face the window. Finally. Maybe Sisters Alcuin and Labenzia had pulled a few strings upstairs to help me out. I'd light a candle tomorrow. But my elation passed, and I was left with a hollow feeling in the depths of my soul. What did it all have to do with me? I wondered. Had these been some of the people I wrote off on the exfiltration memos? Was I involved in some other way? There were no easy answers to any of these questions.

I spoke these words to John Sullivan and to everyone. Most of all, I spoke them to myself. The closer I got, the farther back I traveled to a time of sweat and misery and death. I had known heroes, and I had met villains. My guess was that the latter were involved in Steve Courney's death and the killing of the woman at Northern Illinois Gas. And somehow they had tied me to both. But I still didn't know why.

# Chapter 16

It was happening again. I couldn't escape the explosions bursting inside the compound. The earth shook, and rockets of metal, dirt, and flame roared on all sides. I fell back inside the sandbags and buried my head in the moist dirt. I heard rifles fire, recoil, then fire again. A scream pierced my ears like a sharp pin. I jerked my head up and found the captain's chest a wet tangle of flesh and muscle. I crawled over. His lips were moving; but there was no sound. His body trembled, then stiffened, and a passing light in his black eyes faded to gray. His Colt .45 lay in the dirt to his side. I grabbed it and dove back onto the ground. Jamie was there, his M16 exploding with rapid staccatos of fire and cartridge. Sweat streamed through the stubble lining his chin, his tongue pressed between his teeth. I swept the sweat off my brow and chambered a round. Moisture beaded along the back of my hand. The dirt under my fingernails turned to mud. My breath came in short spasms. My ribs were ready to burst. I heard another scream. When I looked up, a blinding light shattered the night.

I was back home. A stream of morning sunlight swam over my face and down along the white sheets. I had forgotten to close the drapes when I'd gone to bed. Squinting to escape the blaze, I rolled over toward the night table. Seven thirty. The window unit in my bedroom hummed, but the pillow was damp from sweat. I stripped the bed to put on clean sheets, then peeled off my boxers for a shower.

After I toweled myself dry, I threw on a clean pair of shorts and some khaki docksiders, topped with a blue and white striped Oxford dress shirt. It even had some starch in it, but I figured that would last about as long as the first car ride. I made a proper breakfast of toast and eggs over easy, with orange juice and cup of java from downstairs. I didn't really have that much of an appetite, but I figured my body needed the fuel.

As soon as the dishes were clean, I called the DMV in Alexandria, Virginia. I identified myself and referred to the request I had filed for information on a certain Sean Cavanaugh. I repeated the social security number for the heavy voice on the line back east. They gave me the address on St. Asaph for two years prior to the sale of the property, but nothing further on place of employment. He'd driven a Mercedes then, but he appeared to have left the state after the sale of his house. Great. Another dead end.

By ten o'clock I was riding the blacktop to O'Hare Airport. I had missed mass again, but that was a pretty regular habit by now. The buzz of people out for their Sunday morning drive hummed along Ogden Avenue and Naper Boulevard. A panorama of colored neon shone as far as the horizon, its brightness dimmed by the blaze of sunlight. I dodged around shoppers pulling in and out of parking lots, then finally got frustrated enough to stray into the left lane. A familiar looking Grand Am followed. He kept a comfortable distance about four or five cars back as I cruised out to the Tollroad. By the time I caught Route 294, he was gone. Instead, billboards advertising newspapers, toothpaste, liquor, cleaning aids, and radio stations swept past. Rows of small industrial plants, mostly single stories of corrugated sheeting and hard steel frames, blossomed underneath. I opened all four windows to let the wind flush the car of the fetid summer air.

At Route 90 I steered the Volvo through the exit ramp to catch the entrance to O'Hare. About a half-mile shy of the departure lanes, I broke off and drove to the car rental lots that spread beneath the highway like a stillborn lake of bright, colored metal. Gravel and oil stains rested on concrete lots like dull coral on an ocean floor. Breezing past the Hertz and Avis gates, I pushed through the entrance to Budget Rent-A-Car, then parked in front of an office set in a cocoon of dark glass. It looked cool and comfortable inside. Attendants skipped back and forth behind a chest-high counter, talking into their computer screens while customers waited obediently on the other side.

A load of travelers boarded a small white commuter bus around the corner from my parking space. They were dressed for summer travel, about half of them wearing shorts and T-shirts. Some of the men had their legs draped in polyester, and loose polo shirts hung off drooping shoulders and extended stomachs. They looked like they had just gotten in from a round of golf. Nearly everyone had a garment bag to cram into the compartment above their head. That way, they could grab their luggage as quickly as possible and have plenty of time to stand in the aisle while they waited for the plane to unload.

After walking through double glass doors, I strolled through the lanes marked with black ribbon and silver, waist-high poles, and stopped in front of the only available work station. A tall, thin man with a short black brillo pad for hair stood behind the counter. His modest tan and beady eyes reminded me of an overgrown sparrow.

"Can I help you, sir?"

"Yes, you can. I'm investigating a hit-and-run accident for an insurance company. I hope to verify that the vehicle in question did indeed strike a woman and her companion." I smiled as broadly as possible while I pulled a copy of my license from my wallet.

A look of horror swept his face. "Did it strike a pedestrian?"

I smiled to reassure him. "No, no. Nothing like that. I have the license number here, and the people at the Division of Motor Vehicles told me that it belongs to one of your cars."

He studied my license like I had posed in the nude, then leaned as far away from the counter as he could without losing touch with his computer keyboard.

"I'll have to get the manager, sir."

"Of course."

He broke away from his machine, retreating into the inner sanctum of an office that measured about ten feet by eight. A heavier man with tufts of brown hair and fleshy cheeks enclosing a thick, round nose sat behind a gray metal desk. The second individual, whom I took to be the manager, leaned forward and looked at me through the clear glass. Then he pulled his bulky frame from a wooden chair like it was coming unglued, sucked in a sloping mid-section to slide around a desk, and emerged from the office.

His smile was even wider than mine as he approached. Obviously, he'd had a lot more practice. The original attendant stood about a foot behind him in a state bordering on deference. Both men were wearing identical blue and orange ties pinned to their white shirts with little silver clasps bearing the Budget logo.

"I understand you're looking for some information about one of our cars."

"That's right." I reproduced the copy of my license. "I believe one of them was involved in a minor altercation that could cost a client of mine a good deal of money. It was a Chevy Corsica." My hand tucked the license away, then ascended to the countertop. I flipped it open, palm up, the fingers spread apart and curled slightly in a reassuring manner. "I'm sure it was no fault of yours. You just never know who is going to rent a car these days."

I pushed a slip of paper with the license plate number across the counter.

"I see." One hand massaged the double cleft in his chin; the other gathered the paper in. A wedding band lay half-buried on the ring finger of his left hand. "About when did the accident occur?"

His right hand moved from the chin to the keyboard. I could hear the dulcet beeps of letters and numbers registering with the hard drive.

"Last Saturday night. Around ten o'clock."

"Yes, the car in question does belong to Budget, and it was returned that evening."

"I see. Could you tell me when it was acquired?"

He peered at the screen. "Ah, sure. It was Saturday morning. "

I glanced out the window at a busload of new arrivals stumbling down the steps to the sidewalk. The hall was about to get busy.

"Was there any damage to the vehicle?"

His head shook slowly, as though he was pondering a calculus problem. "There's nothing here to indicate that anything was found."

"Hm. That doesn't sound right. Would I be able to talk to whomever handled the transaction for that particular car?"

"Have you been in touch with the police from Naperville?"

"Is there some other problem?" I raised my hand to my forehead.

"Actually, yes. They had some questions about the car as well."

My hand slid to the counter again, pounding it twice for emphasis. "Of course. That must have been Stenson. A good man."

"So, you know the officer. Are you working with him?"

"Yes, I have been in touch with the Naperville police. My client, however, would like to conduct its own investigation. That's often the case with insurance companies."

"I see."

He pulled off a printout from the terminal in front of him. He leaned away from the counter and tipped his body sideways to study the other attendants lined up in a row to his right.

"I suppose you could talk to the agent who was on duty that morning."

He walked down the aisle and tapped a younger man, almost a boy, on the shoulder and gave him the printout. I placed his age somewhere in the mid-twenties. Definitely not more than twenty-five. His light black hair looked like it had suffered through a half-assed attempt at a combing this morning, and he was trying his best to grow a mustache. His hormones weren't quite up to the task, but I was willing to forgive him if he could give me the information I needed.

The kid sauntered over and pointed to a set of chairs against the windows that looked out to the gas pumps and maintenance garage. He flopped into one of the orange chairs standing next to a small steel table with a spider plant backed against the glass. Car and travel magazines littered the tabletop.

"We can sit over here, sir. It should give us a little bit of privacy at least."

I thanked him as we settled in. I repeated the story I had handed his supervisor.

"I never met a private eye before. Can I see your license?"

"Sure, son. What's your name?" I pulled out the copy of my license. This particular exercise was starting to grow tiresome.

"Wow! You really are a private dick." His face darkened around eyes bright with color and excitement. "Oh, I'm sorry. I didn't mean to offend you. Oh, yeah. The name's Mat."

"That's alright. It happens all the time," I lied. "What I really need from you, Mat, is some information about the person who rented this vehicle last week." I showed him the slip with the make of the car and the license plate number. "I have reason to believe that whoever was driving this car last Saturday was involved in a serious accident."

"Really? How serious?"

"Very serious, Mat. Perhaps serious enough to warrant a reward," I lied again. I wondered how often I was going to have to do that with this kid.

He nodded, then studied the sheet his supervisor had given him, waiting for inspiration.

"Let me think...."

He shook his head.

"Do you mean you can't remember?" I shuddered to think how long this might take.

"Oh, I remember the transaction all right." He leaned his head back against the window, his eye squinting toward the ceiling. "I just can't remember that much about the woman who rented the car."

"So, she was a woman? You're sure about that much?"

"Oh, yeah. That and the dark hair. She was really attractive. Chinese or something."

I leaned forward. "Did you say Chinese? Are you sure?"

"Well, no. But she was definitely Oriental."

"Are you sure?"

He leaned toward me, his face shaping itself into a pale, vapid oval. "Oh, yeah. And the hair really did it. Real long, and it hung all the way down her back. Real cool lookin'. Kind of like a model's. You know what I mean?"

"I'm not sure I do, Mat." I pulled a notebook from my coat pocket.

"It went really well with her tall, thin body. Very attractive." He winked.

I winked back. At least that gave me something about her physical appearance. "Can you describe her beyond 'tall' and 'thin'?"

"Well, I'm not sure I can." He smiled. The vapid look did not disappear. There was no sign of recognition behind his pale brown eyes.

I set the pad on the table. "Well, how tall? Orientals are generally shorter than us."

"Oh, she was over five feet, easy. "Id, say at least five four, maybe even five five"

"Anything else?"

He frowned, studying the plant. "Sorry. But I'm drawing a blank on her face."

"It wasn't that long ago, was it?"

"Well, no. But I never got a really good look at her face. At least, that's not what I remember. But I do recall her bein' kinda skinny."

"Skinny? Would you say boney, or just someone who was in good shape?"

"No, not boney. Just thin features, you know."

I picked up the pad and scribbled something. "What is it then that you do remember?"

He shuffled his body further toward me in his seat, his lips curving into a knowing smile. I thought he was going to wink again.

"Well, there was the hair, but I already mentioned that."

"I know. It's right here," I lied, holding the back of my notepad up for him to see.

"But it was really cool. Kinda like long waves of silk."

"Okay. Tell me what struck you about her the most. Her most distinguishing feature."

A soft, dim glow took possession of his eyes. He looked like he was dreaming. "She had a real nice build, man. Up front, if you know what I mean."

"Excuse me?"

He glanced back toward the counter, his head nodding while he returned his gaze to me. "Well, I always thought Oriental women were small. You know, up front. But she had really nice breasts. A great set of jugs, man."

"That's what you remember the most?"

He sat back, a satisfied smirk etched across his lips. "Yeah." His face turned serious. "I'm sorry, but that's all I can remember now."

"Think real hard, please. Wasn't there anything else? Why did you focus so much on that?" Not that I needed to work real hard figuring out the answer to that one.

He leaned forward and surveyed the counter again. When his face turned toward me, the glow in his eyes had blossomed to a deep flame.

"It looked like it was gonna be a really long day. We were busy as hell. Then I see this really exotic-lookin' customer come in, you know. So, I'm hopin' she comes to my station. I mean, like the whole morning's been crazy, and the afternoon figures to be more of the same."

"Yeah, that can be tough on a guy." More scratches on the notepaper.

"Well," he slapped his knee, "I couldn't believe it when she did. So, anyway, I took the information from her driver's license and ran through all the options for her."

"Options?"

"Yeah. You know, whether to get insurance and all that stuff. Anyway, when I ran off the form for her to sign, she takes it and bends over just enough to read through it all." Mat wet his lips. "Well, she was wearin' this low cut summer dress and no bra. Man, it was like she did it on purpose."

"I'll bet." I smiled through gritted teeth.

"Oh yeah. It was all I could think about all day long."

"Do you remember what the dress looked like? The color perhaps?"

"Uh?" He shook his head to wake himself up. "Oh, it was blue, or somethin' like that. Maybe green. I had a lot of customers that day. Sorry."

"Did she speak much? Was there anything distinctive about her voice? Her eyes perhaps?" Fat chance.

"Oh, sure. She had to talk. But I don't remember much beyond her voice being real soft. You know, like a woman's."

"No accent or anything?"

Mat shook his head. "Hard to tell. I don't remember her saying much."

"Nothing else about her looks? Nothing stands out? Scars?"

"Not that I remember." He stared at the distance for a moment, then looked back at me. "I think she was pretty tan. But you see that a lot in the summer, you know."

"Yes, I've noticed that, too. Anything about her manner that struck you. Did she seem nervous, or preoccupied?"

"Nope. She was a real cool customer."

"Where did her license say she came from? Was she an out-of-towner?"

"Oh, she was definitely an out-of-stater."

"Do you remember which state?"

He thought for a moment. "Nope. Sorry. Maybe it was California. I hear they got lots of Asian people out there. No, wait." He looked at the printout. "The address listed here is a local one. She must have been visiting a relative or something."

"How long was the rental for?"

He glanced at the paper again. "Says here for a week."

"But she returned it early. Did she say why?"

"I wasn't working then. Sorry."

I picked up my pad and pen. "Thanks very much, Mat. Oh, just one more question."

"Sure."

"Was she wearing any sort of jewelry?"

He thought for a moment. "Sure. I mean, she was a woman. There were some bracelets and stuff. Why?"

"What about a necklace?"

He pondered that one with obvious pleasure, then shook his head. "Nope. Not that I remember. Nothin' down there between me and the promised land."

That was not what I had expected. Another bus rolled up in front of the booth, discharging a new army of arrivals. They hustled through the door, then filed obediently into the columns outlined by the elastic black streamers to wait their turns. The line had backed up through the maze to the end of the tape. The manager caught Mat's eye and gestured with his head toward the battle station.

I must have looked disappointed. The kid stood up, holding out his hand.

"Good luck, sir. I hope I was able to help you some."

"Oh, absolutely, Mat. You've been a big help." I motioned toward the slip in his hand. "Do you mind if I take that registration form with me?"

He held it up to his face for about five seconds. "No, I guess it's all right. We can always run off a new one if we need it." He flung his arm with the piece of paper in the direction of the counter before handing it to me. "The stuff's all on a computer."

"I see," I said, folding the sheet of printout. "And thanks again."

# ANGEL IN BLACK

I shook his hand and hurried out the door before anyone else in a blue and orange tie tried to stop me. But they were all busy communing with a mainframe somewhere in the entrepreneurial ether.

Outside, the sun was still pushing thermostats to a long, slow bake. A big silver bird, an American Airlines 747, glided by on jet streams and diesel fuel, climbing through the sky to disappear in a haze of blue and white.

It reminded me of the last summer job I had held before the Army grabbed me. I was working in a cement plant in Des Plaines, not far from the airport. They were extending the runways for the 747s, and we were pushing the cement out around the clock. I had the night shift, eight-to-eight, which brought pretty good money, especially for an eighteen-year-old. Early each morning, as the sun rose, I climbed atop one of the railcars that transported the cement to watch the jets lumber in from exotic places, like Rome or Tokyo, Cleveland or Detroit even. At times, I thought all I needed to do was reach out to feel their glistening steel bodies, to catch their tailfins and escape to sights unseen, adventures unknown. At the end of August, I received my draft notice.

I lowered my arm and strolled to the Volvo. After I waved to the security guard at the gate, I cruised through the exit. I pulled the car onto the shoulder of the access road and reached for the computer printout. The humid summer air seeped back into the car's interior through the open windows. A light coat of dust settled on the hood from the gravel lining the sides of the road. Sweat outlined my face, and I swiped at the sides with the back of my hand.

I grazed through the printout and cursed. The registration listed a Joan Deerfield of Wilmette, Illinois. The Naperville police were probably running a trace right now, but I was pretty certain Ms. Deerfield did not exist. If she did, she almost certainly had nothing to do with the events of the last week. For one thing, no self-respecting woman from Wilmette would spend her Saturday nights in Naperville. She probably had planes to catch and places to go. That made two of us. The net from Vietnam was drawing tighter.

# Chapter 17

Once off the Tollroad and back on Ogden, I pulled into the Jewel grocery store and parked next to a handicapped spot at the front. Inside, I walked over to the bank of pay phones just to the street side of the cashiers, dropped in my quarter, and dialed the number of Jamie Krug. After about 60 seconds of monosyllabic conversation, I hung up and walked over spotless linoleum and through a steady stream of industrial lighting, cold air, and piped-in music to the cold beer displays. Despite my earnest lectures and emotional pleas, Jamie liked Budweiser. He always had. Always would, I guess. I had eaten a hardy breakfast, but I knew I needed to keep my tank full, so I grabbed a bag of potato chips and a sandwich in the deli section. While I waited in the checkout line, I read that space aliens were kidnapping the game animals of Africa. Several authoritative sources claimed that this-not pollution, or human greed and indifference-represented the real reason for the depletion of the rain forests. I wondered when the government was going to do something about that.

After I left a ten-spot and a five behind, I returned to the car and propped the twelve pack on the front seat. Thirty minutes later I steered the Volvo over the sparse gravel in Jamie's driveway. He sat waiting on the porch, his butt balanced on the ledge in front and his feet swinging over thin brown shrubbery. His hands twirled a black and white checked dish towel through the air in front of his chest. A sprinkler showered the lawn with pellets of water.

I climbed from the car, beer and chips in hand, and nodded toward the struggling bushes. "Trying to save the landscaping?"

Jamie shrugged. "Have you eaten yet?"

"I hand a nice sandwich in the car on the way over."

"In the car? How American."

"Yeah. I also spent my morning talking to a rental car company."

"Did you find anything?"

"Yes and no." I waved off Jamie's protest. "It's a long story, but I might be able to make something out of it."

Jamie led us back inside, and we took seats on opposite sides of the kitchen table. The worn cushions on the chairs groaned under our weight. Jamie grabbed a beer from the cardboard case, flipped the tab, and swung it toward his mouth.

# ANGEL IN BLACK

After wiping his chin, he ripped open the bag of Lays potato chips, grabbed a mittfull, then pushed the bag in my direction.

"Thanks, Jamie. As always, your hospitality is overwhelming."

"That's because it's always so good to see you, Bill." He took another drink. "Hey, I got some good news."

"What's that?" The chips tasted salty and crisp.

"I start next week working construction again. I got hired as a carpenter."

"That's great, Jamie." I reached into the cardboard and grabbed a Bud for myself. I felt obligated to offer Jamie a toast. "What does Suzy have to say about that?"

"She thinks it's great, of course. It should speed up our movin' in together again."

Jamie stood, then picked up what was now a ten pack. "One's the limit today." He tossed the beer on the second-to-last steel shelf in his refrigerator, where it could keep company with a loaf of bread, a carton of eggs, and a couple plastic containers.

When he returned to the table, Jamie's eyes studied mine over the rim of his beer. The last time we spoke, they were as clear as I'd seen them in years. Today, however, the blue pupils refused to stay focused whenever they looked at me. I told him about the burglary at my apartment and the missing weapon found at the side of another corpse.

Jamie leaned forward. His fingers beat a steady drumroll on the tabletop. "Yeah, I know. Your friends from the Naperville Police Department were here with one of Oswego's finest." His fingers were moving like Gene Krupa's now.

I reached over and placed my hand on top of his to steady his nerves. And mine.

"What did you say?"

"They were here earlier today. That's why I'm so late with the dishes."

"The police? From Naperville?"

His eyes darted about the room. "Uh huh."

"Talk to me, Jamie. Who came and what did they want? Was it Jamieson?"

"No, not him." His free hand went to his nose, wiping away a line of nasal drip with a fresh napkin. "It was another guy. He didn't leave a card, but I think his name was something like Stetson. You know, like the hat."

"The guy's name is Stenson, Jamie. What did he tell you?"

The hand went to the nose again. I looked for some Kleenex.

"They wanted to know about 'Nam too. About you and me. And about how well you adjusted and all that."

"Anything else?" I thrust a new napkin at him.

"Yeah. He wanted to know if you had gotten mixed up in any shit back there." He must have read the puzzled look on my face. "You know. Drugs and shit. Or if you got tight with any of the locals."

"To see if I was involved in any rackets now?"

"Yeah, I suppose so. I didn't tell him anything, Bill."

"There's nothing to tell, Jamie."

"I know that."

"The narcotics would explain why it was Stenson that came. That's his usual beat."

"So, why are they pushing the 'Nam shit if there's nothin' there?"

"They've gotten ahold of some of Courney's records, and they're groping, Jamie. They need to fill in the other half of the card. They've got opportunity...."

"Not to mention a weapon."

"For only one of the killings. But they're looking for motive, at least for the second one. They probably hope that can tie them together afterwards."

Jamie drained his beer, jumped up and trotted over to the refrigerator. He jerked the door open and extracted another beer in one clean movement, like he was gutting a deer.

"I thought you were sticking to one today."

He ignored my comment. "So you think they're tied together?"

"I'm pretty certain of it. Hell, Jamieson's all but admitted it. And there's a witness that thinks so, too. There's just too many Vietnamese around for them not to be." I filled Krug in on my experiences back east. "And Sully has pinpointed the victim's work in intel as an agent handler for networks in the north. I think that's how the Vietnamese back here are involved. I'm just not sure why. But I'll bet he knew them somehow back during the war."

"You think they killed him?"

I shrugged.

"Why?"

"Something must have happened. But it's so hard firgurin' out what with no access to the records."

"So why are you up to your knees in this shit?"

"His wife hired me. And her sister followed up."

"Why?"

"Good question. The widow claimed she wanted him tailed because she suspected he was having an affair. But she knew our paths had crossed, according to the sister. When we were in the 25th. And he may not have acted like it, but those women in his life were afraid for him."

"Afraid of what?"

"They can't, or won't, say."

"Anything else?"

"Sully thinks I may have come across whatever it was when I was in Saigon. Or there's a possibility that it could have happened during a time in between his life as a grunt and his tour in intel."

"But you don't remember?"

"No, Jamie, I don't."

Krug settled back into his chair, his fingers squeezing the aluminum can while he poured what looked like a third of its contents down his throat. The chair cushion squealed like it wanted us to change the topic of conversation.

"I was hoping you could help me fill in some of the gaps, Jamie. What happened to him after he left our division and turned up in Saigon? You're the encyclopedia. You're the one with the contacts."

"What about after the war? What did he do before he died?"

"He worked for one of those firms over on the Tollroad, United Americo Technologies. They claim they hired him from the Pentagon, where he worked in procurement."

"So?"

"But Sully couldn't find any reference to him. He doesn't think the guy ever worked there at all."

"And nobody's seen his records?"

"Some. But Sully ran into a wall there as well. Everything else turns into a dead end, Jamie. It's all been buried. But I think he stayed in some kind of intel work after the war. I mean, the answer could be buried there, too."

Jamie stood, kicking the chair backwards. It teetered for a second, then fell to the linoleum with a bang. He paced back and forth for about a minute, drained his beer can, crushed the thin aluminum in his right hand, then tossed the remnants toward a waste basket next to the refrigerator. He leaned against the sink with his back to the window. I could see the metal wiring of his neighbor's fence extending from each shoulder like a giant web of silver. The grass outside looked almost yellow in the afternoon sun.

"Shit, man." His lips curled into a sly grin. Deep blue eyes peered out from beneath stringy, dirty blond hair. He shook the grin from his face.

"What?" I edged forward in my seat.

"You sure you did everything you could?"

"I've got nothin' else, Jamie. If you can think of any more, tell me." I stood and started to work my way out from behind the table.

"Maybe you let some things slip. Have you checked all of Courney's records on your own?"

I kept my eyes on Jamie as I inched my way out and away from the wall. The bag of potato chips lay on the table, and I grabbed a handful. "Like what?"

"What about the Military Locator Service at the VA?"

"He wasn't on active duty anymore."

"Not even in the reserves?"

I shook my head. "Nope. I got that much in the first week from a quick and dirty background check when I started to tail him. I was going to file an FOI, but I thought Sully would be quicker and get more." I found myself pacing the kitchen. I paused, chewing the chips.

Jamie stepped away from the sink and picked up a napkin. He walked back toward the sink, wiping the grease and salt from the chips off his fingertips. "I gotta take a pee. The beers went right through me. Anything else? Heard anything more from the anonymous caller?"

"There's been another call and an anonymous note. My guess is he was the one behind the burglary."

"You still don't recognize him?"

I shook my head. "Not quite. The voice varies, but there is something about the tone. And he talked about a payback. That points to Sully's hunch, but I still don't see where Courney fits in. It's one of the reasons I'm turning to you. Get me some more from that time, Jamie, and maybe things will fall into place."

Jamie's eyebrows rose. "I'll bet there's money involved. Lots of it."

"People don't always kill for money, Jamie. We didn't."

"Usually they do. It was different for us. We had to."

I exhaled slow and easy to ease my heartbeat. "I wish it were that easy."

Jamie marched past the refrigerator, through the foyer and headed upstairs. I followed and aimed for the front door.

Jamie's footsteps halted, and his voice beckoned from the stairway. "Bill, I've known you since 'Nam. You were the wiseguy fuckup and green ass that rolled into the bush six weeks after I did. And I could see from day one that I was going to have to look after you...." He paused, settling himself on the top step. "...Or you were going to get your ass blown off quick time."

I halted at the foot of the stairs. "And you were right, Jamie. You did save my ass. On several occasions." I drank what tasted like warm swill from the metal can. "I need your help again. And it has to do with 'Nam."

No answer. My friend just shook his head, almost as though he had heard it all before.

"The victim is turning out to be a real mystery man with a sketchy history through the 80's as well. He lived overseas for long stretches, and with a diplomatic passport, which implies he was working for the government."

"Sounds like fun."

"Well, it isn't. I'm wondering if he got involved in something during that period that's tied into this killing as well. Or maybe something resurfaced. If there is anything tying Courney's tour in Vietnam to the events of the past week, we have to find it before the police do. And before my friend shows his face again. I need to get ahead of the curve, Jamie."

Jamie's eyes did not move from mine. I felt myself starting to sweat. Jamie did not have air conditioning, and the small fans oscillating in the kitchen and living room did no more than remind me of cooler air somewhere else in the world.

"What do you think it might be?"

I shrugged. "Almost anything. Gun-running, embezzlement...."

"Drugs."

I nodded. "Narcotics trafficking. Courney appears to have had a habit."

"I can't help you much there. I'll stick with the 'Nam shit and see where it leads."

Jamie crumpled the napkin into a tight ball, which his fist squeezed over and over.

"Describe this guy for me."

Stroking my chin, I struggled to remember Steve Courney with his head intact. "I'd say about six feet tall, with deep blonde hair. He had the kind of baby blues and square jaw that set a woman off. Kind of like Kirk Douglas."

"You mean Spartacus?"

"Same guy, but without the sandals. Anyway, I'd place his weight at about 175, 180."

"I don't know, Bill. That description would fit an awful lot of guys in our unit. Except maybe for the good looks."

"Yeah. I'm sorry, Jamie. It isn't much to go on. But I never had a photograph. Didn't need one."

"I'll make some calls. Try to rack my own memory."

"Thanks, Jamie. And be careful, okay?"

"Why? Is there somethin' you're not telling me, Billy-boy?"

"Not that I know of. But then, there's still something out there, still some unmarked snipers."

"And one of 'em blew away that young woman a couple of days ago?"

I swallowed. "Yeah, it seems so."

"I'll see what I can do." He paused, his teeth working the lower lip. I could tell there was something he wanted to ask.

"What is it, Jamie?"

"Have you been thinking about that woman again?"

"Which one?"

"The one from the hilltop that night near the old plantation."

"I always think of her, Jamie. Just about every night."

"Has it been botherin' you from this case?"

"How so?"

He shrugged, his thumbs hooked into his back pants pockets. "I dunno know. Screwin' up your judgment, maybe. It shouldn't, you know."

I glanced out the front door, then back at my comrade from those days of hell. "I know. It might be, though. Shit, Jamie, it's hard to tell."

"She didn't belong there. It wasn't your fault, Bill."

"I'm not so sure, Jamie. I guess I'll never be sure."

"Just ask yourself why she was there."

"I always figured she was one of the fun girls, or selling stuff. They were always around. You know that."

He nodded. "Uh-huh. And I also know they always got the hell outta Dodge whenever anything was gonna happen. Those people had better intel than anyone else out there."

"So what are you saying, Jamie?"

"Maybe she was workin' for them. Maybe she got what she deserved."

"I doubt I'll ever know." I turned in the direction of the door, then glanced back over my shoulder toward the stairs. "Thanks anyway, Jamie. I'll be in touch."

I flicked him another smile and a wink. Jamie stood motionless at the top of the stairs. He did not smile back.

Outside at the curb, I opened the Volvo door and slid in behind the wheel. But I didn't start the engine right away. Instead, I sat there under the shade of the oak thinking about Steve Courney and the voice on the telephone, sweat still building along my forehead and under my chin.

A mosquito buzzed against the windshield inside the car. I lashed out and crushed the spiny frame in the corner, where the glass drops into the dashboard just above the radio speaker. The image of a dead man in a parking lot minus half his head returned, flies collecting around the mottled mass of brown tissue and red pools stagnant in the dirt. Then the body wore black pajamas, and the feet clung to sandals and grime. The voice from the telephone laughed in a staccato burst of accusation.

Jamie's lawnmower coughed twice, then settled into the low, muffled roar.

A Ford Explorer the color of melted vanilla ice cream roared past. That alone wasn't too unusual. But the Oriental driver behind the wheel got me thinking. I fired the engine and let the Volvo creep away from the curb, then sped down the road in the direction of the Explorer. But it lost me before we reached Aurora. I headed for home, carrying with me the feeling that the few certainties I had returned to in the land of my childhood were fast escaping as the wider world closed in upon me.

# Chapter 18

Driving back from Oswego, I remembered I still needed to call Paul Justin to see what he had learned of my client's movements. I swung by his house in the Moser Highlands development, on what had once been the southern edge of town. It was near the middle now. Justin's wife told me he was out on an errand, and that he'd call as soon as he returned. I steered the Volvo for home.

Climbing the back stairs of my apartment, I heard the telephone ringing on the other side of the door. I figured Justin had finished his shopping. I leaped up the stairs two steps at a time, then struggled to insert the key in the lock. Occasionally, I managed to turn the key and handle simultaneously and swing the door wide and burst into the room, all in one smooth motion. But not today.

When I finally managed to break in, my feet tripped over a small package somebody had set against the door. It tumbled into the kitchen, where I kicked it about five yards further. By this time, however, the ringing had stopped. After flipping on the light switch, I stomped over to the recorder. I pushed the rewind button, waited for the squeal to cease, then replayed the message.

"Habermann! Sorry I missed you. I've been trying to get you all day. Give me a call as soon as you can."

I could almost hear Justin panting through the tape. I flipped on the air conditioner, then dialed his number at home.

"So, what's the big deal? Karen didn't look that excited when I was over there."

"Most women don't, not when you're around. I finally connected on your late friend."

"Courney?"

"How many other dead clients do you have?"

"Actually, he was never my client. But let's skip the technicalities. What did you find out?" I settled into my swivel chair and leaned back.

Justin let a deep sigh escape, like he was about to impart some very profound revelation. He often did this. It probably stemmed from his days as a philosophy major over at Lake Forest College. It was one of the reasons I chose not to open an agency with him.

"Mister Stephen Courney was never in procurement."

"How do you know?" I did not let on that I already knew. Confirmation is always welcome.

"I checked with some of my sources out along our very own Research and Development Corridor." Justin hurrumphed on the other end. It sounded like he was trying to clear his nasal passages.

"Which ones?"

"The usual. AT&T, Northern Illinois Gas, and...."

He paused. I did not enjoy the suspense. "Yeah?"

"...United Americo Technologies."

"Who do you know there?"

"The deputy head of security. And he knew Mister Courney very well."

"How so?"

"Courney was his boss."

I rocked the chair back and forth. "So, that's what he was up to."

"Not all that surprising, when you think about it. I mean, that company does a lot of work for the Pentagon, and God knows who else. So they would need a security department to check on the people, protect access to their projects. All that crap Washington types worry about."

"How large was the security department?"

"The guy didn't say, and I didn't want to push it. I'd say about four or five for a place that size."

"What were Courney's qualifications for that sort of work?"

"The guy wouldn't say. Apparently, the word was out not to dig too deeply into Courney's background."

"Interesting. Do you think he was legit?"

"My source claims he ran a pretty good shop. Very effective. In fact, I heard good things about Americo's security elsewhere."

"Where was that?"

"Out along the Corridor."

Justin hesitated again. The squeaking from my chair continued.

"What aren't you telling me, Paul?"

"Well, people also thought he ran too tight a shop at times. I got the impression the guy could be a real prick."

"Do you think he made some enemies?"

"Definitely. This fellow couldn't name anyone in particular, but I got the impression that Courney was not well liked. Respected maybe, but not about to win any popularity contests."

"Anything in particular?"

"They say he liked to dig real deep into other people's backgrounds. Deeper than necessary. And rumor had it that he collected files of his own, which he kept up to date. That, and the fact that he was so tight-lipped about his own past, pissed a lot of people off."

"How long had he been working there?"

"He started in '91. Came straight from Washington."

"I wonder how he connected himself with Americo."

"That's another interesting tidbit I found."

"And?"

"It was his sister-in-law who recommended him for the job. She even brought him out for the interview."

Both feet slammed into the hard wooden floor, and my thighs bumped against the edge of the desk when I stood up. The blue and gold Notre Dame coffee mug I use for assorted junk tipped over, pencils and pens scattering across the desktop. Several rolled onto the floor.

"His sister-in-law?"

"That's right."

"Deborah Krueger?"

"Unless he had more than one." More hesitation. "Is that your client, Bill?"

Paul's last question whistled by my ears on its way out the door and over the crowd filing through the archways of Saints Peter and Paul. The coming of night had softened the sunlight with a light coating of dusk. A few hardy souls lingered on the concrete steps in front of the church. One young couple stood next to the cornerstone, set when the original church was rebuilt in 1925, three years after it burned down. The really smart parishioners, though, made a line for their cars and the air conditioning. They were the people with a purpose and a goal. Like my client, apparently.

"What did you find out from your tail on the sister-in-law?"

"Not much, guy. Although she does like to spend an occasional afternoon in the city."

"Whereabouts, and how often?"

"She drove in twice while I watched. Once she stopped at the Art Institute, and another time she took the El south."

"How far?"

"She got off at Archer and caught a cab to Cicero. I think she's havin' an affair. I don't know if that's what you're after at this point, though. It's seems to me, Bill, that you've got more pressing business."

"Why do say an affair? Did she meet someone?"

"Yeah. Same guy both times. Tall, heavy shoulders, and deep black hair. Looks like she goes for the tall, dark and muscular types. Which leaves you out, of course."

"Did you get close enough to pick up any conversation?"

"Not really. I almost lost her in Cicero and had to race just to keep up. But at the Institute I was able to stroll past once. I didn't want to risk it twice. I'll tell you, though. If they are having an affair, their conversation is not very romantic. Weird even."

"Why is that?"

"I heard him say something about Saigon, and she just kept shaking her head."

I jumped out of my chair and paced the width of the living room. The spiral cord tugged the telephone from one side of the desk to the other.

"Anything else?"

"Afraid not."

"Thanks, Paul. What do I owe you?"

"Forget it, Bill. Consider it a professional courtesy."

"Bullshit. I'll send something over in the mail. How much time did you spend?"

"Save it for the policeman's auxiliary league. I hear you're in the shitcan down at the department. Hardy's supposedly been steamier than the ozone in this bloody heat wave."

"You heard right. This information helps, though. It helps a lot."

I hung up, then noticed that the message light was still blinking. I rewound the tape, and the deep-set voice of Jack Davis, the assistant personnel manager at United Americo Technologies, broke from the speaker.

"Uh, this is Jack Davis. I hope you remember me, Mister Habermann. Please call me at my office. There is something we need to discuss."

That was it. Very crisp and all business. I like that. And I liked it that Davis wanted to talk. I would try to run him down at home, if he wasn't in the office this weekend.

After cradling the receiver, I remembered the obstacle at my back door. Hustling to the kitchen, I found a packet about half the size of a shoe box, wrapped in plain brown paper. No name, no address.

I scooped the box off the floor and noticed another plain white envelope. This one was square, however, and the back flap held an embossed Hallmark seal. I carried both to my desk, where I sat down with the package in my lap. I let the box rest while I tore open the envelope. Inside sat another plain index card, although this one was tan. Block letters cut from a magazine spelled out a clear and simple message. "Mister Courney got what he deserved for betraying honorable and decent people. Leave us alone. You have something to lose also."

And that was it. No signature. No return address or postmark. No penmanship. Not a damn thing.

I set the card and envelope on the desk and picked up the package. It had the heft and weight of a thick paperback. Something by Tom Clancy, or perhaps another, more profound writer. Like John Fowles. No sound and no movement erupted when I shook it. Definitely not Clancy. The wrapping slid off easily in my hands and tumbled to the floor. The lid followed.

Bundled inside the pages of yesterday's *Tribune* Sports section sat $5000 in neat stacks of $50 and $20 bills. Taped to the top of one pile was a note in the neat, rounded penmanship of a feminine hand. It said, "Your next deposit. No receipt necessary."

The handwriting resembled that on the cheque from Deborah Krueger.

I glanced at my answering machine, where a flashing beacon indicated another message awaited. I hadn't noticed it in my rush to unwrap the mysterious gift. I punched the button, and Miss Krueger spoke to me in the cool dulcet tones of erotic mystery and longing.

"Oh, Bill. I'm so sorry you're not home. I so wanted to talk to you," she sighed. "And we do need to talk. It's about the other night. Please get in touch with me. If it has to wait until Monday, you can come to my office around quitting time. Perhaps we can have dinner. You can add it to my bill. But please call."

It was a voice that beckoned. A siren call worthy of the Lorelei. I tucked the package into the bottom desk drawer and wondered what it would be like to idle my time away with a woman like that on a Caribbean island. And I wondered if the stranger with the notes might try to contact me there. Maybe he or she'd sign one of them, eventually. Before he or she did, though, I was going to have to figure out why the author held such a low opinion of Steve Courney. And why he or she wanted to threaten me. Was it because I was linked to the Courneys? When I had only been doing my job? That's all I had ever been doing. When and where had I crossed a line that followed me back home?

# Chapter 20

After that brief, dreamy moment, I trotted back to my bedroom, retrieved Deborah Krueger's private number, and dialed her home. No answer, just that same recording from the other night. I reheated some pizza for dinner before trying her number again. Sweat moistened my palms. After five rings that damn recording came on again.

I slammed down the receiver, burst for the back door and bolted down the stairs two steps at a time. I climbed into the Volvo and hurled the car out of the alley and onto Benton Avenue. Deborah Krueger's house was fifteen, maybe twenty minutes away. After ringing the bell and pounding on the doorbell for about five minutes, I decided she was not home. Not this Sunday night. Church, maybe? Pretty unlikely.

Downtown, Naperville's streets were filled with pedestrians on their way home from the day's shopping excursions. Many held plastic cups with soft drinks. A hardy few even carried cups from Starbuck's. Some were winding their way to Riverwalk Park, the site of an evening concert of melodies from Johann Strauss.

I drove to the luxury condos Lisa Courney still called home and parked near the main gate, just across from the rental office. I hopped out of the car, trotted over to her building and rang the bell.

When no one answered, I paced the sidewalk in front. I was not having much luck getting anyone to come to their door that evening. About halfway to my car, I whirled in frustration and hustled to the side of the building by the Park. I counted over and up until I found the green patio furniture, then backed onto the lawn to get a clear line of sight to the apartment. Nothing. No movement, no sign of life. But it was too early to give up.

I jogged back to the Volvo, jumped in, and rammed the key into the ignition. I gunned the engine, and the angry pitch of squealing rubber drew startled looks from passers-by. I bolted from the lot, out onto Aurora Avenue.

I glanced at my watch. Seven forty-five. The streets surrounding the Park were packed with Naperville's aspiring music fans, and parking was as rare as good taste in Las Vegas. I had to leave the Volvo in the parking lot at the high school.

I tucked a paperback into the back pocket of my blue jeans and a set of opera glasses into the chest pocket of my madras shirt. Then I marched back down

Webster Avenue, up Aurora, and down Eagle. From there I could enter through the back entrance to the park, just like any other concert-goer. The location also put me in a good position to observe the Courneys' apartment.

Strolling over toward the condos, I set my post at the edge of the parking lot, about ten feet into the Park, and sprawled on the grass. Then my stomach decided that a warmed-over slice of pepperoni pizza was not going to cut it for dinner. I strolled to a sausage stand down by the pond, right across from the McDonald's and somewhere near midpoint in the Park. Jamieson's suggestion for dinner the other night had put my mind on bratwurst, so I scarfed down two of the golden brown sausages in a hot German mustard and grabbed a Coke for the walk back to my observation post.

A handful of clouds swam in the dusk, harbingers, I hoped, of a shift in the weather. The air was stale with humidity, and the scent of mowed grass hung like a blanket over the lawn.

I plopped down and pulled a worn copy of Eric Ambler out of my back pocket. I figured I had about another hour of light to read by, if Lisa Courney failed to return home. One of Ambler's English journalists was experiencing a rough time in Eastern Europe between the wars, and I wanted to see how it turned out for the poor guy. Besides, I was always looking for pointers.

I never got the chance. Around eight fifteen, a light in her apartment flickered. A minute later, Lisa emerged onto her porch, set a candle on the metal table, and wheeled one of the lawn chairs around to face the Park. Then, her sister passed through the doorway, took another chair, and placed it beside Lisa's.

The two women sat alone for less than five minutes. A tall, thin man appeared, bearing what looked like a bottle of wine. White I guessed. Probably expensive. It took me a while, about fifteen minutes, to place the guy through my opera glasses. I couldn't be sure from that distance, and the evening's fading light kept pulling shadows across the image at the far end of my lens, but he looked an awful lot like Mr. Jack Davis.

The music erupted in the night air, like it had been waiting for his arrival. It was a waltz, of course. Easy on the ears of the general listening public. I liked it, too. The guest on the Courney's balcony sat down and let his gaze roam across the horizon. I was sure of it now. He had the same mannerisms, the same profile as the Assistant Director for Personnel at United Americo Technologies.

I rolled over on my back and propped the paperback on my chest. What the hell was that prick doing with those two women? Jack Davis had clearly been lying to me about Steve Courney's work at Americo. But why? Was he hitting on the new widow and figured me for the competition? Perhaps. But then why lie about her husband's work? Professional security? Perhaps. But this involved a murder investigation, and deceiving the police-or even a private detective-could have serious consequences. Maybe the guy was hitting on Deborah Krueger. But even then, why lie to me? And why had he called me back? Remorse? He didn't look very sorry.

I rolled over again and studied Davis through the opera glasses. By now he was pacing the length and width of the patio, wine glass in hand, surveying the crowd below. He looked about as interested in Strauss as somebody on his way to a Rolling Stones concert. His discomfort and impatience shone through on this summer night with the clarity of a full moon. No, romance was not on his mind. From where I was sitting, it looked more like anxiety.

Then he disappeared inside. I waited, glasses poised between intermittent glances in the direction of the music. After a minute or two, he did not reappear. After five, he was still gone. Either he was taking one hell of a leak, or he had left.

I lowered the spyglass in disappointment, only to see Jack Davis marching across the parking lot in my direction. I jerked the glasses down and jammed them into my pocket. Eric Ambler fell open on the lawn, and I pretended to read. The coke tipped over, spilling its half cup of soda onto the grass. Davis's footsteps passed not more than twenty feet from me and continued through the grass in the direction of the Park exit, near Eagle Avenue.

I crawled as lazily as I could into a standing position, stretched my arms in a poor imitation of a yawn, and frowned with disapproval at the music. What's with all this Viennese stuff we have to hear every summer? I pretended to ask myself. You'd think we could have some Brahms or Rachmaninoff once in a while. Maybe even some Wagner. Tucking my book away, I ambled off in the direction of Jack Davis's fading outline.

He was nowhere in sight, so I walked toward the high school parking lot to retrieve the Volvo. Three rows closer to the school and about a dozen cars down, I spotted my quarry. If he had been interested in romancing the Courney-Krueger sisters, the guy had struck out. From this distance I had a pretty good look at his face, and he had the visage of a man who had just been told he would never win the lottery. I did not pity him. I didn't feel like gloating, either.

His head ducked, then dodged into the side of a Pontiac Grand Am the color of dust. That explained my periodic tail. After about a minute, the Pontiac backed slowly out of a tight fit, its driver strapped properly into the front seat. Davis

ANGEL IN BLACK

straightened the car and bumped his way through the pitted lot of packed, dry dirt. I focused on his taillights through the dust swirls covering his trail and crept along in his wake.

He turned right on Aurora Avenue, then headed into town, where he swung left at Washington Street. Davis followed the main drag through the middle of town at the mandated speed of thirty-five miles an hour, just like the good citizen I assumed he had been all his life. He stopped for every red light, never trying to push his luck with a yellow one, which made my job of tailing him so much easier. I was almost grateful.

At Ogden he headed east, and his speed increased to forty. By now, the Volvo could have followed him all by itself. Once on the Tollroad, Davis opened his Pontiac up to a brisk fifty-five, hugging the right lane as though it ran along the edge of a cliff. When he reached Americo, Davis pulled into the parking lot, just like any ordinary assistant director of personnel. But it was Sunday night.

I continued past the Americo building, holding my speed to about fifteen miles an hour, my eyes spending most of that time peering through the rear view mirror. When Americo slipped out of sight, I pulled the Volvo off the road and into the lot at a Red Lion Motel. The clock hovering on a sign said nine-twelve. The motor stilled, and we sat for exactly four minutes in the dark.

When I was sure no one was observing, I restarted the engine and headed through the exit with my lights still off like a sleek shadow from some radio play. I eased the Volvo back along the frontage road the way I had come, sliding over to the curb in front of the building next to Americo. A sign planted among a garden of hibiscus and bluebells said Columbia Industrial. I had never heard of them, but I cursed their architect. The panels of green glass were the worst possible place for a stake out, because the reflections allowed someone on the lookout to check for my reflection without exposing his own position, but it was the only spot that gave me vantage from the road of Americo's building and its parking lot at the back. It also gave me a clear line of sight of Davis's corner office. A steady glow of yellow light told me he was still there.

I prayed that Jack Davis was not an overly cautious man. His driving suggested he was, but judging by the easy trail he had left for me, the man did not possess a suspicious gland in his overstuffed body. Either that, or he was extremely preoccupied. He might as well have left a trail of rye and pumpernickel.

The light in his third floor office burned for over forty minutes. Five minutes after the window panes went dark, Davis swept from the building's entrance at a light trot. He scrambled toward his car, which screeched out of the lot at about fifty miles an hour.

I thrust the Volvo forward, lights still off. When I saw the Pontiac pulling onto the Tollroad, I swerved to follow. All I caught was a fading glimpse of twin taillights dodging in and out of traffic at a distance of half a mile, then a mile, then more. I fed the engine to keep pace, but the traffic was too heavy. A lumbering truck was making a home for itself in the middle lane, so I swung to the far left just in time to see the red specks of light from the Grand Am barrel onto the exit ramp for Route 294 going south.

Something, or someone, had spooked a model of suburban propriety and driving school etiquette into a Richard Petty imitation. I swung wildly to the right, cutting off the truck and a light green Toyota Tercel in the right lane. But I was able to catch the end of the exit.

I barreled onto 294, then glanced at the gas gauge. Volvos can be hell on mileage. I figured Davis had better reach his destination quickly, or I'd be trying to keep up as a hitchhiker.

Then again, maybe he was low as well. The Grand Am didn't lose a cycle as it caromed up the ramp and into the Hinsdale oasis over blacktop patched with strips of tar like scars from a bad operation. I pulled off after the Pontiac and crawled toward the fuel tanks.

The Grand Am stood nearly alone in the middle of the parking lot, forlorn and neglected, like its owner on Lisa Courney's balcony. Apparently gas was not the issue. I stopped next to the pump for some eighty-nine octane and kept one eye on the register and the other on Davis's car. After dropping twenty bucks on the attendant, I steered the Volvo toward mid-lot and parked three rows behind the Pontiac. The exterior was covered with dust and soot dried to a pale brown with speckled bird shit on the hood. The undercarriage was flecked with tar. The interior behind locked doors was immaculate, though. It was also empty. I decided to explore the shops and restaurants inside.

As I neared the curb, a white Explorer barreled by, scattering pedestrians in its wake. I leaped to safer ground, then wheeled around to get a look at the driver and maybe make the tags. The pale metal behemoth flashed down the north-bound entrance ramp. A bush of dark hair hung low over the wheel. Dry shrubs along the metal railing swayed in complaint before the Ford disappeared on the highway. I had gotten next to nothing.

# ANGEL IN BLACK

I ran into the building, jogging past postcard stands and a Baskin-Robbins on the right and a bank of phone booths on the left. The linoleum under my feet was a blend of brown and beige. It was hard to tell where the floor left off and the dirt began. Davis was nowhere in sight. Just to be sure, I stopped at the toilet. Stench worse than anything you'll normally find in a public toilet told me right away what had happened.

The door to Davis's stall swung open with a gentle shove from my elbow. He sat upright and fully-clothed in the middle stall, shoulders pinned back against the wall. His posture was perfect. His clothes were a mess, though, with a carpet of red running along his chest and belly. A pool of blood had settled in his mouth, the rim of thick liquid topping the edges of his teeth. And the back of his skull was missing, much of it scattered like squashed berries across the tiles at his back. A pistol lay at his feet, a neat little Glock that sparkled like polished silverware.

I had seen worse in Vietnam. Smelled worse, too. But I never did get used to it. I forced myself to tiptoe closer to see if I could spot anything on Davis that would explain his activities tonight. The tip of a white index card peeked over the edge of his shirt pocket, and I pulled it free. The same kind of magazine had apparently contributed the same words to a note matching the one I had received. On it someone had written the name of the oasis and figures with a dollar sign. The number was two hundred fifty thousand. I did not see a quarter of a million dollars lying around, though. I wiped the corner of the card with some toilet paper and slipped it back in his pocket. The I used the toilet paper to push the door of the stall shut.

A stranger wandered in, clutched his nose, then ran out. I gulped to hold down a surge of nausea, wheeled to the sink and found a pale, desperate face staring back at me. The vacant eyes of Jack Davis joined a silent chorus of accusation. "Too slow again," they seemed to say. "You're still one step behind."

There was no doubt in my mind that the three deaths were related. Coincidence is not this strong, not when it involves murder. But was the motive behind the killings drugs or money or both? Then again, what had happened in Vietnam to draw all this together, and what role had I played? And Davis, for Chrissakes. Why him? Because he had worked with Courney? Then there were those two sisters, who I was certain knew more than they had told me.

Then everything came rushing back. Images of innocence and guilt, good and evil, twin poles of humanity that I had grown up believing were distinct. All of it raced by in blurred memories and concepts. The discovery of their kinship came to me in Vietnam and had followed me ever since. I wanted to separate the two again, to find where and how to do that, or at least push them far enough apart to make sense of this case. And to do that I had to keep myself from falling in, from being dragged into something that looked like a mix of revenge and greed and convenience. And I had to figure out who from the cast of characters was carrying which goal.

I bunched paper towels in my fist to soak the sweat off my forehead. Then I wiped down the sink and slipped through the double gray doors at the entrance. Out in the lobby, I dialed 911 on a pay phone to report the death.

Outside, I raced to the Volvo and roared out of the lot. I wanted to get as far away as possible, and as quickly as possible. Near the intersection of Ogden and Naperville Boulevard, a Rexall store had a beer sale on. I thought that if I cradled a six-pack of Augsburger or Special Export long enough, I just might figure out what the connection was between Courney's death, the woman at Northern Illinois Gas, and now Jack Davis's killing, and maybe even how Lisa Courney and Deborah Krueger fit into all this. If I figured all that out, I might be able to find out what a way to keep myself out of jail and maybe even alive a while longer.

# Chapter 21

For once since this case began, I did not revisit Vietnam. I tossed and turned most of the night, thinking of Jack Davis over and over again. The poor sap had clearly been playing out of his league, and I had not been able to help. I, too, was confused as hell, but at least I had some idea of the stakes, and of the kind of people involved.

I sat up in bed and stared at the confusing world outside. Night still framed the edges of the window where the drapes did not quite reach. The air conditioner hummed a message of comfort. I remembered shooting even further back into the past, standing in a crooked line, milling about with school friends in the early morning sunlight. A tall, thin nun in a black veil, her face framed in white starch, told Jamieson and me to keep still. One hand emerged from the other sleeve and gripped my upper arm. Then she shook me back and forth. Heads bobbed in our direction, and laughter pealed from somewhere in the crowd of blue uniforms. I couldn't help myself. I laughed back. An open palm followed, and my face burned with anger.

I sat upright again. It seemed like minutes had passed. I rolled free of the bedcovers and strolled through the apartment. Not a sound. Everything was peaceful; the locks were all secure. Streetlights cast broad bands of light across church steps and a deserted playground. In the morning I'd get another gun. Sorry, Sisters. Sometimes you just do what you have to do.

My mind drifted off again, half in sleep and half out. Then I was back in the jungle. The grizzled face of a first sergeant stared hard, stubble sprouting from his chin and cheeks, soot lining the folds of his neck and eyes gleaming with the heat of the Asian sun. I had just pulled latrine duty. Jamie Krug was helping and promised to get me high once we finished. The thought of smoking marijuana with the scent of human waste hanging in our nostrils and death just beyond the perimeter struck me as absurd. I started to laugh, and then Jamie did the same. The laughter lasted for minutes. We couldn't stop, the whole situation was so ridiculous. Then I spilled some of our cargo, and a noncom rushed over. He tore into us with all the abuse and scorn he could muster, his dog tags flapping against the bare, tanned skin. A religious medal bounced off his chest. The glistening silver drew my attention.

"Watch what you're doin', you fuckin' asswipe. Or you shitbirds will draw this job every fucking week. I'll see to that." He thrust a finger at me. "And I'll be watching you especially."

Sunlight radiated from his short blonde hair like the image of a fallen angel. Streaks of white shot from the medal on his chest.

"Fuck him," Jamie says. "He's short anyway. Thinks he's top shit now that he's leaving. Nervous as hell, too." Jamie chuckled again. "And Courney's the guy that sold me the stuff."

I remembered the image in silver. Saint Jude, the patron saint of lost causes. It seemed to fit. Just fifty-one weeks to go.

More ringing. My eyes popped open. I kicked off the sheet and fell from the mattress, struggling to reach the damn telephone. Finally, I stood up, trotted to the desk and grabbed the receiver.

"That you, Habermann?"

"Rick? Glad to see we're still on talking terms."

"I'm not interfering, am I? You don't have a girl over there, do you?"

"Not yet. Why? Have they switched you to vice?"

"They just might, if these murders don't get solved. Anyway, I've got a peace offering."

I lowered myself onto the edge of the mattress. "Peace offering? Has Hardy approved?"

"Susan made me do it. She wants you to come over for dinner tonight."

"Sorry to disappoint you, Rick-or Susan, rather-but I thought I'd swing by Wanda Rathko's to see how she's getting along." After last night I wanted to keep Jamieson at a safe distance for a while longer. For his good and mine.

"Good. She seems like a sweet kid."

"I'm worried about her. That jag-off is still out there, and who knows how many more people could wind up dead before it's over."

"We're tryin', guy."

"I hope you boys are providing some sort of protection for her."

"We've got patrolmen swinging by her place now and then."

"That's it?"

"Come on, Bill. You know we haven't got the manpower for anything more."

"It's still not enough." I sighed and rubbed my eyes. "Is your wife's perennial interest in my love life the only reason you called?"

"Don't you mean the lack thereof?"

"Whatever."

About ten seconds of silence followed. "Not really."

"Well?"

"Look, pardner, I shouldn't be telling you this, but I want to give you a heads up."

"What about?"

"The lab work points to the woman at Northern Illinois Gas as being present at Courney's shooting. A hair sample matched one found on his shirt."

"I figured as much. Wanda pointed in that direction as well. Did you get anything out of the car rental?"

"Not much. The name and address were phony. She must have had some false identification. And she prepaid in cash."

"Great. Do you think the stiff's the same one who rented the car out at Budget?"

"It would fit. How about you?"

"I guess so. Were you able to trace the Makharov?"

"No such luck, pardner, but we did get the report on the firearms test on the woman we found."

"Yeah?"

"It matches your weapon. That's the killer."

"Now you just need a shooter for this one too."

"Or a motive. Hardy wants to see you at the department later today, Bill."

I knew it had to come. "I'll try to fit him in."

Another ten seconds of silence. "Don't piss him off, Bill. I mean it. You're in enough trouble already."

"You know, Rick, this is not what I need to have hanging on my mind."

"I told you to stay away, my friend. But you wouldn't listen."

"What is it now?"

"Do you remember your conversation with a certain Jack Davis, the assistant director for something or other at Americo?"

"As a matter of fact, I do. Why?"

"He was found dead last night in an oasis restroom along Route 294."

It was my turn to stay silent.

"Did you hear me, Bill?"

"Yeah, I heard you. That's pretty shitty."

"That usually follows. This one could be a suicide."

"You're not sure?"

"Not yet, but right now we're guessing murder. Someone you know, as a matter of fact."

That made me wonder what else they had.

After a shower and a shave, I dressed in a pair of khaki slacks and a Hawaiian shirt with big green and blue flowers on a yellow background. It seemed to suit the weather. I tried to raise Deborah Krueger on the phone, but gave up after about a dozen rings. Lisa Courney, however, said that she'd probably be home for a while longer, but once her visitors left she had some errands to run.

I walked over to the parish house, where Father Kramer answered the bell. The thought of so much money in the house after last night's adventure made me nervous, but I didn't want to leave it with a bank. Not yet, anyway. The police had enough incriminating material to hang around my neck already.

The good father was skeptical at first, or perhaps just hard of hearing. He had to be pushing eighty. He had been around long enough to chase Jamieson and me across the playground one day when Rick stroked one of my hanging curve balls through a third grade window at recess. We weren't even supposed to have hard balls at school. I didn't tell him what was in the box. I just mumbled something about personal stuff and a breakin. I promised to retrieve it at the first opportunity and once I had my place safe again.

Twenty minutes later I cruised toward the visitor spaces at Lisa Courney's luxury condominiums. There were no vacancies. I turned to the right and grabbed one of the reserved spaces next to the sloping green lawn of Riverwalk Park. It stood about fifty feet from where I had lain the evening before. I left the back end of the Volvo out just far enough to cover the 636 painted in bright yellow against the edge of the black backdrop.

A young couple with what looked to be a real estate agent swung through the entrance to Lisa Courney's wing as I approached. The agent, a woman whom I placed somewhere in her early thirties, had dusty brown hair that fell in a semi-shag to frame bright crystal eyes that laughed with entrepreneurial pleasure. The couple with her wore loose-fitting, casual clothes: light slacks and even lighter shirts, as though they were on their way from brunch to the golf course. We brushed past each other on the sidewalk, and they nodded in acknowledgment.

They looked young enough to be newlyweds, arms entwined in the embrace of new love. No disappointments or betrayals yet. Some people have all the luck.

The door to Lisa Courney's apartment was open about half an inch. It looked like somebody had forgotten to pull it shut. Polite as ever, I knocked.

"Come on in. It's open."

Lisa Courney's voice wavered with expectation. When she saw me, her face settled into disappointment. "Oh, it's you."

There was a monotonous, almost listless air about her that left me wondering if she would always be recovering from her husband's death, or if there had been other tragedies in her life. I wondered if others had wanted to explore those chasms. I wondered what Lisa Courney's response would be to men who tried.

She sat in the corner of her white leather sofa, next to the spot she had occupied the day after the shooting. But this time she had a flute of champagne in her right hand. The left one held a cigarette to her lips, which she waved in the air in a odd-shaped arc when I entered. Her light brown hair was pulled back tight over the scalp and came together in a braided ponytail that ran down the middle of her neck. She was dressed in white cotton slacks and a loose pullover of white and beige geometric designs. The gold necklace was still there.

"Take a seat, Mr. Ex-detective."

Glazed eyes of contempt surveyed my steps from the door to the white leather arm chair facing her. I slid onto the smooth, slippery furniture.

In bright sunlight the room had looked almost antiseptic. But with the sun ducking behind the roving clouds outside, the atmosphere was somber. The environment, crisp with air-conditioned freshness, held the impersonal aura of manufactured sweetness. This one smelled of lilacs competing with cigarette smoke and alcohol. Two plants in gallon-sized pots near the windows had joined those by the fireplace. The plant life and three oil paintings with an array of multicolored splotches provided the only color in the room.

"Ex?"

"That's right." She sipped from bubbles floating in crystal. "I've talked to the police as well. I've also informed my sister."

"That's good to hear. I tried to reach her this morning, as well. What did the lovely Miss Krueger have to say?"

Shifting eyes roamed my face.

"You like her, don't you?" She didn't wait for an answer, which I was not about to give. "Most men do. They think they know her, or can get to. Eventually."

Lisa fingered the gold chain again. She noted the direction of my eyes. "It was a gift from my sister, years ago. I find it consoling right now. It reminds me of the support I have from my family."

"I'm glad to hear it. Your sister has never seemed all that easy to understand. I know she cares for you, though."

"So, you can figure some things out." Her hand dropped the necklace and held the bottle aloft. "Care for any?"

"No thanks."

Thin legs encased in white stirrup pants and bare feet stretched out across the glass top of the coffee table in front of her, then receded closer into her body. The balls of her feet rested on the rounded metal edge of the table. Her arms circled the knees as she leaned into her legs. She still held her cigarette.

"I can figure a lot of things out," I said, peering straight ahead, "but I still wonder why you lied to me, Mrs. Courney, about why you hired me in the first place."

The eyes left mine to form their own arch, like a dance of conscience.

"So, you think I've been hiding something?"

I didn't answer.

"And you accuse me of lying?"

"You know you've lied to me."

"About what?" The cigarette fluttered near her mouth, the smoke providing a hazy mask.

"About your husband's alleged philandering. You knew he wasn't doing anything of the sort. And then there's his past." I paused. "Your past as well. In fact, your behavior has me wondering about your role in this whole affair."

"How dare you." The eyes danced again, retreating behind their copper glaze. "My past?" She waved the cigarette, now a smoldering butt, in my direction. Ashes flew. "There's nothing there that's very interesting."

"I'm not so sure. Where did you live overseas?"

"Oh, that." Lisa Courney straightened her body, letting the feet fall to the floor. She stubbed the cigarette into a half-filled ashtray, picked up a document from the middle of the table, glanced at it, and then tossed it back down.

"We lived in Paris first, then Munich."

"What were you doing there?"

"Steve had a job in the Embassy and Consulate, working with the military."

"And you?"

"Oh, I was just a dependent in Paris." She smiled, but not to me. She motioned with her chin in the direction of the patio doors behind me. "It looks like rain. They're probably wasting the water."

"Excuse me?"

She didn't miss a beat. "Not a bad place to live as a housewife, actually. That is, if you have the money."

"And did you? In Paris?"

"Enough. Your needs aren't that great when you're stationed overseas. The government picks up a lot of your living expenses."

"Did you have any additional costs?"

I heard no answer.

"What about Munich?"

"I found a job there."

"Doing what?"

"Working in the press office."

"What sort of job?"

"I edited summaries of the East European press."

"Did you translate them?"

"Heavens no! Have you ever tried to learn some of those languages?"

"Not really. That sort of thing doesn't come up often in my line of work." I glanced at the document on the table, which appeared to be a contract of some sort. "Was it in Munich that you ran into trouble? Or was it earlier, in Paris even?"

Lisa Courney's body snapped upright. Her head shot in my direction. "What do you know about that?"

"Your sister mentioned it."

Her lips hardened like red scars. White teeth flashed. "Don't you dare drag her into this." She stood and paced in front of the sofa. "Deborah had nothing to do with any of that."

"Deborah hired me, remember? If your sister wasn't involved then, she certainly is now."

"What's with all these questions? Your interest in our past is a little late, don't you think?"

"No, I don't." I tried to lock my eyes onto hers. "You've been lying to me, Mrs. Courney, from the day we met. You've been hiding something in your husband's past, and it's tied to his murder. You and your sister know what it is, and that means you're both in danger."

She waved my words off like some bothersome insect.

"What about your husband's time in Vietnam? Did he get dragged into something there?"

"He was a soldier and a civilian aid administrator. You don't need to know anymore."

"Why not?"

"Because it's not pertinent to the case."

"What did he do after he left the 25th?"

"He worked with the Vietnamese."

"Did he ever mention meeting me there?"

She shrugged, then nodded.

I glanced toward a row of photographs on the table behind the sofa. A duplicate of the one in Deborah Krueger's office stood in the middle, the one with an ex-soldier, his wife and her sister. In this one, though, the sister contemplated the young man with a look that bordered on devotion. Then my eyes fell to the medallion around his neck.

"That's an interesting photo. I didn't know your husband was Catholic."

Lisa Courney looked at the picture. "He wasn't. Why do you say that?"

"The religious medal. It looks like the kind a Catholic would wear."

"Oh, that. It's a Saint Jude's medallion. He got it from a friend in Vietnam. It was a small joke to them."

"A joke?"

"Yes. You're a Catholic, aren't you? I'm sorry, but isn't he the patron saint of lost causes?"

"I believe so."

"That was the joke, you see. It's how they felt about the war. Steve even gave some to the Vietnamese he worked with. I don't know if he told them why."

"That's why you hired me, isn't it? Because my path had crossed your husband's in Vietnam."

"Look," she waved a hand, "it's over now. I told you, you're off this case."

"Humor me."

"Yes, I did. He said something about it once. So I thought you could help us." Her eyes met mine with the same look of contempt I had seen when I first arrived. "I guess I was wrong."

"How was I supposed to help?"

"I thought you could protect him. You had been there. You knew what it was like. You should have done more."

"That's pretty hard when you don't know what the dangers are."

The contempt faded to uncertainty. "But Steve said he remembered you. He said you knew what it was like back there."

"What did he say, exactly?"

"He said you knew the score and that you got along like everyone else." Her eyes rolled as she repeated each phrase.

"That could have meant almost anything. What was he referring to? Try to be more precise."

She shook her head. "It's too late. I...I can't. I'm leaving." She stared for a moment at a distant spot of time. "It's better this way. Better for everyone."

She stood up and held the document aloft, waving it at me. "It doesn't matter anymore. I'm going."

"And that is?"

"It's a contract on this condo." She slapped the table with the papers.

"Are you leaving because of Cavanaugh?"

Her head dodged up and down, then she looked towards the glass doors leading to the balcony. Lisa Courney shook her head, emitting a light laugh. When she spoke again, her voice sounded suddenly somber. "I never should have come back here. I never should have let Steve talk me into this thing. It's been one hell of a homecoming."

"What thing was that, Mrs. Courney?"

Her eyes glazed over again. I wondered how long she had been drinking. The bottle of French champagne stood half empty in the middle of the glass table top. Fading sunlight pranced across the tabletop and up along her body. Her hand waved me away.

"Never mind. I can't talk about it anymore. It's better for all of us if I leave quietly." She looked over at me. The contempt was gone. "Especially for you, now."

"What does that mean?"

"I can't help you anymore. I can't help anyone. I tried to help Steve. I couldn't even do that."

"This isn't just about me or your husband. How well did you know Jack Davis?"

Her eyes darted back and forth in momentary confusion. She brushed at her hair, although not a strand had moved.

*Bill Rapp*

"Not very well." Her eyes flickered. "He's a nice man, but I wish he would leave us alone."

"What has he been doing?"

"Hanging around. Trying to help. Why?"

"He was here recently, wasn't he?"

"I told him to leave us alone. He can't help. It's too much for him."

"You're right. He's dead."

Lisa Courney's hand shot to her mouth. What little color there was drained from her face. "Oh, my God."

Lisa Courney fell into herself, her back collapsing against the cushions. Her shoulders dropped, while the hands found each other in her lap.

"As best I can tell, that makes three deaths, Mrs. Courney. If you don't tell me what he was after, there may be more."

She muttered through quivering lips. "Please go."

I studied the clouds gathering outside. She was right; they probably were wasting the water. And I was wasting my time trying to lead her through this conversation. I stood up.

"You can't run from this forever, you know."

"I'm not running. I'm just leaving this place behind."

"That doesn't mean it will stop for you, or your sister."

"It stopped for me when Steve died."

I thought about that for a moment. I doubted the choice would be hers to make.

"That remains to be seen. Where will you be going?" I asked.

"Maybe I'll go back to Washington. Maybe I'll go someplace else, someplace a person like me can find work and a future."

"What sort of a person are you, Mrs. Courney?"

"Someone with moderate ambitions and a modest past. And someone who's always wanted the right man."

"And never found him?"

She stood up, blew out her chest as she collected herself. The collar of her sweater fell to the edge of her shoulder, exposing the white strap of her bra. She pointed to the door. "Good-bye, Mister Habermann."

I walked past her, close enough to feel her breath across my face like an icy veil. She stood unsteadily and backed several inches away from me. Her legs bumped the edge of the sofa, and she fell back into her seat.

When I reached the door I turned. "It wasn't this place."

She looked up. "What wasn't?"

"What happened to you and your husband. Coming back here made no difference. It would have happened anywhere."

She studied my face as though she was aware of my presence in her apartment for the first time. Her eyes focused, if only for a moment.

"But it happened here," she replied. A glint of suspicion flashed as she squinted, struggling to pull my form from the blaze of sunlight in the room. "What do you know? Steve said you knew. But you don't. You don't know anything."

"I know a lot more than when I started."

Thin streams of tears ran down her cheeks before they disappeared along the ridge of her chin. I made sure the lock clicked shut when I closed the door behind me.

Downstairs, I halted abruptly when I nearly collided with a tall, husky character in pleated gabardine slacks and a polo shirt of black silk. He was dressed like someone who could buy and sell the realtor and young couple I had seen earlier.

"Oh, excuse me," I mumbled.

Mr. Black Shirt did not say a word. Instead, he flipped an irritated smile in my direction, like he was shedding an inconvenience. His heels clicked along the marble floor inside, metallic taps bouncing off the white wainscoting that covered the lower half of the walls.

When I got to the Volvo I bent low in the car and peered through the back windshield. I counted first up, and then over until I was pretty sure I had found Lisa Courney's apartment. After about five minutes, Mr. Black Shirt appeared, his right hand holding the half-full bottle of champagne. With an air of calm deliberation and firm purpose, he walked to the railing, tipped the bottle upside down, and poured what was left of the fine, golden nectar onto the empty blacktop below.

Silhouetted against the morning sun, something else struck me about this figure. Now I wanted to hear his voice. I jerked the keys out of the ignition and hopped back onto the pavement.

That's when Detective Stenson rode up in his rusty red Plymouth Fury, trailing heat and dust and authority.

"Let's go, Habermann. Hardy wants you at the station. Now."

I waved him off. "In a minute. I want to check on something."

Stenson threw his transmission into park, then jumped from the car. He barreled around the back end like he had just found Lee Harvey Oswald. His hand fumbled at his side for his gun.

"Now, Goddammit! I had to chase all over town to find you. You're late already. A fuckin' Kraut like you should know to be punctual."

I held up my hands. "Easy, Columbo. I'll go peacefully."

The gun stayed in its holster

I strolled to his car and climbed in on the passenger side. I figured I'd check on Lisa Courney's guest later. And get a weapon, too.

# Chapter 22

We rode in absolute silence to the Naperville Police Department. I had no idea how far they would press me this time, or how much they had on me. I didn't even know how far I could count on my friendship with Jamieson.

It was the longest mile I'd ever traveled—aside from some of those I crept through in Vietnam, stalking an unseen enemy. The more I thought about it, the more the similarities emerged: a familiar, yet foreign environment that seemed to change by the day, and the anxiety and uncertainty that comes with the unknown. Even the heat was there, although not quite so heavy. And I didn't have to worry about booby traps or ambushes. At least not any with shrapnel or live fire-not yet, anyway.

The interrogation room had not changed since my visit the night of Courney's shooting. It was a little larger than a principal's office. There were no windows. After the first hour, the four walls of concrete block and bright yellow paint narrowed even further to the psychological space of a phone booth. I sat directly across from the one-way mirror on a metal folding chair. The overhead light bathed the entire room with an unsympathetic glare.

We had a full house: Hardy, Stenson, Jamieson, and Mal Higgins, a deputy prosecutor for the county. And me, of course.

I stuck my index finger in the direction of the ceiling. "Isn't there supposed to be a hot light shining directly in my face?" I asked.

"This is the twenty-first century, Habermann," Stenson explained.

"And besides, we wouldn't want to make you too uncomfortable," Hardy added, "or forgetful. We've got a lot to discuss still." His smile was not comforting.

"Then how about turning the air conditioning up?"

Rick Jamieson leaned against the wall by the door, his eyes exploring the linoleum floor of gray and blue flecks. Higgins had positioned himself to my right, and Hardy sat opposite me, his elbows pressing against the wooden table top. His fingers rolled back and forth, digging furrows against the grain. Stenson sat on the edge of the table to my left. The last two had their white shirt sleeves rolled up at the elbow. They wore no ties, however. We were all here for the duration, apparently. Their identical slacks of charcoal gray fell nearly to their black Oxfords. No cuffs, though. No class. A strip of white skin and sparse leg hair peeked at me over the rim of Stenson's navy blue socks, whose elastic rims had lost their strength. Higgins, on the other hand, wore his ambition in a blue pinstripe suit and a solid red power tie with little interlocking silver squares. The jacket was draped over the back of his chair, and his shirtsleeves still extended to his wrists.

Stenson was working his way through a pack of Winstons. The smoke combined with the scent of human sweat and worn clothes to give the air the stale quality of a mausoleum. I wondered if it was intentional.

My hosts would leave periodically, either individually or in pairs. I shifted my weight from one buttock to the other. Sometimes for amusement, but usually to relieve the pain.

"We're still waiting for an explanation of where you were last night. We can tie you to the Davis murder any number of ways."

"Oh, Christ. This should be entertaining. I'd like to hear them. Especially anything involving a motive." I glanced about the room. "Oh, by the way, does a citizen's rights include the privilege of taking a private pee?"

Stenson actually laughed. "And I was just going to offer you another cup of coffee."

"You can pee, Habermann, when you answer my questions." Hardy said.

"I told you. I was enjoying an evening alone on a Saturday."

"The wild bachelor life." I had never liked Stenson. I had met his wife a few times, and she seemed like a pleasant, if bland, person. Still, I wondered what she saw in his flat head, with its pancake of bristles along the crown, his pale skin and perennially red eyes. The fingernails on his calloused hands had been chewed to frayed stubs.

"How do you two get along, Stenson?"

"What?" His eyes narrowed into thin channels of anger. "What the hell are you talking about?"

I shook my head. "Never mind. Just day dreamin'." I waved my arm. "Anyway, I saw Davis wander through Riverwalk, so I followed. I wanted to follow up on our conversation from last week."

"Why?" Stenson asked.

"Because there were inconsistencies. I thought he was holding something back."

"So you're tellin' us you lost him?" Hardy glanced at his colleagues, a smile spreading across sagging cheeks. "I thought you were better at your job than that."

"No, Frank. I found him, but he raced away like a furry little rabbit in polyester when he left the high school parking lot. I lost him out of respect for our city's laws against reckless driving."

"Bullshit!" Hardy was a tough one to fool.

We all leaned back to take a pause. My stomach growled.

"Any chance I can get something to eat from the vending machines?"

"You forget your lunch over at the Courney place?"

"I guess I forgot to pack one. I was kinda rushed by some asshole in a Plymouth Fury."

Stenson leaned closer at this point, close enough for me to smell his lunch. Lebanon bologna, I guessed. Heavy on the French's mustard, with a pickle as an afterthought. I noted a hint of banana as well. Good. Always include some fresh fruits and vegetables. Now I was really hungry, and it was after one o'clock.

"I'm going to enjoy putting you away, asshole," he said.

"Look, do you clowns really think I killed this guy? I mean, it's absurd. What was the weapon type?"

"A Glock. Nine millimeter." Those were the first words Rick had spoken since I entered the room. Unfortunately, we had not had the chance to talk before I was dragged into my homeroom session.

"Well, you've already got my weapon in custody. Besides," I wagged my finger. "it's the wrong make. And I know you guys carry 357s. So I doubt it's any of us. So just why the hell are we all sitting here?" I glanced at all three.

"Look, Habermann." Hardy's voice rose, approaching shouting stage. "You know fucking well why we're here."

"Enlighten me."

"We have been plagued this summer with a lot of dead people. You are associated in some way with all of them, and you have been lying from the beginning. You were present at the first, your weapon was used for the second, and we know you were present at the third."

Hardy rose from his chair and walked out of the room. He returned a minute later and tossed a box on the table.

"Look familiar?"

It did. It was the same shoebox I'd left with father Kramer. I guess he still hadn't forgiven me for hanging that curve. I looked at Jamieson. After all, he had hit the damn thing. His eyes returned my stare almost as if they were pleading with me to confess, to come clean with everything I knew. I thought back to the jungle trails and the hilltop near the old Michelin plantation, to a woman in black who had appeared like an angel in our own little hell, and who had begun to reappear in other disguises back here in the States. I wanted to ask for redemption and forgiveness for any pain and suffering I had caused. But I did not want to confess anything to these pricks, not until I knew why she was back in my life in one form or another, and not until I knew what it had to do with the death of Steve Courney and all the others. I turned back to the box.

"Where'd you find it?"

"You know fucking well where we found it, Habermann."

"What makes you think this ties me to the third killing?"

"We also have your voice on the 911 tape from last night, Bill," Higgins interrupted. "You see, that's the kind of thing that happens when police in different jurisdictions cooperate with one another."

From what little I knew of the guy, Higgins was a prick. Sharp, but still an asshole. He had come to the county prosecutor's office right out of Northwestern Law School, and he always impressed me as a man determined to make a quick name so he could join one of those large, prosperous firms in Chicago with an office overlooking the Lake and all that crap. The more I studied his smug face, with its two strategically place zits on the right temple and the smooth brown hair that looked like it had been modeled in wax, the more I disliked him. If he was lucky he would prosecute some white-collar stiffs tomorrow, then defend the same assholes in private practice the day after.

"That still doesn't explain the box. So, maybe it isn't as bad as it looks." I even smiled at this point. That was a mistake.

Hardy's hand shot across the table and grabbed a fistful of flowers from my shirt. He yanked against the fabric, pulling the shirt-and me-halfway across the table top. A button snapped free and rattled across the table.

"Listen, shithead. If you want to play smart ass, we can stay here all day and all night. I can even lock you up as a material witness."

"I don't think so." My words hissed out between gasps. Hardy must have been lifting weights in his off hours. He had been a year ahead of me in high school, and had always thought of himself as a tough son-of-a-bitch. Until he tried to play football. He hit like a sack of pebbles.

"I can also lock you up for obstruction of justice. Remember the pictures?"

"The what?" Higgins interrupted. He leaned forward. Hardy glanced at him, then back at me. His grip loosened.

"Look," I said. "I am sorry about the goddamn pictures. I gave them to you the minute I got the film developed. So I haven't withheld a fucking thing."

"What about now?"

"What about it?"

"What about those two sisters, and that stiff Courney and his drugs? What about his service record, and yours? And what about the money?"

I leaned forward. "So what is it about the goddamn money, Hardy? Why is it so important? Who's playin' games now?"

"We received a call, Bill." It was Higgins again. "It was an anonymous tip that you had received a drug payoff, and the caller told us where to find it."

"Male or female?"

"That's not important, Bill."

"The hell it isn't."

"What's important is the recent influx of narcotics and your possible link to that flow."

I stared wide-eyed at this jerk-off in a suit. "What the hell are you talking about?"

"Cocaine, Bill. Some of which we found in your garage."

"Oh, shit. Let me guess. Another anonymous tip, right?"

Higgins shrugged. "True, not the most reliable source. But it's all adding up, Bill. It doesn't look very good for you. I mean, study the case from our perspective." He paused. It was almost as though the shyster was working a jury. "So why not tell us what you know. Work with us on this one, Bill."

"Sorry, I need to talk to my client first."

Hardy's grip tightened again, and his breath spewed forth in short bursts. He turned toward Higgins. "You're wasting your time on this one."

I felt hot and exhausted. Hardy's goading was either going to push me to blurt out the pieces I had assembled about the connection to Vietnam, or throw a right cross at his leering face. It would be hard to miss. And it was something I wanted to do a lot more at the moment than lead them down the path I was on. My breath came hard and fast, and my temples were pounding against the side of my forehead. I felt a rush of blood that must have turned my face crimson.

"I can't help you, Hardy. Not yet."

"Why not?"

"Because I don't know who killed Davis, and I don't know where the drugs are coming from. It makes sense that they're tied to the killings, but it doesn't make sense to try to rope me into that."

"Why not? Was Courney dealing in Vietnam?"

"I'm not sure. Probably."

"No, I'd say definitely," Hardy responded. "And you and he worked together back then more than once. And now all this shit. It fits, dammit."

"Yeah, but it's too damn cute, and you know it. We never worked that closely, especially after he left our unit at Tay Ninh. That was another world, Frank. Forget it."

"I can't. It's back here now."

Jamieson walked over and laid his hand on Hardy's arm. Hardy looked at him like he was an unintended interruption, then pushed me back in my chair.

I smoothed the wrinkles and re-tucked my shirt into my blue jeans. One hand reached high and found my hair, smoothing a patch back into place.

"One more outburst like that, and I won't need a trip to the can."

Hardy glared. Stenson slammed his palm against the table, then walked out of the room. Jamieson strolled over and took Stenson's place at the edge of the table, but on my right side this time.

"You are not out of the woods yet. Not on the other two killings, either," Hardy pressed.

"You can't be thinking of pinning Courney's murder on me, Hardy." I shook my head and waved my hands in front of me like I had just ruled his pass incomplete. "No fucking way, boss man."

"There remains the matter of the woman out at Northern Illinois Gas...."

"She was killed with your weapon, Bill." Thanks, Rick. Like I needed reminding on that point.

"Had you ever seen that woman before?" Higgins asked.

"You mean before the shooting out at the Skylark?"

"That's right. Like in 'Nam," Stenson pressed, sauntering back into the room. He used the worn 'Nam' like he'd been there, like he knew the place and the people. Hell, I wasn't even sure I did. And Stenson had never gotten closer than Omaha, as far as I could tell.

"Excuse me?"

"You never met back there?"

"Not that I remember. There were so many, you know, and not all of them friendly."

"Cut the comedy, asshole," Hardy barked. "There's nothing funny about this shit. We sent a query about her to the FBI's national database when we tried to ID her. The report came in yesterday. There are some nice coincidences here. Some very interesting coincidences."

Hardy stressed the word 'coincidences' like it had fallen off the stage at Second City. I looked to Rick, who avoided my eyes. His index finger was following the grain along the table's edge.

Hardy's fingers snapped. "She's what people call a 'Eurasian.' Her name was Juliette Huang. And the Feds say she's was deported once for illegal entry...."

"I thought if she had an American father...."

"Who just might be...?" Stenson jumped in.

"I have no fucking idea, Stenson." I shot back.

"Easy, Habermann. They have to establish identity and proof of parentage to get into this country," Hardy continued. "And it helps not to have a record. Which, of course, she did after she had been here a while. She had been convicted once for narcotics trafficking. A very interesting woman."

"I still don't think I know her." My eyes refused to focus on anyone, or anything.

"And now this Davis thing," Hardy droned on. "So you can see why we're interested in your whereabouts last night."

"So, what do you think I was doing?"

"You were trying to set something up with Davis."

"Like I said. There were discrepancies in what he had said with some other information I'd acquired. I wanted to run those by him. I think he was lying."

"Lying about what?" Hardy pressed.

"I never got the chance to ask."

Hardy sat back and studied the ceiling. He surveyed my face, which had broken out in a mild sweat.

"I need a smoke," he claimed. He and Stenson rose and left me with Jamieson and Higgins, who shoved his chair close enough to mine so that barely a whisper could pass between us. He was close enough to make me glad I had shaved this morning. He even held up his hand like he didn't want Jamieson to hear what we said.

"You need to level with us on what you know about the Davis killing. I know you're not in this thing alone."

"Who else am I in it with?" I immediately regretted having ended my sentence with a preposition. Higgins might think I had attended a state school or something.

"The woman. Which one was with you?"

"Come again?"

"Don't jerk me around, Bill, like you do with these guys. Your best play is to be open and honest. Things are looking increasingly shaky for you, and it won't be long before they have enough evidence to hold you."

Not enough evidence yet? Jesus, what were they waiting for? "Hold me for what? I haven't done anything."

After a few minutes, Stenson returned with a cup of coffee for Rick. Higgins shot the interloper a glance of disapproval.

It went on like this for another hour. Part of that time, they left me to ponder my errant ways. When we were together, I told them what I remembered of Davis's testimony. And I stuck to my original story about losing Davis in traffic. Then I insisted on having a lawyer present if they wanted me to answer any more questions. I almost asked Higgins when he was going into private practice.

So, they gave me some of the details of Davis's death. A pistol shot through the mouth. Some poor sap from Minnesota on the way east with his family for a vacation in Boston had found the corpse shortly after the 911 call, blood and brains spattered against the tile behind the toilet. The state police had some trouble separating the vomit from the blood and gray matter.

"And that's not all," Hardy pronounced, leaning forward with a gleam of delight lighting his dirt-brown eyes like a Fourth-of-July sparkler. "Your employer's prints were all over the weapon."

I stared with the silence of an altar boy caught at high mass with a condom.

Hardy refused to relent. The sparklers were exploding. He lit a cigarette at the table.

"That's right. Deborah fucking Krueger, big boy."

"So, where is she? Have you guys booked her?"

Higgins stood and came around to Hardy's side of the table. He left his jacket on the chair, though. He had rolled his sleeves halfway up his forearms by now, and his hands sat on his hips like he knew what he was doing. The tie hung so far down the collar I could have put my fist through it.

"She's been at the county office with my boss." Higgins looked at his wristwatch. The gold spandex glistened like a magic wand. "Probably still is. Unless she's confessed."

"So, why am I still here?"

"Because I also spoke to her before I came over here, Bill. She admitted she hired you to investigate the death of her brother-in-law, but also said that she recently released you."

"Oh, really? Did she give a reason?"

"Said she thought you were acting strangely. Impulsive, and overly aggressive. She no longer trusted your judgment."

"And she put you with Davis last night," Hardy butted in. "Saw you two leave the concert at Riverwalk together."

"Still not havin' much luck with the ladies, eh Habermann?" Stenson asked.

"I think they're afraid of my overwhelming masculinity, dickhead."

My fingers toyed with the buttons left on my shirt. The mirror's glare had turned into a smile of malice. My ears rang with the snide laughter of Hardy's voice, and a puff of cigarette smoke floated past my nose. I heard myself coughing.

"And there were traces of cocaine in Davis's car. His garage over in Glen Ellyn also had a nice little stash."

That was enough. I gave them a statement, sort of. I claimed to have seen Davis by chance while I was taking a pleasant evening of Strauss and had decided to pursue him to finish my interrogation from the week before. I told them pretty much everything as I had found it in the oasis. I even told them about the Ford Explorer, but not the suspected occupants. They had me sign the statement, then released me on my own recognizance.

I drove home, careful to observe the speed limit. Hardy's revelation had come as a real shock. There was no way Deborah Krueger had been at that oasis. So now someone was trying to frame her as well? The "him" she had spoken of? And cocaine in Davis's car and house? The lab work on him would be interesting. But there was no way I could see that guy doing drugs, much less dealing.

I wanted to soak for several hours in a tub to wash away the stench of interrogation, betrayal, and death, but a shower would have to do. My second of the day. I thought back to two-a-days at the outset of football practice during my junior year in high school, the first time I had kicked Hardy's ass. One-on-one blocking drills, and I had done it all fall. He had finally gotten his revenge. If he even remembered, that is.

It would have to be a quick shower, though. I had promised to stop by Wanda's and I thought I'd pick up steaks and a six-pack to improve her mood. And mine. We had a lot to talk about. And then I'd find Deborah Krueger. I'd have to be careful, though. I figured the real reason Hardy set me free was their hope that I'd lead them to the pot of gold at the end of this case. That could be a stash of cocaine, another bundle of cash, or a nest of conspirators. What I wanted, though, was the chance to meet with my client alone. I wanted to get to the bottom of her own sorry story in this mess.

Before driving home, though, I stopped at Lisa Courney's condo. No one answered the doorbell, and when I searched for the old coot from Wichita, I found a three hundred pound reject from Weight Watcher's Anonymous behind the counter. He informed me that since Mrs. Courney had not given my name or description to the desk, he was not at liberty to divulge her whereabouts. At least I learned she wasn't home.

At Wanda Rathko's apartment, the sound of the Cubs game on WGN filtered through a crack under her door. I knocked.

"Come on in." The words drifted on a lazy breeze of hinted intimacy.

Her full, tan figure reclined on the sofa, while her eyes followed the listless play of Chicago's North Side anti-heroes. Wanda wore Bermuda-length blue shorts and a sleeveless white oxford dress shirt. The loose cotton spread like waves over full breasts and the small curve of her stomach. Her feet were propped on the teak coffee table.

"I hope you like baseball."

Her face did not move from the television, but her eyes darted in my direction with a flicker of recognition. A spiced heat hung in the air, a bowl of salsa sat amid a platter of yellowish tortilla chips on the coffee table.

"Love it," I explained, "although my mind is elsewhere today. I'm also not too crazy about the Cubs."

Her feet fell to the carpet. Fake anger surged in her eyes. "Don't tell me you're one of those White Sox fans?"

I walked to the kitchen, stashed the steaks in the refrigerator, and returned to the living room with a two bottles of Augsburger.

"They are losers, dear girl. Have been for years. Probably will be for many more. But more to the point, I need to discuss some other things...."

She cocked her fingers like a pistol and took aim at my forehead. "You sound like a disappointed true believer."

"Maybe I am." I winked. "Disappointed anyway. Ever since '69, when Leo Durocher and his boys blew it to the Mets. "

Wanda leaned forward, pressing her breasts between her arms as she grabbed a can of beer sitting in a tiny pool of moisture. A Miller. I frowned and handed her a real drink. She set the can on the carpet to her side of the sofa, then reached for the bottle. Her deep brown cleavage opened like an invitation.

"I should expect as much from some hayseed raised in this town."

"Are we still talking baseball?"

"What else?" The Cubs went down in order in the fifth.

"Well, screw you," I sputtered through a rich layer of foam. "There was more to do growing up in my town than in pits like Oak Lawn or River Forest, or wherever the hell you grew up."

"Yeah. Like sucking on alfalfa, maybe."

I dropped onto the sofa beside her, cradling the cold Augsburger on my knee. I grabbed a chip loaded with salsa and shoved it into my mouth. An explosion rocked deep inside my sinuses, and my head jerked back in a vain attempt to escape some of the heat.

"Good Lord, what have you put in this stuff?"

She laughed and shook her head. "Hick."

"Well, I've been around, too. In fact, I've been to places I never want to see again."

"Like where?"

"Like the Naperville Police Department. I have just had one hell of an afternoon." I rolled my eyes and took a swig of Augsburger. "Last night wasn't too great, either."

"What happened?"

"Somebody was shot. Over in Hinsdale."

"And they think you did it?"

"I'm not sure what they think, but I doubt it. There is a lot of circumstantial and a little physical evidence linked to me. Mostly, though, I think they want me to tell them everything I know in the hopes that it will provide the great clue to solve this mess."

Her hand went to her mouth. "Jesus, Bill. What are you gonna do?"

"Find the real killers. There's not much else I can do."

"How are you gonna do that?"

"Well, you might be able to help."

"How?"

"By helping me remember things. And seeing if there's anything else you can recall from the other night. I need to ask you a few more questions."

Wanda's face darkened. She shuddered.

"I'm sorry. But try to remember the woman at the Skylark. How good a look did you get?"

"Jesus, Bill. It was kinda dark, and I was working."

My head rolled back against the sofa cushions. "I'm stuck on a few points. There may be more than one." I took her hand. "Please. I'll even cook the steaks the way you like 'em."

She nodded. "Medium well. What do you need to know?"

I tried to think about the woman at the morgue, the sighting in northern Virginia, and the customer at Budget. The green bottle of Augsburger rose to my lips. The cold beer felt damn good running down my throat.

"Can you describe her again?"

"Not any better. I mean, what's it been, a week now?"

"Try. Please."

"Shit. I do remember her being thin, but not really skinny. Especially the nose. Nice and sharp, almost like a blade."

"Anything else? Skin? Eyes? Anything to throw a clue on her age?"

"Geez!" She bit her lip in thought. "I never really got close enough to tell for sure. But I'd say already out of her teens. Twenties, certainly no more than her early thirties."

"Anything about her behavior or her movements that ring a bell?"

She shook her head. "Not really."

"Did you hear her speak?"

"Sorry."

"Was she wearing any jewelry?"

"I didn't notice."

"How well was she built?"

"Whatta ya' mean?"

"I mean, did she have a full figure? You said the first time we spoke that she looked pretty thin, without much of a chest."

"Yeah, that's right. She was flat. Like a pancake."

"Did you see her there with anyone else? Another Oriental, perhaps?"

She thought for a moment. "Actually, now that you mention it, yeah." Her face wrinkled with concern. I thought she might cry. "Oh Christ, Bill, I'm sorry. I should have thought of that. But nobody asked to remind me."

"Tell me about it now."

"I just remember seein' the two of them come in. It looked like they were together, but I couldn't be sure. The other one was a little heavier. Taller, too."

"What happened to her?"

"I don't remember. I guess she took off."

I studied Wanda's face. "How about that guy that came by? Has he tried to contact you again?"

Wanda slid closer. I considered another bite of salsa, then decided against it. Wanda's hand dropped and found my knee.

"I don't like to talk about him. I know he's still out there. And that frightens me."

"But what kind of hair did he have? And what about his build?"

"Dark, I guess. And tall." She shuddered. "Don't, Bill."

"Look," I tried to sound reassuring. "I'm pretty sure he's gone under. I haven't heard or seen anything for a few days now." I decided to keep quiet about the break-in and the stranger at Lisa Courney's. But I glanced at her door just to be sure. Two deadbolts. "That could mean he's up to something else. My real problem at the moment is I don't know where to look for him. Not exactly, anyway. I've also gotten the police to add some patrols out here. If anything happens, anything at all that sounds the least bit suspicious, please call. Call me, or the police."

"I thought you said you don't like the police."

"I said that only one of them is my friend. As for the rest, 'liking' has nothing to do with it. They're a competent bunch. They've just got some wrong ideas."

"Which ones?"

"Ones I'm going to correct. But you can trust them to protect you." I paused. "Are you sure you've never seen him before? He never came out to the Skylark that you can remember?"

Wanda shook her head.

"And you never saw him there that night?"

More headshaking. Then her head tilted back toward the cushions, and her hand traveled along my arm, coming to a rest at the shoulder. "Tell me something, Bill."

"What's that?"

"What does all this have to do with Vietnam?"

I didn't answer but swallowed hard. The bump in my throat refused to budge, so I tried to drown it with beer.

Wanda's eyes softened for the first time since we had met. "It's okay, Bill. I understand. Your police friends told me. Maybe it would help if you got some things out."

I shook my head, nodding toward the TV. I waved at breath scented with salt and chili peppers and took another sip of beer. Cincinnati had scored a run. "Like I said, only one is my friend. The others are just men I worked with."

"Okay. But, Bill...?"

"Yes?" I drank again. The bottle was nearly empty.

"Talk to me. Something happened, didn't it? What was it?"

My eyes zeroed in on the label that was peeling from the green bottle. "I don't like to talk about it. Besides, it was a long time ago."

A roar erupted from the TV. I grabbed the remote and turned the sound down. Cincinnati had scored again, but a close play at the plate had gotten the Cubs out of the inning.

"But I do understand. I lost a brother there." Tears formed small pools at the lower rims of her eyes.

I didn't say anything. I didn't know what to say. My insides were churning with years of anxiety and fear. But somewhere, hidden deep in the nausea was a frightening sense of relief. Relief that I had survived. Relief and guilt. I finished the Augsburger.

"He was a Marine. At Khe San."

I stroked puffy cheeks and brushed away pellets of water from a face that suddenly looked aged and weary. "I'm sorry. Most of us lost something there."

"And you? Was it a friend?"

"Friends, sure. And people I barely knew but could have known better." I stared into the empty bottle of Augsburger. "Other things, too."

"Like what?"

"Oh, I don't know. Sometimes I think I lost my innocence back there, my sense of certainty about life and people."

"What happened?"

The walls of Wanda's apartment narrowed like some medieval prison. Harry Carey's voice caromed through asymmetrical dimensions. I could feel the sweat breaking out along my forehead. Breathing became hard, and my chest tightened. Wanda's fingers massaged the muscles in my shoulders and the back of my neck.

"I...I don't know." I was struggling, fumbling for words. "I never got a good look at her." I rubbed temples that were pounding now. I wiped moist hands across my shirt. "Jesus. It all happened so fast."

"It's okay, Bill." Soft hands stroked the hair along the back of my skull and neck. "Tell me."

"There were so many pouring out of the woods and toward our perimeter. We were late getting into line, and it was all so confusing. We were so damn tired. We had humped through that damn jungle all day. Man, you just never got enough sleep. We had finally finished filling the sandbags, and some of us had just laid down when the shit started happening. You could see women and kids mixed in with Charlie. You never knew how to figure them. Maybe they were Charlie's cover. Maybe they were just trying to get away. And there were some in our camp. Inside the perimeter. I remember wondering what the hell they were doing there. It was such a fucking mess."

I stopped and sucked warm air from an empty beer bottle. I heard it thud against the carpet, then roll under the table.

"Did you have to shoot someone? A friend?"

I shook my head and swallowed. "I was carryin' the captain's .45. He had been hit, and the rounds tore up his chest like raw beef. He had just pulled me back down behind cover. His eyes seemed to blame me, while his life drained away in that godawful hole. I was so scared and so angry. I wanted to kill as many of the little bastards as I could. I hit that goddamn wire, and then there's this peasant woman. I was so shocked. I mean, what the fuck was she doing so close? In that spot?"

I swallowed more air from the space in front of us. I licked my lips with a dry tongue. The skin felt like rough wood.

"You shot her?"

"It was an accident. At least, I think so. I was so pumped up, I guess my finger pulled the trigger without me even thinking about it." I hesitated. "Then I froze."

"Who wouldn't?" I saw confusion in Wanda Rathko's young face. Soft, round eyes glistened against smooth, tanned skin. Her cheeks flushed.

"Someone who wants to survive, that's who. Someone who isn't a burden to his unit. Someone who won't get his friends killed, that's who." I shook my head and stared at the carpet. "Jamie pulled me back behind the sand bags. He saved my life. The VC hit minutes later. That would have been the end."

"Who's Jamie?"

"Jamie Krug. A friend over in Oswego. I rely on him a lot."

Then his words came back to me. His last comments about the woman that night and why she was there, why she hadn't left with the others, the ones who were caught in the crossfire. She had known, and she hadn't told anybody. That's why she wasn't out there with the rest.

And I remembered seeing her before. Several times, often with Steve Courney. But I couldn't remember him being there that night. I couldn't even remember if he was still in our unit then. But I knew that an answer to all this lay somewhere in that line, the one that ran from the woman I'd accidentally shot straight to Courney and his work after he left the our division. It went through his time in intelligence when he ran those agents in the north and whatever else he had worked on. And it had all come to an end back here.

I jumped up. "I'll go get the steaks ready. I'm starving." My heart was pounding like the Cincinnati line up working on Cubs pitching. "I could use another beer, too." I glanced around with my head already swimming. My legs felt rubbery, and my feet looked like they were miles away on a distant rug. I stood still, trying to regain my sense of balance. "It's been one hell of a day."

Before I registered her movement Wanda was up too, standing beside me. I stumbled to the center of the living room, closer to the television. I wanted to turn the damn thing off. The fucking Cubs were worthless.

She stayed with every step of mine. We stood like awkward captives in front of the set, a discomforting silence between us until she took my hand and set it on the rounded slope of her buttocks. Then she took my head in her hands, pressing her lips to mine. She tasted so sweet, and her body melted against mine. Our hips rubbed. Hands roamed down my back.

My head slid to her neck and along her shoulders. I pulled at little round pearl buttons, and her shirt fell open. I found myself on my knees before her, like a priest to a goddess, tugging her shorts to the floor. Tan lines across an alabaster skin beckoned along the edges of flowered panties. Her bra fell to the floor between us. I glanced up and saw Heaven descend. The cares of the day drifted to another world.

Wanda dropped beside me. I rolled toward her and buried my face in the soft, fleshy folds of desire. Long, round legs wrapped around mine. I forgot about the steaks. I forgot about Hardy and Vietnam and the deaths of Steve Courney, Jack Davis and anyone else the police had found here. I pushed them away to another world and another time, if only for a little while.

# Chapter 23

Shortly after midnight, I crept along Benton Avenue, finally feeling good about something. Somehow, I figured, we all get by, regardless of the losses and pain and stupidity. Sometimes, we even gain a little satisfaction.

Jamie Krug's pickup brought me back to the present. It sat waiting against the curb across from my building. His rusting hood and dark windshield formed a rich backdrop for a swarm of insects fluttering under the streetlight. When I pulled up close, his arm swung from the open window and pointed to the alley. I parked and then crept outside, alert for trouble. We met around the corner of my garage, in the dark and away from the house.

"What's up?"

His head beckoned toward my apartment. "You've had visitors."

"Any idea who?"

He nodded. "The local law was hanging out down the alley but bugged out about half an hour ago. I can see you haven't gotten any more popular here."

"Anyone else?"

"Some other creep was sneakin' around the back yard when I drove up. He bolted when he saw me pull over, though."

"Did you get a good look at him?"

Krug shook his head. "Nope. Sorry."

"What did the cops do?"

"Nothin'. I got the impression they wanted to see what might happen."

"Did they say anything to you?"

"Nope. Maybe they figured I was waitin' for a late Mass."

"Yeah, maybe."

We moved toward the house like we were back on patrol, our feet treading as light as possible to avoid making any noise. The shadows at the back of the house hung like velvet, still and heavy. When we climbed the stairs, my eyes searched the neighbors' yards for any sign of movement. All they found was an eery stillness hovering at the edge of my back door. My company for the evening appeared to have gone home.

"I'm surprised your alarm didn't go off." Jamie pointed toward the small metal octagon stuck on a thin, gray pole about waist-high in my back yard.

## ANGEL IN BLACK

"I don't have an alarm." I nodded at the sign. "I took that from someone's yard in one of those new developments out near Bollingbrooke."

Krug shook his head and laughed. "You're a hell of a detective, Habermann."

"I didn't get caught, did I?"

We moved into the kitchen, where I pulled a couple Special Exports from the refrigerator. Jamie Krug grabbed his, popped the top, and passed into the living room. There he fell onto the couch. I followed but settled for my desk chair. I set the unopened bottle on the desktop.

"So, what's up, lad? Why'd you stop by and scare off my guests?"

"I found out a few things about Courney's tour. Thought you might need the information."

"And?" I reached for the bottle and twisted the cap. I tossed it at the desk but kept the bottle.

"Well, his tour with the 25th overlapped only briefly with ours. He got transferred out after only eight months. You had only been there a couple of months."

"Where to?"

"Intel work."

"That soon? I thought he went to Saigon later."

Krug shook his head. "Saigon came later. But that's why his VA records are incomplete. They end with his first transfer."

"What was he doin'?"

"It took a few calls, but I finally found out that someone that had put him in Phoenix."

I leaned so far forward, I was about to fall on the floor. "Phoenix? The Agency thing?"

I stared at the floor, trying to recall images and personalities of the few people I had met who were associated with the Phoenix program. It had become shrouded in mystery and myth shortly after its creation, with new layers added each succeeding year. A lot of it had been promoted by those involved to enhance its prestige and power to frighten. But it had been tightly controlled, from what little I had seen.

"Jamie, Courney couldn't have been with the Agency. I knew some of those guys. No way."

"Didn't have to be. By then the Agency was gettin' out of it. Lots of military types we're movin' in. It came under CORDS later on, remember?"

"Yeah, okay. But even then." I shook my head. "Was he on any of the patrols we made with those people, when we provided cover?"

Krug nodded while he gulped about a third of his beer. "Yeah, he was. And one of 'em was the night at the plantation."

"I thought we were out setting ambushes."

"We were. But there was another mission, one not everyone knew about. The Phoenix patrol hooked up with us later. Only a couple guys were told. Courney was the American advisor."

"And the woman? She was with them? That's what you were referring to the other night?"

He nodded. "Yeah, I heard something about it a while back, but I never told you because I figured it wouldn't make it any easier for you."

"What do you mean?"

"Man, you had enough to dwell on. I thought it all might fade away quicker this way. Especially if you thought you had shot a friendly."

I sat back and tried to think between sips of the Special Export. "But what happened to Courney that night? Why wasn't he around when the NVA hit our perimeter? I don't remember him in the firefight."

Krug shrugged. "Hell, Bill, I don't know. I was too busy savin' your ass to worry about Courney or any of those hard-ass Phoenix guys." His eyes drifted off to some distant memory. "Jesus, man, do you remember those guys? I mean, they were some tough motherfuckers. I saw them go into a village once, ask around, then just pull some guy from his hut and blow his ass away. Man, if the ARVN drips had been more like that, we would won that fuckin' war in about a year."

Jamie Krug's word floated by. I was too far gone in thought to pay much attention to my friend's ruminations. If Courney had deserted his asset, did someone hold him responsible for her death? Had it been intentional? Did that explain the involvement of the Vietnamese family back east? I flashed on the business card the brother had slipped into my pocket outside the church in Virginia. The kid had said something about us and his family having done their duty by our country.

"Jamie, does the name Sean Cavanaugh ring any bells?"

He drained the Special Export and studied the empty bottle. "Not really. Why?"

"It's a name that's cropped up in this case. I think he may be the one bugging me and trailing Lisa Courney. Did anyone remember anything about Courney's buddies? Anything about his dealing?"

"There was one guy, a grunt I met in therapy. He had gotten hooked on smack back there, and he remembered Courney."

"As his dealer? I thought he only handled grass."

Jamie Krug shook his head. "He dealt the heavier stuff once in a while. This guy's connection was normally someone else. I think Courney just hung around. He may even have been Courney's supplier."

"Did he have a name?"

"Not that this guy could remember. He did remember that his supplier was a deserter, though, and that he had been sent to the stockade at Long Binh. The grunt had gotten really upset, because he had to find a new source for his habit."

"Army, eh?"

"Yeah. Anyway, he broke out during a VC mortar attack one night and set himself up like some kind of mafia don in Dogpatch. Narcotics, prostitution, the works."

"Which one?"

"Mostly up in Da Nang. When it got too hot there, he'd move on to someplace else."

"I'm surprised he survived. The competition could be pretty stiff."

Jamie shrugged. "The guy probably worked the right people, made it worth their while. There was a lot of that shit goin' on, at the end. Funny thing, though."

I stared hard. "What's that?"

"The grunt claimed he took a strong interest in this orphanage run by some French nuns. Used to send 'em lots of money."

"Anyone know why?"

"Nope. Maybe he had a kid there."

I jumped up and marched into the kitchen. There were four Special Exports left. I pulled two out of the refrigerator, opened both, and passed one to Jamie when I returned to the living room.

"You found all this out from one grunt?"

He took a long drink from his bottle. About another third of the beer disappeared. "I also called a friend who works at the VA office in Saint Louis."

"Who you met in therapy?"

Krug nodded.

"Jamie, you are better than any locator service I ever found."

He smiled. "Thanks, man. Anything for a pal. One other thing, though."

"Yeah?" I sipped.

"I don't remember anyone named Cavanaugh, but I do recall some asshole named Callahan now that I think about it."

"You think it's tied in?"

He shrugged. "Could be. I used to see him with Courney."

"Could you call your buddy in Saint Louis to see what happened to this Callahan?"

He nodded. "No problem. You think it could be the same guy?"

I studied the peeling beer label. "There isn't much else to go on right now. This other stuff really helped, though." I hoisted the bottle and gazed at my friend. "You may have saved my ass yet again."

"Hell, Habermann. Someone has to. There's a pile a shit rollin' downhill here." He winked. "And it's headed right at you."

I nodded. "I think you're right. And I think it's about time to unload all this on Hardy and the gang."

Krug nodded. "No shit, man. What finally did it for you?"

"A combination of things. But mostly it was the realization earlier tonight that I'm up against a crew of professionals." I told Krug about the possible involvement of a second person in Courney's shooting. "It looks like one may have acted as bait, while the other one nailed him. And they've got to have lots of support to get away as cleanly as they did."

"Except for the woman that got killed at the Gas building."

I nodded. "Yeah. All that proves is just how ruthless they are. And if there's a lot of narcotics trafficking and money involved, I'm not surprised."

"So why haven't you gone to the cops yet?"

"I need to talk to Deborah Krueger first. I owe her that much, and I need to see how she fits into all this."

"What the hell for? Let the cops sort it out."

"I'm not just doing it for her, Jamie. It's also for her sister. And me." I pointed at his beer bottle. "Need another?"

"Sure. And something to eat, too. You got anything here?"

"Let's see."

When we reached the kitchen, however, Rick Jamieson and Frank Hardy were waiting.

"Come on in," I said. "Don't let the door stop you."

Jamieson and Hardy strolled over to the kitchen table, where they pulled two chairs out. Jamie Krug slid between the two cops and took up a post in front of the sink. He and Jamieson nodded at each other. I leaned against the doorframe, while Hardy collapsed into the chair he was holding. Rick followed his boss.

"Was your friend leaving?" Hardy asked.

"Nope. He was going to fix something to eat."

Hardy craned his neck to look around the kitchen, then he focused on me. "Somebody doesn't like you."

"No shit, Frank. You figure all that out by yourself?"

Jamie Krug laughed. Hardy shot him a dirty look, then turned to me. Before he could say anything, Rick Jamieson cut in.

"Have you seen Deborah Krueger lately?"

I shook my head. "Not yet. She's sort of dropped out of touch. I thought you guys had the bead on her."

Hardy blew out his breath. "Not anymore. We were hoping you could lead us to her."

"Is that why you had the patrol car outside?"

Jamieson nodded.

"And you probably never got those statements from her at the DA's office, did you?"

Hardy and his deputy exchanged glances, and then Rick Jamieson smiled. "That was Higgins's brilliant idea."

"That guy's a dickhead."

"Yeah, but he'll probably be a rich dickhead soon," Hardy said.

He stood and approached me. He moved slowly, like he was carrying extra weight. I couldn't see where he could hide it, though. His fingers wrapped around my upper arm and applied about as much pressure as it takes to open a jar.

"Let's go for a walk."

I peered through the doorway at the night sky. "Now? Do you realize what time it is?"

Hardy let go of my arm and kept walking. The back of his light brown checked sport coat was wrinkled like he had sat in it all day. His brown loafers scuffed along the tops of the stairs as he descended toward the backyard. I sighed at Jamieson, waved to Jamie, and then followed.

Hardy had halted in the middle of the stone pathway that bisected my back yard. His head sat back on his neck, while his eyes roamed the stars. His hands were buried in his pockets.

"A couple of us used to sit on the deck of our carrier in the South China Sea at night, when there were no missions on."

"That must have been rare."

"Yeah, it was. But it was really beautiful when we did get the chance. I always wondered what it would be like to watch them stoned." The words seemed to slip out from some persona Hardy had occupied in the past. Distant and foreign.

"I couldn't tell ya'. I was never on a carrier." I followed his gaze toward the pinpoints of light far off in a dark, brooding sky.

Hardy lowered his face. I did the same, and our eyes met. We still had light years between us.

"That was another time and another world, Bill. You know what I mean?"

"I think so."

"I heard plenty of stories about how you grunts spent a lotta time gettin' high. It always amazed me. A lot of guys said you all had earned it, fighting in that fucked-up war."

"Some felt that way. Others didn't really give a shit."

"Like I said, that was then. I'm not going to judge. I know you did your job over there, along with your friend upstairs." Hardy's head bobbed in the direction of my apartment. "But I can't have any of that shit comin' to roost here, Bill."

"Just why are you telling me this, Frank?" Hardy's eyes and lips did not move. I guess he was looking for answers too. The problem from where I stood was that too many things pointed in my direction. "Do you suspect me of dealing drugs? Or knowing someone who is?"

Hardy turned to study the church across the street and blew out a long breath of stale air. He glanced at the ground, then roughed his hair. It must have been a long day for him. "I'm not sure what to suspect right now, and maybe I shouldn't tell you this. But your friend Jamieson keeps stickin' up for you, and deep down inside I suspect he's right. Right now, you're our best link. So many things point your way. I know we've had our differences in the past, but I also know that something like this doesn't fit for you. At least I never would have thought it did."

"But you do now?"

Hardy shook his head. "Let me tell you somethin' else that better not go any further." He paused, studied the sky again, then glanced back at me. "That woman we found out at Nothern Illinois Gas probably wasn't Courney's shooter."

"Go on."

"The county had a forensic specialist study the blood spatterings at the Skylark. She was too short. It had to be somebody taller to get the right angle of entry." His eyes focused on mine. "You have to follow the leads, Bill. You know that. The opportunities have been there for you. And as much trouble as I have seein' it that way, you've got the closest thing there is to a motive."

I raised my hand, thinking of the woman at Budget. "Wait a minute, Frank."

"I know, I know. It's still pretty vague, though, and somehow it just doesn't fit you. But even if you aren't involved in the killings, it still looks to me like you're coverin' something up. Something from those days and nights out there, way back when."

"You're right and you're wrong, Frank. I've turned over to you guys everything I've run across. The one thing I haven't given is something you've already got." I told him about the woman who rented the car. "That jerk Stenson never talked to the kid behind the counter. And Wanda Rathko told me she thinks she remembers another woman who was at the Skylark that night, one that fits the description of this second person." I paused to suck in some breath. "But that's not all. There is something else, and it is from the past. But it's something I've got to settle myself."

"We'll check it out. I can still give you the benefit of the doubt, Bill. But I can't give you much more time. And if it does turn out you're in deeper that you've indicated, in any way, I'm coming down on you like the world's biggest shithouse."

"I never expected anything else."

"Where are you goin' from here?"

"I've got to find Deborah Krueger and she if she can lead me to another vet and some more Vietnamese."

"Be careful. And don't fuck it up. We haven't got a lot of time here. The pressure's building to see if we can go to a judge with probable cause. Higgins doesn't want to wait. This would be a nice feather in his cap."

"Thanks for the warning."

Footsteps bounced behind me, and I turned to catch Rick Jamieson stepping off my back stairs and rambling in our direction. When he passed, Rick's hand caught the same spot on the arm that Hardy had grabbed earlier. Jamieson's fingers squeezed the muscle like a steel vise, but his grip held no hostility. He waved at Jamie, who had come out on the porch. Then the two cops disappeared in the alley.

# Chapter 24

Jamie Krug trotted down the steps and out of the yard to his truck. "Be right back," he called.

When he returned, his palm held a small pistol. He thrust the weapon at me with one hand, while the other fished in his shirt pocket for some rounds.

"It's not much. A twenty-two I use for target practice. But it's better than nothing."

I stared at the weapon. "I don't know, Jamie. If anything happens, this could draw you in more than you'd like."

He shrugged. "Man, I can't just leave you stranded in the bush." He watched my face. "You ever thought of doin' something like carpentry or pottery for a living?"

I took the pistol, weighing it in my right palm. It had all the heft of a slingshot. He was right, though. It was better than nothing.

"Thanks, Jamie. I'll try not to lose this one."

He turned to leave. "Let's hope not. And try to keep your eyes focused on where the best cover is." He stepped toward the alley. "Just like in the bush, man. Just like in the bush."

Then I was on my own.

Back upstairs, the rounds slid into the .22 as easily as if I had been doing it for a living. Just like at boot camp. Maybe it's like riding a bike. Then I called my old pal John Sullivan to ask for another favor.

"Jesus, Bill, I gotta work in the morning. It's the middle of the fucking night. I can't just run over to the Memorial because you got some hunch."

"Sully, this is critical. If I'm right, more people are in danger here."

"Including you?"

"Sully, I'm already in this up to my ears."

A pause followed, during which I could hear my friend's breath come and go in a slow cadence of frustration. I glanced at my watch. Twelve thirty. I heard him mumble something to Hannelore, then come back on the line.

"Goddammit, Habermann. You owe me big time. I'll go check. That is, if I can find my shoes."

"Thank you, my man. I'll be waiting at the phone right here."

"You're fuckin' right you will." Then he hung up.

I spent the next hour sipping coffee and trying to get in touch with Deborah Krueger and Lisa Courney. It was after two when Sullivan finally called back.

"Damn, I'm getting to hate this town. There was even traffic at this time of night. I cannot believe it."

"So what did you find? Was I right?"

"Looks like it. There is a Sean Cavanaugh listed, who bought it in '69."

"What about a Callahan?"

"There are a couple listed, but no Sean Callahan. Does any of this really help?"

"Yeah, Sully. It helps a lot. I owe you big. Maybe when this is over, I'll come back east and buy you and Hannelore dinner."

"Great. I'll make reservations right away. But first I'd like you to stay out of my life long enough for me to get some sleep. The American taxpayer would shit if he or she knew how much time I've spent helping you over the last week."

"Don't forget, Sully, I'm one of those, too."

After I cradled the receiver, I grabbed Jamie Krug's peashooter and headed for the door. My first stop was Lisa Courney's condo.

A half hour later I parked the car at the River Place condos and tucked the gun into the small of my back. Good ol' Wichita was back at the desk and sound asleep. I knocked at the Courney apartment, which remained shut and quiet, like the gate to a fortress. I leaned against the door, hoping to catch a sound of movement or a voice on the other side. Nothing. I stared at the mounted brass numbers on the door and the tiny peephole for what seemed like minutes.

I tried the knob. Locked. I pulled my extra key chain from my pants pocket, the one with the metal pins that trip most door locks. I figured if no one was home, the dead bolt would be off. The knob revolved with the turn of my palm, and the door slid open. My heartbeat echoed off barren walls, and I wondered why my lips felt so dry when my forehead was so moist.

A maze of brown cardboard lay scattered throughout the apartment. To my right, half a dozen open boxes stood stacked on the dining room table, with about a dozen more spread on the floor around it. Others rested on the soft felt cushions of dining room chairs, and roughly two dozen more, taped and sealed, stood piled in front of the patio doors. In the kitchen, the cabinet doors stood open, their contents exposed. Dishes and pots were strewn across the countertop and the floor.

I followed a long corridor lined with red flowered wallpaper and half a dozen landscape watercolors in wooden frames of gold lacquer toward the back of the apartment. The air conditioning hummed through vents spaced at either end of the hallway. An open door to my left led to a powder room, where a dripping faucet beat a sharp, steady rhythm against the porcelain sink. Someone had left the light on.

At the end of the hallway, another shaft of light erupted from a vacant door-frame. I crept toward the room. I waited, listening to the absence of sound. I peered around the corner.

In the center of the room stood a desk, a dark-stained piece with a red leather inlay at its center. A desk lamp with its light still beaming perched on the corner. The wall across from the desk had a built-in bookcase, but it was empty. Someone had piled small square book boxes unevenly on top of each other, so that those in the bottom rows had bent along their upper edges from the weight. Spread at uneven intervals on the other three walls was an array of discolored squares, the spaces a shade lighter than the walls around them. I glanced at one of the open boxes on top. American classics, mostly, laid in neat perpendicular rows. The top layer included Raymond Chandler's *The Little Sister* and *The Wycherly Woman* by Ross MacDonald

There was no sign of Lisa Courney, but a note from her sister lay on the desk: "Lisa, I need to see you right away. Deb."

I left the desk lamp on when I departed. I left all the lights on. I didn't want my prints anywhere in this apartment. I even wiped the handle when I shut the door on my way out. I knew my next stop.

---

The rain finally broke as I drove to the other end of Naperville. Nature's tears, my mother used to say. The Volvo's wipers strained to keep those tears from the windshield, while small rivers washed against the wheels. No Ford Explorers or other cars followed. Instead, I had the pitch of night and the drumbeat of rain for company. Faceless images floated in the dark, misted by the rain, and then erased by lightning only to reappear again. I had to blink to escape the empty sockets and splintered skulls.

Deborah Krueger's Dutch colonial sat silent and dark, a mysterious shadow drifting on a black lake in the heart of suburban prosperity. I parked the Volvo around the corner and away from the main point of entry into the subdivision. Then I pulled Jamie's twenty-two caliber from the glove compartment and put it back into the slot at my back. Tombstones resting under a full moon in the nearby cemetery cast distended black shapes across the backyards. I hustled along the sidewalk and up the driveway to the front door. No one answered the bell, so I walked back to the kitchen door and knocked. Nothing. I looked through the kitchen window just to make sure, then I checked on the garage. Her red BMW was there, which added to the mystery. Screw it, I thought. I'm going in.

I returned to the kitchen door, picked the lock, then cracked the door open. The dead bolt was off, and there was no chain. I figured no one was home.

I snuck into her living room. A desk that looked like an eighteenth-century replica beckoned. I pulled out the middle drawer. Deborah was behind on her payments to Saks and Marshall Field's, but not by much. There was only a balance of a little over $300 on each statement. The BMW was paid for, and the mortgage booklet had enough stubs to round off the year. The woman was careless about household security, but her finances were in decent order.

Headlights flashed across the picture window in the living room, and I dropped. It's amazing, sometimes, how lessons learned and lost can return in less than seconds. It's supposed to become instinctive, a reflex instilled by good training. And to think I had hated the army.

After the lights passed, I rolled over and returned to the desk. The side drawers yielded boxes of stationary and canceled checks, none of which struck me as suspicious. The bottom drawer, though, held several folders with newspaper clippings. One contained stories about Steve Courney's shooting. One held background material about me, including a copy of a local newspaper clipping on my discharge from the Army and my Distinguished Service medal. It almost made me proud. Another file had a series of articles on the Vietnamese boat people and the Phoenix program. I whistled louder than I would have liked. Deborah Jaeger had unusual tastes in reading material. The main thing, though, was the absence of the daily planner her secretary had mentioned. She probably carried it with her, which meant I was still playing a guesing game trying to figure out where she was.

I slid the folders back in the drawer, then slipped upstairs. It took about a minute for my eyes to adjust to the darkness. I moved to the bedrooms first. She must have had a subscription to *Vogue* and *Bon Apetit*. Old magazines cluttered the underside of the bed. The jewelry boxes lining the dresser and chest of drawers surrendered nothing of value to me. Just a lot of expensive jewelry. Her drawers held nothing but clothes. Her long walk-in closet revealed more of the same. Most of the boxes contained shoes. Lots of them.

The other bedrooms weren't much different. The closets were full of dresses and coats and shoes. Deborah Jaeger was a clothes horse. I could understand why, looking as she did when she dressed for effect.

I decided to skip the bathroom. I had no desire to wade through feminine toiletries and scented soaps. Instead, I strolled down the stairs and headed for the kitchen. At the edge of the linoleum floor I stood and thought about my next move. I considered just waiting at the house. I mean, she had to come home sooner or later. I could be wasting valuable time.

The internal monologue was academic anyway.

The blow fell without warning, without a sound or breath of movement in the air. The hard metal edge struck me just behind the ear. A sharp stabbing pain shot through the back of my skull and burst out through my temples. I reached for the pistol hidden inside my belt and grabbed at air. My knees buckled, and mysterious shapes swam in circles around me. I fell against the doorframe, then tumbled toward the floor in a freefall. I pushed my hands out, but there was nothing to grab.

At the bottom of a long dark pit, I heard sounds of laughter. But then I escaped on a rocket that shot me out into the damp night. I hung on tight as it caught an arc and circled the moon. Then it flung me out of the lunar orbit, farther and deeper into a vast pool beyond, where I swam in an ocean of deep, painless oblivion.

# Chapter 25

There were explosions everywhere. I ducked and dug for cover. Too damn much confusion. Rounds thudded into the dirt and sand. I reached up and fired over the sandbags. I couldn't see a damn thing through the phosphorous and rain. But I heard the screams, shrill and piercing. The Colt rested in my right hand, finger hooked on the trigger.

One dead body lay near the perimeter. No, several. Cries for medic echoed in the background. Outside the wire, black pajamas swarmed with patches of red. Drops of water exploded against the sandbags. A baby cried. People were running back toward the tree line. Some had weapons slung over their backs. I hurled my body over the barrier, telling myself to watch for booby traps. Some NVA were probably still around.

Then a human shape loomed, covered in black rags. The pistol fired. The slender body crumbled, then twitched and grew still. I moved in closer. A tight web of shiny black hair framed a woman's face of light, gentle features. Brown vacant eyes leered at me. The hair changed to blond, then deep brown, then back to black. It started to grow and flowed down past the shoulders, on toward the waist. A beautiful round face melted into a corpse, hideous and decomposing. A skull laughed. Hands of bone reached up to pull me down. Suddenly an American face smiled under a crown of thick, dark hair, pistol at his side. Then he disappeared again.

"Well, well. He's finally waking."

I tried to open my eyelids, but they weighed too much. I rolled over, lost in confusion and pain. My head spun, pounding in a world of miniature explosions that came every few seconds. I squinted against a beam of flashing brightness and groped through sweat and darkness in search of my bearings. I struggled to suck in some oxygen. The light burned too damn much, and I had to shut my eyes. Words floated by on a faraway river. I knew that voice, but I couldn't find the body. I decided to go back to sleep.

A foot nudged my shoulder, and my eyes popped open. A long phosphorescent tube burned overhead. A set of steel pincers somewhere inside my head tried to force my eyes shut again.

"You are a very sound sleeper."

Peering through the haze, I focused on an angel and found Deborah Krueger sitting crossed-legged in front of me. She looked relaxed, her back to a brown wooden desk, one arm draped over a metal folding chair. Her thick, dark hair sat in a braid that curled around her shoulder and fell forward across her breast. The dark, sleeveless dress clung to her like gift wrapping, with sequins across her neck and a split that reached to her thigh. A smile softened the fear in her eyes. She hovered, like some fallen goddess. Beautiful white legs shimmered under the curve of well-trimmed muscle. I wanted to reach out and touch them.

The hammering inside my head argued against it. My stomach rose, then plummeted. I gasped for more air.

"Jesus, Habermann, I was wondering how long we were going to have to sit here. I was about ready to make some coffee."

"Go right ahead."

"Forget it. Maybe your girlfriend will do it."

I tried to raise my head from the floor to find the asshole that went with the voice. It hurt too damn much, so I rolled over in the direction of the noise and found the same husky son-of-a-bitch I had seen at Lisa Courney's apartment. His dark hair was pulled back into a ponytail that glistened in the room's light like a sick eel. A steady drum roll of rain beat against a roof of metal sheeting.

"Debbie, get this jerk a glass of water or something while we wait for our gook friends."

Deborah Krueger uncrossed her legs to stand up, and they parted just enough for me to catch a glimpse of white linen at their core. She noted the direction of my eyes. The look of fear in her deep blue eyes melted into a smile of concern.

"I'm sorry, Bill. I wish you had stayed away like the police asked."

Those words hurt more than I could have imagined.

"Don't tell me you're in this thing with that creep. You're breakin' my heart."

"No, please. I tried to break away. But he threatened to kill Lisa."

I rolled over and propped myself on one elbow. "Let me guess. You tried to get rid of him, maybe even pay him off to keep quiet. That's why you've been traveling into the city to meet with him, isn't it?" I closed my eyes for a moment to focus my thoughts and lowered my voice to a whisper. "Or better yet, you were hoping to get even."

"Why would she do that, Habermann?"

I aimed the words over my shoulder and at the voice. It hurt too much to move my head. "Because she was in love with him." I looked up at Deborah Krueger. "It's true, isn't it?"

She nodded, tears collecting at the rims of her eyes. "I know it was stupid. I guess I got trapped."

Somehow I was able to move my hand to my head, where it rubbed the back of my skull. A small knot the size of an after-dinner mint felt sore and very sensitive. I decided to work on my temples and forehead instead.

"No, you were scared and desperate. You didn't see anything else to do. You just got in over your head."

"I thought you could help. That's why I hired you. Lisa told me it wouldn't do any good, though. She said you couldn't do anything about all this, that you weren't a part of this back then after all."

The fluctuating confidence the two sisters had in me was underwhelming. "I understand all that now. But it's not over yet."

I forced myself into a sitting position and surveyed the room. We sat in an office paneled with cheap plywood, about forty yards long and maybe twenty wide. The floor felt like thin linoleum spread over hard concrete. I shook my head to free it of the odor of fear that kept surging through the smell of industrial cleaner. Sean Whatever ambled into the picture.

"Oh, Shithead here was a part of it alright. He killed your brother-in-law's access agent. That's why the gooks want his ass."

Deborah Krueger regarded the man who spoke these words with an impression of permanent distance and disgust.

I considered the voice. It crept out from a smile wreathed in contempt. His right hand slid along the lapel of a navy blue, double-breasted jacket to reveal a .44 Magnum. A big gun for a big guy.

"Let me guess. You're Sean Cavanaugh-no. Sean Callahan, U.S. Army deserter, drug dealer, and all around asshole."

"Score one for the private dick. Good for you, shithead. But I think it's gonna be your last hit."

Deborah Krueger's footsteps echoed behind me as she left to find something to drink. Tap water ran in the distance, and I glanced in her direction. It looked like she had gone into a restroom for my glass of water. I turned back to Sean Whatshisface.

"So, tell me why Courney had to go? Did he get too greedy, or did the Vietnamese family want their revenge, too?"

Sean strolled over and grabbed me under the arms. With a sigh, he pulled me off the floor, then pushed me into a hard, straight-backed chair across from the desk.

"You got it. I sure as hell didn't kill anyone. I just wanted to make sure that dipsy broad from the bar didn't go talkin' to the cops." He shook his head. "Those gooks do not forget a thing. They said Courney had to die for betraying them. Man, he never shoulda bugged out that night. You, too. I guess they see you two as the personal representatives of the great screw-up back there."

"What happened to him on the hilltop?"

"Hell, I don't know. Probably got wasted."

"And you gave them the two of us so they would plug you into a network out here. One of the Vietnamese gangs operating in the city, no doubt."

"Not bad, dickhead. Not bad at all."

"And the woman whose body was discovered at Northern Illinois Gas? She had to be kept quiet?"

He nodded. "That's right. But I didn't do it. It was the gooks again. Same with that stupid Davis prick."

I rotated in the chair to study the room. The explosions of pain had dropped to one burst every minute or so. I massaged my temples, trying to concentrate on a way out of this predicament.

"So, why am I still alive? Because it made more sense to frame me for the killings?"

"Right again. That was my idea. I told those hungry bastards that what we did not need was another corpse. Instead, we needed someone to get the cops' attention. I guess you could say I saved your life. For a little while, anyway."

"It was pretty transparent. I don't think the police bought it."

He shrugged. "Still good enough to confuse those clowns. That's all I needed. Some extra time to get connected, to make some sales. I'll see later if it's worth sticking around. There's a lotta money around here, these days."

"That's a pretty rough crowd. You sure you can handle them?"

"Oh shit, man. I'm shakin'." A brittle laugh burst from thin lips the color of old meat. "I learned how to deal with those fuckers in the war. I can handle myself."

I slumped in the chair and blinked at Deborah, who stood at my side. Her eyes held an iron coldness that remained fixed on Sean. She looked like she wanted to nail him to the door. I took the water and thanked her. It was warm, but it tasted good.

"What's your next move, Sean?" she asked. "How long do we have to wait?"

"Until the gooks show." He nodded at me. "He belongs to them now."

"What about me? What happens then?"

"I haven't figured that one out yet. The gooks don't care about you, so I can probably let you go."

I knew that was bullshit. Form the look of desperation in her eyes Deborah Krueger knew it too. She knew way too much by now.

"At least promise you won't harm Lisa. You can do that much."

He shrugged again. "Sure. The gooks don't care about her, and I don't even know where she is."

Deborah Krueger glared at the hulk for several seconds. "Do you have to keep saying that? It's so racist."

Another shrug. That seemed to be his principal form of expression. "Whatever. It doesn't matter to me. Just habit, I guess."

His hand groped in his pants pocket and came out with Jamie Krug's twenty-two caliber pistol. "Look at this useless thing. What did you think this was gonna do, Shithead? You might as well piss at someone."

"Not if you know how to aim. Hand it over and I'll show you."

His eyes rolled, and Sean Callahan laughed. "Oh, right."

I stood. "Mind if I use the restroom?"

The prospect appeared to cause him some concern. His forehead wrinkled with thought as he wondered how I might use the toilet paper roll as a weapon.

"Naw. Go ahead."

I took one step toward the rear. It served as a sort of wind-up. Then I wheeled and fired the glass at Callahan's head. I ran three steps closer and lunged. He threw an arm in the air to block my shot, while the other reached to his chest for the forty-four Magnum. The glass shattered against the wall at his back.

Everything collided at about the same time. My head rammed up hard against his chin, and I heard something crack. I figured it was a tooth but hoped for something more. His free arm wrapped around my neck and spun me off. I rolled to the floor and kicked at his knees. Something crunched. Callahan howled and fell to one knee.

I could feel shards of glass stabbing at my back as I lay on the floor. My head was pounding again. I rolled over and moved towards Callahan. Blood trickled from the corner of his mouth and one nostril. I felt pretty damn good about that, until I saw the gun in Callahan's hand. The rain began a new drum roll against the metal sheeting overhead, and I started to pray.

"You motherfucker. I'm not waiting for the gooks. You're dead now, Shithead."

"Sean, no." Deborah Krueger's voice swept toward us. "Please. I'll do anything you want, anything. Please."

"Too late."

"You're right, Sean. It is too late. But not for him."

These words came from a new, yet familiar voice. I rolled over through bits of glass that stung like little bees. Staring straight in the face of Sean Callahan was the ugly end of a Walther PPK. It rested easily in the smooth white hand of Lisa Courney.

# Chapter 27

"You came back."

"I never left, Mr. Habermann. I was just hiding until I figured out what I had to do."

Lisa Courney surveyed the room through brittle, blinking eyes. Their hazel pupils looked like dull granite, hardened by the distance they had traveled over the last two weeks.

Sean Callahan did not move. He still knelt about two feet from me, the Magnum aimed at my chest.

"Well, it looks like you got here just in time," I said.

Her pistol stayed with Callahan, as she leaned against a spot in the wall just inside the door. The light brown hair, clipped shorter and brushed back along the top, pressed against the plywood. The eyes stayed hard and unmoving.

"Yes, it does. Drop it, Sean."

A malicious smile crept across his face. The rain slackened again, and a heavy silence settled over the room. I could hear Deborah Krueger's breath ease to a steady, solemn flow. Callahan squinted at Lisa Courney. The gun did not move. The knuckles whitened under his grip.

"You know he's responsible for your husband's death," I said.

Lisa Courney nodded. "Yes, I know that. He's responsible for a lot more, too."

"Such as?"

"Such as dragging Steve back into that muck after I worked so hard to pull him out."

"What do you mean?"

"He showed up again when we were in Europe, but I got Steve to send him away. I didn't want him to ruin what Steve and I had built."

"You mean your careers with the Agency?"

She nodded. The Walther didn't move. "That's right. We were doing fine. We had left that damn war behind. I taught Steve how to beat the polygraph, so his drug dealing wouldn't come up and we could get the security clearance." She gestured at Callahan with her head. "And he disappeared. For a while, anyway."

"Then you moved back here."

"Yeah. Go figure. We come home, and that crap follows us here. I thought we were rid of it for good."

"I found it doesn't always work that way."

"Friggin' right, Dead Man," Callahan said. "My cavalry's comin', too."

"Shut up, Sean." Lisa Courney's words sounded hard and filled with hate. "If anyone's a dead man, it's you."

He shook his head. "I don't think so. I got friends on the way. You guys are all finished." His smile broadened. "You're the one who's too late."

"Shouldn't we call the police?' Deborah Krueger's voice rose just above a whisper. The words sounded brittle, and the sound seemed to crack in the tension surrounding us. I had forgotten she was there.

"Anyone got a phone?" I asked.

Lisa Courney's free hand dove into the pocket of her sun dress and emerged with a cell phone. "Later."

"Why, Lisa?" Deborah Krueger sounded scared. She was not alone. Her voice wavered while the words tripped from her lips. "Call now, so they can come get us."

Sean Callahan let a hard, guttural laugh escape. It was ripe with overconfidence. "She can't. She's scared shitless. She doesn't know what to do. If the cops come, everything about her precious husband will come out."

He stood on his one good leg, then stumbled for balance. His weight tipped to one side, like a sinking ship. His gun swung from me to Lisa Courney.

Two shots rang out. The sound bounced off the metal walls all around us. I covered my ears and turned toward Callahan. He had a look of total surprise on his face, the eyes wide and round with the whites glaring at something in the distance. His cheeks were puffed and pale. A carpet of red spread across his chest. He glanced down, then up at Lisa Courney.

"You fuckin' bitch."

His feet gave way, and Callahan dropped first to his knees. His bad knee tipped his weight further to the side, and he coughed once, then twice. Blood shot from his mouth the second time, spraying the floor to his front.

"You goddamn slut."

He fell face first and hit the hard cement floor like a statue of stone.

"Lisa!"

Deborah Krueger rushed across the floor to her sister. I scrambled up and over. Lisa Courney lay on her back, a red stain at her upper chest and shoulder. We knelt together at her side. Lisa Courney blinked and seemed to fall in an out of consciousness. I jumped up and ran over to Callahan, took his weapon, ripped off his jacket then spread it over Lisa Courney's upper body.

"She looks like she may be going into shock." I pulled the phone from her hand and looked at Deborah Krueger. "Do you know where we are?"

She nodded. "Somewhere on Butterfield Road, not far from Route Eighty-three. It's a warehouse of some kind." Her eyes never left her sister as she stroked Lisa Courney's hand.

I called 911 and gave as much information as I had about our location. Then I bent low over Lisa Courney and caught the gasping sound of labored breathing. I scrambled outside, where I found the BMW parked about twenty feet from the warehouse entrance. A Honda Civic sat another ten feet to the side, at the edge of the gravel driveway.

A search for a first aid kit came up empty. I ran back inside to the restroom, grabbed a handful of paper towels, and returned to the sisters. Lisa Courney's breathing came in short staccato bursts. I pressed a bundle of the towels against her chest and shoulder and ripped off my shirt for an ersatz bandage.

"We can't wait long. I hate to move her, but we may have to if she gets any worse."

"Oh God, oh God." Deborah Krueger's chant slipped out between sobs. Tears streamed down her face and spotted Callahan's jacket.

Then a low, hungry moan rose from the lump that had been Sean Callahan. Deborah Krueger glanced over, then reached around her sister and picked up the Walther. It took her just four steps to reach Callahan's body. She stood still and silent for ten, maybe fifteen seconds. Then she bent low and aimed the pistol at Callahan's skull. I didn't say a word.

It took only one shot. She coolly blew a hole through his brain, probably not a very big target. She looked like she had been practicing.

"That was for Sean, you son-of-a-bitch."

I was real glad she was on my side.

A minute or so later, the sound of tires crunching on gravel drifted in from outside.

"Well, it sounds like somebody's here," I said. "Let's hope it's the good guys."

It wasn't.

# Chapter 28

There were four of them. Their footsteps moved slowly through the hallway outside, suggesting they were careful but not particularly worried. Or in a hurry. I grabbed the forty-four and stood over Lisa Courney. Her sister came to my side.

"What should we do?"

"I'm not sure. Just try not to look too scared when they get here." I motioned toward the gun still in her hand. "And keep your finger off the trigger. I don't want to set anything off by accident."

"Will they try to shoot us?" Her eyes bounced back and forth in their sockets. Her hands shook.

"Relax. We'll be okay as long as we don't loose out heads. Besides, it's me they want." I didn't tell her that people like this usually don't like witnesses, either.

Our visitors paused outside the door, and I heard weapons being drawn. A couple rounds were chambered, which probably meant they were wondering why their ally Sean hadn't spoken up to welcome them.

I stood with both arms at my hips, the Magnum in my right hand but the finger pointing up the barrel. Two toughs in black leather jackets slid around the doorframe like Oriental snakes, bodies lean and hard and brown. Two more followed. They were all armed, of course, but with weapons trained at the floor like professionals. One of them covered me the instant he saw my weapon.

"You guys bring the white Explorer?"

Faces of stone just stared in response. Underneath the jackets, the group wore black T-shirts over black jeans. Except the last one to enter the room. He looked to be in his late twenties, give or take five years, and he wore a white dress shirt and sunglasses. The shades came off when I spoke. He smiled in response. Then he pointed at Callahan.

"What happened to him?"

I nodded at Lisa Courney. "She shot him. A revenge thing. I guess he turned her husband over to you boys."

He nodded. Then his lips puckered in thought. "Somebody's a pretty good shot."

"Sometimes people get lucky. It was also a case of self-defense. She needs medical help, fast." I gestured toward the telephone on the floor next to Lisa. "An ambulance is on the way. Police, too. I'm curious, though."

"About what?"

"Why did the others have to die?"

"Business is business. Some families take revenge very seriously."

"But why did the girl have to die, or Davis? What did they have to do with any of that?"

"You mean the fat guy? He threatened to go to the cops." Boss Man made an empty gesture with his hands. "We had to protect our interests."

"And the girl?"

His head rolled back with a laugh. "She wanted to warn you. Said you hadn't done anything wrong. Thought he was the one who would cause us trouble." He pointed toward Callahan. "He said we needed to remove her."

"She's the one that lured Courney out of the bar?"

He nodded. "That's right. He was supposed to be meeting her."

"Was she from here, or the family back east?"

"No, she's one of his." He considered Callahan's corpse for a second. "He sold her out, too. I guess we're better off without him." He paused in thought, lips puckered again. "We're supposed to take you with us."

I shook my head, slipping my finger down toward the trigger. "Not today guys. Not without a fight. And I'm ready this time."

He smiled. "We're not supposed to kill you. Not yet, anyway."

I shrugged. "Doesn't matter. I think we got another stalemate."

Big Daddy shrugged in response. "Then maybe later. It's all the same to us."

"No, I don't think it's gonna happen then either."

"Why not?" A smile split his smooth face. His features looked like they had been carved from amber then polished. I was willing to bet he didn't even shave yet. "You think you're too tough for us?"

I let a light laugh escape. "Not really. I've been through too much to get that stupid. No, I'm gonna try to set things right with the family. See if I can talk them off this thing."

He shrugged again, and the shades slipped back over his eyes. "Good luck. We'll hear either way."

He motioned with his head toward the door and said something in Vietnamese to his buddies. They slid back out the way they had come, silent and stone-faced. Except for the head honcho, of course. He smiled all the way out the door, stepping backwards, his eyes locked on mine.

"Later, Bill Habermann, ex-grunt."

"That'd be okay by me," I muttered under my breath. "There are still some scores to settle."

Then we were alone in the room again.

"Shouldn't we get their license or something? For the police?" Deborah asked.

"Honey, we're lucky we're still standing. I'm not going to risk that by playing hero while your sister is bleeding and unconscious on the floor."

Tires crunched on gravel in the distance as the Vietnamese tough guys drove away. Our side arrived a few minutes later. I guess my directions were okay.

# Chapter 29

This time the rental car company gave me a Plymouth Neon. A nice blue color, very masculine. The car sat at a metered spot in Arlington, Virginia, about a block from the Nam Dinh restaurant. I stood by the front door, rehearsing my lines. It was still hot as hell in Washington. Our heat wave had broken. It didn't feel like theirs ever would.

After about five minutes I swallowed my fear and pushed through the front door. It was just after two o'clock, and the last of the lunch crowd was filing out the door. There were maybe three tables still occupied. The brother who had confronted me outside the Catholic church sat at the cash register. The first three buttons on his white shirt were unfastened, and a silver Saint Jude medal rested against his light brown skin. His upper lip curled when he saw me approach.

"My sister not here."

"I need to talk to the other woman."

"She does not speak English."

"Then you translate."

He shook his head. "Why should I?"

I was all set to threaten the kid, to tell him that we could have some more deaths and keep the cycle of violence and hatred spiraling on and on until we were all devoured. But I didn't have to. His sister was there after all. She wore a black sarong and passed through the thick curtain that hung behind the register to hide the kitchen and stood next to her brother.

"I'll translate for you."

She reached out with a small hand that looked as though it had been woven from yellow silk. I took her fingers in mine, and her eyes softened with pity and understanding. I thought for a moment of the woman I had shot thirty years ago, and cursed myself and my fellow man for our collective stupidity. I choked back a tear, and my heart jumped. I had killed an angel of this family, and now I was about to be assisted by another. Fortunately for me, this one was smarter and more thoughtful than all of us. She had moved beyond the grieving and sorrow and fear that had trapped the rest of us.

We stopped in front of the old woman, who sat on a stool at the back of the kitchen. Her eyes hardened when she picked my face out of the steam and noise around her.

"This is my grandmother. She brought our family out of the north after the war. She has suffered terribly. You must understand that."

"I do. Believe me, I do." I turned to her grandmother. "You know why I'm here, don't you?"

She nodded after her granddaughter translated.

"And you know what I'm going to say, don't you? That it has to end. That your daughter's death was a horrible accident. And it's one that could have been avoided. But things like that happen in war. They happened to too many people, back then."

A stream of Vietnamese poured forth. The granddaughter struggled to keep pace.

"Yes, of course, it could have been avoided. If your people had not come. If the French had not come before you. If the Communists had not come. But mostly if you had not been there that night."

"No," I said. "There was nothing I could do about that. Try to understand. She should not have been in the camp that night."

More Vietnamese flowed. "She had to be there. That was her job."

"No, she worked for Mister Courney in the villages, identifying the Viet Cong cadres."

The old woman nodded, her head bobbing up and down vigorously. "Yes, yes. She helped with Phoenix. But she also helped the Communists. She had to give them information on your movements."

I stood there in silence for a few minutes, letting it all sink in. "She was a double agent? She worked for both sides?"

"Yes, of course. That's how we survived. That was our only goal. We didn't care who won. We just hoped you all would leave eventually. We survived the Americans, the French, and the Chinese before them. We will survive the Communists also. That is what we do best."

Pots and pans and dishes rattled behind me. My head swam in confusion and heat and steam. Voices barked at each other in Vietnamese. The scent of spices drifted in the air around us. I glanced at the girl. She must have read the uncertainty in my face, because she squeezed my fingers with a touch of reassurance. Then the old lady spoke again, just a few words this time, and in English.

"You go away now. Leave us in our peace and sorrow."

An angel led me back to the door, her fingers holding mine.

"How did you know I was in Alexandria the other day?"

"My grandmother told me. They called from Chicago. They wanted to know if they should follow you."

"But she left it to you, didn't she?'

The angel smiled. Then she kissed my cheek, and I left.

I stumbled toward the car, holding my hand against my forehead to ward off the sunlight. I dropped in behind the steering wheel and started the engine. Then I waited a few minutes for the car to cool off, the air conditioning going full blast. I was in no hurry. I planned to meet the Sullivans for dinner-I figured he'd had enough time to catch up on his sleep. Then I'd call Wanda Rathko, later that night. If I was lucky, she'd invite me over. I knew that when I slept I'd still see my angel in black some nights, but I didn't think I'd see the Ford Explorer when I was awake anymore.

THE END